FASTER

ALEX SCHULER

MJ HOWSON

The author of this book is solely responsible for the accuracy of all facts and statements contained in the book. This is a work of fiction. Names, characters, places, events, and incidents are either the product of the author's imagination or used in an entirely fictitious manner. Any resemblance to actual persons, living or dead, is entirely coincidental.

This book is printed on acid-free paper.

Published by:
Level 4 Press, Inc.
13518 Jamul Drive
Jamul, CA 91935
www.level4press.com

Library of Congress Control Number: 2019908659

ISBN: 978-1-93376-984-4

eBook ISBN: 978-1-93376-985-1

Printed in USA

Other books by Alex Schuler

CODE WORD ACCESS
CODE WORD BRAVO
ROGUE
CODE WORD CHARLIE
CODE WORD DELTA

DEDICATION

This novel is a work of fiction and facts, woven together to tell a story. The inspiration comes from the brilliant visionary women and men working tirelessly to advance the state of transportation and develop new ways to design and build vehicles. We are on the precipice of moving from a world dominated by personal vehicle ownership to a way of life where transportation as a service is the new normal. Change is never easy, and not everyone can agree on the best way to make this transition.

1

Ted Wolff smiled as he revved the rebuilt engine of the classic black 1990 Pontiac Trans Am. Once the tachometer reached 4,000 RPMs, he released the clutch and the car jolted forward into the dry desert of Nevada, sand firing out behind the tires. Ted had named the car Frankie because of the hand-painted, bright lime-green portrait of Frankenstein across the hood in place of the Firebird "screaming chicken" emblem, the car's hood pin latches doubling as neck bolts. One wide green stripe stretched down the middle from just above Frankenstein's head, over the roof, to the back of the vehicle.

Movement in the rearview mirror caught Ted's eye and he grinned at the sight of his co-worker, portly Kevin Hallaway, waving his arms frantically as he ran after Ted and Frankie. Ted kept driving, watching Kevin and the dusty, drab exterior of the workshop and garage get smaller behind him. He had a kickass job—designing and building desert-racer vehicles for Fisher Tuner, the best company around of its type—though he knew it would only be temporary. He turned his attention back to the road ahead. The five-speed manual vibrated in protest beneath his right hand. He had never bothered to put the Pontiac on a dynamometer to determine how much additional power the supercharger generated. He knew the transmission wasn't built to handle this kind of load, but figured it really didn't matter. The puffs of blue smoke spitting from the exhaust also indicated the engine didn't like his modifications.

Less than a mile north of Fisher Tuner was what Ted called the playground. Several impossibly massive dunes dotted this region, making it a perfect test site. As he pulled into the area and slowed to a halt, the transmission stopped shaking and the engine settled to a quiet burble.

"Okay, Frankie. Let's see if we can go three for three today."

Ted, just two months shy of turning twenty-three, was lean and lanky, deep blue eyes, chestnut hair cut above the collar, parted to the right and longer in front with one lock that always fell in front of one eye. His pale complexion covered a square jawline and ski-slope nose. His passion for rock-n-roll matched his intense attention on the world around him. "Intense"—there was a word that followed Ted. Currently, his lasered attention was on this test vehicle at Fisher Tuner.

The interior of the Pontiac was a mess. The airbags had been removed; the top of the caramel-colored dashboard and door panels, faded and cracked. The passenger seat was cluttered with three different notepads filled with scribbles and mathematical formulas. Fast-food wrappers and crumpled napkins filled the floor and accounted for the slightly nauseating smell of deep-fried food. Half of the warning lights on the instrument panel flashed or glowed solid amber or red. Ted ignored the warnings.

Grabbing a red ballpoint pen and yellow notepad from the bottom of the pile, he scanned quickly through his calculations, nervously tapping the pad before tossing the pen and pad onto the seat. He knew his figures were as good as they could be.

In the middle of the mess, secured in the passenger seat, was the brand new 2005 IBM ThinkPad T43 laptop resting against a small black canvas bag. A cable ran from the back of the laptop to one end of a metal box screwed beneath the dashboard, the other end of which had several more cables dangling toward the floor. These multi-colored wires looped back up and disappeared through the firewall, the area between the dashboard and engine.

The ThinkPad's screen, divided into four sections, showed the status of each of the wheels and a list of components for the custom air-suspension system Ted was about to test. All four sections had green status indicators. The lower part of the screen, labeled MAG SETTING, focused on the magnetic shock absorbers. Ted changed the setting from "Standard" to "Off-Road."

Shoving his hand into the small black bag next to him, he pulled out a clear plastic CD case. Inside, the Memorex CD-R disc was labeled ROCK IT in red marker next to a hand-drawn small rocket in black and blue, red flames thrusting from the bottom. He slid the disc into the aftermarket Pioneer stereo system jammed into the car's dashboard. As the CD loaded, Ted shifted Frankie into first gear and rolled the car forward, spinning the steering wheel to aim for the first dune.

The opening guitar strands of "Limelight" by Rush ripped through the cabin. Ted smiled and turned up the volume almost as high as it could go. Once the drums kicked in, the Velodyne subwoofers crammed into the back hatch thundered to life. The bass pounded through his body.

He revved the engine and dropped the clutch. The fifteen-inch rims of the Trans Am had been replaced with twenty-inch aftermarket steel wheels carrying all-terrain A/TX tires. They barely fit inside the wheel wells, scraping against the edges. As the car raced toward the first dune, Ted tapped a few keys on his laptop, triggering the air suspension to engage.

Frankie began his transformation. Ted's air suspension had a maximum articulation of fourteen inches. When fully deployed, the Trans Am was an odd sight to behold—a lifted muscle car off-roading on desert sand.

He nudged the music up to full volume and upshifted, bringing the speed to forty miles per hour. The music completely engulfed him. What he saw in the rearview mirror was blurred by the rattling glass of the rear hatch caused by the vibrations coming from the twin Velodynes as the music blared. Even so, he could make out the sun beginning its descent behind the mountains behind him. He looked over at his laptop to check the car's status. All four sections showed full deployment to fourteen inches, and air pressure steady within the suspension.

"Number one," Ted announced to the empty car while stamping down on the accelerator. Frankie lunged toward the first dune. Despite the extended front and rear overhangs on the Pontiac, the jacked-up suspension allowed the car to claw straight up the first dune relatively easily, launching all four tires into the air at the peak. "That's it!" Ted screamed.

The car hit the ground and took a few rebounds against the custom suspension before settling down and heading to the next dune. Ted gripped the wheel harder, turning it twenty degrees to the right.

The old Pontiac edged up to fifty miles per hour and Ted glanced at his computer screen. Again, all four indicators showed green. He took a deep breath as the Trans Am vaulted up the steep dune. This second one had a thirty-five-degree incline and a steeper drop-off on the other side. He held his breath as Frankie again took flight, landing smoothly a ways down the backside. Still immersed in the music, Ted couldn't hear the warning beeps coming from the ThinkPad.

He spun Frankie ninety degrees to the left, allowing the car to do a wide sideways drift through the sand, and accelerated to fifty-five miles per hour, heading toward the final dune, a beast, with a forty-five-degree incline and even steeper fifty-five-degree decline. Just before the final ascent he turned to the computer. The front right air bladder was running at seventy percent, and the status had changed from green to yellow. He frowned but shrugged it off and pressed forward.

"Come on, Frankie, don't let me down."

Moments later, he and the car began their climb. At the top, in the air, Ted closed his eyes and waited. The landing this time was much harder than the last two. He tightened his grip on the steering wheel and braced his knee against the driver's door as the Pontiac rocked a couple of times before steadying itself.

Holding on, he looked at the laptop. Three of the four wheels read green, with only the front passenger side still in the yellow. As he slowed Frankie to a halt, the pressure was down to sixty percent. He could tell the front right corner of the car was dipping compared to the rest of the vehicle. "Talk to me, Frankie."

He clicked through the settings of the failing suspension. After a brief pause, the pressure readout slowly began to rise as the hiss of a compressor filled the cabin. Within moments, the readouts were all back to normal.

"Yes!" Ted shouted again. He slid the gearshift into first and cranked the steering wheel to head back to the shop. Turning his head to stare at the area he had just conquered, he thought the dune had never looked more beautiful, bathed in the fading orange light of the setting sun. Bringing Frankie to an abrupt stop, he studied the deep tire marks on the rear side of the dune where the car had impacted.

"I wonder," he said. He looked at his laptop to confirm all systems still green. Turning down the music and grabbing his pen, he rifled through the pile of notepads. His hands landed on the small five-by-seven white one with corners frayed. Flipping to the last page, he quickly scanned the formulas, tapping his pen impatiently as he stared down. A smile crossed his face. "Why not?"

Pumping up the volume, he floored the gas pedal as he headed toward the backside of the dune he'd just come down. The transmission shuddered as he shifted into second gear. Blue smoke trailed anew from the exhaust pipe of the old Pontiac. Laughing out loud and singing at the top of his voice, he slammed the transmission into third.

The Trans Am raced up the steep hill, the A/TX tires tearing through the sand, when once again, Frankie went airborne. Ted straightened his arms against the steering wheel to brace himself. He glanced at the speedometer, shocked to see he had hit sixty-five when Frankie launched. He waited for what felt like an eternity until the car finally hit ground.

The car landed hard and rocked sideways to the left onto two tires, almost going all the way over before coming back down and rocking up on the other two, throwing Ted back and forth within his racing harness. The front right suspension gave out, collapsing that corner of the car into the sand. Tearing out of its restraint, the laptop flew off the passenger seat and crashed to the floor. The steering wheel rotated violently, ripping itself from Ted's grip. The IBM's warnings rang out uselessly in the loud music, lights flashing as one by one the systems began to fail, plunging from green to yellow and finally all to red.

It seemed like an eternity before the Pontiac ground to a halt. And as if he had choreographed the damn thing himself, just as the car stopped moving, the song on the stereo played its last notes. Ted chuckled. Instead of the silence he expected, though, the urgent blaring of warning alarms from the ThinkPad overtook the interior. The front right air suspension showed "Offline," as did the magnetic shocks. He killed the engine and tossed the computer back on to the passenger's seat. A little shaken and not without some effort, he stepped out of Frankie.

The car was lowering itself toward the passenger side as he began his inspection. The driver's side showed nothing out of the ordinary. He walked around to the back of the vehicle, his eyes following the bright lime-green stripe. He kept walking around and let out a sigh when he got to the front corner of the passenger side. The lowering had stopped and the front, right nose of the car was flush with the sand. As he bent down to take a closer look, a loud hissing sound shot out from the opposite front side of the vehicle, followed by a lowering of that side to the ground. Both front wheels were now sunk deep within their wells.

"Shit." Ted stood and pounded his fists against the hood several times. "You should have made that last jump, Frankie. What did I miss?"

He dropped to his knees and tried to look beneath the front of the car, but the suspension was fully collapsed. There was no way he was driving the Trans Am back to the garage. He stood up and glanced toward the main road. Way in the distance, he could just barely make out the Fisher Tuner workshop building.

Sighing, he popped open the passenger's side door. Then he noticed the blood. "Shit," he said as he followed the red streak along the edge of the doorframe with his eyes. He turned his right palm up, revealing a gash just below his thumb. Inside the cabin, the back of the laptop was smeared with blood. So was the steering wheel and parts of the driver's door. He looked from his bleeding hand to the blood throughout the car as he thought about what to do.

Shit. I gotta call Kevin. But as he formed the words in his head, he remembered that his cell phone was back at the workshop. He and Kevin had planned for this though and always brought radios out here as a backup. He reached into the car for the black canvas bag, which had been thrown to the front passenger-side floor during the hard landing. With his good hand, he grabbed it and began rummaging through. The image of Kevin in the rearview mirror waving at him as he drove off appeared in his mind. "Oh, shit! He was holding the radio!"

He shoved his laptop and notepads into his bag, grabbed a handful of crumpled napkins, and slammed the door shut. He slid the edge of his bleeding hand into his mouth and headed toward the dirt road several hundred feet away. The last rays of sun disappeared behind the mountain range, and a cool breeze kicked in, spitting sand across his face. The moon, now fully visible, glowed in the darkening sky. Venus began to make her appearance. Ted looked at his watch and hoped Kevin would still be there when he got back. He was going to need a tow.

2

It was just after 8:30 p.m. when Ted finally made it back to the Fisher Tuner garage. He was happy to see the bay door still open, and Kevin busy at work. Ted inspected the gash on his hand and frowned as he licked the blood away before going in.

Fisher Tuner was founded in San Luis, Arizona, just outside Yuma, a small town along the border of Mexico. The company designed and built trophy trucks and other vehicles for desert racing as well as cutting edge components for more general off-road tools and technologies. They had both polished customer-facing stores and testing and development sites. Fisher Tuner's Nevada Skunk Works shop, where Ted and Kevin worked, was one of the latter. It was located near Pyramid Lake, roughly sixty miles from Reno. The closest real town to the facility was Nixon, a sleepy place with fewer than four hundred residents. The building was a dull, two-bay wood and tin garage, weatherworn and full of dust. The only indication of its purpose was a small hand-painted sign nailed above the front door. Otherwise, it almost looked to be an abandoned building, alone at the end of a winding dirt road.

Inside, two separate workspaces sat along the back wall lit by rows of incandescent bulbs dotting the ceiling. The work area on the left was organized and relatively clean, depending of course on one's definition of "clean." The tables to the right, closest to the office, were in shambles. Stacks of suspension components, wiring, and tools were scattered everywhere, leaving very little of the tabletop exposed. Pinned to the wall behind the mess was a 2005 muscle car calendar. May's picture, surprisingly current given its run-down surroundings, was a 2005 sonic blue Ford Mustang GT with twin white stripes from front bumper, across the hood, and onto the roof.

"Where are the keys to the tow truck?" Ted asked as he stepped into the garage, scuffing his feet across the sand he'd fired into the building earlier that evening.

At 5'8", Kevin was a few inches shorter than Ted. The slightly overweight thirty-year-old Irishman had been with Fisher Tuner for over six years. Ted found him behind a large black mask, sparks parading up in front of him as he welded a custom control arm. Some of the tools and components around him had yellow sticky note warnings—Do Not Touch. Kevin killed his torch and removed his mask. He looked at Ted and the empty bay surrounding him.

"Where the hell is Frankie?" Kevin asked.

"Obviously not with me," Ted replied flatly. "Why do you think I need the tow?"

"How bad is it this time?"

"Nothing a little duct tape won't fix."

"Holy shit, Ted. You're bleeding!" He pointed at the blood dripping from the cloth around Ted's hand. He reached out and uncoiled the rag to expose the cut. "That's a bit deep. You should get that stitched up."

"I've seen worse," Ted said, shrugging.

"We need to at least get you bandaged up. Follow me."

Obediently, Ted shuffled behind him to the main office and sat down at the front desk in the small dingy room. The chairs were covered in tattered, cracked navy vinyl, and the faux wood covering the particleboard desktop was peeling away from the chrome edges. Fisher Tuner's main showrooms, such as the one in Reno, were sleek and modern but their workshops were not intended for the public. Very few customers ever got to see them. Ted scanned the trophy-filled case on the opposite wall. Fisher Tuner designs were renowned for their excellence and had the awards to prove it.

Ted grabbed a tissue from the box on the corner of the desk and wiped his face while Kevin rummaged for a first aid kit in the storage closet. Tossing the oil-stained tissue into the trash, Ted again shoved the edge of his bleeding hand into his mouth and turned his attention beyond the dust-covered windows to glance at the stars. *No clouds.* The loose-fitting front door rattled as a gentle breeze buffeted against its frame.

Kevin returned, a box of gauze bandages and roll of adhesive tape in his hands. Looking around, he spotted an old napkin on the desk next to Ted and used it to clean the wound. The gash was just over an inch long and ran from the base of Ted's thumb to just above his wrist.

"That's going to leave a scar," Kevin said. "I wish we had some rubbing alcohol to disinfect it."

"Or whisky," Ted added with a grin.

Kevin chuckled as he retrieved a pair of scissors from the top drawer.

"Let's get you patched up first. We can have a drink when I'm done."

"Don't forget about Frankie. It's getting dark out. He needs to be towed back."

"I tried to stop you before you left." Kevin frowned and shook his head as he sliced the adhesive tape into strips. "No helmet. No radio. You should know better, Ted. You're taking unnecessary risks."

Ted winced as Kevin pressed the gauze against the wound.

"Relax, Kevin. What's a little spilled blood in the name of progress?"

As Kevin finished bandaging Ted's wound, the shop phone rang. "Who would be calling at this hour?" Kevin said as he left the office and went over to his workstation to pick up the handset on his desk.

"Fisher Tuner," Kevin said. "Kevin here. How can I help you?"

Ted smiled at the drawl of Kevin's heavy Boston accent and his inability to pronounce the letter "R." As Kevin spoke, Ted went to his own workstation to put down his things.

"That was sent out yesterday," Kevin continued. He held the

handset away from his ear and looked at Ted. Kevin waited several seconds before returning the phone to his ear and speaking. "Sure thing. Not a problem. My apologies."

Kevin slammed the phone down and shook his head.

"Why are people so impatient?" Kevin asked as he stared at the phone.

"You're asking the wrong guy," Ted replied. "Tell me something, Kevin. How many people call here thinking they somehow got a fish market?"

"What?"

"Fish a Tuna?"

Kevin smiled and flipped him the middle finger. They both burst out laughing.

"So, what happened out there, Ted?"

"Frankie did great. I finally got through all three dunes. I just pushed him a bit hard when I was done."

"Of course you did."

Walking to the rear of the garage, he leaned against the workbench next to Kevin and shoved his injured hand into the front pocket of his faded denim jeans.

"I'm probably going to need to raid the supply room." Ted pointed to the door in the back corner of the garage. "I have a feeling once we get Frankie on the lift, there's going to be a lot that needs replacing."

"Just 'a little duct tape,' right?" Kevin chuckled. "If you take anything from the warehouse, just be sure to log it."

"I know. Hey, when is Kyle due back?"

"The boss is flying into Reno next Wednesday. He's got business in town and then plans to come by here on either Thursday or Friday. Why?"

"That gives me plenty of time to fix Frankie. I don't want him walking in here seeing him in a mess."

"What in God's name were you testing today?"

"God had nothing to do with it. I wanted to supplement the air suspension I've been designing with magnetic shocks."

"So that's your latest secret gizmo. And they failed?"

"I'm not sure. I think it may be something structural attached to the chassis. I won't know until we get him up on the lift. I got the idea to try that last dune in the opposite direction and ended up coming down pretty hard. The decline and airtime were severe."

"I know that one. Why take last-minute risks like that?" Kevin said, shaking his head. "Maybe if you had more carefully planned for the test you could have prepared the structure and calibrated the system to handle it."

"I did the math. It should have worked." Ted could see the disapproval on Kevin's face. "I've told you before. The only way to know the limit on something is to break it."

Kevin rolled his eyes and walked over to the royal blue Toyota Tacoma in the bay behind his workbench. He shoved his arm over the top of the huge forty-inch tire and tapped his index finger against the bright yellow coil shock absorber.

"I still don't get why you test your stuff on an old muscle car, Ted. People don't race those in the desert."

Ted was about to answer when his cell phone rang out from his workstation on the other side of the garage. He started to walk across as he pulled his injured hand from his pocket. The cut was still fresh and bleeding. He frowned when he noticed the blood stain on his jeans.

"I told you, Kevin. If I can build it small, it's much easier to scale up. If I can get Frankie to take a beating, then something like that Toyota will be a breeze to customize." Ted grabbed his Nokia cell phone and answered the call. "Hello?"

"Ted, it's your father," John Wolff said. The connection was weak, and his voice crackled through the speaker. "How are you, Son?"

"I'm fine, Dad." Ted took a moment to inspect his wound. His temporary bandage of soiled napkins was now saturated in blood. "What's up?"

"I've got good news. I know you don't want to work at corporate. You've made that very clear. But with your skills, I think you can make a real difference at the plant. I talked with my boss and told him all about you. He's ready to bring you on board. Just say the word."

Ted lowered the phone and sighed. John Wolff worked at a General Motors assembly plant and had been badgering Ted to take a job with GM ever since Ted left college. His father's demanding attitude was one reason Ted had decided to move from Ohio to Nevada.

"This isn't a good time, Dad." Ted rubbed his bleeding hand against his stained jeans. "Can we talk later? I'm busy at the shop."

"Why are you still at work? I thought you'd be home by now."

"I'm just wrapping up a few things."

"They've got you working crazy hours. I bet you don't get paid overtime. Do you?"

"No, Dad. Look, the way it works is—"

"For the life of me, I still have no idea why you ran off to the West to work in that stupid shop." John's tone was terse. "Desert-racers? You're wasting your skills, Ted."

Here we go again, Ted thought. He lowered the phone and squeezed it with both hands. The last thing he wanted to do was get in another argument with his father. He grabbed the bag he'd brought back with him and retrieved one of the notepads and a pen. He began reviewing his data, ignoring the sounds coming through the earpiece.

"Come back home and get a union job, Son," John continued, his tenor now sounding more consoling than lecturing. "You need to think about your future."

"I came here for a better future, Dad. I've told you that many times. You don't understand."

"I understand your mother and I broke our backs to get you a college education. And this is how you repay us? Why can't you be like your brothers?"

"I need to go, Dad."

"Run away as always, Ted. You call me when you're done dicking around out—"

Ted ended the call and sent the phone tumbling across a mess of papers and tools onto his workbench. He felt his body tremble and eyes well up with tears. Frantic, he looked around for a towel or napkin. Landing on a rolled-up terry cloth rag splattered with oil stains, he grabbed it and pressed hard against his eyes to prevent the tears from falling.

"My father's an ass, too," Kevin said from across the garage. "Do you two ever have a conversation that doesn't end in a fight?"

"Rarely. My parents don't get me." Ted sighed as he lowered the rag, leaving smears of grease across his cheeks. "They never have."

Ted wrapped his wound in the dirty rag and walked over to Kevin at his desk.

"My dad wants me to follow in his footsteps," Ted continued. "He thinks I can make a big splash at GM. But I know my future lies elsewhere. I'm sure of it."

"Is that future here?" Kevin asked as he turned to face Ted. "Don't get me wrong. You're brilliant. The customers love you. But we both know you're wasting your skills here. I hate to say it, but I kind of agree with your dad. You could easily work your way up the chain at GM. You've got the skills and education. Tell me something. Where do you see yourself in five years?"

"Five years?" Ted looked around the garage, taking in the vehicles, tools, and equipment. The scent of oil and gasoline brought a slight grin to his face. "Maybe in five years I'll be Kyle's right-hand man. Or maybe own my own chain of custom tuner shops."

"Well, don't tell the boss that." Kevin gave him a reassuring smile. "I always plan my life in five-year chunks. It's good to have goals. It sounds like your dad is trying to help you aim for a better future."

"Thanks. I'm sure he means well. He and I just don't see eye to eye. You're a good friend, Kevin." Ted wiped his nose as he surveyed the various components spread across Kevin's desk. "What are you working on?"

"Just some suspension components for the Toyota."

"Not that." A large metallic cylinder, over two feet tall, was jammed in the far corner of Kevin's desk. Ted pointed at it and said, "That."

"The boy genius doesn't know?"

Ted ignored Kevin's dig and walked past him to inspect the unit. "This is a lidar system."

"It was—before I dismantled it."

Kevin's workstation was covered in motors, lenses, mirrors, and circuit boards. Ted studied the components with a mix of envy and curiosity.

"Looks like I'm not the only one with secret projects." Ted's eyes widened in awe as he ran his fingers across the equipment. "What are you planning on doing with it?"

"The boss got a request from some prince in Qatar. The guy wants to dominate the next Dakar Rally. He's setting up his own road course and wants to map the entire area digitally. Kyle, of course, tells him we can do it. The guy doesn't know the word 'no.' So now I'm trying to make it desert-worthy."

"How's that working out for you?"

"Too soon to say. The problem is these things only see in one direction. The detail they can give you is incredible. It's just limited to where they are aimed. They are also fragile as shit. Very temperamental when you shake them around."

"Maybe I can help you with it." Ted picked up a scanning mirror to study the design.

"Maybe. But before anyone's helping with anything, we gotta go get Frankie. After that, you need to get a doctor to look at that wound."

"This is fine." Ted said holding up his thumb, blood already beginning to seep through the bandage Kevin put on. "Nothing a good cleaning and bandage can't fix. Let's go get Frankie."

"If you say so, Ted."

3

Within a few days of the accident with Frankie, Ted had the car back up and running. Thumb still bandaged, he stood hunched over his workbench engrossed in thought. With his good hand, he frantically flipped through piles of notebooks he'd kept from college. A tap on the shoulder brought him out of the pages and focusing on Kevin standing behind him.

"What are you looking for, genius?" Kevin asked.

"I've got a problem I'm trying to solve," he replied, his voice a bit nasally. He turned back to his pile of papers. "I know I figured this out in school. I'm just trying to find it."

Kevin frowned as he let his eyes scan across the cacophony of items scattered around Ted. A stapled group of yellowed papers resting on Ted's oscilloscope caught his eye. Kevin picked them up, curious.

"What's this?" he asked.

Ted snatched the papers from Kevin's hand and glanced at the front page. "It's an essay by Vernor Vinge. You familiar with it?"

"Not in the slightest."

"He wrote it in the early nineties. I did a research paper in college on the history and future of artificial intelligence and this essay was one of my major sources. Vernor believed AI would become so advanced it would replace humans in the intellectual pecking order on the planet."

"You mean like in those *Terminator* movies?"

"Who knows?" Ted chuckled and tossed the weathered pages onto his desk. His smile faded as he scanned the opening paragraphs of the essay. "I have to admit, he's gotten quite a few things right. It's pretty amazing how quickly AI is advancing. I think we've only scratched the surface."

"So, no robot domination on the immediate horizon?"

"No."

"Good." Kevin turned and walked back to his side of the garage. His bald head glistened beneath the harsh light. "I like being at the top of the food chain. Speaking of food, are we still on for dinner this weekend with the girls?"

"Dinner?" Ted said absently as he searched for his notes. He picked up a small three-by-five-inch notebook and flipped it open to the first page. "Was there something planned?"

"No, I just assumed after last weekend, we'd all go out again."

Ted closed the notebook and let out a heavy sigh. As much as he enjoyed working with Kevin, he preferred to keep the non-work socializing to a minimum. Especially when it came to dating. There were times when Kevin reminded him of his mother, always pushing him to be with women who didn't interest him. Last weekend, the two of them had gone to a dive bar for some cheap wings and met two women, sisters, who had ended up joining them for drinks and a few games of pool.

"I'll pass."

"Why? Katie likes you."

"Was that her name?" Ted grinned at the disapproving glare Kevin shot him. "She was nice and all, Kevin. But, she's not my type."

"Another one not your type. You're too picky, Ted."

"I know what I like. And what I like is to be challenged—pushed. I'm looking for an equal. That wasn't Katie."

"I don't get you, Ted."

"Few people do."

"So, then, what are you going to do this weekend? Don't even tell me you're going to be back here with Frankie."

"Maybe."

Kevin rolled his eyes and began organizing the tools spread across his workbench.

"It depends on how tonight's playground run goes," Ted said. "I want to get in one last test run before the sun goes down."

"Really? What's the rush? There's no deadline."

"I know. But I'm trying something new."

"Care to share?"

"Not really. I'll show you when I'm ready." Ted slowly turned his gaze to the notepad in his hand and scanned the mathematical formulas scrawled across the page. "It's that last hill. I just can't nail it."

"You'll get there, Ted." Kevin came back over to his workbench and placed his hand on Ted's shoulder and spun his chair around. "The systems you create are amazing. You build shit I couldn't even dream of. I still don't understand why you are out here in the Nevada desert in the middle of nowhere."

"I have my reasons." Ted stood up and grabbed his small black canvas bag from beneath his desk. Sorting through the papers piled on his desk, he selected a few notebooks along with some pens and tossed them into the bag. "You know I won't rest until I figure this out. Don't wait around for me. I'm not sure how long I'll be out there."

4

Gary "Rusty" Abrams leaned back in his chair and glared at his computer screen. The spreadsheet listing key project deliverables was peppered with cells shaded dark red, flagged as past due. He glanced at the October picture of the USS *Ronald Reagan* aircraft carrier on the 2005 wall calendar pinned to a corkboard beside his screen. Below that, each day of the first week had a bright red "X" through it.

Taking the marker, Rusty stood to cross out Friday the seventh—another day complete. Crossing to the bank of windows overlooking the David Silver University Robotics Lab on the main floor below, he gazed intently at the dozens of workers, mostly students, milling about the massive garage, hard at work on what he believed to be ground-breaking technology. He noticed that several stood around the faded red 1988 Humvee, the focus of all this work. As he watched, he had a momentary flood of disbelief. Heading up the robotics lab for DSU was a role the veteran had never imagined himself taking.

Gary's bright reddish-blond hair had earned him the nickname "Rusty" in his younger days. He was an imposing figure, standing 6'4" and built like a linebacker. His head was a bit small for his frame, and his hands oversized. These odd features gave him the appearance of being physically larger than he was. At fifty years old, most of his hair—cropped short since his military days—had begun turning white, though his beard and trademark handlebar mustache still had bits of red mixed in with the white and gray.

DSU, based in Pittsburgh, Pennsylvania, had campuses on three continents. The Pennsylvania campus comprised over fifty buildings spread across one hundred acres. The robotics lab, unlike many of the historic structures housing classrooms and students, had the appearance of an abandoned automotive repair shop. The two-story cream-colored concrete building had four standard-sized garages on one side, and one on the other side big enough for a semi-truck. The windows, original to the 1950s building, did little to keep the brutally cold winter temperatures from seeping in. Inside, a massive workshop floor was offset with a few small classrooms.

Turning from the windows, Rusty looked across the second-floor workroom to the line of desks in the opposite corner. Harry Palmer and Lori Preston, two of his students, were quietly at work with their heads down, eyes focused on their multi-screen terminals. Above them, the walls were covered with printouts of project plans and schedules. A white poster with black lettering hung on the wall behind them:

CAUTION—M.A.D. ROBOTS AT WORK

The periods had been hand-drawn as lightning bolts and the letters rendered from parts of robotic arms. M.A.D. stood for "Mobile Autonomous Development" and the project name, M.A.D. Robots, proudly appeared on screen savers, signs, T-shirts, and bags.

Rusty walked over to the two at the terminals. For such a large man, his approach was silent, despite the slight limp that often plagued his right leg. He paused less than a foot from Harry, a young bald African American man, and stared over his shoulder.

"Is there a problem?" Rusty asked.

"Shit!" Harry jumped in his chair, knocked over a cup of coffee, and spilled it across a pile of papers. He grabbed a stack of napkins to mop it up. "No. No problem at all."

"Really?" Rusty spun Harry's chair around. "Then, why is my project plan covered in red?"

Harry kept his head down and glanced over at Lori, a few feet away. Lori maintained her focus on her work, ignoring the conversation.

"Don't look at her!" Rusty bellowed. "Look at me."

"I'm on track," Harry replied as he stared at his clasped hands. He adjusted his eyeglasses and looked up at Rusty. "So is Lori."

"Not according to my project plan."

"We're not at fault," Lori said as she calmly pushed back from her desk. "The problem is the hardware."

Rusty took a few steps back to place himself equally between Harry and Lori. He folded his arms and stared down at his two students.

Lori was not the least bit intimidated by Rusty. Having studied at MIT, she'd transferred to DSU to get her master's degree. The always calm twenty-three-year-old relished the challenge before her. She rarely smiled, yet her bright red hair and freckled face gave the appearance of just another sweet girl-next-door.

"Harry's software and my mapping programs are both on track," Lori said. "The hardware team keeps changing their configurations. Every time they do, we need to make adjustments. Our delays are due to theirs."

"So, you're throwing Nico and his team under the bus?" Rusty asked.

"More like under the Hummer," Harry said with a chuckle.

"Do you find all of this to be a joke?" Rusty asked as he leaned down toward Harry. "I didn't enter us in the DARPA FAST Challenge for fun. This isn't just another learning opportunity. This is one of the greatest challenges the military has ever put out there."

Rusty's face was mere inches from Harry's, his hot breath cascading across the nervous student's glasses. Harry kept his eyes focused on the floor, bracing for Rusty's punishing loudness.

"It's the shaking," Lori said calmly.

Rusty stood upright and turned his attention back to Lori.

"The sensors on the Hummer can't take the pounding from the

off-road terrain," Lori said. "We haven't even gotten to real-world testing yet, but all the simulations show failure. They keep making tweaks, or in some cases, changing the tech."

"They?" Rusty asked. "You mean Nico's team?"

Lori and Harry nodded in unison.

"Nico," Rusty said with disdain. "I should have known."

"We're only a few months into this." Lori crossed her arms defensively and leaned back in her chair. "In my opinion, we're doing our best."

"Well, your best isn't good enough." Rusty spun on his heel and marched to the exit.

He shoved the door open hitting the damp, stale air of the hallway and descended the stairs to the main level. As he made his way down, he favored his bad leg and gripped the handrail for support. He went past the door that led outside and barreled toward the entry to the workshop floor. Grabbing the door and whipping it open, Rusty slammed it against the backstop—the rattle of the metal door sending shockwaves throughout the garage.

Nico Lee was standing with a group of five other students next to the Hummer, holding a clipboard and reviewing a task list with his team. At the sound of the door, everyone stopped talking and turned to see Rusty stomping his way across the garage. One by one, they took a step away from Nico, until the Chinese American student stood alone beside the Humvee.

Rusty stopped a few feet from the hulking military vehicle to study the gear strapped to the roof. The DSU team had spent the past few weeks installing multiple sensor arrays on top of the old Humvee. The equipment would be used for mapping terrain and controlling the robotics yet to be installed.

"Harry and Lori tell me we have a problem down here," Rusty said as he shifted his gaze to Nico. "Do we?"

"Nothing that can't be solved," Nico replied flatly. He glanced back at his fellow team members as they inched away from him.

Absentmindedly, Nico pulled a pen from his clipboard and began twirling it between his thumb and fingers. "We just need more time."

"Time is something we don't have. What's the delay?"

Nico stepped past Rusty and grasped a door handle to haul his lean frame up the side of the Humvee, balancing his right foot on a small step stool. The roof of the vehicle was covered in a series of metal support struts running front to back and across the top. A variety of sensors and cameras were secured to the rigging. He slapped his hand against a large black conical sensor attached to the front beam.

"This lidar unit is overly sensitive. I know you've used it on other robots, but speeding across the desert opens up a whole new set of variables."

"Why are you talking to me like I don't know what we're up against?" Rusty stepped closer to Nico. Despite the young student's perch several inches off the ground, Rusty was still able to look him in the eye. "I've built robots to explore mines, nuclear reactors, volcanoes, and other planets! Are you trying to teach me about lidar?"

"No. No, I'm not." Nico glanced up at the second-floor office windows to see Lori and Harry watching the drama unfold. He turned his attention back to Rusty. "All I meant was that adapting the sensors to work at high speed is proving to be a real challenge."

"That's why it's called the FAST *Challenge*, Nico. If it were easy, it would've been done by now." As he finished his last words, Rusty abruptly spun and began walking back to the stairwell door. He looked up and glared at Lori and Harry before turning to face the students scattered throughout the garage. "All of you need to start thinking outside the box. The solutions of the past will not work with what lies ahead of us. I expect nothing but perfection from all of you. If you can't cut it here, then I'm sure Berkeley or Princeton or some other shit school will be happy to take your second-rate talent. Our goal is to win this event. Win! Coming in second is not an option."

Nico lowered his head as he gently stepped off the stool. He walked over to the rest of his teammates huddled at the back of the Humvee.

"Nico," Rusty continued. "If you can't find a way to smooth out the readings from those sensors, I'll find someone who can."

Rusty shook his head in disgust as he again marched to the stairwell door and back upstairs to the second floor, pausing briefly to rub his throbbing right hip. Once inside the second-floor workroom, he found Harry and Lori back at their workstations. Rusty said nothing as he took a seat at his desk and picked up the phone. He opened a faded red leather contact book to the tab marked "F" and ran his finger across the list. Rusty smiled as he dialed the number and waited for the call to connect.

"Hello," said Kyle Fisher.

"Mr. Fisher," Rusty said as he leaned back in his chair. "How nice of you to take my call."

"Rusty! I saw the area code and had a feeling it might be you. Not many people have my personal cell number. How are things at DSU?"

"An endless joy as always," Rusty replied. He glanced across the room to confirm neither Harry nor Lori were listening to his conversation. "I'm calling in a favor, Kyle."

"You name it."

"Have you heard about the new FAST Challenge DARPA announced?"

"DARPA?"

"The military's research group. Defense Advanced—"

"I know what DARPA is, Rusty. I also know all about the challenge they're doing."

"Perfect. I knew you'd be the man to call. DSU has entered the challenge, and I plan on winning the event."

"Rusty, I need to stop you right there. I can't talk to you about the event."

"Why not? It's a desert race. Who better to advise me than the guy who created an empire on building desert-racing vehicles? You're the go-to guy on this stuff, Kyle."

"And that's the problem, Rusty. DARPA beat you to it. They came to me to help them design the Challenge."

There was a long pause before Rusty finally spoke.

"Well, shit, Kyle. I mean, congratulations to you, I guess. But that doesn't help me."

"Sorry, Rusty. I've been working with them for the past year. In the beginning, they just wanted me to advise them on the race portion. I ended up designing all three challenges planned for the competition coming in two years."

"I assume you've been well paid for your services?"

"We just expanded our headquarters here in San Diego."

"How many millions are you worth now?"

"I have my own plane."

"Of course you do." Rusty shook his head in amazement but also felt a bit of pride for his longtime friend. "Wait. San Diego? So you've shut down San Luis?"

"No, I still have a workshop there. I have a dozen development shops around the globe now."

"You've come a long way from those days we used to hang out in Yuma."

"I took you to your first Baja 1000 race, didn't I?"

"Indeed, you did." Rusty grinned as his mind recalled the adventure he'd had with Kyle. "I remember the tequila bars more than the races."

"Those were good times in Arizona, Rusty. How many years were you stationed with the Marines in Yuma?"

"Long enough to have seen three Baja races with you and saved your ass from at least a dozen bar fights."

"I never could hold my tequila," Kyle said with a chuckle. "You were a good friend. You still are, Rusty. Look, I won't be able to give you any info about the FAST competition. But tell me why you called. I'll do my best to help in any way I can, without breaking the rules."

"You know my history with robots."

"Of course I do. You're a legend."

"The issue we're having has to do with speed. The sensors we're using are fantastic when you've got a robot crawling at one mile per hour across the rim of a volcano. They don't do so well when going forty miles per hour across rough roads. I thought you might have something in your catalog we could maybe adapt to our vehicle."

"That's a tough one. It would depend on how stable you need the equipment to be."

"We're struggling to nail that down ourselves." Rusty stood up and walked over to the bank of windows overlooking the lab. He glared at Nico now leaning over the roof of the Humvee. "Unfortunately, I can't give you specifications. Not yet, anyway."

Rusty waited for him to reply. He could hear Kyle clicking his tongue against the roof of his mouth. It was something he did when he was lost in thought. Rusty took this as a good sign.

"I might have something for you, Rusty. Actually, someone."

"I'm listening."

"I've got a guy you might like. In fact, you might love him. He works at one of my development sites outside Reno. He's fresh out of college. The kid is brilliant. He can build just about anything. I'm amazed at some of the things he designs. The guy's a great problem-solver, too. Customers are starting to ask for him by name."

"If he's so brilliant, what's he doing working on desert-racers?"

"Listen, Rusty. This guy isn't some grease monkey. He got his engineering degree from the University of Michigan. I don't know why he hasn't started working on his graduate degree yet. Trust me. You want this guy. Hold on while I get his number."

"So, you're just willing to give him up?" Rusty sat back down at his desk and grabbed a pen and piece of paper. "That's not like you, Kyle."

"Like you said, Rusty, you saved my ass many times. Besides, as much as I love him, I feel his talent is going to waste at my shop. It's only a matter of time before this kid realizes just how good he is. The DARPA Challenge might be a wake-up call for him. Give him a buzz. Talk to him. Pick his brain. Then you can decide for yourself."

"I'm going to need to do more than just talk to him, Kyle. I want to see what he's built and how he thinks. I run a tight ship. Although I trust your judgment, I'm going to need more than just your word. The DARPA project is going to be intense. We're going to be breaking boundaries. I need to know he can handle it. Most people can't handle me."

"I won't argue with that. Then you need to get to Reno. The shop is about an hour or so outside of the city, near Pyramid Lake."

"Give me the details, Kyle. I'll fly out as soon as possible."

5

Rusty stood at the entrance to the Fisher Tuner workshop and stared at the bright lime-green face of Frankenstein inscribed across the hood of the Pontiac Trans Am. The wind ballooned and rippled his olive-green T-shirt, and the intense rays of the desert sun made the seventy-degree temperature feel warmer than it was. The weather was a nice change from the cold front he had left behind in Pittsburgh.

Kevin Hallaway emerged from the restroom, wiping his hands across the back of his jeans. He looked up at the imposing figure standing in front of Frankie at the edge of the garage. Kevin glanced over at Ted sitting at his workbench, earbuds in. He sighed and headed to the front of the bay.

"I'm Rusty," Rusty said as he stepped forward and extended his hand.

"Been expecting you," Kevin said. The two men shook hands briefly. "I'm Kevin. The boss said you'd be here around noon today. I see you're punctual. When did you get in?"

"Yesterday. I fly back tonight. Red-eye."

"Quick trip. Come on in. Ted's in the back."

He led Rusty past the old Pontiac to the workbench at the back of the garage. Ted seemed oblivious to what was going on behind him. An Apple iPod rested beside his keyboard. The black music player with the red click wheel was the U2 Special Edition iPod Apple had recently released. The white headphone cord swayed as Ted bopped his head back and forth to the strains of Blue Öyster Cult's "(Don't Fear) The Reaper."

"Ted!" Kevin yelled as he flung a roll of duct tape, hitting Ted on the back of his head. Luckily, the roll was almost used up.

Ted yanked his earbuds out and tapped pause on his iPod. He spun around in his chair and stared at Kevin and then looked beyond him at the behemoth standing behind him.

"Ted, this is Rusty. The guy Kyle told us about."

Ted stood up and stepped forward to shake Rusty's hand. Rusty was silent as he kept his eyes locked on Ted's and grasped the young man's thin-fingered hand. Ted continued to smile as Rusty increased his grip.

"Welcome to nowhere," Ted said. He relaxed his hand and waited for Rusty to let go. "It's nice to meet you."

An awkward silence followed as Rusty said nothing and folded his arms across his chest. He towered over both men standing in front of him. Rusty could see that Kevin felt uncomfortable, but Ted seemed relaxed. Aloof even. Rusty turned his attention to the Toyota Tacoma on the lift in the adjoining bay.

"I'm not sure what Kyle told you about me," Rusty said, his eyes turned to the truck's sophisticated suspension system. "He's said good things about you, Ted, and the work you do here. Is that one of yours?"

"The Taco is mine," Kevin said. He walked over to the truck and slapped the passenger's side door but then pointed at the Pontiac behind Rusty. "That one belongs to Ted."

Rusty raised his right eyebrow as he briefly studied the heavily customized Trans Am. He shook his head in confusion and returned his gaze upon Ted.

"I'm sure Kyle told you I head up the robotics group at DSU," Rusty said. "But my work goes beyond the education offered at the school. I've worked with NASA and other government and private firms to design and build custom robots."

"Kyle mentioned that. He said you had a job for me."

"A job? I wouldn't put it that way."

Kevin realized he was no longer going to be part of the discussion, so he nodded toward Rusty and went back to working on the Toyota's front suspension.

"Have you heard of DARPA?" Rusty asked Ted.

"They're part of the military, right?"

"Correct. It stands for Defense Advanced Research Projects Agency." Rusty leaned back against the workbench and motioned for Ted to sit down. "It dates back to the fifties when the Russians launched *Sputnik*. Nobody shows up America. The military decided to join forces with the private sector and tap into the wealth of knowledge out there in our universities and corporations. The hope was that the research and development coming out of DARPA would benefit everyone, not just the military."

"And what's DARPA have to do with the work you want me doing at DSU?" Ted asked. "What's it pay?"

"Pay?" Rusty frowned and stared at him. "The *opportunity* is the pay. The *challenge* is the pay. DARPA's latest project is a contest to build a self-driving vehicle."

"Why would the military want a self-driving car?" Kevin asked as he stepped forward from the underside of the Tacoma. "Do they want to build robot tanks?"

"Maybe," Rusty replied. "The world is changing. Those planes taking down the twin towers a few years ago sparked a whole new approach. That type of aggression was uncharted territory. Now we've got IEDs killing our troops over in the Middle East. Dogs have been trained to sniff out those bombs buried beneath the dirt. But it's not enough. Instead, imagine an intelligent robot. Something heavily armored that could scout ahead of our soldiers and trigger or immobilize IEDs. The Air Force has unmanned drones doing strikes. But piloting a vehicle across a desert floor at high speed requires a completely different set of controls and variables than flying an aircraft."

As Rusty spoke, Kevin had inched his way over to stand beside Ted.

The two men were now leaning against the workbench, both riveted by what Rusty was saying.

"What's the DARPA project called?" Ted asked, his voice filled with curiosity.

"Back in May, DARPA announced the FAST Challenge."

"Fast?" Kevin asked. "As in the timeline or speed?"

"It's an acronym. Fully Autonomous Self-driving Technology."

"Is there a prize?" Ted asked.

"There is," Rusty said. The young man's interest in money was beginning to annoy him. "The winning team gets two million dollars."

"Wow." Kevin let out a long whistle. "That's a lotta lobster."

Rusty and Ted stared at Kevin, neither saying a word. Kevin shrugged and walked back to the Toyota.

"Do you divide that up among team members?" Ted asked. "How does it get split?"

"You seem to be missing the point. This isn't about the money. The money will go to DSU and back into the robotics program."

"Oh." Ted paused and furrowed his brow, flicking his hair away from his eyes. "What about the technology that gets created to build the self-driving car?"

"This is where it gets interesting. The military will get to use whatever intellectual property we create. But the winners can go to market in the public or private sector. If money is what you're after, then there will be ample opportunity down the road." Rusty glanced around the dusty garage, slowly inspecting the vehicles and tools. "I can tell you that creating a self-driving car will be much more profitable than building desert-racers."

"What are the details of the FAST Challenge?" Ted asked. "Is it a race? I mean, we do desert racing so that must be why Kyle sent you here."

"There are three parts to the challenge. First up is a qualification stage. This is where DARPA will filter out the hobbyists from the serious players. Second is a desert road race—130 miles of brutal terrain.

The last test will be an urban challenge navigating city streets. DARPA is holding back many of the details. All we know right now is it will take place somewhere in the Mojave. It's a points-based system, with the final winner across all three challenges taking the grand prize."

"Three unique tests," Ted said quietly. He looked around at the vast array of vehicle components littered across the garage. After a few moments, he looked up at Rusty. "You said they announced this in May. What sort of progress have you made?"

"I bought a 1988 Humvee. I've got a team of almost three dozen back at DSU. More join every week. I'm also in the process of getting private backing and donations."

"Why did you pick a Hummer?"

"It's old tech, but it's also unstoppable in the desert. The robotic controls to manage the driving will be relatively easy to do."

"Kyle said you were a legend."

Rusty suppressed a smile as he studied Ted's eager demeanor.

"The robots I've built have each been designed for a specific task. The last one was completed two years ago. There was a collapse in a diamond mine in Africa and the workers were trapped almost a mile down."

"I remember that. They used a robot to map the shaft to plan the rescue. Wait—that was *your* design?"

"Indeed, it was. We used a mix of radar and lidar to see the walls and build a virtual map. That robot traveled at a maximum speed of less than two miles per hour. Every robot I've built has been slow by design. Our Humvee is going to need to be able to perform the same basic navigation functions as that diamond mine robot, but traveling much faster."

"How fast?"

"Forty, maybe fifty miles per hour. Let me be clear, Ted. DSU is going to win—at all costs."

"It's not just the speed that's the problem, is it?" Kevin asked as he emerged from behind one of the Tacoma's tires dangling from above. "It's the terrain."

"Exactly," Rusty replied. "Right now, we're running basic simulations but the lidar is proving to be a real bitch to tame."

Kevin walked to the back corner of his side of the garage and motioned to Ted and Rusty to join him. He leaned against his desk and pointed to a pile of equipment.

"That's a lidar unit," Rusty said with surprise.

"It was," Ted says. "Kevin and I have been playing around with it. Some guy is paying Kyle a hefty penny to make this work in the desert."

"My students have been struggling with getting it to work the way we need it to."

"So have we," Kevin said. "Our resources here are limited."

"Mine are not," Rusty replied. "As I said, I intend for DSU to dominate this competition."

"I'm going to need to think it over." Ted stared at the lidar components strewn across Kevin's workbench. "It would be a big change for me."

"Think what over?" Rusty asked. "I haven't invited you to join the team yet."

"Ouch." Kevin laughed as he strolled back to the underside of the Toyota.

Rusty shoved his hands in his pockets and walked over to Ted's Pontiac. Ted quickly followed, keeping his head down.

"Tell me about your education, Ted. Kyle tells me you graduated from the University of Michigan?"

"I did a double major in civil and mechanical engineering."

"Why didn't you pursue a graduate degree?"

"A few reasons. Mostly, I was bored."

"Bored?" Rusty asked with surprise.

"I was tired of studying. I wanted to get out there and get my hands dirty."

"But with your degrees, you could easily be working elsewhere. If you love customizing cars, why not get a job with Detroit?"

"You sound like my dad." Ted folded his arms defensively and lowered his head. "I just don't see me working for some big corporation. There are too many rules. They move too slowly."

"Are you saying you don't like to follow rules? You need to know I run a tight ship, Ted. I have no tolerance for failure. Zero."

"I don't like to follow unnecessary rules—red tape. I set high standards for myself. I set deadlines. I've never met a problem I couldn't solve. But I like to do it my way. Like I said, some place like GM would be too restraining for me."

"I see."

"Every vehicle or component I've designed for our customers has been a winner. You can ask Kevin."

"He's a mechanical genius," Kevin yelled out, his head buried deep inside the underbelly of the Toyota. "The stuff he comes up with is amazing."

"So, you're all about the hardware?"

"Yes and no. I mean, you need to control the hardware. So, obviously, there's a software side to it all. I did a research paper on AI in college. But my passion is the mechanical side of things."

"Is that so?" Rusty tapped his hand on the curved glass of the Trans Am's rear hatch. "Tell me, Ted, why did you pick an old muscle car to test desert racing equipment?"

"I love pony cars. The small size also lets me easily scale up. In my experience, it's harder to shrink technology than expand it. If I can make the tech work on this old Pontiac, I can easily apply it to something like that Tacoma."

"And what tech do you have going on here?"

"Frankie's got—"

"Frankie?"

"Don't you name your cars?" Ted pointed at the giant graphic of Frankenstein emblazoned across the Pontiac's hood and grinned proudly. "Frankie. Frankenstein. Get it?"

Rusty remained stone-faced, staring intently at him, and waited for him to join him at the back of the vehicle. Ted kneeled beside the rear tire and began pointing out the customizations.

"Frankie's got a custom air suspension integrated with magnetic shocks."

"Magnetorheological shocks? Interesting."

"They blow away anything in production today," he said as he stood back up. "I designed them myself. The response time is twice as fast as what's on the market. They can also take a beating."

"Do you think something like that would smooth out our lidar issue at DSU?"

Ted folded his arms and leaned back against the car, taking a position next to Rusty. He looked over at the lidar components scattered across Kevin's desk.

"I'm not convinced. I'd need to see the entire configuration and run the numbers. My gut tells me it wouldn't. Not without something else to better control the lidar. That's the issue Kevin and I have been trying to solve." Ted ran to grab his notepad and pen and frantically flipped through the pages. "I have some ideas that might work. But, as Kevin said, our resources here are limited."

"You told me you never met a problem you couldn't solve. And that you only build winners."

"Our computer power here is a joke. I end up doing most of the calculations on paper or in my head. But I stand by both of those statements. The trophies in the other room prove it."

"Don't make promises you can't keep."

"I never do."

Rusty slowly walked around Frankie, studying the oversized tires jammed into the wheel wells. He got to the passenger's side and noticed the crumpled fender ahead of the front wheel. Several pieces of duct tape were covering the damaged bodywork.

"It looks like you've pushed Frankie a bit too hard."

"You sound like Kevin. I tell him he's too cautious. You need to take risks. If you don't push something to the breaking point, how will you know when it will fail?"

"Indeed." Rusty paused and scratched the underside of his beard. "Do you worry?"

"About what?"

"The consequences."

"Of breaking Frankie? No. I can fix anything."

"I meant the consequences of pushing things beyond their limit."

"Not really. I mean, how else can you succeed?"

Rusty nodded in agreement and took a few steps back to admire the bizarre design of the customizations made to the Pontiac.

"Now I understand why Kyle recommended you. You remind me of someone."

"Who?"

"You seem to have a nice little gig going here, Ted." Rusty reached into the pocket of his khaki pants and pulled out a piece of paper. He tucked it under the wire holding the hood pin latch—Frankie's neck bolt—in place. "But if you are up for a real challenge, come to DSU."

"I'd want to think it over. I mean, you basically said the pay is zero. How would I live?"

"We'd provide room and board and a small monthly stipend. But don't waste your time worrying about trivial matters, Ted."

"Trivial?"

"You've got forty-eight hours." Rusty turned and headed toward the open garage door. The wind gusts whipped desert sand across his weathered face. Once outside, he stopped and turned back to face Ted. "Opportunities like these don't come often. If you decide you'd like to change the world and be a part of history, you've got my info."

6

Ted gripped the steering wheel with his left hand, his right resting on the five-speed manual transmission as he cruised along. The roadway ahead of him was empty. He glanced at the clock—just after 6:00 p.m. He'd be in Wadsworth within twenty or thirty minutes, assuming traffic stayed light. Lucky for him, the cops never patrolled this barren part of town so he could easily go well beyond the speed limit.

Route 447 was a winding two-lane road that ran between the eastern side of Pyramid Lake and the dried-out bed that used to be Winnemucca Lake. The roadway connected multiple small desert towns, including Nixon and Wadsworth. With Nixon fading away in his rearview mirror, Ted pushed hard on the gas pedal. The 4.6-liter V-8 of his 2002 Mustang GT roared as he accelerated past fifty miles per hour. Reaching for the Mach 460 stereo's power button, he stopped himself just a few inches away.

No. He shook off the impulse. *No music tonight.*

Resting on the empty passenger seat was the paper Rusty had tucked under Frankie's hood pin latch. All Ted had thought about since Rusty left Fisher Tuner earlier was the FAST Challenge. His initial disappointment about the distribution of the two-million-dollar prize had worn off. He knew Rusty was right about the long-term possibilities. He'd been with Fisher Tuner less than a year. Going from building desert-racers to robotic self-driving cars at a university would be a big change.

I can only imagine what my parents will say.

The seventeen-inch performance tires on the Ford hummed as he made his way home. The scenery was bleak and desolate. Tufts of dead grass covered the edges of the roadway and the hills were strewn with rocks and sand as far as the eye could see. It was a lonely, empty place, lost in the middle of nothing.

After a while, he reached the edge of Wadsworth's town line, happy to have the long drive behind him. He downshifted to third and slowed his car to twenty-five miles per hour, as he turned off Route 447 and wound his way through the small roads before finally reaching home.

At less than four square miles, Wadsworth was a tiny town with a population fewer than a thousand people. Ted had decided on this spot mainly for the inexpensive rent and because it was just about equidistant to Reno and Nixon. Kevin lived in Spanish Springs, just north of Reno, and just could not understand why Ted had chosen to live in such a desolate place. Ted liked the privacy. But every few weeks, he would meet Kevin in Reno for dinner or drinks. Most of the time, though, he would tinker away in his apartment or drive back to Fisher Tuner outside Nixon to work on his latest project.

He smiled as he parked his Mustang in the dirt driveway, spotting his landlord, Ms. Lawrence, in a rocking chair on the front porch smiling and waving at him. A widow of many years, she was a nice enough elderly lady. He killed the rumbling engine and grabbed the paper with Rusty's information.

"Good evening," Ted said as he nodded hello. "How are you feeling tonight?"

"A bit chilly," Ms. Lawrence responded. "You're home early."

"I've got a lot going on."

As he passed the cracked concrete steps that led to the porch of the pale blue ranch, Ms. Lawrence said, "My oven's on the fritz. Would you have time to check it for me?"

"I need to make a couple of phone calls, but I'll try to come by a bit later."

"Thank you, Ted. That would be much appreciated."

He made his way away around the side of the old house, stopping at a cracked white wooden door connected to the garage. The yard, like most of the properties in town, was filled with dirt and weeds and a few sickly desert trees. He reached into his pocket and pulled out his key ring, fumbling until he found the one for his apartment.

Several years ago, before his passing, Ms. Lawrence's husband Oscar had converted the garage to a rental unit. It was the most basic of living spaces. The bathroom was the only room with a door. The rest of the place was wide open, with a simple kitchenette area tucked into a corner. The apartment came fully furnished with a collection of mismatched furniture—a brown and red plaid couch, small end table, wooden coffee table, and twin bed. A silver metal table with two chairs served as the eating space. One small window beside the entrance was the only source of natural light.

Ted stepped inside and flipped the wall switch that connected to the tattered cream-shaded lamp on the end table next to the couch. He dropped his keys and the paper onto the metal kitchen table.

The clock on the small countertop microwave glowed 6:28 p.m.—9:28 p.m. at his parents' place in Ohio. Taking out his cell phone, he checked the LCD screen—one bar. He tended to get a better signal by the door, so he crossed the room and checked again. The screen now wavered between one and two bars. He sighed as he dialed.

"Hello?" Barbara Wolff said cheerily.

"Mom, it's Ted."

"Teddy!"

He stifled a grin at his mother's use of his childhood nickname.

"It's so good to hear from you," she continued. "Is everything okay?"

"Everything's fine. Great even. I need some advice. I hope I didn't call too late."

"Nonsense. You know we are always here for you. Hold on while

I get your father. He's got exciting news for you." She held the phone several inches from her face and covered the receiver. "Jack! Jack, it's Ted! Pick up the other extension. Jack?"

"How are things with you, Mom?" Ted asked as he waited for his father to join the call.

"Not much changes around here. We had a lovely day today, but I know winter is coming. The temperature will be below freezing soon. You don't have that problem out in the desert, do you?"

"It gets below freezing at night here in the winter. But the only snow we get is up in the mountains."

"And are you dating? Is that why you called?"

"No, Mom." He sighed, crossing over to the couch and sinking into its softness. The line responded with crackles and pops as soon as he stepped away from the window. "I wanted to talk to you about work."

"Jack!" Barbara screamed out. "I don't know what's taking him so long. Listen, Ted, you turned twenty-three a few months ago. Do you know how old I was when I married your father?"

"Let me guess. Twenty-three?"

"Twenty-two. How do you expect to meet a girl and raise a family living in the middle of—"

"Ted?" John Wolff said as he joined the call. "Is everything okay?"

"Everything's great, Dad."

"Did your mother tell you the news? I've been promoted to floor supervisor."

"No, she didn't. Congrats."

"You should see the quality we are getting with the new Cobalt. GM is heavily investing in our plant. Chevy's never been better. You're missing out on a lot by not being here."

Ted held the phone away from his face and glared at the tiny screen. He felt his grip tighten as frustration poured over him. He closed his eyes and took a long deep breath.

"I have news of my own," he said as he struggled to ease his anger. "I have an offer to work on a project for DSU."

"DSU?" Barbara asked.

"David Silver," Ted replied. "It's a university in Pittsburgh. The guy that heads up the robotics lab personally came out to see me. My boss Kyle is friends with the guy, and Kyle recommended me for the project. Impressive, right?"

"What kind of project?" John asked.

"As in Pennsylvania?" Barbara added. "I thought you moved to the desert to get away from the snow?"

"There's this national competition, sponsored by . . . by the government."

"What's it pay?" John asked.

Ted sighed and lowered the phone. He was beginning to regret making the phone call. "The pay comes at the end, Dad. For the team that wins."

"And if you lose?" John said.

Ted paused as he struggled to come up with a response that would not escalate what was quickly turning into an argument.

"But how will you live if you don't have an income?" Barbara asked, her voice filled with angst. "Where will you live?"

"The school will take care of that. If I have to, I'll sell my Mustang, but I'm hoping—"

"Good," John interjected. "You should be driving a Camaro, anyway."

"What's this school like, Teddy?"

"It's the best. The guy, Rusty, who I would work for has built the most amazing robots. Remember the diamond mine collapse? He's the guy who—"

"I think this is a bad idea, Ted," John said. "You've been wasting your time on race trucks in the desert less than a year. Now you want to go play with robots?"

"You don't understand," Ted said. "This is an amazing opportunity to work with a legend."

"You should be here working beside your brothers," John said. "Michael and Steve are doing great. All they did was go to a trade school and they are making more than you with your fancy degrees. You can be so much more, Ted. Do so much more."

"I know, Dad. That's why I'm seriously considering this project. You're not understanding."

"I'm not understanding? I'll tell you what I understand!"

Ted lowered the phone and placed it on the cushion beside his thigh. He could hear his father's voice bellowing through the earpiece but could not make out what he was saying. He looked across the room at the paper Rusty had given him. He picked up the phone.

"I'm sorry," Ted said. "This isn't your problem. I shouldn't have called. We can talk about it another time when it's not so late."

"I thought you wanted our advice," Barbara said with disappointment. "Did you already decide what you want to do?"

"He never listens to us," John said. "You keep making these poor choices, Ted. I'll never understand why. If you go out there and fail, remember I can get you into the Lordstown plant. Okay?"

"Sure thing, Dad."

"You really need to think this over, Teddy," Barbara added.

"Of course," he stood up and walked over to the kitchen table. The connection crackled. "I haven't decided anything yet. Honest. Rusty said I have two days to decide."

"Two days?" John asked. "That doesn't seem fair. You need to tell him you need at least a week to think this through."

"Okay, Dad. I'll call back another time so we can talk about it. I promise. Have a great night."

Ted was done being lectured by his parents and ended the call. The silence felt like a weight lifted from his shoulders. He smiled as he grabbed Rusty's paper from the table. Walking back over to the door, he stepped outside to get a stronger signal and dialed Rusty's number. After several rings, it went to voicemail.

"Rusty, hey, this is Ted. Ted Wolff. I know we only talked earlier today, but I've made up my mind. I'm in. I just need at least a week or two to wrap up my job with Kyle. I have a few projects to finish. I can plan to be there the first week of November." Ted glanced down at the paper in his hand. Printed in neat almost block letters beside Rusty's phone number was his email. "I will send you the details once I've talked to Kyle. Thanks again for the opportunity. I won't disappoint you."

He ended the call, let out a sigh of relief, and felt himself grinning widely as he walked back inside. The kitchen area had a dozen walnut-colored cupboards. Six on the bottom below the gold Formica countertop, and the others hanging somewhat unevenly on the wall. Ted opened the one below the sink and grabbed a bottle of Chivas Regal. The glass he'd used for his morning orange juice was resting in the dish rack. Flipping it onto the counter, he filled it with a few ounces of the whisky.

He raised the goblet to his nose and inhaled the scent of grains, flowers, and vanilla, smiling as he gazed into the deep amber liquid.

"Here's to changing the world."

7

Rusty leaned against the side entrance to the DSU Robotics Lab and stared across the parking lot toward the road. The gray early November sky and low clouds threatened to unleash rain at any moment. A strong gust of wind sent his navy windbreaker flying. Rusty shrugged off the nearly freezing temperature and glanced at his Seiko chronograph watch. It was a few seconds before 9:05 a.m. A whirring sound caught his attention, and he turned toward the road to follow the sound.

Just as he did, Harry Palmer rounded the corner on a Segway, weaving his way through several parked cars. He came to a stop a few feet from Rusty and hopped off, leaving it parked beneath a small overhang beside the entrance.

"I know," Harry said as he nervously adjusted his backpack. He didn't wait to hear what Rusty had to say. Instead, he flung the door open and stepped inside the building. "I'm late. Sorry."

The hinges on the door squealed as the door closed. Rusty turned back to the road and glanced again at his watch with a frown as he saw Ted Wolff slowly making his way across the parking lot.

"Good morning," Ted said cheerily. He held his hand out to greet Rusty. "I forgot how damp and cold it gets out here. It's a big change from the desert."

"You're late." Rusty did not extend his hand. Instead, he turned and opened the door. "Don't let it happen again."

Ted's smile faded as Rusty opened the door to the building and went in without waiting for him. As Ted ran to catch up, he bumped into Harry's Segway, almost knocking it over, noticing the dangling key fob before stepping into the dimly lit hallway.

"The team leads are upstairs waiting for you," Rusty continued. "But first, I want to give you a quick history lesson."

He opened one of two doors at the end of the hall. As they made their way in, Ted saw it was some sort of storeroom, dark with no windows. Rusty flicked a switch and a dozen overhead fluorescent lights sparked to life. The cold white light filled the room.

Ted looked around in awe. Floor-to-ceiling display cases, six in total, lined up along the back wall. Each showcased a robot mounted on a heavy-duty steel shelf. Ted walked straight over to the one on the far left and read the plaque on the outer glass door. The NASA emblem immediately caught his eye.

"Is this the robot they sent to the moon?" he asked in amazement.

"No," Rusty replied. He was standing in the doorway with his arms folded across his broad chest. "It was the prototype. The one they sent to the moon is still there."

"Oh. Right."

Ted moved to the next station. Inside was a six-wheeled vehicle painted olive-gray. The robot was just over three feet long and heavily armored. He saw the USMC stencil of the Marine Corps along the side beneath an array of sensors and cameras.

"These are truly amazing," he said as he studied the knobbed heavy-duty tires.

"What they are is amazingly slow. Those sensors on that military drone are incredibly accurate. It's like I told you in Nevada, they can't collect data above a couple of miles per hour. Imagine an assembly line, and you have someone tasked with sorting the items coming down the belt. Keep adding speed, and eventually, no matter how many bodies you throw at it, the system is going to fail."

"My dad builds cars," Ted said as he nodded in agreement. He looked back across the collection of robots. "I'm all too aware of assembly lines. So, are all of these prototypes?"

"Not all of them." Rusty pointed to the case to the right of Ted. "They let me keep that one."

Ted looked at the plaque on the next door.

FOREVER-007—BOTSWANA, AFRICA—2003

"From the diamond mine collapse," Ted said softly. He turned and faced Rusty. "I thought you didn't name your vehicles?"

"The team always does."

"What's the name mean?"

"It's a James Bond reference," Rusty said, disappointed he hadn't already picked up on that. "Now that you've seen the past, let's go take a peek at the future."

They returned to the hallway. Rusty killed the lights in the display room and pushed the other door open. He grabbed Ted's arm to prevent him from entering the garage.

"We'll come in here later," Rusty said as he held the door open so Ted could see inside.

Dozens of people scampered about the expansive workshop floor. A faded red Humvee sat in the center of the commotion near a group of people clearly consumed in some sort of heated discussion. Three people were crawling across the roof of the Hummer, perched on the roof rails like birds. Six others huddled around a computer screen. The workstation was one of several desks located on the opposite wall of the garage.

"Technically, the FAST Challenge is a graduate seminar class," Rusty said. "That's our vehicle. The one I'm going to need your help with."

"Sure thing."

"Ted, you should know I'm very selective on who I allow on this team. Don't take any of this lightly."

"Of course not."

Rusty closed the door and headed to the staircase at the far end of the hallway. Ted smiled as he ran his hand along the door that held the collection of robots Rusty had built. As Rusty began climbing the stairs, Ted followed behind, staring at Rusty's heavy-duty Caterpillar boots that pounded each metal step as they ascended. Rusty winced and rubbed his thigh as they approached the top of the staircase.

"What's with the limp?" Ted asked, noticing the older man's difficulty.

"It's not your concern."

The door at the top of the stairs announced watch tower, scrawled in blue and red block letters on a yellow poster board. Rusty twisted the handle and flung the door open.

Harry, Lori, and Nico were inside the room, standing around Harry's terminal. Nico had a glazed look about him as he twirled his pen across the tips of his fingers. Harry and Lori were in a hushed discussion but stopped their conversation as Rusty and Ted entered. A white plastic bowl filled with leftover Halloween candy was on the table closest to Lori. Harry grabbed a Snickers bar and ripped it open.

"I need everyone's attention," Rusty said as he closed the door behind him. "This is Ted Wolff. Ted's an engineering whiz from the University of Michigan. He also has expertise in building desert-racers. *Winning* desert-racers. With the three DARPA challenges being set in the Mojave, Ted will give us an edge the other teams won't have."

"I'm Lori," Lori said as she stepped forward and shook hands with Ted. "Lori Preston. I'm in charge of mapping."

"Mapping?" he asked.

"DARPA won't tell us where in the Mojave the challenges will take place. Assuming it will be within the range of a military base, and knowing they plan to do a 130-mile race, we've started mapping where we expect it to happen. Fifty thousand square miles, to be precise."

"That's a lot of desert," he said. "Is it just you?"

"No. I have a team. We've divided it up into fifteen hundred sections. We're using military photos as well as topographical digital maps. On race day, DARPA will give us the GPS points for the event and we can refine our maps then."

"That's impressive."

"Thanks," she said as she flicked her red ponytail over the shoulder of her bright pink M.A.D. ROBOTS sweatshirt. "It's exciting work."

"I'm Harry Palmer, software lead." Harry stepped forward and wiped his candy-covered hands along the sides of his white Apple sweatshirt. Streaks of dark chocolate permeated the cotton-poly blend. "Woz up?"

"Wazzup?" Ted asked. He furrowed his brow as he and Harry shook hands. "As in the beer commercial?"

"No," Harry said with a bit of a frown. He pointed at the rainbow logo on the front of his shirt. "As in Woz. *The* Woz! Steve Wozniak."

"Harry's a bit of a geek," Nico said as he greeted Ted. "You'll get used to him. I'm Nico Lee. I've got the team doing the sensors and hardware on the Humvee, calibrating everything it will see. I work closely with both Lori and Harry on all aspects of the system we're putting together."

Nico was a couple of inches shorter than Ted. He was dressed in indigo denim jeans and a black long-sleeved T-shirt pushed up to his elbows. Ted pointed to the tattoo on Nico's right forearm—6D6F6D in black ink.

"What's it mean?" Ted asked.

"It's hexadecimal," Nico said.

Ted reread the tattoo and chuckled. "That spells out 'MOM.' Cute. And you said Harry was the geek?"

"Oh, it gets worse," Harry said. "Nico made the artist use a specific font—Segoe."

"What's that?" Ted asked.

"Enough with the small talk," Rusty said as he flung the door open.

"Ted, feel free to grab a coffee. I want everyone downstairs in five minutes. I'll be waiting for you by the Hummer."

Ted watched Rusty head back downstairs and looked around the watch tower. Various printouts hung on the walls, and the whiteboards were covered in mathematical formulas. The military calendar was turned to the November photo of an F-15 fighter. It wasn't a particularly large room. He walked over to the bank of windows and glanced down at the workshop floor. He smiled as he watched the crowd of students parting as Rusty marched over to the faded red Humvee.

"Coffee?" Lori asked as she tapped him on the shoulder.

"Sure," he replied.

Nico was at the table of snacks and drinks filling an orange Caltech mug with hot water. Ted joined him just as Nico placed a green tea packet into his water.

"I'm guessing we'll be working together a lot," Ted said to Nico. "We started using lidar back in Nevada just before I left."

"Started?" Nico asked. "So much for the boy genius. See you downstairs."

Ted frowned as he watched Nico turn and leave the room.

"Don't mind him," Lori said. "Rusty's been riding his ass for months. He thinks you're here to replace him."

"Replace him? No, I'm here to help—and to learn. Rusty never said anything to me about replacing anyone."

"Of course not," Harry said. "It's all part of the game."

"What do you know about Rusty?" Lori asked. She emptied three packets of raw sugar into her red DSU mug. "You had to have researched him before agreeing to this."

"Well, I know he's a robotics genius. And this DARPA project sounds amazing."

"So, you really don't know what Rusty's like." She finished stirring her coffee and tossed a tarnished silver spoon onto the tabletop. "I hope you're ready for this."

"Ready?" Ted asked with confusion. Lori grabbed her coffee, turned around, and left the room. Ted looked to Harry. "Ready for what?"

"You're in the Marines now," Harry said. "Rusty is a complete drill sergeant. I swear he thinks he's still in the military. I've never been to boot camp but I think it would be easier than this."

"If it's so bad, why are you here?" Ted asked.

"Are you kidding?" Harry pulled out a can of Red Bull from a small refrigerator beneath the snacks table. "It's the opportunity of a lifetime. I was thrilled to get on the team. I'm just warning you. He drives someone to tears at least once a day. Three students have already left the project in the past two months."

"Really?" Ted grabbed a Styrofoam cup and filled it with coffee. He'd been in Pittsburgh less than two days and was still adjusting to the time change. He added a few packets of sugar and some nondairy creamer. "I don't know. Rusty seems a bit stiff to me, but otherwise not so bad."

"You've been warned," Harry said as he grabbed a handful of snacks from the candy bowl. "We need to get downstairs. Our five minutes are up."

Ted held the door open for Harry, and the two made their way down. Harry stopped at the entrance to the workshop floor and turned back to Ted.

"One more thing," Harry said. "About Nico's tattoo."

"What about it?"

"Segoe is the original font used by the Windows operating system."

Ted laughed as he swung the door open. Rusty was on the other side of the lab next to the Humvee, surrounded by over two dozen students. Ted and Harry joined Lori and Nico, who were standing several feet away.

"Did we miss anything?" Harry asked.

"No," Lori said. "He's been studying the latest hardware upgrades."

Although he was at least twenty feet from the Hummer, Ted could easily make out the assortment of sensors secured to the roof. The main lidar array was much larger than the one he and Kevin had been working on at Fisher Tuner. He studied it for a few minutes, walking around the vehicle to get a look from all sides before turning his attention to the whole vehicle.

“That thing is huge,” Ted said. “I’ve never seen a Humvee up close before. Did you name it yet?”

“The vehicle?” Harry asked. “No. Not yet. I’ve made suggestions, but Rusty’s shot them all down. He keeps telling me it’s a low priority.”

Rusty pounded his fist against the Hummer’s rear fender. The burble of loud voices instantly responded, switching first to a low murmur and then silence. The only sound remaining was the hum and whir of the electronic equipment.

“I need everyone to pay attention,” Rusty said sternly. “We’ve got a new team member. Ted, where are you?”

Harry shoved Ted from behind, forcing him to stumble a bit. Ted handed his coffee cup to Harry to hold and joined Rusty beside the Humvee.

“Ted Wolff is an expert in building desert-racers. Think of the vehicles you’ve seen running the Baja 1000. They are built to take a pounding. Ted’s also been designing a system to get lidar to work with those machines.” Rusty slammed his hand against the rigging that straddled the roof of the Hummer. “He’s here to tame this beast so that the sensors are usable at high speed. Something that none of you have been able to do so far. Isn’t that right, Nico?”

All eyes turned to Nico as he pushed his way past his fellow team members and joined Rusty and Ted next to the vehicle. Nico quietly sipped his tea and stared blankly into the crowd, refusing to respond to the question.

“Nico, tell Ted what we’ve got so far,” Rusty continued.

“We’ve got short-, medium-, and long-range sensors.” Nico placed his tea on the concrete floor beneath the Hummer and hopped onto the closest stool. “Lidar. Radar. Cameras. Each has their field of vision. We have most angles covered and can see about one hundred and fifty feet ahead. When steady, we get a crystal-clear view of our surroundings. The issue is stability."

"What about dust and sand?" Ted asked. "Are they a concern?"

"They shouldn't be. Everything's in pairs. We've got redundant systems, and Harry's software can compensate for false images—most of the time. The issue is this guy." Nico pointed to the large black cylinder at the front of the roof. "The data coming from the lidar becomes unreadable the more the vehicle shakes."

"I thought speed was the problem," Ted said.

"It's both," Rusty said, interrupting their discussion. "So, Ted, what's the fix?"

Ted suddenly felt everyone in the room staring at him. The point-blank question shocked him. He felt his clammy palms as he stepped closer to the Humvee and used his foot to snag a step stool and haul himself up to get a view on top of the Hummer. He spent a few moments studying the collection of devices strapped to the roof, his eyes masked by a lock of hair that had fallen to his face. Up close, the array of gear was impressive. He grabbed the metal rigging supporting the equipment and shook it.

"There are fluid mounts between the rack and the roof," Nico said. "They aren't effective over fifteen miles per hour."

"These mounts won't do," Ted said as he ran his hands across the cylinders supporting the gear. He tapped his fingers on the lidar. "We dissected one of these back at our shop in Nevada. It's way too delicate."

"I didn't bring you here to state the obvious, Ted," Rusty said with frustration. "I want it fixed."

Ted looked over at Nico but found no solace. He looked into the crowd of students. Harry and Lori appeared to be miles away. Ted felt his face flush as he raced to come up with a solution.

"If given enough time, I'm sure my software can figure out the false readings," Harry said. He began to step forward. "All I need is—"

"Is your name Ted?" Rusty bellowed.

Harry froze in place and lowered his head before melting back into the crowd.

Ted looked around the room as all eyes shifted from Harry back to him. He felt the disappointment, even hostility, toward him in the room. He remembered Harry's warning about Rusty running things like a military boot camp, and recalled the less than warm welcome he'd received from Rusty when he'd arrived earlier. He closed his eyes as he strained to come up with a solution he thought might satisfy Rusty. A grin spread across his face. He let go of the gear atop the Humvee and jumped off the stool.

The robotics lab had four large garage doors that led out to the main parking lot. In the far corner beside the row of workstations was an exit door. Ted walked with purpose past Nico and Rusty, taking the step stool with him, and headed to the exit. He pushed the door all the way open and wedged the stool against it to prevent it from closing. The ice-cold air blasted into the workshop floor, and those closest moved toward the center of the room. Ted disappeared outside.

"Where the hell is he going?" Harry whispered to Lori.

"Beats me," she replied.

Thirty seconds went by before Ted re-entered the building, riding Harry's Segway. As he went past the stool propping up the door, the wheel knocked the step stool loose, allowing the door to slam shut behind him. The crowd parted as Ted glided the two-wheeled vehicle to a halt next to the Hummer.

"Software can't solve this," Ted said as he glanced at Harry. "This is a hardware fix."

He stepped off the Segway and rested his arm across the handlebars.

"A Segway uses a sophisticated assembly of gyroscopes to keep itself balanced," Ted continued. "Basically, what you are going to need to do is construct a three-axis gimbal, but on a much larger scale. Not only will you be able to keep the lidar steady, but you'll be able to rotate it."

"That would increase the field of vision," Nico said, as he nodded in approval. "That may solve a number of problems."

An undertone of voices broke out in response to Ted's idea.

"It would work like a spotlight," Harry whispered to Lori. "Oh! That's what we can name the Hummer. Spotlight!"

"Quiet," Lori hissed.

Rusty began to clap his huge hands together—a slow, rhythmic clap, never increasing in intensity. He stepped forward and approached Ted and Nico. Nico hopped off the stool and waited for Rusty to finish his applause. Silence again returned to the room as everyone turned to Rusty.

"*This* is what I call thinking outside the box," Rusty said to the crowd of students. "All of you need to be on your game. I had to fly out West to find someone who could do the things you can't. The next time I have to pull in someone new, one of you will be gone. Am I clear? Everyone get back to work."

As team members gathered to discuss what had just happened and how to move forward, the noise crescendoed, overtaking the whir of the background equipment.

Ted climbed on the stool and pounded a fist against the Humvee's roof. The vibrations echoed loudly throughout the garage. Ted looked at Nico.

"Have you considered removing the roof?" Ted asked. "The vibrations may be a factor."

"You can't remove the roof, Ted," Rusty responded. "It would make it illegal to test out on public roads."

"Oh. Right." He hopped off the step stool and ran his hands across one of the mounts holding the roof rack in place. "I'll call Kevin out in Nevada. Maybe he can ship me some components we use on our trucks. That'll let me construct a better support system for the rest of the gear."

"Do whatever it takes," Rusty said. He looked down at Nico. "You need to step up your game, Nico, before Ted replaces you as my hardware lead."

Rusty turned and made his way across the lab to the door that led upstairs to the watch tower. Harry and Lori joined Nico and Ted by the Humvee.

"That was fun," Harry said.

"That was brutal," Ted said. "For a guy who was in the military, he's really not big on teamwork, is he?"

"Get used to it," Nico said. "He may be praising you now, Ted. But it won't last. You'll see."

8

Rusty watched intently from the watch tower as one by one, his team filed into the conference room he referred to as the war room. Years ago, when Rusty first pushed DSU to create a dedicated lab for robotics, senior administrators proposed multiple options, including building an entirely new structure or renovating existing administrative buildings. They were shocked when Rusty insisted they convert an old automotive shop. The lab was gritty, old, and drafty. In many ways, it reminded Rusty of his old Marines base in Yuma.

The copier in the corner of the room near where Rusty stood buzzed and rattled as it spit out the status report he would be distributing shortly at the team meeting. He glanced around the empty room and let his eyes settle on the calendar beside his computer. March's picture featured an M1 Abrams tank catching air time over a desert dune. The first twelve days, completed, were marked with their red Xs. The DARPA FAST Challenge was now eighteen months away. As soon as the copier went silent, Rusty grabbed the stack of papers and descended the staircase to the main floor.

The war room, a converted section of the original garage, was much larger and more modern than the watch tower. At the back, a separate food area doubled as a small cafeteria and break room. Five rows of tables, each with ten seats that faced a smaller table and an old walnut podium, had been set up for the meeting. The wall behind the podium had four whiteboards, and a pull-down screen hung ready for use with a video projector suspended from the ceiling.

Rusty paused in the war room doorway to find about half the team already seated, and the rest gathered in the food area. Three large coffee makers, creamers, sweeteners, pitchers of ice water, and six Dunkin' Donuts boxes of donuts sat on tables. The aroma of freshly brewed coffee with notes of vanilla and chocolate pastries filled the room.

Rusty walked over to the donuts, noiselessly coming up behind Lori and Ted, who were busily eyeing the chocolate glazed donuts.

"How are you settling in, Ted?" Lori asked. "It's been just over four months, right?"

"Honestly, couldn't be happier," he replied. "The stress is insane, but the progress we are making is fantastic. I've even gotten used to sleeping on a fold-out couch with a bunch of loud students."

"Do you miss home?"

"Not at all. If it's this or working with my dad back in Ohio, I'll take the couch."

"You don't talk much about your family."

"I know. They don't get me. Especially my dad. That's one of the things I like about being here. I feel like he gets me."

"Who? Rusty?"

Rusty tapped Lori on the shoulder.

"Do you plan to talk all morning, Ms. Preston?" Rusty asked as he turned to make his way toward the front of the room. "It's nine o'clock. Time to start."

"Good morning," Ted said as Rusty marched by them.

"We'll see about that," Rusty responded.

"We'd better sit down," Lori said quietly to Ted. "He looks like he's in one of his moods."

Ted pointed to the two empty seats in the front row. Harry and Nico were already seated up front. Rusty was very strict about where everyone sat, down to the specific seat. The pair made their way to the front and took their places. The seating order was Lori, Harry, Ted, and Nico.

The faint exchanges in the room subsided as soon as Rusty stood behind the podium, which looked oddly small in front of his towering presence. Clearing his throat, Rusty gazed around the room, taking a mental count of those present.

"Good morning," Rusty said. "You know the drill. Lori, you're up."

Every day, the team met at 9:00 a.m. to go through the project and highlight areas falling behind. Rusty had little interest in doing a deep dive into the project plan or discussing upcoming tasks. Achievements were irrelevant. The meeting was always focused on what should have been met that wasn't.

"The mapping team is at thirty percent complete," Lori said as she stood up. She glanced at her team's status report she'd brought with her. "We're on schedule and have no issues to report."

"Are you having delays or problems with other teams?" Rusty asked.

"None," she replied.

She returned to her seat and took a sip of coffee, looking over at Harry to her right. He groaned as he stood up, licking his chocolate-covered fingers.

"So, um, we're behind," Harry said. "Still."

Rusty leaned forward over the podium, which creaked under his weight. He gripped the edges and dug his nails into the wooden underside. "Can I ask why?"

"It's the new hardware," Nico said from his chair. "We have to—"

"I was asking Harry," Rusty thundered, cutting him off. "Harry?"

"It's like Nico said," Harry replied. "The gimbal and revamped lidar that Ted designed are taking longer to integrate than expected. My team and I have been trying to patch the old code, but it's been cumbersome. Half the subroutines have been rewritten. Ideally, we would start over, but we are too far into it."

Rusty stood upright and stepped away from the podium. He made his way to the back of the room to the food area, grabbed one of the pitchers of water and a glass, and filled it halfway. People in the room began glancing at one another, wondering what he was doing.

"So, Harry, are you blaming Nico and Ted?" Rusty turned as he took a sip of water and made his way back to the podium as he talked. "Is it the software or the hardware? Ted?"

Ted lowered his coffee and stood up. He looked at Harry, but Harry's head hung low. Ted frowned as he flicked his hair from his eyes. "The new hardware is exactly what we discussed. The lidar now has a field of view of two hundred and seventy degrees. The gimbal controls are proving to be a bit tricky. It's just a matter of getting everything in sync."

"So, you're blaming Harry?" Rusty asked.

"No," Ted responded. "Nobody is to blame. Look, this is a big hardware change. I agree with Harry that he's got a lot of rework to do. We're all on the same team."

"Both of you sit down. Ted, I brought you here to solve problems. It's about thinking outside the box. You've proven you can do that. Better than most." Rusty glanced down and stared at Nico until he looked away. "It seems to me we have an integration problem nobody wants to solve."

Rusty held out the glass of water at chest height.

"I'm giving everyone in this room two choices. I'm holding four ounces of water in an eight-ounce glass. The glass is either half empty or half full. Raise your hand if you think it's half empty." Rusty watched as team members looked back and forth and over their shoulders. "Are you telling me *nobody* is going with this option?"

A handful of students in the back two rows raised their hands, followed by Nico in the front. Rusty did not bother to acknowledge any of them.

"Okay, now raise your hand if you think it's half full." Rusty nodded as those remaining thrust their hands into the air. "Is there anyone who didn't raise their hand?" He watched as one by one everyone slowly lowered their arms and looked around the room. "Nobody?"

He walked around to the front of the table less than three feet from the front row, taking the glass with him. Again, holding the glass directly out in front of him, he looked around the room.

"Well, I have news for you," he continued. "All of you are wrong. It's not a question of whether the glass is half full or half empty. It's a question of design. All I need is four ounces of water. This is a wasteful and poor solution. What's needed is a new, properly sized glass."

Rusty's facial features remained cast in stone as he squeezed the glass. After a few seconds, the goblet shattered in his hand as gasps went up around the room. Shards of glass scattered to the floor, and water splattered in all directions, hitting the carpeted floor and Rusty's thumb and fingers. Those in the front row barely missed getting hit.

"If something's not working the way you need it to, then replace it with something else! Start clean. This is about finding the right solution for the right problem. If you need to revise the hardware to fit the software, change it. If you need to throw out your code and start from scratch, start over. If we do this half assed, it will only come back to bite us later."

Rusty glanced at his hand. Two small cuts on the inside of his thumb glistened red, and a few remnant shards sparkled on his skin. He wiped his hands against one another to shake off the glass and looked out at the room, ignoring the stunned looks staring back at him. He picked up the stack of papers he'd brought with him from the watch room and handed the pile to Lori before returning to the podium.

"Here's today's punch list of critical items that, if not addressed, will completely derail our critical path in the project plan. I've listed the name of the person at fault, as well as who I've decided will fix it. As always, that person may not be the one to blame."

Lori took the top sheet and passed it to Harry. Harry pointed at the bloodstain on the upper edge of the paper before giving the pile to Ted.

Rusty walked behind the podium to the center whiteboard. Grabbing a marker, he wrote COMPETITION across the top.

"There are forty copies in that pile," Rusty said. "But only thirty-nine people in this room. We lost another one—another quitter. I won't bore you with his name, and his work has already been reassigned, as noted in the report. I've been busy collecting intel on who else besides DSU has signed up for the DARPA competition next year. Does anyone in here know who Vinod Malik is?"

"He's from here," Lori said. "DSU. He worked under you, didn't he?"

"Indeed he did," Rusty replied. "He was my protégé. Vin was my best student. His software skills are beyond anyone's in this room. Vin helped me design the NASA moon rover. I mention this because Vin is now at Ashton University. And before you ask, yes, he's heading up their team for the DARPA competition."

Several groans went around the room. Ted was about to speak but raised his hand instead. Rusty pointed at him and motioned for the rest of the room to settle down.

"With all due respect, there's no way Ashton has a gimbal system as sophisticated as ours. Some of that tech is proprietary from what I built back in Nevada."

"Be that as it may, Ted, I've learned never to underestimate Vin. Going forward, I want everyone to assume that Ashton will be our biggest competition. I'm going to continue to try and squeeze whatever I can out of Vin, but I don't expect him to give away any secrets. Just consider them our top rival going forward."

"Do you know what they're driving?" Harry asked. "I doubt anyone has anything as brutal as our Humvee."

"We can just roll over the competition," Ted added.

Many in the room started to laugh, and a few even applauded. Rusty slammed his bloodied hand on top of the podium and waited for the room to quiet down.

"Do I have to remind all of you of the rules?" he asked. "This isn't *BattleBots*. If we damage any other vehicle, we are disqualified. Teams can't run each other off the course. And we can't pair up against others or block vehicles faster than ours. Every other team out there is trying to solve the same problems we are. There is no predicting what we will find in the Mojave next year. That's why I want all of you working beyond full capacity."

Rusty took a moment to grab a napkin from the table in front of the podium. He methodically set about wiping the blood from his hand. Out of the corner of his eye, he noticed Harry raise his hand. "Yes?"

"I know it's not on the project plan, but when can we name the Hummer?" Harry asked.

"This again?" Rusty let out a heavy sigh. "All right, Mr. Palmer. Go for it."

"I know everyone has different ideas." Harry jumped from his seat and glanced around the room. "But now that we have that big rotating lidar unit on top, I thought we should call it Sauron."

Several students looked around the room with confusion.

"Sauron!" Harry continued. "From *The Lord of the Rings.* He sees everywhere."

"Actually, Harry, the lidar can't see a full three hundred and sixty degrees," Ted said. "I do like your idea of a big eye looking around. How about—"

"Gort!" Harry said.

"You really are a geek," Ted said. "Let's keep it simple. How about Cyclops?"

Rusty surveyed the room, relieved to see everyone nodding in agreement. Everyone except Harry.

"Cyclops it is," Rusty said. "All right, people, you've got the punch list for today. Getting the new gimbal and lidar integrated with our core controls is top priority. Any other questions?"

The team members sat silently, many focused on Rusty. Several were busy scanning the status report. Some appeared lost in their coffee mugs, looking defeated.

"Look, I know I'm pushing all of you hard. You knew when you agreed to be on my team the goal was to change the world." Rusty walked around to the front of the table and leaned back. "DARPA had Lockheed Martin and General Dynamics working on self-driving technology for over a decade with no progress. Now they're looking beyond military contractors. We're not just competing with Ashton. There are dozens of schools out there clamoring to lead the way forward. There are also private sector businesses. Corporations. We have no idea what sort of competition we're facing. All I know is the most brilliant minds are on this. Everyone sitting in this room is part of this. These big companies have proven they are slow and out of touch. They can't innovate, no matter how much money they spend. Let's show these corporate bastards how we get things done here at DSU."

9

The DSU Robotics Lab's workshop floor was cold and empty of team members. The industrial heaters hanging from the twenty-five-foot ceiling struggled to keep the space warm. Outside, the early morning temperatures, typical for January, were below freezing and not expected to get much higher. Snow and ice pellets hammered the windows at the top edges of the walls, their thin panes covered in crystallized dew. The tin roof sang as it deflected the tiny bits raining down from the gloomy overcast sky.

Rusty glanced at his Seiko as he made his way across the workshop floor. The watch showed him the year—2007. He always felt the passage of time for weeks every January—the shock of the new numbers only slowing fading. The thud of his heavy boots echoed against the concrete walls surrounding the garage. It was fifteen seconds before 9:00 a.m. when he entered the war room. He marched past the small group of people mingling around the food area and walked behind the front table, dropping the forty-four copies of the status report next to the podium.

The war room was warmer than the workshop floor, thanks to the lower ceilings. Even so, most were bundled in sweatshirts, and some even wore hats. Bagels and cream cheese from a local bakery spread across the food table.

The center whiteboard directly behind Rusty was filled with

mathematical equations. He grabbed an eraser and wiped the board clean as several groans rose up around the room. With a marker, he wrote three dates in large letters across the board.

JANUARY 24

AUGUST 19

SEPTEMBER 9

Turning to face everyone, he tossed the marker onto the desk. The last two getting coffee hurried to their seats. Rusty glanced down at Lori, Harry, Ted, and Nico in the front row.

"We have less than seven months until we arrive in the Mojave for final prep and testing," Rusty said. His voice had grown hoarse over the past week, a result of too many heated arguments. "Three weeks later, on September ninth, the DARPA FAST Challenge begins with the qualification round. Where are we at? Lori, you're up."

He walked around to the front row and handed Lori the stack of papers to begin passing around. She took the top sheet and handed the rest to Harry.

"DARPA has confirmed all teams will get GPS data with a thousand waypoints exactly two hours before the start of the road race," Lori said. She slowly stood up as she studied her team's latest project summary report. "The course will include only ten percent of paved roads. The remainder will be barren desert, including rocks and a small stream to forge through.

"Going through the latest info, we've come up with five areas that could be the potential course. One has an overpass, and two have train tracks. We've therefore expanded our original area to survey. We've got 37,000 of the 47,000 square miles of the Mojave mapped, and less than 400 of the 1,600 sections to go. I'm projecting we will be done ahead of schedule."

"Ahead of schedule?" Rusty asked. "Finally, some good news. Harry?"

"The interior of Cyclops has been maxed out with seven Pentium computers," Harry said as he hauled himself out of his chair. Bits of sesame seeds were wedged in the corners of his mouth. He licked cream cheese from his fingers before continuing. "We just passed one million lines of code. The simulation software is running perfectly. Lori and I are in sync. Every new map profile can immediately be run through the simulator. We've started running the simulations on the final urban challenge this week."

DSU had elected to do their early testing using simulation software. Harry and his team built a virtual world based on the map detail from Lori and her team. Because these were topographical maps, they were aware of hills, valleys, and changes in elevation. The team then built a virtual Humvee they could drive across the terrain. The sensor arrays and outputs on Cyclops's roof were also simulated, allowing them to drive the vehicle through any part of the desert they had mapped. This approach proved invaluable, as it allowed them to determine how to get the short-, middle-, and long-range "eyes" of the vehicle to interpret what they saw properly. This information would be relayed to the servos controlling the steering, accelerator, and brakes inside the Hummer. Doing this in the virtual world allowed them to develop the bulk of the software before taking Cyclops out on the road.

Rusty gave Harry a slight nod, and looked past Ted and over at Nico. Harry took his seat and returned to his bagel. Nico twirled his pen across his thumb and fingers, then let it roll into the palm of his hand.

"Working with Harry, we've been able to adjust the sensors to get Cyclops to go faster without losing visibility." Nico adjusted the sleeves on his Caltech sweatshirt, exposing his hexadecimal tattoo. "We have him at just under forty miles per hour right now with no problems. Once we get past forty, he, well, starts to get a bit confused."

"That's still too slow," Rusty said. "We need to be faster."

"We're ahead of the deadlines on the project plan," Nico continued.

"Ted's rotating lidar is working brilliantly. Every week we bump our speed up a notch. We will hit forty-five ahead of schedule."

"Make it fifty," Rusty said. Two of Harry's teammates gasped from the back of the room. Rusty ignored the theatrics. "You're all getting a little too comfortable—too sure of yourselves. I guarantee you the competition is not."

"There's no way anyone else has this level of technology," Ted said abruptly. "I guarantee it."

"There are no guarantees," Rusty said. "Last night I talked with Vin at Ashton. The bastard still won't cough up any details on what they've got, but he somehow knew we had a modified Humvee. I have no clue how he found out. I'm guessing one of the quitters snitched. He seemed overly confident in what his team was building."

Rusty walked behind the podium and leaned forward. Half the students were busy studying the report. A few small sidebar conversations had broken out. He stood patiently, resting against the old walnut lectern. He lowered his eyes to see if any of his team leads had looked at the status report. He knew right away they had not.

"As some of you may have noticed, I moved up the outdoor test schedule." Rusty watched as Harry dusted bits of sesame seed from today's report. He smiled as Harry's jaw slowly fell open. "I've secured a testing site not too far away. It's in an abandoned train depot along the Allegheny River. The dean had to call in a few favors, but we will have it for as long as we need."

"Starting tomorrow?" Harry practically squeaked.

"Tomorrow," Rusty replied. The room erupted and he slammed his fist against the podium. "Is there a problem?"

The room responded with silence. Nico slowly raised his hand.

"We've designed this equipment for the desert and extreme heat," Nico said. "Snow and ice were not in our plans."

"We work with what we've got. What we've got right now is cold. I know the plan was to begin outdoor testing in April, but that conversation with Vin told me we need to be ready for anything. As far as I'm concerned, temperature extremes are extremes, one way or the other. We have no idea what DARPA will hit us with. We must be ready for the unexpected."

Harry shook his head, his eyes darting wildly as he flipped back and forth between the first few pages of the report. His hand shot up.

"What now, Mr. Palmer?" Rusty asked.

"You didn't just move up the timeline to start earlier. You cut the duration. A lot. We have a lot less time to complete the testing."

"What's your concern?"

"That's . . . that's impossible. I mean, we'd have to work night and day to hit these dates."

"Then I suggest you pack a sleeping bag. It can get chilly once the sun goes down."

Harry was about to speak but changed his mind, lowered his head, and sunk deeper into his chair.

"Any other questions?" Rusty scanned the room, taking inventory of his flock. Most had their heads down. Some were reading the report, others simply looked exhausted. "The status report lists the teams and schedules for testing. Dismissed."

He turned his attention back to the whiteboard. The room filled with unhappy groans as people pushed their chairs back and headed for the exit. A few stopped to top off their coffee or grab a bagel or two to take back to the lab. The whiteboard to the far left listed major project milestone tasks and dates. Rusty erased the dates for testing and replaced them with the modified ones he'd just shared with the team. When he turned around, he was surprised to see Ted quietly standing behind him.

"Do you have a problem with the new test schedule?" Rusty asked.

"Nah, I grew up in Ohio. I can deal with the snow and cold." Ted looked over his shoulder and waited for the last of the team members to leave the room. "I had a question. About Ashton. More specifically, about Vin."

"Vin?" Rusty folded his arms across his chest and looked Ted up and down. The lanky young man had proven himself resilient since he had joined the team a little more than fourteen months ago. Rusty was surprised to see a look of genuine concern and confusion on Ted's face. "Why do you ask?"

"I got an email from some guy named Sam over at Ashton. He said he's working for Vin on the DARPA project. According to Sam, Vin said you offered to help them configure their hardware. Is that true?"

Rusty closed his eyes as he replayed last night's phone call with Vin. It was well past ten o'clock when they'd spoken. Rusty remembered a tennis match of boasts lobbed back and forth, each trying to impress the other with hints about the breakthroughs their teams were making.

"Shit." Rusty dragged the palms of his hands from his eyebrows to his chin, finally letting out a long sigh. He sat down on the edge of the desk and began to chuckle. "Vin was telling me his software lead was doing amazing things with their sensor array to try and tame the environment we'll be facing later this year. Something to do with their hardware being too fragile. I told him we solved that over a year ago. I might have even mentioned you by name. If my memory is correct, I told him that if they hit a dead end with their hardware configuration to let us know. But I meant it as a joke. Vin had to know that."

"So, what should I do about Sam?"

"Nothing. Don't respond."

"But this might give us some insight into—"

"What part of 'don't respond' don't you understand?" Rusty crooked an arm toward the revised testing dates he'd just scrawled across the whiteboard. "We have more important things to focus on. Vin is just calling my bluff and using this guy Sam to try and figure out what Ashton's up against. I said enough on the phone last night. Give them nothing. Am I clear?"

"Crystal."

"I'm serious, Ted."

"It's a promise."

Ted struggled to open the door of the watch tower. One hand was clutched around his DSU coffee mug. The other had a napkin with a cinnamon-raisin bagel generously smeared with peanut butter, as well as a folded copy of Rusty's status report. He managed to get the door open a crack and used his foot to push it the rest of the way. Harry was the only one in the room, intently focused on his set of three computer screens.

"I need some guidance," Ted said. He took a seat in Lori's chair and dropped his bagel, coffee, and report beside her workstation. "I also need you to swear secrecy."

"What now?" Harry spun around and rolled closer to Ted. "I don't trust that grin on your face."

"I got an email from some guy at Ashton," Ted continued. "He's working on the DARPA project just like us. Apparently, Rusty and Vin got in some pissing match, and Rusty told Vin if they needed help tuning their hardware to give us a yell."

"That was stupid," Harry said.

"Rusty wasn't serious. He told me to ignore the email." Ted took a huge bite of his bagel and continued speaking with his mouth half full. "This guy Sam reports to Vin. Seems like a total dick. After raving about their groundbreaking software, he tells me they're having trouble smoothing out the readings from the sensors and that Rusty said we had the fix."

"But you just said Rusty told us not to. Ashton is supposed to be our biggest competition."

"That's exactly why I want to respond to Sam. If Ashton wants to play games with us, then we should give those . . . those *ash*-holes something weird. Something to confuse them."

"Ash-holes." Harry laughed and nodded in agreement, but then shook his head. "Ted, it's totally fine to ignore their email but rules of protocol are clear. If we provide information to them, it must be good information. It's unethical to provide misinformation. Rusty will find out and we could even be disqualified."

"I didn't say we needed to give them *bad* data, Harry. We could just give them *old* data—with a little twist. Maybe from before we installed the gimbal. Do you still have those algorithms?"

"I have it all backed up." Harry paused and stared at the project plan charts covering the walls. "But Ted, if you're going to give them information, it has to work. Old is okay, a little gray in the ethics department, but still okay. If you "twist" it too much, you will have crossed a line."

"Relax, Harry." Ted licked some bits of peanut butter from his fingertips and gulped his coffee. "I think Sam's fishing—probably under orders from Vin. It sounds to me like Ashton is trying to size up the competition. I think we should do the same."

"Meaning?"

"Meaning we ask for something in return."

"Like what?"

Ted clasped his hands above his head and leaned back as he stretched. Leaning forward again, he pursed his lips and exhaled loudly, his hair falling in front of his eyes. The springs on the underside of the chair creaked as he rocked back and forth in thought.

"Are there any software issues we're still having?" Ted propped his elbows on his knees and cradled his chin in the palm of his hands. "I know we told Rusty that Cyclops sees perfectly. But I thought there were still some hiccups."

The two men stared at each other for several seconds.

"Short trees," Harry said. "And people."

"Is that supposed to mean something to me?"

"It has to do with our simulator." Harry adjusted his glasses and scratched the top of his bald head. "Nico and I were doing dry runs through the Mojave maps Lori built. We're especially worried about the Urban Challenge when Cyclops will be going through city streets. Lori gave us some maps of the DSU campus to use in our simulations for that competition. We're getting Cyclops to see things like people and signs. Most of the time it does great."

"But?" Ted asked cautiously. "What? Short tree people confuse it?"

"Pretty much. We put people along the side of the street to make it as real as possible. Cyclops couldn't tell the difference between trees and people that were the same size and shape."

Ted laughed as he imagined people shaped like shrubs and bushes covered in leaves but with human faces.

"I don't get why that's a problem," he said. "It's not like there will be trees crossing the street."

"It's the opposite. Cyclops kept getting hung up at the same intersection because it thought the small tree in the center island was a person crossing, and it just sat there forever. He just kept waiting for them to move out of the way."

"Well, on the plus side we have a very courteous self-driving vehicle." Ted frowned and ran his hands across his scruffy chin. The long days and nights were taking their toll, and he hadn't bothered to shave since the weekend. "So, you want me to ask Sam if they can help us tell the difference? Shouldn't we ask them something we know the answer to?"

"Nico and I think we have it figured out. I've got someone working the subroutines. But let's see what Ashton has to say. You said this guy Sam bragged about their software superiority. So let's see what they've got."

Ted smiled and stood up, pushing the chair and letting it roll across the floor until it banged against Lori's desk. He grabbed his coffee mug, status report, and the rest of his bagel and headed toward the door.

"Sounds like a plan, Harry. Let me know when you have those old algorithms I can send to Sam."

"Do you want me to just forward them along? If you give me his email, I could also explain the tree problem to him."

"No, let me handle it."

"Why? Ted, I'm really serious about not giving them bad information. You have to swear to me that you will not give them bad data."

"I promise," Ted said as he stuck his right hand in the air. Inside his pocket, his left hand had crossed fingers. *It won't* be bad, just *tweaked*. He already had an idea of how he would scramble what he sent.

"Okay, I'll get you the algorithms then."

"I'll make it sound like we're struggling with that tree problem. Sam will think Ashton is lightyears ahead of us. He will be completely shocked when we roll into the Mojave with Cyclops."

"What if Sam tells Vin what we sent—and then Vin contacts Rusty?"

"I'm going to tell Sam the truth—that Rusty said not to answer him. I'm going to pretend we are struggling and that Rusty doesn't know. I will beg for Sam's help."

Harry laughed and clapped his hands a few times.

"Remind me to never play poker with you, Ted."

10

Ted awoke to tingling at the tip of his nose. Buried deep within his sleeping bag, his head was hidden behind the cool zippered edge. He had left a four-inch crack open near the top corner to allow in some fresh air. Bracing himself, he slid his hand through the opening and pushed against the zipper, spreading the sides apart. The air that greeted him was shockingly cold. He looked at the electric heater several feet away. The power light was off.

"Shit," he said as he crawled his way out of the bag.

The interior of the abandoned freight train car was nearly pitch black. Ted could barely see Nico and Harry fast asleep in their sleeping bags on the opposite side of the dead heater. One of the doors was ajar just enough to allow a power cord inside. The morning sun was still below the horizon, but the sky had taken on a faint pale blue glow, casting a sliver of light across the inside of the car. Ted used the light to find and lace up his snow boots.

Crawling over to the heater, he flicked the switch a few times. Nothing. Dirt and sand on the floor of the train car clung to his hands and sweatpants as he continued on all fours and followed the power cord to the side door. He paused, sticking the side of his face against the opening. The crisp wind bit at the curved edges of his ears. He let out a sigh as he shoved his body against the door. The wheels groaned in protest as the massive metal door slid open.

"What the hell?" Harry asked from beneath the depths of his sleeping bag.

"Why is it so cold?" Nico asked as he popped his head through his zipper. He looked back and forth between Ted and the heater. "Are we out of gas?"

"No clue." Ted shrugged, then turned and jumped from the railcar.

The Eastern Atlantic Depot facility was tucked along the banks of the Allegheny River, far from DSU's main campus. During the 1920s, the site had served as a repair facility for the major train lines that ran along the East Coast. Nowadays, it was used to store old, broken, and abandoned freight cars. Half a dozen rows of dilapidated tracks stored over fifty different cars and several engines. Adjacent to the tracks sat a hollowed-out maintenance building, the neglected roof gaping with holes.

For Ted, Nico, and Harry, this was day three of this brutal cold. Lori and her team had stayed behind, contending with their own challenges at DSU. Rusty's schedule required the three men to first design the course Cyclops would navigate, followed by actual testing. On the first day, the team had agreed on a basic route through the seventy-five-acre site. Testing on day two had gone poorly.

The brutally cold weather that greeted Ted on day three was most unwelcoming. Snow was falling, and the temperature was well below freezing. The snow was also mixed with small ice pellets being driven sideways by heavy gusts of wind. Each of the railcars sang at different frequencies as the various-sized ice capsules bounced off them on their way to the ground.

Ted held the heavy-duty extension cord in his hands and followed it back to the Ford Econoline van borrowed from the DSU maintenance department and parked several yards away. Ted, Harry, and Nico had loaded it with spare parts and the bulk of the support gear they would need to test Cyclops. Ted's brow furrowed as he reached the van. The engine was off, which explained why their portable heater had no power.

After fumbling through his pockets, he pulled out a spare key for the van and hopped inside. Nico and Harry were standing in the doorway of the train, buried deep in the sleeping bags they had wrapped around them. Ted made a couple of attempts to get the engine to turn over, but it was completely dead.

Nico disappeared from the doorway briefly, returning without his sleeping bag and a heavy coat in his hands. He jumped from the freight car and ran over to join Ted, pulling his heavy coat on as he moved. He opened the back of the van to check the inverter he'd installed and followed the leads to the van's battery to make sure everything was connected correctly.

"We're out of gas," Ted said as he stepped out of the Ford. "Do you have any in your Civic?"

"I've got three two-gallon jugs in the hatch." Nico slammed the rear doors of the van shut. "We forgot to top the tank off before going to sleep."

Ted made his way back to the freight car as Nico ran off to get the gas to refill the Ford. Harry was back inside, still wrapped up in his sleeping bag. Ted closed the freight door most of the way to block the wind and snow, but left it open a crack to allow in a bit of light.

"This sucks, Ted." Harry's voice was shaky. "This is inhumane. We shouldn't be out here. Rusty is out of his mind."

The team had brought a foldable card table and set it up along the back wall of the train car. Ted walked over to it and began gathering everything he would need to make a pot of coffee. He stopped when he remembered they still didn't have power.

"When you told me we'd ended up in boot camp, I really thought you were joking."

"When did I say that?" Harry stuck his nose through his bag. "Oh, that first day you showed up. I remember. I thought you were going to trash my Segway that day, too."

Ted laughed as he opened a cooler and pulled out a bottle of Red

Bull. He waved it at Harry, but Harry declined and slid back down into his cocoon.

"This schedule is a joke," Harry continued. "I wonder who we could complain to?"

"You want to file a complaint?" Rusty asked.

Ted spun around, startled to see Rusty looking through the doorway of the freight car.

"Who said that?" Harry asked. He popped his head out of his sleeping bag and stared at Rusty in total shock. "Nothing. We, uh, had trouble with the van running out of gas. Nico has it fixed."

"Everyone outside," Rusty said. "I need a status report."

Harry thrashed himself free of his sleeping bag—his bright yellow Cheerios shirt practically radiating light—grabbed his glasses and yanked on a pair of boots. In dual layers of sweatpants and sweatshirts and a heavy winter coat and hat, Harry followed Ted outside, where they met Nico and Rusty beside the van.

"How was last night's testing?" Rusty asked, his handlebar mustache accumulating snow. He kept his hands shoved deep inside his pockets. Rusty didn't bother to wear a hat, despite the bitterly cold wind. "When I left last night, you still hadn't gotten Cyclops to complete the first milestone."

"We just woke up," Harry said.

"Did I ask about your sleeping schedule?" Rusty responded.

"Cyclops still shuts down after about five laps," Nico said. "We want him to run that first course for fifty laps, but he keeps going offline."

"So, you've made no progress?" Rusty began to pace back and forth. "I left here at five last night. Why isn't it fixed?"

Ted could see Nico's anger rising, while Harry looked ready to collapse. Ted shared both of their concerns, and took a couple of steps forward, positioning himself between Rusty and his teammates.

"It's the cold," Ted said. "We'll be facing extreme heat in the Challenge, not cold. Cyclops isn't designed for this."

"Are you trying to tell me how to harden my robots? My rovers have gone to the moon, Ted. They have to face both extreme heat *and* extreme cold. It shouldn't matter."

Rusty moved closer to Ted until the two were less than a foot apart. Ted stared up at the hulking man, refusing to be intimidated.

"Show me," Rusty said, his voice a deep baritone.

Ted turned and led everyone over to Cyclops. The vehicle was covered in a giant tarp to protect the fragile equipment covering the roof and fenders. Nico helped Ted release two of the ropes staked to the ground, and together they carefully peeled back the navy blue sheeting covering the Humvee.

"These cameras are the issue," Ted said as he pointed to one of two small black cameras mounted on the front fenders. He tried to temper his anger. Rusty's twice-daily visits had become more than a little annoying. "We need them for short-range data gathering, but the data feed is inconsistent. It's the cold temperatures. Harry's been playing with the code to try and compensate for the data issues."

"How many robots have you built . . ." Rusty asked as he stepped closer to Ted. "Before you started working for me here at DSU?"

"None, but—"

"Then why the hell are you telling me how these sensors work? I brought you here because you said you'd never met a problem you couldn't solve." Rusty pushed Ted aside, almost knocking him to the ground. He bent over and yanked one of the stakes from the ground. "How many times do I need to tell you that if something isn't working, throw it out and start over?"

In one swift move, Rusty thrust his arm out wide and rotated his torso, swinging around and driving the tip of the stake into the lens of Cyclops's closest camera assembly. The glass lens shattered instantly, and the entire assembly tore loose from its mount.

"Have you lost your mind?" Nico screamed.

Rusty lowered his arm and unclenched his fist, allowing the stake to fall to the ground. It bounced a few times against the cold hard ground before coming to a rest between his boots.

"Start over," Rusty said. "Those cameras have been causing you issues since before Ted arrived, Nico. There's no excuse for them to be failing at this late stage. None!"

Rusty walked between the three men, knocking Ted and Harry to the side.

"Where the hell do you think you're going?" Ted said. He reached out and grabbed Rusty by the shoulder. "You can't just break our shit and leave!"

Rusty spun around and grabbed Ted's jacket with both hands. He plowed forward and pushed Ted backward. Ted stumbled to keep from falling and wrapped his hands around Rusty's huge wrists. He tried in vain to get Rusty to release him. Ted groaned as his back slammed against the side of the Humvee.

"*Your* shit?" Rusty said. He leaned forward until his nose almost touched Ted's. "I can break whatever shit I want. This is *my* team. *My* vehicle. *My* shit. And who are you to tell me not to break shit? Isn't that your M.O., Ted? You love to break things to get them to work. Push them to their limits until they fail. Or did you forget the sales pitch you gave me in Nevada?"

Rusty and Ted glared at each other, neither willing to look away. Rusty finally said, "Consider yourself pushed."

Rusty gave him one final shove against Cyclops before releasing him, then swiveled to face Nico and Harry. Both were standing with their hands in their pockets, frozen in fear. Harry immediately looked away, his glasses crystallizing from the cold. Nico stared at Rusty in anger.

"My robots have gone a mile underwater and to the surface of the moon." Rusty headed toward Nico and Harry, who stepped aside to let him pass. "If you jackasses can't solve a little cold, then you have no business being on this team. I'll be back tonight at five, and I expect this to be resolved."

Ted was seething with anger. He clenched his fists as he pushed himself away from the Humvee. Tears streamed down his face. He walked up to Harry and Nico but never took his eyes off Rusty.

"I thought you understood who I am," Ted cried out. "You're . . . you're worse than my dad."

Rusty paused a few yards from his Ford Expedition and slowly turned around.

"I'm not your friend, Ted. And I'm certainly not your daddy. I don't give a shit about whatever baggage you've got rattling around in that head of yours. You are here for one reason and one reason only. DSU is going to win the FAST Challenge. We will do it with or without you." Rusty glanced at his watch. "That applies to all of you. I'll be back here in exactly ten and a half hours. Get to work."

Ted wiped the tears from his face as he watched Rusty drive away. He was both taken aback, and a bit embarrassed at how emotional he'd become. He kept his eyes focused on Rusty's green SUV as it slowly disappeared. Several seconds of silence passed as the wind and snow continued to blast their way across the train yard.

"We've all been there," Harry said softly. He pulled his hand from his pocket and gently let it rest on Ted's shoulder. "It's his thing. He finds this way of just crushing your soul."

"Thanks," Ted said. He lowered his head and glanced at Nico. "You warned me. You both did. He gets to everyone, doesn't he?"

"Everyone," Nico replied. "Even Lori."

"Lori?" Ted said as he wiped his nose dry. "She's like a block of ice."

"It was the first month she was here," Harry said. He shoved his hand into his pocket. "She tried to tell Rusty how much time her team would need to do the mapping, and he ripped her to shreds. He started insulting MIT where she came from and telling her that men are better at math than women."

"Wow," Ted said.

"I walked in on her half an hour later upstairs," Harry said. "It was the only time I've seen Lori get emotional. Don't tell her I told you. She'd probably beat the shit out of me."

Ted chuckled and nodded in agreement. He turned and looked back at Cyclops. The right side camera assembly was dangling from the fender, banging back and forth in the wind. Ted walked slowly toward the Humvee with Nico and Harry close behind. They stopped beside the vehicle to inspect the damage.

"Do you have a spare camera in the van?" Harry asked Nico.

"I do," Nico replied. "But it won't make a difference. It won't solve the problem."

The wind gusts were increasing their intensity, the snow and ice were becoming even harsher than they had been earlier. Harry buried his hands inside his coat beneath his armpits to warm them. Ted caught a glimpse and smiled.

"Nico, can you take a drive back to DSU?" Ted asked.

"Gladly. But do I have to come back?"

"Sorry, but you do. I need you to see what we've got in storage to use for insulation." Ted gathered up the tattered bits of the camera assembly and pushed them together as best he could, positioning the equipment back onto the fender mount. "We need to make a nice set of sleeping bags for these cameras."

"Yes!" Nico clapped his hands together and slapped Ted on the shoulder. He gave Harry a quick thumbs-up before sprinting off to his car.

"And if someone did a food run on their way back, it wouldn't bother me," Harry called out.

The snow had stopped falling just as Nico returned at 2:00 p.m. Though the sun was out, it was not strong enough to cut through the subfreezing temperature and melt the two inches of snow covering the ground. Nico joined Harry inside the Econoline van. The heat and fan were both set to high, keeping the interior toasty warm. Harry was fixated on his laptop, monitoring the telemetry they were receiving from Cyclops. He had one hand hovering over the keyboard and another clutching a glazed chocolate donut.

"Can you see him?" Harry asked. "He's only got two laps to go."

"Not yet," Nico replied. He lowered his mug of green tea, raised a pair of binoculars to his face, and scanned the area ahead of them. "Ted should be in view by now. Unless—There! There he is!"

Cyclops emerged from a crop of barren oak trees on the other side of the compound. Ted was inside, riding shotgun in the passenger's seat. The robotic controls occupied the area that used to be the driver's seat. The servos whirred and hummed as they navigated the Humvee down a small hill and across a set of train tracks. The steering, accelerator, and brakes all received precise adjustments based on the commands being sent from the bank of computers loaded in the rear. Ted could not wipe the grin from his face as the Humvee approached the van with Harry and Nico inside. He waved as Cyclops turned and passed by them.

Ted's smile was short-lived. Just after the turn, the lights on the control panel began blinking red. Cyclops began accelerating. Ted was well aware that this part of the course was not meant for speed. The Humvee veered off course to the right and straight toward a row of parked freight cars.

"Shit!" Ted yelled. He waited a few more seconds to see if Cyclops would take corrective action, but the vehicle continued accelerating. The train cars were rapidly closing in on Ted's side of the Hummer. "Damnit!"

A large red button on the control pad was labeled "Kill." They were so close to completing their milestone that Ted hesitated. With a heavy sigh, he slapped his palm on top of the button, taking the AI and robotic controls offline. Instead of slowing, however, Cyclops just got faster. Panic set in as Ted realized he was less than ten yards from slamming into a thirty-ton freight car. A secondary kill switch was on top of the dashboard directly in front of him. Ted smacked it and closed his eyes. Several alarms went off before Cyclops finally began to decelerate.

Ted braced himself against the passenger door as the Humvee slowed and ran over a set of train tracks. The rails nudged the front wheels just enough to turn the vehicle away from the train cars. Cyclops rocked back and forth so violently, it jumped one of the tracks, just missing a Norfolk Southern engine. After several seconds more, Cyclops rolled to a stop and Ted let out a big sigh of relief.

His body racing with adrenaline, he did a quick inspection of the control panel to try and figure out what had gone wrong. The roar of an engine drew his gaze over his shoulder, and he watched as the Econoline came skidding to a halt. Harry and Nico burst from the vehicle and ran to the Humvee. The whole scene suddenly struck Ted as funny, and a giggle began to take hold.

"Are you okay?" Harry asked as he whipped the driver's door open. "What the hell is so funny?"

"Two laps! We were so damn close." Ted leaned back in his seat and began to laugh uncontrollably. "I really thought we had it this time."

"I thought you were going to die." Nico opened the passenger's side door and did a quick visual of Ted, looking for injuries. "Are you hurt? Why weren't you wearing your seat belt?"

"I'm fine, Nico. Cyclops is the one you need to worry about. He just took off. The main kill switch failed, too. Do we know what happened?"

Harry ran his hands across the robotic servos anchored in front of the steering wheel. A maze of wires connected the actuators to a matrix of circuit boards, mounted to a rack bolted to the vehicle's floor. These, in turn, connected to the seven Pentium computers jammed into the backseat.

"Maybe your robot got mad you didn't give him eyes in the cockpit," Harry replied jokingly. "You were so close to making a Johnny Five."

"His eyes are on the fenders and roof. There's no point in giving this thing a face." Ted flipped his control pad over and traced the cabling, hoping to figure out why the kill switch had failed. "And if I gave the robot inside Cyclops eyes, Harry, I'd want him to look more like a terminator, not that dorky *Short Circuit* robot."

"Rise of the machines!" Harry laughed as he started checking the wiring coming from the computer array in the backseat. "I think we're a long way from artificial intelligence taking over the planet, Ted. Don't you?"

"I found the problem," Nico said from outside the Humvee.

Ted stepped down from the passenger's seat and let out a moan. His right thigh ached from bracing himself against the door during the wild ride against and across the tracks. He stopped to massage it momentarily before slamming the door shut. Nico was standing next to him, pointing at the camera mounted on the right front fender. The camera was wrapped tightly in the new insulation Nico had designed for it. It had pivoted sideways and was pointed at the sky. Harry ran over to take a look, too.

"Well, if it's looking at the sky, of course it thinks you've got clear roads ahead," Harry said. "But the assembly on the driver's side is intact. They work together to eliminate false readings. It should have realized something was way out of whack."

"Why are you telling us?" Ted said. "You're the software guy."

"I know!" Harry shook his head in frustration. "I'll run through the programs and see what I missed, but from inside the van where it's warm. Then I'll upload the changes back into the computers in Cyclops."

"It's a hardware problem, too," Nico said. "The camera shouldn't have worked its way loose. I replaced the entire assembly that Rusty broke. I must have screwed up. We can't afford these mistakes. I'll check the van to see what we've got to repair this."

"I'm sure there's some duct tape in there," Ted said.

Nico frowned and stomped off toward the Econoline. Harry shoved his hands into his pockets and started to follow Nico, when something caught his attention. There was a thick metal post, about five feet tall, a few feet between the Humvee and the Norfolk Southern engine car. Most of the gray pole was caked in ice, except for one section that was red. Harry bent over to inspect it, wondering what on earth it had originally been used for, and looked back at Ted.

"What?" Ted asked as he joined Harry. He ran a fingernail across the red streaks.

Harry pointed to the Humvee's right front fender. A large scrape ran from just behind the wheel to several inches back across the bodywork.

"It's just some paint, Harry. Aren't you planning to give Cyclops a fresh coat before the competition?"

"Well, sure, but . . . Ted, if that post hadn't been there, you probably would have slammed right into the train. Or worse, rolled down the hill into the river."

"I didn't even see the post." Ted looked past the Norfolk Southern engine and for the first time, noticed the embankment that led to the Allegheny River. "It all happened so fast."

"Nico said you weren't wearing your seat belt. We can't afford to lose you—or Cyclops."

Ted smiled at how concerned Harry was. He scooped some snow from the ground beneath the post and began to roll it into a ball. The heat from his hands melted the edges, which froze once they were exposed to the frigid air. Ted ran the snowball up and down the side of the pole, removing the streaks of red paint.

"Relax, Harry. What's a little spilled blood in the name of progress?"

11

August in California's Mojave Desert could sometimes see early morning temperatures hovering around the sixty-degree mark. As the sun began its slow ascent, the wind that had been pummeling the sandy landscape for days continued its assault. Rusty did his best to ignore the plinking of sand against the aluminum siding of his temporary home. He had more important things to focus on.

He followed a strict routine every morning regardless if it was a weekday, the weekend, or a holiday. He attributed his discipline to his military training. First was a series of stretches his physical therapist designed around his hip injury for him to do before even leaving the bedroom. The exercises warmed up the muscles in his lower back, glutes, and hamstrings. It took Rusty precisely fifteen minutes to complete the routine. Once done, he would immediately shower, trim his beard and handlebar mustache, and follow with a cup of strong black coffee. Then, he could move forward with whatever the day had in store for him.

Working out in the cramped quarters of the thirty-four-foot-long National RV LX-6320 was a bit of a challenge. He made the best of it, though, as he silently and methodically went through his routine undistracted, even by the rocking of the RV, buffeted by the wind.

Once his coffee was in his US Marine Corps travel mug, he stepped outside, checking his watch—6:30 a.m. Rusty took a sip from his mug and smiled as he looked a dozen yards away at the three tents staked to the ground next to the second RV in their fleet. With the forecast calling for a high of one hundred degrees, conditions would be perfect for the day's test schedule.

He went back inside and rummaged through the kitchen. The RV was one of a handful of vehicles DSU had rented as part of their desert camp. He was grateful to have the space all to himself. He had flown from Pennsylvania to Las Vegas a day earlier to rent the RV and make the two-hour drive to the DARPA campsite in the Mojave. The RV, geared for families vacationing in the nearby national parks, came fully stocked. Rusty found what he was looking for—a two-quart aluminum pot and soup ladle—and headed out.

Harry, Nico, Lori, and Ted had driven across the country in a rented SUV as part of a convoy, made up of the Ford F-250 pickup and trailer transporting Cyclops and a semi-truck housing the DSU rolling lab, to make sure all arrived unscathed. The 2,200-mile journey took them four days. Once in Las Vegas, they swapped the SUV for a National RV, similar to Rusty's but a slightly larger model, LX-6342. The four of them would share this space for the next month. The rest of the DSU team flew out yesterday and were staying in a total of three tents, four to a tent, arranged in a semi-circle. To help keep their occupants cool, the tents included ventilation and reflective covers. Each tent represented a team of four that supported each of one of the three team leads—Lori, Harry, and Nico.

Rusty walked into the middle of the encampment and started clanging the spoon against the pot. After a good twenty seconds, the first zipper opened. One by one, the team members filed out, bleary-eyed and dazed.

The door to the RV opened and Lori, hair disheveled, stuck her head out and frowned. Rusty stopped banging and pointed the giant spoon at Lori.

"Get everyone out here," Rusty said. "We have a long day ahead of us."

Rusty paced back and forth, his feet imprinting a path in the silty desert sand. He checked his watch repeatedly as he waited for everyone to assemble. Sand blasted across his forehead as he grew more and more impatient with each passing minute. Harry was the last to arrive as he struggled to keep the wind from blowing his *12 Monkeys* T-shirt above his stomach. Rusty looked at his watch one last time and frowned.

"I don't need to tell all of you how important today is," he said. "Three weeks from now is September ninth, the start of the DARPA FAST Challenge. This means we have exactly twenty-one days to complete our final testing. I know this sounds like a long time, but trust me, it's going to fly by quickly. We have a strict schedule to follow each day. That schedule will not change no matter what comes up. Lori, you're up."

The support team members stood grouped behind each of their leads. Lori took a couple of steps forward and turned to face everyone. Her bright pink M.A.D. Robots sweatshirt rippled in the wind.

"The first thing we'll do is verify the accuracy of our maps." Lori's long red hair whipped wildly across her face. She pulled an elastic from her sweatshirt pocket and tamed it back into a ponytail. "We've mapped over fifty-five thousand acres the past two years, including this exact section of the Mojave. DARPA still hasn't told us where the individual challenges are going to take place. I want to send Cyclops out for some real-world scans of the area so we can confirm just how accurate our maps are. We will send the findings back to the team members at DSU for any map calibrations needed on the mainframe computer system. Then we can adjust the maps loaded inside the computers in Cyclops."

"My guess is the three challenges aren't far from our testing area," Rusty said.

"I've been studying a radius of fifty miles around us. Assuming the competition sites are all fairly local, I think I've been able to narrow down where they might occur." Lori searched the skyline for several seconds and then turned to look at Rusty. "We aren't allowed outside this test area, are we?"

"No." Rusty began to pace back and forth once again, focusing his eyes on the dozen people standing behind their team leads. "If we leave the test site, we're disqualified. There are to be no hunting expeditions anywhere. We aren't even allowed to talk to the other teams. Harry?"

"I'm at the mercy of Lori and Nico," Harry said. The wind gusts rolled through the camp in waves. Harry tilted his head sideways to block the sand trying to get into his right ear. "My team and I are ready to handle whatever adjustments are needed. I've also confirmed the link and protocols to communicate with the rest of the software team back in Pittsburgh. Our remote computer center is ready to go."

Rusty nodded and stepped in front of Nico and Ted. Nico turned to avoid the wind and to face the group.

"The big test will obviously be how Cyclops performs in this heat and sand," Nico said. He remained calm with his gaze set on his team members. "The winter conditions we experienced earlier this year were brutal, but I'm confident we can handle whatever the Mojave throws at us. We've run simulations with winds gusting over forty miles per hour, including debris. Our main focus is on this dust and sand to make sure we have things covered—literally."

"Good." Rusty turned his attention to Ted. "Anything to add, Mr. Wolff?"

"No." Ted's response was short and curt, and he refused to make eye contact with Rusty.

"Are there any questions?" Rusty asked, his voice raised, his eyes looking at each DSU member. "Anyone? Now's the time to ask. I don't want anyone coming to me in a week or tomorrow with any issues we can address today."

Several seconds passed before Harry raised his hand.

"Have you learned anything else about the competition?" Harry said. "I mean, there are dozens of other camps out here just like ours. But they're so far away it's hard to tell what we're up against."

"All I can tell you is there are a total of forty teams, including ours." Rusty turned and walked a few yards away, with his back to everyone. He scanned the horizon, allowing his gaze to momentarily pause on the clusters of tents and trucks far off in the distance. "I know that we're up against some major university talent besides Ashton. MIT and Princeton are out there. So is Berkeley. I've also heard rumors that we will have some impressive competition from military suppliers."

Rusty glanced at his watch and frowned. He spun around and walked back to the DSU team. His limp wasn't particularly noticeable this morning, partly due to having just finished his physical therapy exercises, but Rusty was thinking it also had to be the desert heat. The momentary relief from constant pain felt good.

"Our journey is almost at an end." Rusty paused to study the faces of the sixteen people standing in front of him. He took note that a few had visibly aged over the past two years. "We've got three weeks to test Cyclops and confirm he's battle-ready. Today's wind and sandstorms will push all of you. Everything, from how secure the rig is to how accurate the sensor calibrations, mapping, and software running the robotics are, *must* be nailed down by the end of the month.

"I know you've all sacrificed a lot these past two years. I may not say it often, but I'm proud of this team and what we've achieved. I've built many robots in my lifetime but none are close to the size and scope of Cyclops. This is more than just a competition. The technologies we've pioneered have the potential to change the world as we know it. You know what we have to do as a team. You know your role. Trust in each other. Work together. Let's get this done."

As Ted scanned the desert for other camps, he jammed his earbuds in deeper. Ozzy Osbourne's "Crazy Train" came into sharper focus. The desert wind played with the cord to his iPod, nestled in the front pocket of his Levi's. To prevent it from whipping against his skin, he tucked it beneath his chin. Bopping his head to the beat, he raised a pair of binoculars to his eyes. Even with the zoom set to maximum, Ted couldn't make out any details of the other teams.

DARPA had carved out a holding area for all forty teams central to where the three different challenges would take place, one hundred miles south of Las Vegas. The teams were evenly dispersed across a twenty-mile grid. Ten test areas allowed each of the teams to give their vehicles their final shakedown. Because only one vehicle could test at a time, DARPA set up a strict schedule and closely monitored the situation to ensure everyone complied.

Ted felt a tap on his shoulder. He lowered his binoculars, yanked the earbuds from his ears, and turned around. Nico was standing beside him, sporting a huge pair of wraparound sunglasses.

"I need your help getting Cyclops unloaded," Nico said. The wind puffed up his oversized black windbreaker, making his thin frame look like a balloon. Nico looked past Ted toward the camps dotting the horizon. "What's the competition look like?"

"They're too far away." Ted held the binoculars up one more time and adjusted the focus ring. He sighed and lowered them. "I've counted only four other camps. And even fully zoomed in, I can only make out bits and pieces. Cars. Trucks. Vans. I can't tell the transport vehicles from the robots."

"I guess we'll have to wait until the start of the event."

"I wonder if we should do a scouting mission." Ted gave Nico an evil grin. "Maybe after the sun goes down?"

"And risk disqualification? Or worse, the wrath of Rusty?"

"You know I don't give a shit what he thinks."

Ted shoved his hand into his pocket to power down his iPod and leaned into the wind to head back to camp. Nico kept pace with him across the desert landscape.

Almost seven months had passed since Ted had blown up at Rusty during winter testing at the train depot along the Allegheny River. Since then, Ted had diverted all of his time and energy toward perfecting the lidar and gimbal assembly on Cyclops's roof. He was incredibly proud of what he and Nico had achieved. After being forced to work together in the dead of winter, Ted had bonded with Nico and considered him a close friend. Ted had also distanced himself from Rusty. He no longer saw him as a "tough love" type of mentor, but as just another angry middle-aged man telling him what to do, no different than his father.

Once back at camp, Ted and Nico paused to take in their home for the next few weeks. DSU was, by far, the largest team in both staff and financial backing. Their camp dwarfed the size of their closest competitor. With millions in funding, they had four support vehicles at their disposal. Two were the rented RV units. They also had the truck and trailer used to transport Cyclops across the country. The main vehicle was a semi outfitted with a wall of computers and office equipment on one end and a break area on the other with a couch, stove, and fridge.

"Do you think anyone else has this level of support?" Nico asked Ted.

"Even if they do, they don't have Cyclops. Let's get him down."

Cyclops was strapped to a trailer parked behind the semi-truck. Harry and Lori were standing under the awning of their RV reviewing a report Lori had printed. Ted waved his arms to get their attention and pointed to the trailer.

The Humvee was wrapped in three layers of heavy-duty tarps and had remained covered since departing the DSU Robotics Lab last week. The bindings were tight, and it took a few minutes for Ted and Nico to loosen them. Lori arrived first, this time in a bright red M.A.D. Robots T-shirt. She perched a box of Entenmann's raspberry danishes on the hood of the Ford F-250 attached to Cyclops's trailer. Right behind her, Harry clutched four bottles of water to his chest to help him combat the dry desert air and ruthlessly intense heat.

Together, the four of them slowly peeled back the tarps, taking care not to disturb any of the equipment attached to the Humvee. As each section of the vehicle was revealed, they paused to check each and every sensor to make sure nothing had been damaged during the long trip. Nico had been meticulous with securing the gear, wrapping each sensor individually. The wind fought against them as they tried removing the tarps. Finally, after what seemed like half the day, they completely freed Cyclops from its cover.

"That is one nice coat of fire engine red, Harry," Ted said.

Cyclops stood atop the trailer, looking like the meanest Hummer ever assembled. Before leaving Pittsburgh, Harry and two other students had spent a weekend meticulously taping off and covering the equipment on the roof and fenders to paint the vehicle. Harry had picked a particularly high gloss coat of red, one more suited to a Ferrari than a military vehicle. Cyclops's standout feature was the white three-foot-high rotating lidar array perched on the roof.

"I'm particularly proud of the brush guard," Harry said. "I never asked Rusty for permission. Do you think he'll get mad?"

Ted walked to the front of the Humvee and slapped his hand on the six-post metal guard wrapped around the nose of the vehicle. All of the bars had been painted silver except for the sections just below the headlights. Harry had painted them bright orange in the shape of Rusty's trademark handlebar mustache.

"Cyclops is big, mean, and crushes everything in his path," Ted said with a grin. "If anything, Rusty should see it as a compliment. Let's hope Cyclops is as brutal in the competition as our leader was in getting us here."

12

September ninth marked the beginning of the first week of the DARPA FAST Challenge. The first of the three events would be the Qualifying Stage. Kyle Fisher had worked with lead members of DARPA to design a set of nine tests in this event that would verify the basic controls for the autonomous vehicles. Some of the tests resembled standard handling tests, such as navigating a slalom or doing emergency lane changes. Most, though, were geared toward assessing more detailed maneuvers, including performing a three-point-turn and cresting hills with turns or barriers as impediments.

DARPA began escorting the forty teams from their testing campsites to the competition site at 7:00 a.m. Crews were brought over in groups of four. DSU was part of the first group and had arrived at the site shortly before 7:30 a.m. The twenty-mile trip had been exciting for the team, especially Lori, as she tracked their movements against her digital maps. She was surprised to find that the Qualifying Stage was in an area she had not predicted.

DSU was packed into a tight holding area. The semi-truck, two RVs, and the truck pulling the trailer with Cyclops secured under his tarps barely fit. After a few tries, DSU figured out how to fit it all and deploy the awnings on both RVs. Rusty's RV was at the front; the team leads' was tucked in the rear.

Ted took up a space under Rusty's awning to watch as other teams pulled in. No one else was decked out with a semi that doubled as a rolling computer lab.

"Seen anything interesting yet?" Rusty was standing in the door of his RV, clutching his USMC insulated mug tightly. "How's the competition looking?"

Ted didn't bother turning around. "So far, all seem fairly basic," he said with more than a hint of smugness. "Some tricked-out pickup trucks with a van as the support vehicle. No other team with more than six people."

"It's still early." Rusty stepped down from his trailer and closed the door. He joined Ted at the edge of the awning. "DARPA has quite a few more trips to make to get all forty teams here."

"If what I've seen is any indication . . ." Ted paused as the ground began to rumble. He looked over at Rusty. "Earthquake?"

A mechanical roar began to fill the air. The clatter and whine of a powerful engine echoed off the mountains surrounding the DARPA site. Harry, Lori, and Nico flew from their trailer and ran to join Rusty and Ted.

"We saw it from out back!" Lori said.

"Saw what?" Ted asked.

The shaking and snarling grew louder. DARPA had enclosed the entire test site in temporary fencing. A sliding gate marked the main entrance where all vehicles entered. All eyes turned toward the gate, just as a dust cloud rose in the distance.

"Holy shit," Ted said. He took a few steps forward to the middle of the road. "What . . . what the hell is that?"

The early morning sun rising in the east caught the narrow windshield of a monstrous vehicle as it crested the hill several hundred feet from the gate. The glint of reflecting sunlight was soon overpowered by the monster's neon green paint.

"That would be our first serious competition." Rusty stepped forward to stand next to Ted. He squinted to keep the dust from obscuring his vision and reached out to grab Ted's shoulder to pull him back from the road. "It's a military contractor."

Lori draped her arm around Harry's neck and watched in awe as the team from Oshkosh Defense rolled past the DSU camp. The Caterpillar C12 diesel engine powering the six-wheeled behemoth was deafening. The vehicle itself weighed over fifteen tons and was nearly as tall as DSU's semi.

"No, seriously, what the hell is that?" Ted asked. He coughed and waved his hands across his face, clearing away the dust kicked up by the vehicle's massive tires. "It's bigger than a tank."

"That's an MTVR." Rusty walked into the roadway and watched the bright green behemoth come to a halt a dozen yards away. "'Medium Tactical Vehicle Replacement.' It's a multi-purpose vehicle for carrying man and machine—and a total beast off-road. Did anyone catch what they had for tech?"

"I saw multiple radar and lidar arrays up front," Nico said. "But I can't imagine something that big can be as fast or maneuverable as our Humvee."

"You'd be wrong." Rusty kept his gaze on the MTVR. "It can easily go over fifty miles per hour. Top speed will max out around sixty-five."

"I didn't see a gimbal," Ted said. "There's no way they can go as fast as Cyclops without data corruption."

"And how will they do the Urban Challenge in that thing?" Lori asked. "It can't do tight turns with six wheels."

"That's enough speculation," Rusty said. He walked back under his RV's awning, guiding the other four to join him. He took a sip of coffee, continuing, "We need to stay focused. In less than twenty-four hours, DARPA will give us the details on the nine tests of the Qualifying Stage. We'll then have two hours to enter that data into Cyclops to get him ready to compete. We can't waste time today watching every vehicle roll through here. I want all of your teams ready to meet in half an hour."

Ted led the way back to the other RV. Once all four leads were inside, he pointed to the small dinette booth and waited for the others to sit down. He leaned back against the kitchen counter on the opposite side of the tiny room.

"There's no way we're ignoring the competition," Ted said. "Let's get the teams together and have Rusty's little pow-wow. We can set them to work on whatever needs to get done. Then the four of us can go on a scouting mission."

"Shouldn't we wait until all forty contestants are here?" Harry asked. "DARPA's moving everyone over here in waves. They should be done by noon at the latest."

"Then let's plan to head out at eleven." Ted sat down next to Harry, forcing him to slide up against the wall. "This holding area is fairly compact. I walked it earlier as soon as we got here. It's basically a giant U-shape. We can split up into two groups. Harry and I take our side, and you two start across from us."

"Hardware and software pairs," Harry said with a grin. "Great strategy!"

"Nico, make a mental note of what each team has. Specifically, see if anyone has a gimbal like ours."

"I'll find out what they did for mapping," Lori said. She turned and looked at Harry. "And what kind of computing power they've got running their systems."

"I think we should keep Cyclops under wraps as long as possible," Nico said. "Not until later today, after we've checked everyone else out. I'll make sure our team members know they aren't allowed to take the tarps off."

"Excellent idea," Ted said. "Under no circumstances do we give up the details on Cyclops. We need to wow everyone tomorrow, the day of the competition. They are going to freak when they see the huge gimbal and lidar array."

The window in the RV's kitchen slide-out faced the road that ran beside the mountain range to the west. Ted watched as another puff of dust rose in the distance. His initial feeling of shock and intimidation at the site of the MTVR was replaced by the realization that this was quickly turning into a real challenge.

He stood up and grabbed his iPod from the counter beside the sink. Putting his earbuds in, he scrolled through the music list before settling on "School's Out" by Alice Cooper.

"Okay," Ted said as headed toward the door. "Let's give the drill sergeant what he wants and then go size up that competition."

Ted stopped a few yards from the Ashton camp and waited patiently for Harry to catch up. Harry removed one of the bandanas from his back pocket and wiped the sweat running from his bald head. The temperature had soared twenty degrees since the sun had risen, now approaching ninety. Harry pulled a bottle of water from another pocket and chugged half of it down.

"Do you see this?" Ted asked Harry. He tried not to laugh out loud. "They have a Prius."

"Why bring a hybrid to a desert challenge?" Harry removed his glasses and wiped them against his T-shirt to dry them off. "It doesn't even have four-wheel-drive."

"I have no idea. So far I've been unimpressed with most of the competition. MIT seems like the only threat, other than Oshkosh."

"I agree. They both had multi-lidar systems. Fortified all-wheel-drive vehicles. And the teams seemed sharp."

"But I also agree with Lori that Oshkosh will be too big to win the Urban Challenge. Even this week's obstacle courses may trip them up," Ted said.

"Why would they enter such a brute if it can't win all three?"

"Who knows. Maybe they just want to show the military what it can do in the desert. Isn't that what started this whole DARPA thing in the first place?"

"I guess."

Ted was about to enter the Ashton camp when he noticed Nico

and Lori approaching. Both were grinning and waving. He and Harry walked over to meet them.

"How'd you make out?" Ted asked Nico. "Do we need to worry?"

"It's a mixed bag," Nico replied. "Almost half the teams have deployed some type of lidar system but nobody has anything close to our gimbal."

"What about the other universities?" Harry asked. "MIT seems pretty strong."

"Princeton looked solid," Lori said. "Would you believe that Berkeley showed up with a motorcycle?"

"Are you shitting me?" Ted asked. "I want to see that MTVR race the bike. I honestly think we have nothing to worry about. Ashton is our last stop. Let's see if Rusty was right about them."

Ashton, like most other teams, came with a support team much smaller than DSU's. They had four Chevy Express 3500 vans, all painted royal blue with the red and white Ashton University logo on the side. The school's emblem was a series of three circles with an eagle in the middle, the name wrapped across the top, and their motto, *quod superius soram*—"soar higher"—around the edge. These vehicles were the property of the college. They did not rent any equipment to make the eight-and-a-half-hour trek to the Mojave. One van was a dedicated passenger van that could carry all eight team members. The other three were for equipment and spare parts.

Ted led the way as all four headed over to the Ashton camp. As they approached, a short, portly man in his mid-twenties dragged a step stool over toward the Prius. Climbing up, he hoisted a small red metal toolbox over his shoulder, setting it on the roof of the vehicle. He spun the latch to open the top and as he did, he slipped, sending a dozen tools scattering on the ground. Ted burst out laughing.

"That has to be Sam," Ted said. "First, the Prius. Now this klutz. Man, this just keeps getting better."

Ted watched as the guy jumped from the stool and quickly gathered the spilled tools. A few of the Ashton teammates helped. One, a shapely blonde wearing oversized aviator sunglasses, caught Ted's eye. He couldn't help but let his eyes wander down her backside and across her tight-fitting denim jeans.

"When you said we should check out the competition, I thought you meant the vehicles." Lori grinned as she took up a position just behind Ted. "Don't be so obvious."

Ted blushed and gave Lori a mischievous grin.

"Don't worry," Ted said. "I only have eyes for Cyclops. All right, follow me."

As they walked, Ted glanced over at Harry. "Harry, did you end up doing anything with the info about the short tree people thing Sam sent us?"

"What are you two talking about?" Lori asked. "I'm confused."

"Me, too," Nico added, looking back and forth between Ted and Harry.

Ignoring his teammates, Ted added, "I didn't bother to read what Sam sent. I only forwarded it to you."

"I looked at it. I was so swamped I didn't spend a lot of time with it. To be honest, I figured it was complete garbage, just like what we sent them."

"Yeah, you're probably right. Let's go check out the Prius." Ted snatched the bandana from Harry and used it to dab Harry's forehead. "And relax, Harry. I'll do the talking."

As they reached the Prius, Harry nodded to Portly Guy. "Welcome to the Mojave," Ted said. "Nice set of gear you have on the roof. Mind if we take a look?"

"Sure thing," the young man replied.

The Prius had clearly been heavily modified. The upgraded off-road, all-terrain tires first caught Ted's eye, followed by the front-mounted roof rack that held four lidar arrays, stereo cameras, a radar unit, and a center-mounted camera. Ted was surprised at the limited number of sensors mounted on the vehicle. Unlike Cyclops, the Prius had no gear mounted on the fenders or bumpers or any other part of the vehicle.

Ted didn't need the step stool to reach any of the equipment. He ran his hands against the roof rack, grabbed the corner of the mount with both hands, and gave it a good pull. It wouldn't budge.

"Aren't you worried about the rough desert terrain?" Ted asked. "I thought you were having trouble with steadying the sensors."

"Excuse me?" the young man asked. He stepped back and looked Ted up and down. "Do . . . do I know you?"

"I'm Ted. Ted Wolff from DSU."

"I'm Ralph." The young man grabbed Ted's hand, shaking it vigorously. "Ralph Lorenski."

"Oh. Sorry," said Ted, taken aback. "I'd exchanged sensor configuration emails with someone named Sam from Ashton. I assumed it was you."

"Oh, *you're* the guy." Ralph smiled and briefly glanced at the rest of the Ashton team, standing off to the side. "I do the hardware configuration. Sam does software. I heard about those emails."

"Was our code helpful?"

"You'd have to ask Sam." Ralph looked at the top of the Prius and then back to Ted. "What were you looking for with the roof rack? How did you end up solving the shaking?"

"We built a custom gimbal." Ted leaned back against the Prius and folded his arms across his body, puffing out his chest. "There's a lot of proprietary tech in it. We can show it to you after the competition tomorrow."

"A gimbal?" Ralph asked. "Does it spin?"

"Yup. It lets us see almost everywhere."

Ted looked over at Nico, Lori, and Harry. All but Harry, who looked nervous and uncomfortable, were smiling along with Ted.

"Same here," Ralph said. "We have an extremely wide field of view, front to back."

Ted's smile faded. He lowered his arms and slowly turned to again inspect the gear secured to the top of the Prius. Nico joined him, pointing to the individual mounts supporting each sensor array.

"Is that how you're dealing with the rough terrain?" Nico asked. "Instead of a gimbal?"

"We use a digital gimbal," Ralph replied. "The software steadies the images for us."

"A digital gimbal?" Ted asked. "I'm guessing Sam wrote that code."

Ralph nodded. His broad smile was beginning to annoy Ted.

"So, where is he?" Ted continued. "I'd like to talk to him."

One of the members of the Ashton team stepped forward. His black hair was cropped short. He stood well over six feet tall and had the build and presence of Rusty. The large man, along with the rest of the Ashton team standing beside the Prius, stepped aside, allowing room for the blonde with the aviator sunglasses to emerge from behind them. She walked in front of her team and stopped a few feet in front of Ted. Her hair was pulled through the back of her royal blue Ashton baseball cap. She lowered her glasses and peered over the gold metal upper rims.

"I'm Sam. Sam Lavoie."

Ted felt his cheeks flush once again. He was suddenly aware the entire Ashton ensemble was staring at him accusingly. He quickly looked over toward his team. Nico had no expression on his face. Harry was sweating and staring at his feet. Lori had her hand over her mouth, desperately trying to suppress her laughter. Ted stepped forward and shook hands with Sam.

"So, it's Samantha?"

"Everyone calls me Sam. Even my family." Sam flipped her sunglasses over the visor of her cap and walked around to the back of the Prius. She opened the hatch and waved the DSU team closer. "So, what do you think of Athena?"

"Athena?" Lori asked. "As in the Greek goddess of war?"

"Also of wisdom. It seemed an appropriate name given the level of technology we were building for the competition." Sam waited until everyone from DSU was standing beside her. "We've got eight Pentium computers crammed in back here. In addition to the upgraded tires, we've also raised the suspension and reinforced the entire underside with skid plates."

Ted glanced around the vehicle's interior. He was shocked at how organized everything was. The lack of mechanical hardware inside the car confused him and he felt an overwhelming wave of anxiety. Harry was standing beside him. Ted snatched a bandana from Harry's pocket and used it to dab the beads of sweat forming across his brow.

"How does it steer?" Harry asked.

Ted was relieved he didn't have to ask the same question.

"It's all drive-by-wire," Sam replied. "We try to use as little hardware as we can. Hardware can break too easily, especially in these conditions. But you guys must know that, right?"

Ted's nerves began to subside as Sam's cocky attitude became more apparent. She was a few inches shorter than Ted. He stared into her eyes in an attempt to look dominant. Her bright green eyes sparkled in the desert sun. Ted looked away to hide his confusion and anger.

"I mean, you guys couldn't tell the difference between trees and people." Sam smiled as she closed the back hatch, almost catching Ted's shoulder. "Did our code help?"

"We figured it out on our own," Ted said dismissively.

Sam shoved her hand into her pocket and pulled out an iPhone. Ted tried to suppress his excitement over seeing the device. Apple had only launched it a few months ago. The DSU team had been so busy prepping for the trip to the Mojave that no one had gotten any hands-on time with an iPhone yet. He tried to ignore it. Ashton's tech already seemed formidable enough. He didn't want to start gushing over Sam's cell phone.

"Wow!" Harry shoved Ted aside and grabbed the phone from Sam. "I am dying to get one of these. Do you love it? Is it as amazing as it seems? I watched the keynote address Steve Jobs gave. I have to have one. I *have* to!"

"It's the future." Sam gently pried the phone from Harry's sweaty hands. "Do you have one, too?"

The question was directed toward Ted. Sam was pointing at his jeans. Ted looked at the earbud wires peeking out from his front pocket. He slid his fingers inside and pulled out his iPod.

"An iPod?" Sam grinned. "That's cute. So, what vehicle do you guys have under that tarp back at your camp?"

"Did you try and sneak a look yet?" Ted asked.

"No. I'm too busy preparing for tomorrow. Other teams have said you guys have something big hidden. MIT thinks it's a tank. So, what is it?"

Ted slipped the iPod back into his pocket and looked over at Harry, Nico, and Lori. They were obviously going to let him take the lead on the response.

"We have a Hummer." Ted did not attempt to control his anger at this point. Sam's smug attitude had become annoying. "It's been heavily fortified. Lori's team has mapped this entire area down to the inch. Our gimbal system is superior to everything else out here. You can count on it."

"Wow, you have a brand new Humvee?" Sam asked in feigned surprise.

"No. No, it's, um, it's an older one. But that doesn't matter."

"It's a 1988," Harry said. "Rusty got a great deal on it and—"

"And it's going to crush everyone!" Ted shot Harry a look of disappointment. "Including that beast from Oshkosh."

Ted glared at Sam one last time, hoping she would drop her smile. Her facial features remained unchanged. She stood there, smiling, happy, and confident. He turned around and pushed his way past his DSU teammates.

"Ted, can I ask you one more thing?" Sam took a few steps forward and waited for him to turn around. "Do you really spell your name with two 'F's? That's how it was on the emails."

"Yeah, why?"

"I was wondering what the extra 'F' stood for?"

"Oh, that's easy." He smiled a wry grin as a wave of confidence poured over him. "It stands for first."

"Really? Huh. With that ancient iPod and twenty-one-year-old Hummer, I would have guessed it stood for 'futile'."

The Ashton team erupted in laughter and applause. Sam began to high-five Ralph and the others standing around her. She slid her aviator glasses back on and put her arm around Ralph to lead him over to the front of Athena.

Ted spun around, unable to contain his anger and embarrassment. Beads of sweat ran down his face. His floppy lock of hair seemed to be permanently plastered to his forehead. Clenching his fists so hard his fingernails bit deep into his palms, his strides were long and rushed as he made a direct line back to the DSU camp. Harry, Nico, and Lori ran to catch up to him.

"Slow down, Ted," Lori called out.

"They named it Athena," Harry said. "Remember Rusty telling us someone told them we had a Hummer? Do you think they knew we went with the name Cyclops?"

"I don't know, and I don't care." Ted stopped and spun around, casting a worrisome glare back toward the Ashton camp. "We're going to crush those ash-holes at Ashton. Do you hear me? Crush them!"

13

Ted grabbed his iPod and shoved it into the front pocket of his faded denim jeans. He sat down at the edge of the RV's dinette, drumming his fingers on the white Formica tabletop beside him. The coffee pot across from him hissed and sputtered as it finished brewing a fresh carafe. The digital clock on the small microwave over the stove showed 7:50 a.m. as the scent of hazelnut and cinnamon filled the RV's interior—Lori had picked the flavor of coffee. As soon as the pot stopped brewing, Ted filled two Styrofoam cups, slapped covers on them, and stepped out of the camper.

In the DSU site, Ted needed only a few dozen long strides across the sandy desert floor to reach the back end of the semi. He passed Nico and Harry busy inspecting the sensors on Cyclops. They were so focused, they didn't even notice him as he walked past.

A tiny staircase led from the ground to the back end of the semi. As he carefully pulled himself up and inside the truck—making sure not to spill the coffee—the chaos of activity engulfed him. The whirs and hums of equipment competed with the arguments of four students who were running back and forth between a computer and a whiteboard. Lori was seated at a workstation hunched over her keyboard, staring at her computer monitor. He chuckled as he placed one of the two cups of coffee beside Lori.

"Thank God." Lori popped the top off the lid and took a sip. She looked at the four students. “Some people don’t understand the value of flavored coffee.”

The arguing students stopped talking, looking back and forth for several seconds, then picked back up, but at a lower volume.

“How’s everything looking?” Ted asked. He pulled up a chair and took a seat next to her.

“It’s fine. I mean, it’s more than fine. DARPA gave us the details on the nasty nine a couple of hours ago. There’s some debate about the last one, but I think we’re all set.”

The “nasty nine” was the nickname the team had given to the nine tests along a five-mile course of the Qualifying Stage.

“What’s the problem with the last one?”

“The first test is a slalom course. The last one is another slalom course, but it will be through ruts and puddles. DARPA was vague on how deep the ruts are and how much water will be involved.”

“Cyclops is tough, Lori. What’s the concern?”

“They’re debating over what speed to have him run the course. DARPA’s been tight-lipped on scoring, too. The slalom courses have a minimum speed of fifteen miles per hour. We’re just not sure if we will score higher if we go faster.”

“Cyclops is a beast. We ran lots of slalom simulations with him doing twenty-five, sometimes thirty, depending on the radius and spacing of the cones. Even real-world testing showed he could handle higher speeds.”

“But Ted, we don’t want to push it. We only get three tries.”

“Set it to twenty-five, okay?”

“If you say so.”

He flipped back the plastic tab of his coffee cup and took a sip, closing his eyes and allowing himself to take a moment to enjoy the warm nutty flavor. When he opened his eyes, he noticed a table beside the whiteboard had a box of Entenmann’s danishes opened. The team had packed both RVs and the semi-truck with plenty of packaged foods before their arrival in the desert. DARPA was supplying food and meals for all participants, but Rusty made sure DSU arrived fully stocked. Ted stood up, snatched a napkin, and balanced a couple of pastries on top.

"Rusty wants us at the big top on the hour," he said to Lori. "Are you ready?"

"Almost." She grabbed her coffee, putting the lid back on, and then turned her attention to the four. "If any of you touch my data, you're dead."

Ted laughed as Lori marched past him and out the back of the semi. Cyclops was parked a short distance away. Nico and Harry had moved him to the front of the site. Members from several other teams were gathered around the vehicle. Ted grinned as he watched Harry, smiling for once, perched on a step stool pointing out the vehicle's technology.

"Sorry to break up the party," Ted said as he walked between Nico and Harry. "The event starts soon. We need to get to the tent."

Harry hopped off his stool and briefly shook hands with a few people as they turned to leave.

"You look happy," Ted said. "Should I assume the competitors are impressed?"

"Half the teams have only one lidar," Nico said. "A few have multi-arrays, sort of like Ashton. But honestly, Ted, I think our rotating gimbal with your magnetic dampers is lightyears ahead of anyone else here. Even the Oshkosh guys were impressed."

"I think we made everyone nervous," Harry added.

A familiar figure caught Ted's eye. He looked over Harry's shoulder to see a tall, lean man approaching the DSU camp. The man was dressed in a green and white checkered shirt with the sleeves rolled up to his elbows, exposing his heavily inked arms. His lightweight khaki pants fluttered in the gusty winds cutting across the desert. A narrow-rimmed olive hat with a black band covered his head. He had the rear back-flap lowered to protect his neck from the extreme sun that would soon dominate the sky. Despite the extended flap, his signature blond ponytail managed to dangle across his back. He stopped and briefly admired Cyclops.

"You've built one hell of a vehicle," Kyle Fisher said. He stepped forward and gave Ted a big bear hug. "You look good, Ted. How's Rusty been treating you?"

"Guys, this is Kyle Fisher. I worked for him before I came to DSU."

"So we have you to blame for this guy?" Lori asked with a grin. She winked at Ted just as Kyle stepped forward and hugged her. "Oh. Uh, okay."

"You'll have to forgive me," Kyle said as he let go of Lori. "There's just not enough love in the world, you know?"

"Sure." Lori went into smile-and-nod mode and glanced at Ted with a raised eyebrow. "So, you worked with Ted in Nevada?"

"My headquarters are in San Diego. Ted worked at one of my test sites outside Reno." Kyle put his arm around Ted and pulled him close. "Kevin still gets calls from clients asking for this guy by name. He does great work."

"Thanks, Kyle," Ted replied.

Kyle quickly shook hands with Nico and Harry before doing a quick stroll around Cyclops.

"I'm impressed." Kyle slapped Nico on his back. "I need to go find Rusty. Should I assume he's already in the main tent angry you aren't there yet?"

"Probably." Ted ran his fingers through his hair, trying to keep his locks out of his eyes. The wind was starting to pick up. "We're heading over there soon."

"Best of luck."

"Nice to meet you." Harry waited until Kyle Fisher was out of earshot. "*That's* the billionaire who owns Fisher Tuner?"

"Yup," Ted said.

"He looks like he just emerged from the Australian outback. Why do people with tons of money never look rich? I swear, sometimes"—Harry paused mid-sentence.

"Sometimes what?" Ted asked.

Harry's jaw was open, and his eyes were fixated just behind Ted. Ted turned around to see a heavyset man rapidly approaching on a Segway. The personal transporter slowed to a halt a few feet from Ted. The man did not step off. He ran his fingers across his short beard as he studied DSU's vehicle.

"Is that a three-axis gimbal?" Steve Wozniak asked. "With a lidar on top?"

"It is," Ted said. He didn't recognize the man, but given Harry's reactions, he had a feeling Harry did. "Harry?"

Harry took a few steps forward until he was standing less than a foot from the Segway. He started to raise his arm to run his hand across the tiny vehicle but stopped himself. Harry cleared his throat and looked up in awe at his idol.

"Woz up?" Harry asked with a nervous grin.

Steve Wozniak glanced down at Harry, but did not react to his question. He turned his attention back to Cyclops and nodded each time he noted one of the other sensor arrays.

"Good luck today." Steve leaned forward, piloting his Segway to the next campsite.

"Was that?—" Nico began to ask.

"It was," Harry interrupted. He walked a few feet away to watch Steve drive off. "That was *him*! That was Steve Wozniak. The Woz!"

"And even he didn't get your dumb joke." Ted put a reassuring hand on Harry's shoulder. "You need some new material, Harry. And all of us need to get to the tent. Lori and I can head over now. You and Nico finish prepping Cyclops. You can get the final data updates from the team inside the semi. The competition is about to start."

Rusty stared at his watch—a few minutes before four—as he paced back and forth in front of the DSU team table. The last seven hours had been filled with much drama, none of it from his team. Cyclops was still on deck, waiting to enter the competition. DSU was fourth in line, and it had taken seven hours for the prior three vehicles to perform. The third entrant was still on the course. DARPA did not have time limits for the Qualification Stage, and so far, the teams had taken full advantage.

DARPA had spared no expense with the FAST Challenge event. The main operations tent was a climate-controlled shelter spanning 40,000 square feet. Portable generators ran air conditioners that helped keep the interior at a comfortable seventy-five degrees. Each of the forty teams had two tables with anywhere from one to four workstations, depending on the size of the team. The tables all faced the main stage, where the DARPA personnel, in communication and coordination with key members from each team, were set up. Four huge overhead screens filled the area above the stage. One screen served as the leaderboard, showing the results of each contestant. Two other screens streamed live camera feeds from the DARPA pursuit vehicles. DARPA had both ground and air support monitoring the competition. The last display was from a small camera placed inside the vehicle currently competing to provide a "behind-the-wheel" view to the audience.

This DARPA-supplied point-of-view (POV) camera proved to be a huge point of contention for the participants. Most teams did not want the added tech in their vehicles, fearing it would interfere with their vehicle's performance. DARPA provided each team the choice of opting out of using the camera if they determined it would introduce risk into the system. DSU, after a much-heated debate, agreed to install the system.

"We may not get to run today." Rusty stopped in front of Harry. "Have you been taking notes on the errors these other teams have made?"

"Of course," Harry replied. "We can run through some simulations tonight to make sure Cyclops won't get tripped up."

Only two teams had completed the course so far: Oshkosh Defense and Berkeley. Rusty was still in shock that Berkeley's motorcycle, dubbed Easy Rider, had performed so well. He looked up at the screen to watch Gator once again attempt a three-point turn. Gator was a heavily retro-fitted 1998 Mitsubishi Montero SUV run by Florida Gulf Technical College. They were a small team of only three people. Gator had been on the course since just past noon and had suffered numerous setbacks. The course itself was having problems of its own, with the desert winds sometimes blowing cones and other markers out of position. Rusty hoped DARPA would fix these issues before Cyclops ran the course tomorrow.

Between the four screens was a huge digital clock above a series of lights—red, yellow, and green. The color of the light indicated the status of the current competitor. Florida Gulf had obviously opted to include the internal DARPA camera inside their vehicle. The status light changed to green, and all eyes under the big top shifted to the screen on the far left.

Gator once again started his three-point-turn attempt. As with most of the turns in the nasty nine, this was no ordinary three-pointer. DARPA had constructed a series of barriers made of concrete blocks, cars, cones, posts, and poles. A human could easily differentiate between these and find the proper spot to make the turn. Gator was having a difficult time.

The POV screen showed Gator driving into the dead-end area and coming to a halt. After several seconds, the SUV went into reverse and slowly turned ninety degrees. It came to a stop, pulled forward, and stopped again. Several seconds passed. A murmur built throughout the tent, as those watching were trying to figure out what the autonomous vehicle was doing. Cheers erupted from the Florida Gulf table as Gator performed another ninety-degree reverse turn and stopped. The joy proved to be short-lived.

"No!" The cry came out from one of the young men at the Gator table. His two teammates peered over his shoulder at his monitor, then looked at the overhead screen. Gator was moving forward—rapidly. "We've lost GPS!" They shouted.

The bottom of the screen showing the POV from Gator also

revealed its speed. The SUV was accelerating past thirty miles per hour and not slowing down.

"Florida Gulf, control your vehicle." The monotone male voice crackled through the overhead speakers. It came from a DARPA technician somewhere at the front of the room. "You have five seconds to comply."

DARPA had required mandatory secondary kill switches in addition to the optional internal camera within each vehicle. Although each team had remote controls to disable the vehicle, DARPA had installed military-spec equipment that would basically blow the brains of any entrant that malfunctioned.

"Oh, my God," Lori said softly as she stood up from her chair. "It's heading toward the bleachers."

A set of bleachers stood next to the first of the nine tests. The covered seating was reserved for VIP guests and the press. DARPA had advertised the event heavily, and the bleachers were fairly full, but not packed.

Gator was now up to forty miles per hour and closing in on the seating area. A mass of gasps and shrieks arose, as those who had been seated began running every which way. Rusty looked over at the Florida Gulf table and wondered why they hadn't hit the kill switch.

"It won't stop!" The leader of the Florida Gulf team smashed his fists onto his keyboard. "Kill it! Kill it!"

The screen displaying the view inside Gator showed the vehicle's speed begin to slow. The image gradually became murky as the SUV's cabin filled with smoke. You could still see the bleachers through the haze as the Montero crashed into the front corner of the seating area. Luckily, it had been reinforced with concrete barriers and sandbags. The interior image, now sideways and cockeyed, remained up after the vehicle finally came to a halt, the bottom three rows of the bleachers on screen. A reporter from *Wired* magazine walked up, looked inside the vehicle, and started laughing.

"DSU, prepare your vehicle." The monotone voice from DARPA once again crackled overhead. "You have ten minutes."

The message through the loudspeakers stunned Rusty. He turned and looked at the two DSU tables. Ted, Nico, Harry, and Lori all seemed to be in shock. The rest of the DSU team was back in the semi-truck. Rusty stood between the two tables and folded his arms.

"You heard the man," Rusty said. "What are you waiting for?"

Nico and Harry jumped from their seats and ran toward the exit. Ted slid his chair closer to Lori so he could better see her monitor. As he did, he looked up to notice Sam Lavoie approaching. She was with two other people from Ashton. Rusty realized Ted was distracted and spun around to see who he was watching.

"Rusty, you old dog." Vin Malik walked up to his old mentor and shook his hand enthusiastically. Speaking with a faint Indian accent, he said, "It's so good to see you again."

"Vin!" Rusty replied. "You're looking fit as always."

Vin was a slender man. With almost delicate features, his tawny skin was flawless, and his teeth, almost unnaturally white. He spoke with an upbeat optimism and smooth delivery and seemed to never suffer a loss for words nor a lack of confidence. His dark hair was gelled back and collar-length. He and the rest of the Ashton team were decked out in royal blue Polo shirts sporting the Ashton University logo.

"We just wanted to come by and wish your team luck. These are truly exciting times, aren't they?" Vin stepped to the side and motioned toward Sam. "My team tells me you've done wonders with your lidar array."

"I'm looking forward to seeing how it performs today," Sam said. She shook Rusty's hand. "Sam Lavoie. Software lead."

"Nice to meet you. Wait. *You're* Sam?" Rusty turned and looked down at Ted. Ted was refusing to acknowledge their conversation and instead was scrolling through the songs on his iPod. "Well, I can honestly say it's a pleasure to meet you, Sam. Vin only works with the best people. I'm sure Ashton has come fully prepared to win this event."

"Indeed, we have my friend." Vin pointed to the overhead screen that was still displaying the view from Gator. The smoke had cleared, and the faces of the Florida Gulf team members could be seen peering into the windshield. "Let's hope we both fare better than others. Take care."

Rusty briefly watched Vin and his people head back to their table. Once they were out of earshot, he turned and looked down at Ted, "I hear Ashton built a digital gimbal. I told you we had to watch out for them." Rusty looked up at the clock at the front of the tent. "Ted, go outside and check on Harry and Nico. Lori, let the rest of the team know we are about to start. The last thing I want is to see Cyclops go wild and run down a bunch of spectators."

During the next forty minutes, the 322 people inside the big top sat in near silence watching Cyclops run through the first four of the nasty nine tests. The Humvee nailed each test on the first try. The only noise inside the tent came from the DSU team as they erupted in cheers at the end of each test. Everyone, that is, except Rusty. Rusty barely moved, standing and facing the POV screen, hands clasped behind his back. He never spoke. He never moved. He knew they still had a long way to go before they could cry victory.

The next test required Cyclops to ascend a forty-five-degree incline and make an immediate sharp right turn at the top of the hill. There were no barriers to prevent it from continuing forward once it crested the peak. This test was designed to assess the vehicle's ability to understand changes in elevation in relation to winding roads without barriers. Cyclops accelerated up the hill briskly and then slowed as it reached the top. The Humvee drove past its intended turn and went down the other side of the embankment. After several feet, it came to a stop.

Rusty spun around and clenched his hands into two tight fists, his knuckles turning white from the blood draining away. He glared at Nico, then Harry, and finally Ted.

"Is this a mapping issue?" Rusty kept his eyes on Ted, despite the question being meant for Lori.

"I'm . . . I'm not sure." Lori scanned through the data on her computer screen. "No. I'm good."

Harry, Nico, and Ted were frantically surfing through the information on their computers. Despite the cool temperature inside the big top, Harry began sweating profusely. He grabbed one of his bandanas and dabbed the beads of sweat forming on the back of his neck.

"It looks like we're blind," Harry said. "But I don't know why."

Rusty leaned forward, resting his fists on the table between the monitors Nico and Ted were using. His breathing was controlled and rhythmic. The minor conversations occurring throughout the operations center sounded miles away. Rusty's eyes ping-ponged back and forth between Nico and Ted, waiting for one of them to respond.

"It's the gimbal," Nico finally said. "It looks like it's locked. I have no idea why. Cyclops is confused."

"The gimbal." Rusty sat on the edge of the table, twisting his body to face Ted. "Your magic gimbal, Ted. Are you telling me we have you to blame for this failure?"

"We've got two more tries." Ted rolled his chair back and stood up. "I've taken Cyclops offline. Nico and I can go out there and fix it."

"You realize we only get three shots at each of these tests, right?"

"I know."

"You two better pray that miracle gimbal and lidar don't prove to be our downfall." Rusty stood up and glared at Nico. "Go work with DARPA ops so they can get you to Cyclops. Don't come back unless you are willing to bet your lives it will work the second time."

It took Ted and Nico only twenty minutes to get Cyclops sorted out. The Hummer completed test number five on the second pass. The next three tests proved to be a mixed bag, with Cyclops stumbling on two of them. Luckily, the team was able to correct the issues remotely. The overhead clock showed the time to be 6:17 p.m. Cyclops and DSU had one final test to go.

"We are a go for number nine." The voice of the DARPA technician crackled throughout the tent's speakers.

Despite the late hour, every other team member had remained on site. Even with the handful of re-runs, Cyclops was performing far better than any other contestant so far. The other teams were busy documenting where and how Cyclops failed so they could go back tonight and make any changes necessary for their future runs over the next few days.

All eyes were glued to the POV camera. The last test of the nasty nine was the slalom course run with the ruts and what DARPA called "water hazards" which were a series of puddles of undisclosed depth. Based on what they saw with those vehicles before them, the DSU team estimated the puddles ranging from two to six inches deep. Contestants were required to maintain a speed of at least fifteen miles per hour.

Two sets of traffic cones marked the entrance to the slalom. Cyclops entered the course going twenty-five miles per hour. There were twelve gates to maneuver through, half with the water hazards, and four with deep ruts. Only two gates—the first and last—were smooth. Shortly after passing the fourth gate, Cyclops took the next turn wide, crushing the traffic cone delineating the edge of the gate.

"Failure number one." The announcement seemed deafening as it echoed throughout the tent.

Rusty turned his attention from the screens, once again setting a menacing glare upon Lori, Harry, Nico, and Ted. Each of the four could feel his anger, frustration, and disappointment. Rusty folded his arms across his broad chest and waited, maintaining his focus on his team despite the many stares directed his way from around the tent.

"I've got it," Harry said. "We need to slow him down. I'm bringing him down to fifteen. That's the minimum to pass the test. He should—"

"He should be able to go faster," Ted said. "Set him for twenty."

"Are you sure?"

"Completely."

Harry quickly banged out the corrections needed to adjust Cyclops's software. It took him less than ten minutes to complete the change and transmit it to the vehicle. When finished, Harry stood up and nodded toward the DARPA operations group at the front of the tent. The row of lights changed from yellow to green.

"DSU, begin your second run."

Rusty did not bother to turn around to watch the POV monitor. Instead, he shifted his gaze repeatedly from Ted to the rest of the team members. Lori kept her eyes glued to the giant screen showing Cyclops's progress. Harry and Nico nervously looked between the front monitors and Rusty. Ted kept his eyes locked on Rusty. Eventually, Rusty stopped looking at the other three and focused on Ted. They stared at each other for less than ten seconds before the overhead speakers crackled to life.

"Failure number two."

Rusty's facial expression did not change. Out of the corner of his eye, he could see Harry and Nico frantically scanning through information on their computer screens. Rusty kept his anger focused on Ted. It was a game of chicken. A game Rusty knew he would win. Ted blinked a few times before slowly lowering his head.

"Harry," Rusty said as he continued to stare at Ted. "Set the speed to fifteen."

It took another ten minutes for Harry to compile and transmit the changes to Cyclops. Rusty stomped off, spending that time at the Ashton table chatting with Vin. The two men could be heard loudly laughing as they shared memories from when they were together at DSU. Rusty kept his eyes fixated on his team most of the time he was talking with Vin. As soon as he saw Harry stand up and point toward the DARPA control group, he shook hands with his good friend and wished him well, returning to the DSU table just as the overhead speakers erupted.

"DSU, begin your final run."

Rusty positioned himself behind the DSU table, standing directly between Nico and Ted. With his hands clasped behind his back, he directed his attention to the POV monitor. For the first time since the event had begun, Rusty found himself feeling nervous. Although he wouldn't admit it to the team, Rusty thought Cyclops had performed brilliantly until this final test. Yet, here they were on the final test with only one more chance to go.

The inside of the big top was eerily quiet as Cyclops started his run, the only sound the whir of the industrial cooling fans at the back of the tent. Everyone watching could see that the Humvee was being much more cautious this time around in its approach. Harry had throttled back the acceleration so that Cyclops entered the course at exactly fifteen miles per hour.

All eyes watched as the big Humvee slowly glided from gate to gate. Turn four was the one that had tripped up Cyclops during the first two attempts. Ted and Nico remained motionless as the Hummer effortlessly made the turn and headed toward the next gate.

"Yes!" Harry cried as he leaped from his chair.

The rest of the DSU team remained quiet and seated. Harry stayed standing. Rusty worked his way to the front of the table, his back toward his team. His eyes remained fixed on the POV screen. As Cyclops passed the tenth gate, Lori stood up. There were only two gates to go. Gate eleven proved to be the most difficult. The water hazard's depth varied between four and eight inches—slightly beyond what DSU had estimated. Cyclops took the turn wide, clipping the outer edge of the puddle, but the vehicle quickly corrected itself to remain inside the cones. Ted and Nico were now on their feet. The last gate was a smooth section of silty desert sand, with no ruts or puddles to trip up the vehicle. Cyclops threaded the cones right down the middle and exited the slalom.

"Course complete."

The DSU team exploded in cries of joy. Ted, Nico, Harry, and Lori all took turns hugging one another. Applause rang out throughout the big top. Lori, who rarely showed emotion, had tears running down her face. She grabbed one of Harry's bandanas and blew her nose as she laughed loudly. Rusty turned to face his team. Their laughs quickly faded as they saw his expression.

"That was close," Rusty said. "Too close."

"But we did it," Ted replied. He pointed at the leaderboard. It now showed Cyclops in first place, knocking Oshkosh Defense's TerraCrusher down to second. "I told you. My gimbal and lidar are game-changers. Nobody will beat us."

"That arrogance almost cost us the race." Rusty, not wanting to make a big scene, kept his voice low. The overhead speakers were announcing the final rankings and the schedule for Tuesday morning. Many of the other teams had already started to leave. "Who decided Cyclops should run the final course so quickly?"

"I did," Ted said. He folded his arms across his chest. "It was built for speed. We needed to show the other teams what we could do."

"Wrong. We needed to win."

"You said to win at all costs."

"You took an unnecessary risk, Ted. When Cyclops failed the first time, you should have dialed it from twenty-five down to fifteen." Rusty looked down at his watch. "I want to see all four of you back in the semi at nine o'clock. I want to know why Cyclops faltered on each test that required a repeat run. I want answers."

"Nine tomorrow morning?" Harry asked.

"Tonight," Rusty replied. He spun around to review the final rankings on the overhead screen. "Dismissed. You have your orders."

14

The following two days of the Qualifying Stage proved to be the most entertaining of the Challenge. Twenty-five of the remaining contenders completed the event. But "completed" for some meant being disqualified. Fifteen entrants in those two days had failed to finish the nasty nine. Of those, six never even made it past the second test.

Four days in, Rusty glanced at his watch—a few minutes before 5:00 p.m. He topped off his USMC mug and stepped down from the semi. The team members inside were hard at work preparing for the following week's 130-mile road race. Another blustery day, gritty sand kicking up everywhere. He shielded his eyes as he made his way over to the big top. The closer he got, the louder the noise from inside became. Rusty hastened his step, his right leg wobbling as he pushed his injured hip to move faster than it preferred.

The leaderboard still showed DSU in first place. MIT's entry, Talon, had bumped Oshkosh Defense down to third late the previous day. DARPA still refused to reveal the points each team had earned out of fear someone would crack their scoring system. Rusty ignored the monitors and marched over to the DSU table to find Harry, Nico, and Lori reclined in their chairs watching the POV monitor.

"Where's Wolff?" Rusty asked.

"He's over at Ashton's table," Lori replied calmly to Rusty, mumbling so that only Nico could hear, "with his new blond girlfriend." Nico chuckled, but was quickly hushed when glancing up at Rusty.

"This is going to be close," Lori said turning her eyes to the leaderboard.

Rusty spun around to check the massive overhead screens up front. Athena, the Ashton Prius, had just completed test number eight and was about to make its first attempt at the final slalom course test. Rusty squinted as he read through Ashton's results. He felt his heart begin to race as he counted the number of attempts Athena needed to complete each section of the course. The little Toyota had faltered very few times, although it did require three attempts to complete the three-point turn. Rusty slowly turned around and looked at Harry.

"When I left here an hour ago, they were in the middle of test six." Rusty's cheeks became flush with anger. "How the hell are they already at the end?"

"They aced the last two," Harry replied. "They told DARPA they could immediately move to the next test. No prep needed."

Rusty pounded his fists on the table, toppling Nico's green tea onto his lap. He glared at Nico before heading toward the Ashton table. Rusty could see Vin standing behind his team, arms crossed, with his gaze locked on the POV camera. Vin looked at Rusty briefly, and then back up at the screen. Just as Rusty arrived at the table, he noticed Vin frown. Suddenly, a familiar voice boomed from overhead.

"Failure number one."

Rusty looked back at the screens to see the POV image showing Athena facing a concrete wall. The status light changed from green to red. He tried not to smile as he walked closer to Vin.

"This last one's a bitch, Vin," Rusty said with a wry grin. Ted was sitting on the edge of Ashton's table next to Sam, only a few feet from Rusty. Rusty directed his next statement to Ted. "My team botched this one big-time."

"Not now, Rusty," Vin said as he waved Sam closer and pulled his team into a huddle.

Rusty smirked and went and sat next to Ted.

"You better hope they screw up this final test," Rusty whispered to Ted. "With DARPA keeping quiet on the scoring, I have no clue how close they are to beating us."

"That's why I'm over here. Collecting intel."

Rusty stood up and headed back to the DSU table. Deep down, Rusty fully expected DSU to win the challenge. He also felt it was imperative to keep his team focused and alert. Ted's attitude earlier in the week disappointed Rusty. He knew an overconfident team would get comfortable and allow mistakes to happen. He couldn't let that happen. Rusty returned to the DSU table to find Nico drying his tea-stained shorts with a handful of paper towels. He was about to speak when the overhead speakers cracked and popped.

"Ashton, begin your second run."

"That was fast," Harry said. He turned and looked back toward the Ashton table. "How are they getting Athena reset so quickly?"

"How, indeed?" Rusty asked. Rusty took a sip of coffee and watched as Athena maneuvered through the second gate of the slalom course. "Whatever the outcome today, by my calculations, Ashton has completed the first eight tests smoother and better than Cyclops."

"But we don't know what DARPA is factoring into the scoring system." Nico tossed a ball of paper towels into the wastebasket beneath the table. "We will have no idea where we stand until they've finished."

"Regardless of the scoring outcome, we should not be getting outgunned by a Prius!" Rusty sat on the edge of the table between Nico and Harry, keeping his back to the front monitors. "We built Cyclops to conquer the desert. The static tests this week may not come into play during the road race, but I guarantee they will be crucial for the Urban Challenge in the final week. Tomorrow I'm going to want detailed reports from each of you identifying how you will remedy Cyclops's failures from this week. We know why things went wrong. Now we need to fix them. Harry, I want you to—"

"Guys," Lori said, interrupting Rusty. "You need to pay attention. All of you."

Rusty stood up and turned to face the POV monitor. His jaw fell open as Athena exited the final set of cones and took aim at the course exit. The overhead speakers popped to life.

"Course complete."

The Ashton team exploded in cheers. Several other teams began to clap as well, possibly out of relief that the Qualifying Stage was finally over. Rusty searched the room looking for Ted, but couldn't see him. He looked up at the leaderboard and waited.

The cheering and applause in the room died down as all eyes focused on the screen showing the vehicle rankings. The scoreboard had four columns: Rank, Team, Vehicle, and Score. All week only the first three columns had been displayed. DARPA was waiting until the end of the competition to give out the individual scores. DSU, MIT, and Oshkosh Defense held the first three slots. Thirty seconds passed, and the board didn't change. Forty seconds. A full minute. Suddenly the board flickered on and off before going dark completely. The other three monitors also went dark. When the four came back to life, the rankings for all forty teams were displayed, ten per monitor with twenty teams on the right shaded in red. Ashton was ranked first, DSU second. Ashton had seventy points to DSU's sixty-eight.

Lori, Harry, and Nico sat in stunned silence. Nico, who'd been spinning a pen across his fingertips, opened his palm to catch it, but timed the move poorly and the pen fell to the ground. Harry grabbed a bandana from his pocket wiping the sweat from his face. Lori simply stared at the scoreboard, rereading the rankings to herself repeatedly.

Applause, gasps, cheers, and cries rang out through the big top as the hundreds of participants digested the information. Confusion slowly spread throughout the crowd. No one understood completely what the red shading over the twenty teams on the right side signified. The overhead speakers snapped and popped briefly.

"This marks the end of the Qualifying Stage. Only those twenty teams scoring fifty points or higher will be moving on to week two. Those shaded in red on the scoreboard are disqualified. Team leads, please report to the DARPA operations center up front for next steps. Thank you."

Someone at the back of the room flung a chair, smashing it against one of the vents supplying cool air to the tent. The murmuring in the room approached a roar as discussions erupted over the news that half the teams had failed to move forward.

Rusty remained silent as he watched Ted emerge from the throngs of people wandering through the big top. Lori, Harry, and Nico were sitting in their chairs, patiently waiting to hear what Rusty had to say. Once Ted arrived, Rusty pointed to the empty chair and watched intently as Ted took a seat. Rusty was about to speak when Vin came running over.

"That was a nail biter," Vin said as he shook Rusty's hand. "The road race should be quite a challenge—best of luck to all of you. Great job. Really impressive."

Vin nodded, smiled, and quickly jogged back to the Ashton table.

"Second place," Rusty said as he shook his head in disgust. "We lost to a Prius. A Prius! In the desert!"

"It was only by two points," Ted said.

"You." Rusty stepped closer to Ted and leaned down until he was mere inches from Ted's nose. "I brought you here for one reason and one reason only—to win this event. You told me you built winning desert-racers. Your magic gimbal and lidar just got its ass kicked by a goddamn Prius. I don't care if we lost by one-tenth of one point. Second place might as well be last. If we don't win the road race next week, you'll be of no value to me."

"No value?!" Ted stood up, but Rusty did not back down. "You'd be in last place if it wasn't for me. Probably even disqualified!"

Rusty noticed out of the corner of his eye that a crowd had begun to form around them. Team Ashton, including Vin and Sam, were now standing several feet away. Rusty frowned as the crowd around them grew larger. He wasn't big on being the center of attention, but he needed his team to know his disappointment—especially Ted.

"You told me you built to win, Ted. What does that board show? Huh? All I see is a loser." Rusty could see the anger and tears forming in Ted's eyes. "I told you when I dragged you from that shit shop outside Reno that my goal was to win at all costs. You need to step up your game. If we lose next week, I will personally put you on a one-way ticket back to daddy at GM. You can go build Chevys with your family. Maybe that's all you're meant for."

Rusty took a few steps back and glared at Lori, Nico, and Harry. All three had their eyes down, trying to act as if they were not paying attention to the argument. Ted stood up, tears forming in his eyes. Rusty shook his head in disgust as Ted turned and pushed his way through the crowd and ran toward the exit.

15

Ted groaned and arched his back and stretched his arms before going back to the task at hand. The servo controls and actuators taking up the driver's area inside Cyclops were a tight fit, and Ted had to scrunch himself in impossibly tight positions to reach everything. Nico was across from him, checking the control panels crammed into the passenger's side. Wind gusts wrestled with the doors, bumping them repeatedly against both men's bodies as they tried to maintain their focus on completing the final inspection.

"How are things looking on your side?" Ted shook his arms vigorously as he fought with an actuator buried deep beneath the dashboard. "I'm almost done here."

"Same." Nico pulled himself upright and grabbed hold of the bars running across the roof of the vehicle. A pelting sheet of golden desert sand threaded through his silky black hair. He squinted to keep his eyes clear. "When do you think the race will start?"

"They have to announce it soon. There've been way too many delays today."

"This sandstorm killed over an hour this morning. And then those two teams that can't get the DARPA equipment to work. It's been a bit of a cluster."

"If you ask me, DARPA has gone overboard with their tech." Ted uncoiled his body from beneath the dashboard, stretching again as he stood, and gently slapped the military-supplied camera installed near the base of the windshield. "They keep trying to make this into some infomercial. Transmissions from these cameras keep screwing things up."

"I think it's kind of cool, especially for this second challenge, the 130-mile race. All twenty vehicles will have onboard cameras modified this time. It's going to make it exciting to watch. Especially for the press."

Ted looked over at the bleachers along the edge of the racecourse. The crowd size was twice as big as last week's. One end of the bleachers had a tarp added to block the pummeling winds. There were also four seventy-inch screens set up in a grid pattern facing the seats in front to duplicate the feed sent to the monitors inside the big top.

"We should be glad this storm showed up on Sunday and DARPA called the delay," Nico continued. "That gave Lori and Harry two extra days to run simulations."

"It also gave Rusty two more days to ride our asses. I swear, Nico, as soon as this competition is done, I'm gone. Two points. Two! That's all that separates us from Ashton and we've got the whole event in front of us."

"I'm with you, Ted. The gimbal and lidar assembly on Cyclops are brilliant. I'm confident we'll win this week's race. Rusty is just being an asshole. It's his thing. Try not to let him get to you."

"Easier said than done. Let's check on Harry."

Ted slammed the Humvee's door shut and walked to its front. Harry was on his knees, facing the bumper, holding a small can of paint in one hand, and a one-inch wide paintbrush in the other. Nico joined him on the other side, leaning against the fender just as a gust of wind pushed him even harder against the vehicle.

"How's it going, Picasso?" Ted asked.

"Finished." Harry stood up and took a few steps back. He glanced down at the orange paint splattered across his hands and forearms, the fluorescent glow popping against his ebony skin. Harry frowned as he noticed spots of orange on his bright white T-shirt. "Shit."

Harry's fresh coat of orange brightened up the handlebar mustache that went along the sections of the brush guard just below the headlights, covering up the scrapes and bruises the Humvee suffered in the Qualifying Stage.

"Is it just me, or is that brighter than usual?" Nico asked.

"I forgot to shake the can," Harry replied. "So the pigments are a bit off. I kind of like it."

"Me, too," Ted said. "And the orange goes well with your shirt."

The top of the paint can was resting on the ground covered like pretty much everything else in tiny bits of sand. Harry dropped the brush onto the upside-down lid and pulled his shirt away from his stomach. The iconic Apple rainbow logo was now surrounded in dollops of neon orange paint.

"Good thing I brought half a dozen of these." Harry smeared his hands across his protruding belly. A smile spread across his face as a familiar face walked up behind Ted. "Sam!"

At the mention of Sam Lavoie's name, Ted felt a rush in his chest as his heart rate picked up. He immediately flushed, but tried to play it cool as he turned toward Sam. She was standing less than three feet away decked out in her team uniform, admiring the Humvee.

"So I finally see Cyclops up close," Sam said pushing her aviator sunglasses back to rest above the rim of her baseball cap. "He's a big boy, isn't he?"

"He's unstoppable," Ted replied as he made his way closer to Sam. "What do you think of our hardware?"

Sam spent a few moments walking along Cyclops's perimeter, stopping to inspect one of the sensor arrays secured to the vehicle. Without a word, she stepped back, eyes still fixed on Cyclops to study the huge lidar on top of the gimbal.

"Is that a multi-beam lidar?" Sam asked. "And it rotates?"

"Yes to both," Ted replied.

"I heard someone at Berkeley talking about it. I thought they were full of shit. Huh." Sam took hold of one of the roof rails and hauled herself up, securing her feet along the side of the vehicle. Ted followed, pulling himself up, keenly aware of her leg brushing against his. "What's securing the gimbal?"

Forcing himself to focus on Sam's question, Ted answered, "It's a secret. Something I was working on before coming to DSU."

"So mysterious." Sam turned looking directly into Ted's eyes, their faces only a few inches apart. The wind picked up and blew Ted's hair across his eyes. Sam reached toward his face to flick the locks away. "I must admit, Ted, you have me curious."

Ted found himself smiling as he stared into Sam's green eyes, then allowed his gaze to wander across her petite nose, flawless complexion, and beautifully shaped mouth. His eyes rested just for a moment on her lips which seemed dry, a little cracked, but were slightly curved and full. Another gust of wind broke his concentration as sand blasted against his face. He squinted and started to chuckle. Ted stepped backward and held out a hand to Sam to help her down. As Sam grabbed Ted's hand and stepped down, Ted felt a jolt of electricity throughout his body. He had to force himself to focus on what it was she was saying.

". . . a rotating multi-beam system?" Sam continued, her cheeks now slightly red. "You must get a lot of data from it."

"We do!" Harry seemed to have appeared from nowhere and quickly maneuvered himself between Ted and Sam. "It lets us see not just where we're going, but also what might be coming from the sides. It sees almost everywhere. Like Sauron."

"Who?" Sam asked.

"Ignore him," Ted said. "Come check out our control system."

Ted casually pushed Harry aside and opened the driver's door of the Humvee. Sam paused briefly as she looked at the cacophony of wires, servos, and actuators in the driver's seat.

"What the hell is all this for?" Sam stuck her head inside and ran her hands along the gear. "Is this to drive the thing?"

"Of course," Ted said with a broad smile. "Pretty amazing, isn't it?"

"Amazingly outdated."

Ted's smile vanished. He put his left arm around Sam to pull her closer to the equipment inside Cyclops.

"What are you talking about? This is a robot inside a robot. We can steer, brake, and accelerate. Not only that, but—"

"Ted, I get how it all works. Like I said the other day, all this extra mechanical hardware is just begging to break down. I can only imagine how difficult it was to not only build this to work, but to tweak it each time it needs to be re-calibrated. We do all of this in Athena with software."

Sam pulled herself away from Ted and took a few steps back as another wild gust rose. She lowered her aviators to shield her eyes.

Aware that a certain amount of bravado was all part of the fun, he still found her condescending attitude more than a little annoying. "Software is only as good as the hardware it's connected to, Sam. You need both."

"Of course you do. But you also need to use the correct hardware and software in the right areas. You have to play to their strengths. It all comes down to efficiency." Sam pointed to the towering lidar atop the Humvee. "That's some impressive hardware you've got up there. But I can tell you that our digital gimbal is just as good, and with less mechanical parts to break."

"Bullshit!" Ted felt himself getting angry. "There's no way Athena's lidar can do what ours can."

"Really? Funny, last time I looked, you came in second."

"Ash-hole," Ted mumbled under his breath.

"What?" Sam asked.

Ted folded his arms as he clenched his fists behind his elbows. He glared at Sam for several seconds. With her aviators on, he couldn't tell what she was thinking or feeling.

"So it's your birthday?" Harry broke in as he nervously positioned himself between Ted and Sam again. "Or someone else's?"

"What?" Sam seemed confused. "Why would you ask me that?"

"Your hat." Harry pointed to her royal blue cap with the Ashton logo emblazoned on it.

Sam's ponytail holder caught and came loose as she took off her baseball hat and sunglasses. Blond strands rippled in the wind reminding Ted of a kite. Sam spun the hat around and frowned at the sight of a white sticker that proclaimed BIRTHDAY GIRL in pink letters.

"Ralph must have done that. I told that little shit to keep his mouth shut."

"Is it today?" Harry asked.

"It doesn't matter. I never celebrate it." Sam shoved the hat over her head, popped her aviators back on, and slid her hands into her pockets. "Anyway, both of our teams should be proud. If the Qualifying Stage is any indication, we're farther ahead than the rest. Good luck today."

Ted remained silent as Sam turned and walked away.

"Good luck! And happy birthday!" Harry called out. He waited for Sam to turn back, but instead, she lowered her head and continued on toward Athena. "I wonder what that was all about. Who hates their birthday?"

"Who cares," Ted said. "She's wrong about our hardware. She'll see."

Cyclops was parked with the nineteen other vehicles at the start of the racecourse, roughly fifty yards from the bleachers. The course was a ten-mile loop, covering thirteen laps. DARPA had placed the start/finish area behind four rows of concrete barriers for security. A series of loudspeakers were mounted nearby, similar to those inside the big top where the four DSU leads and Rusty had watched the scoreboards during the Qualifying Stage.

"Attention all teams." The speakers sputtered from overhead, the announcer's voice echoing against the mountain range on the far side of the field. "All people, clear the field. Team representatives, report to your stations in the big top. The race will begin shortly."

"Harry, clean up that paint can." Nico slid on his wraparound sunglasses to deflect the sand swirling around his face. "I'm heading to the tent. Ted?"

"I'll meet you there." Ted was leaning against Cyclops. He pivoted to his left and slammed the driver's door closed. He peered through the window to admire the elegance and complexity of the robotic controls adorning the interior. "She's wrong."

"Who's wrong?" Kyle Fisher asked.

Ted turned around, shocked to see his old boss standing behind him. Before Ted could reply, Kyle pulled Ted into a bear hug. "Good luck, Ted!" From the confines of the embrace, Ted glanced over at Harry frantically working to secure the sand-covered paint lid to the can before eventually just giving up and rolling the brush inside a rag. With a second rag, Harry wrapped the small can, covering the top.

"Are you heading inside?" Ted asked as Kyle released him. "Or are you toughing it out in the bleachers?"

"Neither. I'm in a chase vehicle."

The twenty vehicles were spread out in five rows of four vehicles spaced ten feet apart. To help minimize the risks of hitting one another, they would be released in groups of four, in ten-minute intervals. Each vehicle would be timed based on its start time. Off to the side of each row of autonomous vehicles sat four black Chevy Tahoes. A total of twenty were poised to serve as chase vehicles. Some had cameras mounted on extendable cranes to film the race. Others had localized remote kill switches to disable the vehicles with the push of a button. Each group also had one Tahoe with a massive brush guard in case they needed to run an out-of-control vehicle off the course. The DARPA vehicles would remain on the far edge of the course, so as not to interfere with the competitors.

"Which group are you in?"

"Yours. I'm driving the rig with the video mount." Kyle glanced around to be sure nobody else was around. "I'm betting this race will come down to you and Ashton. I'm really proud of you, Ted. Good luck."

"Thanks."

Ted smiled and watched Kyle make his way over to the fleet of Chevys on the opposite side of the field. A whirring that sounded like it was coming from Cyclops sent Ted's heart to his throat. Frantic and ready to spring to action, he spun around only to see Steve Wozniak slowing to a halt on his Segway. Harry was immediately by Ted's side, smiling and pointing to the paint-stained Apple logo on the front of his shirt.

"Woz up?" Harry asked with hope.

Steve remained stone-faced before looking up at the lidar array perched atop Cyclops.

"Are you getting a full three-sixty view with that thing?" Steve asked as he kept his eyes focused on the sensors.

"Almost," Ted said. "We have gear on the back that fills in the blanks for us."

"I see." Steve glanced back and forth between Ted and Harry and then nodded slightly. "Good luck today."

Steve leaned forward, sending his Segway on to the next team. Harry, who had been holding his breath, let out a long and loud exhalation.

"He hates me," Harry said softly.

"He doesn't even know you, Harry." Ted chuckled and put his arm around Harry's shoulder. "I'm sure he says the same thing to everyone. Let's get to the tent."

As they began walking, Harry stopped and turned to watch his idol zip from vehicle to vehicle, spending less than ten seconds at each one. It was a truly odd mix of competitors. The monstrous Oshkosh MTVR towered in the front row. Directly behind it in the second row was the motorcycle from Berkeley. In between were various trucks, SUVs, cars, and custom-built machines of all shapes and sizes.

"It looks like the pod race from Phantom Menace," Harry said. Ted just shook his head.

The tension inside the big top was palpable as people were settling into the first complete hour of the first event of the DARPA FAST Challenge. To nearly everyone's surprise, most notably DARPA, all twenty competitors were still in the race. The vehicles released in waves combined with the different speeds at which each one was operating had created a fairly even spread across the course. DARPA's concern that contestants would crash into one another like bumper cars had not come to fruition.

Ten giant overhead screens hung in a checkerboard at the front of the big top. The five on the left had split-screen images from inside each vehicle's POV camera. Two were devoted to the leaderboard to show the real-time positions of each vehicle, taking into account when each vehicle left the start line. The last three alternated feeds from the different chase vehicles as well as the two overhead helicopters.

An hour in had Cyclops in first place, followed by Athena and Berkeley's Easy Rider in third. As with the last challenge, the scoreboards displayed only very limited information on each vehicle's performance, leaving scoring calculations a mystery once again. The teams realized you could use the POV images to determine where a vehicle was in relation to the other groups' entries. Berkeley's bike had just sailed passed TerraCrusher from Oshkosh Defense and was closing in on Athena.

"That thing's fast." Ted glanced at the calculations he'd made on the notepad resting in front of him. He nervously tapped his pen several times as he verified his formulas. Nico was sitting beside him, his eyes fixed on the display from one of the chase vehicles following Easy Rider. "Nico, if my math is right, there's no way we can win this."

Ted slid his notepad over to Nico. Nico picked up a pen and spun it across his thumb and fingers as he reviewed Ted's figures. Nico's ability to twirl a pen or pencil along the tips of his thumb and index and middle fingers was truly impressive and he could even do it to a fixed rhythm.

Lori approached the DSU table carrying a tray filled with sandwiches, placing it in front of Ted and Nico.

"Thanks," Nico said without stopping his twirling.

As Lori reached over to grab a turkey club sandwich, she flipped her hand out, sending both Ted's and Nico's pens flying to the floor. "You two need to calm down." Lori put the sandwich on a plate and took a seat beside Ted. "We're an hour into this with a hundred miles left to go. Cyclops is doing fine."

"Cyclops isn't our problem," Ted said. "Berkeley is."

Lori looked up at the leaderboard. Easy Rider was now in second place.

"That group left ten minutes after us." Lori took a bite of her sandwich and grabbed Ted's notepad, quickly scanning the numbers scrawled across the page. "Shit."

One of the DARPA monitors switched to the lead chopper. Easy Rider was closing in on Cyclops. The POV displays showed DSU's Humvee running at forty miles per hour, but the motorcycle was at forty-five miles per hour and accelerating.

"Even when that stupid thing falls down, it gets right back up with those automated kickstands." Harry grabbed a bag of potato chips from the tray and tore it open, shoving a few into his mouth. "Cyclops, Athena, and a few others have all run into some impasses that make them stop or slow down. Easy Rider's recovery time is insane. That damn bike is possessed!"

"If he maintains that pace, he's going to not only come in first but will do it by several minutes." Ted looked around on the ground until he found his pen. He picked it up and snatched the notepad from Lori. "Cyclops will get up to forty-five on the open straights, but Easy Rider is maintaining a much higher speed overall. That bike accelerates faster than anything else out there."

Rusty, who'd been up at the DARPA operations center, approached the DSU table. He surveyed the tray of food and opted for a roast beef sandwich.

"How are we doing?" Rusty asked.

"What kind of question is that?" Ted replied. "Look at the screen!"

A roar exploded from the Berkeley table as the leaderboard showed that Easy Rider had moved past Cyclops for first place. The bike had yet to pass the Humvee, but based on the time of departure, it was now in the lead. The POV camera mounted between the motorcycle's handlebars produced an extremely unsteady image. Still, the closest chase vehicle showed that Cyclops was approximately two hundred yards ahead of the bike and losing ground quickly.

"It's early in the race," Rusty said calmly. "Everyone should relax."

Ted looked over at Nico and Lori, and then to Harry. He started to open his mouth to speak but stopped himself. Ted couldn't understand why Rusty seemed so relaxed. They were early into the competition and losing to a motorcycle. Rusty should be livid. Ted debated showing Rusty the math he'd done but decided it was best to keep quiet.

"Shit." Lori took a sip of her bottled water and pointed at the overhead monitor on the far right. "It looks like we may have our first casualty."

The screen was showing the feed from the Tahoe following a Jeep Grand Cherokee from Team Skynet, a venture capitalist–funded entry. The heavily modified SUV was veering wildly back and forth across the course. Luckily, there were no other vehicles around it aside from the Chevy.

"The lidar and GPS are offline!" The panicked voice came from Team Skynet's table at the back of the room. "Sarah's running blind! We can't stop her!"

DARPA switched three of the screens to track the Jeep. One monitor was from the chase vehicle, another from a chopper, and the last, the POV camera inside the SUV. The Grand Cherokee was making a run for the side of the course and accelerating. So far, she was up to forty miles per hour. The edge of the track was littered with small ruts and vegetation. Sarah bounced as she refused to slow down. The grooves got deeper and more difficult for the SUV to navigate. Suddenly the Jeep flipped over, rolling end over end. Chunks of sensors and gear scattered in every direction. The SUV crashed into a cluster of boulders and burst into flames.

"Team Skynet, you are disqualified." The cold monotone voice echoed from the overhead speakers.

"So much for the rise of the machines," Harry said with a smirk.

"One down," Ted said. "I'm still worried. How come Rusty's not freaking out over Easy Rider?"

"Don't poke the bear, Ted," Harry replied. "Do you really want Rusty yelling at us? A lot can happen between now and the end of the race."

Three more hours passed. During that time, two other vehicles faltered, both due to equipment failure. The remaining seventeen were spread across twenty miles. Easy Rider had stayed close to the math that Ted had projected, and was now several miles ahead of the pack, with Cyclops a distant second, followed closely by Ashton's Athena.

Ted had resorted to chewing on his pen, redoing his calculations every thirty minutes to confirm his theory that DSU could not win the race. Ted could see that Nico was suppressing his desire to twirl his pen, thanks to the glares Lori was giving both of them. Rusty was sitting at the far end of the table with his legs crossed and elevated. Ted grabbed his notepad and slid his chair around Harry to sit beside Rusty.

"You seem especially calm," Ted said.

"Someone has to be. The four of you are completely on edge."

"But I've been running the numbers, and Berkeley is—"

"That stupid bike is not our problem. Ashton is. They always have been."

"I've been doing the math, and you're wrong." Ted held out his notepad. Rusty glanced at it briefly and then looked back at the overhead screens. "You need to see my figures."

Rusty waved his hand and motioned Ted to go away. Ted felt his blood pressure rise and was about to object when he felt Harry's hand slapping against his thigh. He turned around to see what Harry wanted.

"What?" Ted asked with frustration. Harry pointed at the monitors on the right side of the operations center. One was showing the feed from the Tahoe following Easy Rider. The bike was located in a wide-open section of the desert with very few obstacles. "What am I looking at, Harry?"

"Easy Rider's POV view. Check out the speed."

The image from the motorcycle's POV was jittery, but Easy Rider's speed was falling rapidly. Ted's eyes darted back and forth between the images from the chase vehicle and POV cameras. As the bike's speed dropped below twenty miles per hour, a murmur began to roll across the tables in waves. Ted scooted his chair around Harry's and flung his notepad onto the table.

"What the hell is going on?" Ted asked Nico. "Why are they slowing down?"

"I have no clue," Nico replied. "Lori, what's the scoop with this part of the course? It doesn't look like a huge incline."

"It's not," Lori said. She glanced back toward the Berkeley table. "Whatever it is, they don't seem too happy."

Ted stood up to get a better look at the other side of the room. Team Berkeley was in a huddle around one of their workstations. The murmurs had risen in volume throughout the room. Ted looked up at the bike's POV monitor. The image from the camera was now crystal clear. Easy Rider had deployed its kickstands and come to a complete stop.

"I'm going to go get the scoop," Ted said. He bolted off toward team Berkeley.

Rusty slid his legs off the table and stood up, stretching and twisting his back as he did. He walked around to the front of the DSU table, massaging his injured hip along the way. He turned his back to the monitors so that he was facing his team. Nico and Harry were watching Lori scroll through the mapping data for the section of the course Easy Rider had been navigating before it came to a halt.

"It looks flat and rather barren," Lori said. She looked up at Rusty. "Any guesses?"

"I've told you all day that Easy Rider was not our competition." Rusty looked up to see Ted returning to the DSU table. "And here's why."

Ted's grin was wide and infectious. He struggled to keep from laughing, so as not to look rude, having just left the other team's table. Ted took a position at the end of the table with his back facing Berkeley.

"You're not going to believe this," Ted said.

"What failed?" Nico asked. "The GPS? One of their sensors?"

"Their gas tank." Ted could not help it and began to chuckle. He covered his mouth to drown out his laughter. "They ran out of gas!"

"What?" Lori cried. She looked back at the Berkeley table. "Are you serious? How? Why?"

"They told me they never expected to get past the last challenge. They were truly shocked they made it to the road race. Berkeley never bothered to figure out how much gas they would need to complete the one hundred and thirty miles." Ted looked up at Rusty. "You knew, didn't you?"

"I had a hunch." Rusty remained stone-faced as he spoke. "I talked with their team lead last week. The guy couldn't stop gushing about the innovations they'd done with the bike. I'll admit that getting a two-wheeler to ride upright is impressive. The gear that bike is carrying weighs a lot more than a human rider. I did my own back-of-napkin calculations and figured that with the three-gallon tank filled to capacity it would get ninety, maybe a hundred miles before it ran out of gas."

"Look!" Harry was on his feet. "Cyclops!"

DARPA switched the primary POV screen from Easy Rider to Cyclops. The Humvee's camera feed showed it approaching the Chevy Tahoe chase vehicle parked several yards from the motorcycle. Cyclops's speed slowed to twenty miles per hour and then ten. The crowd beneath the big top became silent as they watched the Hummer gracefully maneuver between the Tahoe and the motorcycle parked on its twin kickstands. With the two vehicles safely behind it and a clear road ahead, Cyclops roared forward and quickly reached forty-five miles per hour. The DSU table erupted in glee, and even Rusty allowed himself a brief smile of approval.

"Don't celebrate just yet." Rusty turned and looked at the leaderboard. Easy Rider had dropped to third place, with Athena in second and Cyclops in first. "We still have Ashton on our tail."

16

The clock above the DARPA operations center read 4:06 p.m. The only sound inside the big top was the hum of the industrial air conditioners. The end of the race was moments away and more than half the team members had left the big top and were crowded in the bleachers and behind the concrete barriers at the edge of the finish line, waiting anxiously to see who would win. The blazing dry heat and blustery wind did nothing to subdue the excitement buzzing throughout the crowd. Ted pushed his way through the crowd away from the monitors to get a front-row, in-person view of the finish line.

The course circled a set of mountains, with the last two miles a relatively flat and winding road that gently snaked its way to level ground. The competitors were on their final lap. A glint of light sparkled in the distance. Ted raised his binoculars to focus on the first vehicle to come around the corner. His heart sank at the sight of Athena. The Prius was cautiously descending the last hill, using its regenerative braking to slow its descent and recharge its batteries. Ted lowered his head, his throat closing as he struggled to inhale the dry, sandy air.

The faint clatter of the Humvee's 6.5-liter diesel engine clamored in the distance. Ted raised his binoculars once again. Cyclops was now in view and gaining speed as it descended toward Athena.

"Come on!" Ted screamed. He released his binoculars and let them fall against his chest. He pushed a few people aside so that he could be flat against the barrier. Nico, Harry, and Lori quickly joined him. "Can he make up lost ground?"

"We programmed him for speed," Harry said. "He goes full throttle once he makes that final turn."

"But Athena's in the way," Lori added.

"I told you Ashton was our biggest threat." Rusty had quietly made his way up behind everyone. "Now, we'll see how well all of you did."

Ted gave Rusty a brief glare before turning his attention back to the course. The rough concrete scraped against his palms as he gripped the barrier harder and harder. Athena and Cyclops were half a mile from the finish line. Cyclops slowed as he detected the Prius ahead of him.

"Move!" Ted cried. "Go around!"

Ted's heart was racing. His eyes darted back and forth between the DSU and Ashton vehicles. As each second passed, he became more and more frustrated at the Humvee's choice to simply follow the much slower Toyota.

"Why won't he pass?" Ted asked. He turned to Harry. "Why?"

Harry stood motionless, staring out at the dusty barren field ahead. Suddenly, cries of "Go Athena!" rang out. Ted glanced around the crowd lining the barrier. Thirty feet away was team Ashton. Sam was crammed beside Ralph and Vin, all cheering for the Prius.

Ted raised his binoculars to get a closer look at the action. The path from the two vehicles to the finish line was clear. The gusting winds blasted sand across the field, reducing visibility. Ted knew that Cyclops, and most likely, Athena, would have no trouble seeing through the sand. He focused on the sensor array atop the Toyota. All Ted could think about was how Sam had told him her digital gimbal would be the superior technology. As Ted scanned the lidar array, the Prius suddenly fell from view. He adjusted his binoculars and zoomed out. A series of large tumbleweeds were blowing across the field. Athena had slammed on the brakes to avoid a collision. Ted smiled as Cyclops swerved to avoid rear-ending the Prius.

"Yes!" Ted screamed. "Go, Cyclops! Go!"

Cyclops, now clear of the Toyota, roared ahead, quickly passing Ashton's entry. The tumbleweeds that had flummoxed the sensors on Athena did not hinder the Humvee. Cyclops blasted through them, and past the Prius, as the vehicle accelerated to forty-five miles per hour. Athena, now free of debris, began to increase speed. The Humvee, however, was already far ahead.

Ted flung one arm around Harry and his other around Nico and pulled them both against his chest. Lori jumped up and down, clapping and screaming. Rusty stood silent, nodding, and smiling as Cyclops continued to pull away from the Prius. DARPA had rolled out a black and white checkered tape to mark the end of the course. Cyclops, almost as if savoring its victory, accelerated faster as it snapped the tape in half, crossing the finish line well ahead of Athena.

"DSU is first." The outdoor speakers crackled their announcement. Roars and cheers erupted across the hundreds of people clamoring inside and outside the tent. The group of reporters in the bleachers were all on their feet applauding. Several seconds later, Athena crossed the line. "Ashton second."

Both vehicles, following their programming, slowed to a halt in a small staging area far away from the finish line. DSU and Ashton were the only two vehicles competing for first place. The rest of the entrants were over five to ten miles away. It would be quite some time before DARPA would know who came in third.

"Did we win?" Lori asked. "What's the final score?"

"DARPA's damn points system is still a mystery." Rusty looked at the oversized outdoor monitors beside the stadium seats. The screens remained pitch black. "We came in first time-wise, but I don't know if there were any penalties or deductions. Both vehicles had hiccups along the way. Who knows how long—"

"We now have the results." A hush fell over the crowd as many eyes looked up toward the overhead speakers. Ted looked over at Sam. She smiled and nodded. Ted's heart pounded in his chest. He closed his eyes as the DARPA announcement rang out. "The winner of the road race is DSU, followed by Ashton."

Ted opened his eyes and screamed. Lori, Harry, and Nico jumped up and down, clapping and cheering. All four held one another. Tears ran freely from Harry and Nico. Ted turned and looked at Rusty. He was busy looking at the monitors next to the bleachers. The leaderboard flashed to life, showing DSU ahead of Ashton by two points.

"Well?" Ted asked Rusty.

"We still have the third and final Urban Challenge ahead of us. Let's not get too excited."

Ted frowned but began to chuckle. Rusty's refusal to enjoy the victory would in no way prevent him from savoring the moment. Cyclops was idling several dozen feet away. A jet black Chevy Tahoe chase vehicle carrying a roof-mounted camera crane that jutted out ten feet from its side followed the action into the staging area. Ted, filled with pride as he gazed upon the towering lidar array perched atop the custom gimbal he'd designed, saw the Chevy keep coming as it approached the Humvee.

"Stop!" Ted screamed. But his cries were too late. The camera assembly slammed into Cyclops's gimbal supporting the central lidar system. "No! Cyclops!"

Still screaming, Ted jumped over the concrete barrier as he sprinted to Cyclops. Harry, Nico, Lori, and Rusty were close behind. As Ted neared the Hummer, the Chevy's door opened, and Kyle Fisher emerged from the driver's seat.

"What have you done?" Ted grabbed Kyle by his shoulders and threw him back against the Tahoe's rear door. "Look! Look! What the hell is wrong with you?"

From nowhere, Rusty's hands appeared, taking hold of Ted's shirt collar to jerk him away from Kyle. Rusty held on to Ted for several seconds, allowing Ted to calm down.

"Jesus," Kyle said as he noticed the end of the crane jammed into the top of the Humvee.

"You built an empire on driving off-road racers, and you can't even park a Chevy?" Ted yanked himself free from Rusty's grip and stepped within inches of Kyle. "You better pray you didn't cause any permanent damage."

Ted spun around to check on Cyclops. Nico was already hanging from the side of the SUV, inspecting the impact point. Ted hauled himself up beside Nico.

"Well?" Ted asked Nico.

"Duct tape won't solve this one."

The camera at the end of the crane was demolished. All that was left was tattered shards of plastic and wire. The assembly connecting the camera to the crane was jammed into one of the magnetic mounts supporting the lidar's gimbal. Ted tugged gently at the beam to try and free it. After several pulls, it popped loose. The gimbal shuddered, finally free from the pole.

"How's it look?" Kyle asked cautiously, nervously flicking his tongue against the roof of his mouth. He stepped closer to the Hummer. "Can you fix it?"

Ted struggled to control his anger. He found it difficult to focus on how to repair the damage. His hands trembled as he tried to sift through the torn metal and broken connectors. He squeezed his hands into fists to try and stop them from shaking. Part of him wanted to turn around and punch Kyle in the face. Wind blasted sand into his eyes, causing even more tears to flow down his face.

"What's the damage, Ted?" Rusty asked. His voice was calm, cool, and controlled. "Give it to us straight."

"I'm . . . I'm not sure." Ted's eyes darted back and forth as he made a mental inventory of the parts that would need to be replaced. He took a few deep breaths to try and calm himself down. "The gimbal looks fine. There's a slight bend where it connected to the magnetic damper. But the mag shock itself is toast. It was sheered from its mounting point. I don't know if we can repair that. And the servo controls. They look shot."

"I can make it work," Nico said confidently. "We have spare shocks in the truck. Servo controls, too. I should be able to rig something."

"Nico, the system is programmed specifically for the magnetic dampers and gimbal." Harry was sweating profusely a few feet away. He removed his glasses, and nervously wiped them dry. "It has to be an exact match. Otherwise, we will have a lot of code to adjust."

"I know!" Nico leaped from the top of the Hummer. "I'll be right back."

A large crowd had formed around the Hummer and Chevy. Competing teams were grouped together, all wearing their coordinating shirts and hats. Many were pointing at the camera and the DSU team inspecting the damage. Sam pushed her way past the Oshkosh team and stopped beside Cyclops's front fender. Ted let out a sigh when he saw her and slid down from the side of the vehicle.

"How bad?" Sam asked. She stepped forward and ran her hand across the Humvee's doors.

"Nico's convinced we can fix it." Ted glanced over at Kyle. He and Rusty were having a quiet discussion beside the Tahoe. "Twenty autonomous vehicles battling across the desert, and we get taken out by a human driver."

Sam let out a chuckle and quickly stifled herself. Ted allowed a grin to escape.

"Well, . . ." Ted said. "I'll probably think it's a whole lot funnier later."

Sam pulled herself up alongside the Humvee and inspected the damaged gimbal.

"For what it's worth, congratulations on the win. I hope you can compete in the final test."

"You do?"

"Of course. We've all worked hard to get to this point. We are pushing boundaries here. All of us." Sam slid her aviators off, her green eyes dancing. "Besides, I don't want to win because you had to default. I want to beat your ass fair and square."

Ted smiled. He felt a bit of his anger and anxiety subside. He was surprised to realize that Sam's playful taunting and genuine concern brought him comfort. He was about to say something about it when Nico came running back, carrying a crushed box.

"That was fast," Ted said to Sam. "Too fast."

"Bad news." Nico hunched forward and dropped the box he was carrying. He was panting heavily and took a few deep breaths to regain his composure. "The box with the magnetic dampers was crushed."

"What do you mean, crushed?" Rusty pushed his way past Ted to confront Nico. "How?"

"Everything in the storage locker was fine when we left to come to the race but the equipment stored above the box with the dampers worked its way loose during transit."

"How bad is it?" Ted asked. He fell to his knees and began sorting through the components inside the box, his hands shaking as he extracted a collection of wires and struts. "What the hell did this?"

"Toolbox," Nico replied. "More like three of them."

"What's the damage, Ted?" Rusty asked.

Ted and Nico spent a few moments scrounging through the contents.

"All four dampers are destroyed," Ted said. "They look to be in worse condition than the one on top of Cyclops."

Ted stood up and looked toward the horizon. He slammed his fist on the hood of the Humvee. Sam slowly began to step away from the DSU team. Lori and Harry took her lead and moved away from Ted, Nico, and Rusty. Walking over to Ted, Nico put a comforting hand on his shoulder.

"So it's over," Ted said. "Without the dampers, we can't control the gimbal."

"Relax," Rusty said calmly. "We can call DSU back in Pittsburgh. They can express ship a replacement part overnight."

Nico lowered his head and shoved his hands into his pockets.

"We do have more dampers, don't we?" Rusty asked.

"No," Nico replied. "I thought it made sense to bring all of them with us."

"And now they're all destroyed?" Rusty did not wait for a response. His calm temperament was gone in an instant. He stepped forward, forcing Nico against the Humvee's fender. "You're telling me that our ace in the hole gimbal is now a piece of shit because you didn't have a backup plan?"

Most of those who had gathered to check out the crash began to disperse. Rusty's bellowing and bright red face told them this was a discussion strictly for DSU. Sam stayed, though, standing just behind Lori and Harry. Rusty turned his attention to Ted.

"You've got five dampers to work with, Ted." Rusty's temples throbbed as his voice escalated. "The four in the box and the busted one on top of Cyclops. Are you telling me you can't patch them into a single working unit?"

Nico grabbed the box and placed it on the Hummer's hood. He and Ted began to lay out the broken components. Ted used his arm to shield the wind and sand from blowing the pieces away, doing a quick inventory of each piece and closing his eyes to work out a solution. He began to shake his head and sigh. He took one last look at the damper crushed on Cyclops's roof before turning to face Rusty.

"It's a long shot," Ted said. "All of the key mounting points are bent. I'm going to have to see what else we have in storage to try and slap something together. But this isn't a quick fix. To properly repair, calibrate, and test everything is easily a week."

"A week?" Rusty yelled. "Unacceptable! We don't have that long."

"I can try and cut that in half, but not without introducing a ton of risk," Ted said.

"There has to be a solution!" Rusty was now pacing back and forth, his limp appearing to be quite aggravated. Ted was standing beside Nico for support. Both men looked exhausted and defeated. "Think! We didn't come this far to win the road race only to be taken out by a goddamn camera! How can we get control of the gimbal?"

"It's an integrated system," Nico said. "The magnetic dampers are Ted's design. We can't just swap some other tech in there. This is my fault. I should have double-checked that everything was secured. I thought bringing all of the parts with us was the right move. I'm sorry."

"I don't want to hear apologies," Rusty said. "Everyone focus."

Ted put a hand on Nico's shoulder. He let his eyes wander past Rusty and settle on Sam. She was standing a few feet behind Lori, looking quite concerned. Ted then looked over at Kyle, leaning up against the side of the Chevy. Kyle was busy pulling the video cabling running along the crane atop the Tahoe. To Ted, it looked as if Kyle were reeling a huge fishing pole line.

"Fish a tuna," Ted said softly. "That's it!"

"What?" Rusty asked with confusion.

"Kevin will have what we need." Ted ran over to Kyle. Rusty and Nico followed him. "Kevin's a packrat. He's insane about version control. The back room in the Nixon facility will have a shitload of magnetic dampers. Every iteration."

"Are you sure?" Nico asked. "If it's not an exact match—"

"It will be close enough." Ted struggled to contain his excitement. "The final versions I used on Cyclops are based on my original prototypes. I can make adjustments to get those to work. I know I can. Kevin will know which ones I need and can express ship them to us."

"There's only one problem," Kyle said. "Kevin's in Boston. He had a death in the family. The shop's closed."

"Don't you have another shop in Reno?" Rusty asked. "Just have someone drive out and get what we need."

"The guys at the Reno shop don't have access to the test site," Kyle said.

"Then they can break the door down!" Rusty yelled, his temples throbbing in anger.

"It's not that easy," Ted said, his enthusiasm quickly fading. He spun around and leaned back against the Chevy. Sam, Lori, and Harry had now joined the group. "Kevin will have dozens of different versions stored away. It's not something I can talk someone through."

"So, then we drive up and get it." Bits of potato chips fell from

Harry's mouth as he excitedly grabbed another handful from the bag he was holding. "We can rent a car or take the RV. How far can it be?"

"It's probably a ten- to twelve-hour drive," Kyle said. He and Rusty were busy staring at one another. "Depending on traffic."

"Okay, so we take turns driving and load up with caffeine." Harry now seemed genuinely excited at the prospect of a road trip. "What's today? We can leave early tomorrow morning. That should still give us time to—"

"No." Rusty stepped forward until he was beside Kyle. "I'm not sending half my team on a road trip. This isn't a problem we created, so it's not our problem to solve. Kyle, a word?"

Kyle lowered his head and followed Rusty around the other side of the Tahoe. Ted, Nico, Harry, Lori, and Sam gathered around. Ted placed a hand on Sam's shoulder and nodded quietly to thank her for her support. Harry was busy looking over his shoulder, his gaze seemingly fixated on the underside of the Chevy.

"What are you looking at?" Lori asked.

"I'm waiting for the blood to flow," Harry responded. "I know that look in Rusty's eyes."

Kyle and Rusty were gone less than two minutes before returning to the group.

"Ted, I'm going to fly you to Reno." Kyle spoke slowly, reflecting on the task he'd just agreed to do for Rusty. "My plane is only a few minutes away at the airbase. I can have you there in two hours. You'll be back by midnight."

"A private jet to Reno?" Harry licked the salty canola oil from his fingertips. "Can I go?"

"No, none of you will go." Rusty said, still angered by the damage and delays caused by Kyle. "There is too much prep we have to do here. That replacement part won't be an exact match. You need to be ready to make it work. Besides, the Urban Challenge is just around the corner. All of you have a lot of work to do to get ready for that event."

"Do you need to run this by DARPA?" Ted asked Kyle. "Aren't you breaking some kind of rule by helping us out?"

"I will speak to them and explain what happened. This is a DARPA error. My error, yes, but I'm representing DARPA here. I will ask for two-day delay to allow time for the repair and I will see if I can get permission for Ted to leave to go pick up the parts he needs. I am confident they'll agree to all terms. . . . And, as Rusty so eloquently pointed out to me on the flip side of the Chevy, I broke it, so now I own it." Kyle smiled as he slapped Rusty on the shoulder. Rusty did not smile back. "Meet me at the operations center under the big top in fifteen minutes, Ted. I'm going to get the ball rolling on this, including arranging a rental car for you in Reno."

Kyle turned and headed off to the tent. Rusty pointed at Nico and motioned him toward Cyclops. Nico led him over to show him the damage in detail. Harry and Lori walked away and began discussing their next steps, leaving Ted alone with Sam.

"Do you think you'll be able to fix it?" Sam asked. "Or was that just to shut Rusty up?"

"No, I'm sure of it. Kevin's so methodical, I know he's going to have the pieces I was working on or something very close to what we need."

"Sounds like my kind of guy." Sam let out a laugh. Ted managed a smile. "I'm looking forward to seeing Cyclops back up and running."

"Me, too."

"Okay, let me get back to my team. They're throwing a surprise birthday party for me."

"A surprise that you know about?"

"Ralph told me there was an emergency team meeting back at our camp. But I already found the cake they stashed away. It's fine. I'll fake a smile and get through it."

"You really don't like birthdays, do you?"

"It's a long story." Sam slid her aviators back on. "Good luck, Ted."

Ted was worried but hopeful. He was also genuinely surprised at Sam's concern for him and the DSU team. An idea suddenly hit him.

Looking toward the big top, he spotted Kyle still making his way across the dusty field. Most of the other teams had cleared out. Ted bolted to catch up to Kyle.

"Hey Kyle, how big is your plane?" Ted asked as he gasped for breath.

"Why?"

"Do you mind if I bring someone with me?"

17

Sam Lavoie was born and raised in California. Her mother, Catherine, a self-made millionaire, demanded the best education for her only daughter, but was overly protective. Traveling, considered risky, was something they only rarely did. Sam could count on one hand the number of times she'd been in an airplane.

From the tarmac, the plane had seemed small and confining. Although she didn't consider herself claustrophobic, Sam found herself a bit concerned over the private jet's tiny size. The few times she'd flown with her mother, it had been first class in commercial jetliners. Despite the luxury accommodations inside the private jet, she couldn't help but feel this was a step down from what she was used to.

"Prepare for takeoff." Kyle's voice sounded thin and frail over the cabin speakers.

She closed her eyes and with her right hand, felt for the small heart charm pendant on the gold chain around her neck, clutching the armrest on the seat with her left.

The engines roared to life and the jet accelerated down the runway. Within minutes the tiny plane was off the tarmac and banking upward. The landing gear doors whirred and whooshed and then thumped and closed. Sam opened her eyes and exhaled.

"Are you okay?" Ted asked. He was seated to her right, a narrow aisle between them.

"I'm fine. I just get a little nervous."

The plane banked right as it climbed into the evening sky. Ted cupped his hands beside his eyes and pressed his face to the glass as he stared at the ground far below.

"I can see the airbase," Ted said. "Do you think we can see where the Urban Challenge will be?"

"That would be cheating."

"It will be a few more minutes before we reach cruising altitude," Kyle said through the speakers. "We should be in Reno well before six. A rental car will be waiting for you two. There are drinks and snacks in the bag at the back of the plane. Help yourself once we level off."

"I wonder if he has any whisky," Ted said.

"Whisky? I don't think we should be drinking. We have a long night ahead of us."

"One glass won't kill you."

Ted unlatched his belt and knelt in front of his seat.

"Ted! What are you doing? We're still climbing!"

"Relax."

The space between the seats was tight. Kyle had strapped a duffle bag into the rear bench seat. Ted slid past Sam and sat on the floor behind her. His body bobbed back and forth as he struggled to keep himself steady. He managed to get the top of the bag open and thrust his hand inside. After a few moments, he pulled out a box of sesame crackers and a bottle of wine. He passed both to Sam.

"You're insane, Ted. I hope you know that."

He came back to his seat, wine opener, napkins, and two plastic cups in hand. Once his seat belt was secured, he flipped out the tray stored beside his seat and set about opening up the box of crackers.

"Why are you doing this?" She asked as she gripped the bottle of wine.

"We'll be level in no time. There's no reason we can't start to enjoy ourselves early."

"No, I mean me. Why did you want me to come along?"

He tore the foil cracker pouch open and scattered some across a napkin. The nutty scent of sesame wafted through the cabin. He grabbed the bottle of wine from Sam and removed the foil covering the cork.

"Well, I certainly didn't want to take this trip alone."

"You could have been up front in the cockpit with Kyle or insisted with Rusty that one of your teammates be allowed to come."

"I think Rusty was pretty adamant about everyone else staying behind to prep. And two hours listening to Kyle's stories? No thanks." Ted laughed, then grimaced as he struggled to remove the cork from the bottle without splashing red wine across the tan leather interior.

"The question I have, Sam, is why you decided to come?"

"Well, it was the perfect escape from the surprise birthday party, and . . ."

"And . . . what?"

"I thought it might be a fun adventure. And a way to be a good sport and help a fellow competitor get back up to speed so Ashton can win spectacularly, fair and square."

"Oh, yeah?" Ted said looking directly into Sam's eyes. "Well, I'm sorry to have to be the one to disappoint you then. . . ." He paused, his expression hardening a bit. He moved away from her slightly, suddenly seeming to change tack and taking on a more professional air. "Actually, speaking of your expertise and knowledge, I did want to learn more about Athena. That is one impressive vehicle. I was hoping to hear about what you went through to build her."

As he spoke, Sam thought that the deep blue shade of his eyes reminded her of the deepest blues of the Pacific on one of those priceless cloudless days. She could feel a heat deep within her that made her a little giddy, and she could not stop smiling. She reminded herself that this was a professional trip—for a colleague in need.

He smiled as the cork finally popped from the bottle. The jet was slowly beginning to level off. He pointed to the bin against the wall beside Sam. She opened it and unfolded her tray for Ted to place two plastic cups in front of her and pour the merlot.

"I was also wondering why Vin let you come tonight."

"Oh, Vin had no problem with me coming whatsoever. With the extra time we have to prepare because of the delay, he could afford for me to go tonight. Besides, he wholeheartedly agrees with the idea of helping when needed, even when it's for the competition. What happened to DSU today could have happened to any of us." She held up her acrylic cup and passed the other to Ted. "Cheers."

"Happy birthday, Sam."

She took a sip of wine, looking down, and ignoring his birthday wish.

"If you get to learn about Athena, then I get to hear about the great Cyclops machine that DSU built. Tell me, Ted, is Rusty as big of an ass to work for as he seems?"

"Bigger." Ted tossed a few crackers into his mouth and washed them down with the wine. "It's like he never left the military, and we're all in this neverending boot camp. He made us test Cyclops overnight in sub-freezing weather."

"Why?"

"Because he's an ass. A big giant ass." Ted rolled his head sideways and stared out at the darkening sky. "What's Vin like?"

"Vin's amazing. He—"

"Hey guys," Kyle's voice interrupted. "We've leveled off. Feel free to help yourself to some snacks. I'll let you know when we're getting ready to land."

"Vin pushes us, but not like Rusty, it seems. He's always asking us to think outside the box. We bring him solutions, and he will tell us they're great and then ask us if they could be better. Our team is completely in sync. We support and encourage one another to go further."

"It sounds delightful."

"Do I detect a note of jealousy?" Her smile faded as she realized Ted seemed genuinely upset. "Hey, sorry. Is it that bad at DSU? All joking aside, Cyclops is also quite impressive."

"It's just that when I agreed to get on board with Rusty, I thought... I thought he got me. That he . . . understood."

"Understood what?"

"Me."

She shifted uncomfortably in her seat, watching as Ted sipped his wine, keeping his gaze fixed outside at the horizon. She was suddenly aware of how intimate the interior of the jet was, and how little space separated her from Ted.

"I take it the brilliant Ted Wolff with two 'F's' is a tough nut to crack?"

"I guess you could say that." He spun sideways in his seat so that he was facing her. "You tell me. What do you see when you look at me?"

"Oh, do you really want to go there?"

"I do. Go for it."

"Okay." She realized she had finished half her wine. A slight buzz was beginning to set in. She took a handful of crackers from the napkin in front of Ted, doing her best to ignore the piercing stare of his blue eyes. "You come across as confident, but borderline egotistical. I mean, you seemed very dismissive of the digital gimbal we built. I never once heard you compliment the tech we've got on Athena. You're obviously a smart and talented engineer, Ted. Cyclops kicked our ass in the road race and came very close to beating us during the Qualifying Stage. You have every right to be proud. But there's a fine line between pride and arrogance."

She paused to gauge his reaction. His gaze was focused on the cup of wine in his hand, so she couldn't get a read on him.

"You told me to go for it," she added.

"I did. I didn't expect you to go that big." He grinned and smiled at her. "Look, I know I can be impatient now and then. And maybe I do tend to be a bit overconfident from time to time. I just . . . I just want a better life."

"We all do. Do your parents support you?"

"My parents?"

"Sorry. If I'm getting too personal, tell me."

"No. No. It's fine. At least . . . with you." Ted briefly draped his hand on her knee. "My dad is very old school, you know? I have two older brothers. They basically did what my parents wanted. Trade school. Working at the factory. Do as you're told, and you get all the praise."

"And is that something you seek? Praise?"

"No, it's just that I feel like the life I want, and the dreams I have, aren't the ones my parents have for me. They . . . they don't understand." He grabbed the bottle of wine and emptied some into his cup. He motioned toward Sam to fill hers, but she waved it away. "How about you? Are you close to your family?"

"Family means everything to me. My parents divorced when I was four years old. I barely remember my dad. He went off and found someone half his age."

"I'm sorry."

"Don't be. I think my life turned out all the better because of it. My mom was so broken that she vowed to reinvent herself and went on to form her own company. She's been the best mother—the best friend—a daughter could ask for. I wouldn't be where I am today without her."

"That's amazing. Any siblings?"

"No, it's just my mother and me. And, well, I . . . I also have a daughter." Sam waited a few moments to see if Ted would say anything. He just sat there with a blank look on his face. "Danielle. Dani. She'll be four in December."

"A daughter. Wow." His eyes drifted to her hands, which were wrapped around her cup of wine.

"I'm single, Ted." She lowered her cup, and unconsciously slid her hand over her ring finger. "Dani was . . . Dani *is*, a long story. She's my world."

They sat in silence for several seconds, each staring ahead. Sam wondered if she'd revealed too much too soon. She finally said, "I'm guessing you don't have any kids."

"No." Ted shook his head and grimaced. "The thought hasn't really crossed my mind. So, um, is it, uh, hard being a single mom?"

"Yes and no. We live with my mother in Fremont. I commute to Ashton, and my mom and the nanny care for Dani when I'm not there."

"You have a nanny?"

"My mom arranged for one to help out. She sold her cosmetics company years ago. Now she's on the board of directors in an advisory role, so she's got plenty of time to care for Dani. But the nanny helps out as needed."

"Must be nice," Ted said with a bit of contempt.

"It's not like that, Ted. We came from nothing. My mom struggled. I wasn't born with some silver spoon in my mouth. She built what she has."

"I didn't mean to hurt your feelings."

The roar of the outside air rushing across the plane's fuselage hummed throughout the cabin, filling the silence left by the sudden lack of conversation. Sam slid her empty cup to the far side of her tray table. She'd had enough alcohol for tonight. She spun around and reached into the duffel bag with the snacks, retrieving two bottles of water. Passing one to Ted, she opened the other for herself.

"That's all I'm trying to do," Ted said. "My family is blue-collar working class. I want more."

"It may seem like we come from different worlds, Ted, but we are both pushing for a better world. Despite the struggles you've had at DSU, you must be proud of what you've achieved. The rotating lidar array you've built is revolutionary."

"Thanks." He smiled and leaned closer to her. "My plan was to make it spin, not just rotate, but we ran out of time."

"Spin?"

"Kevin and I went back and forth on it for months before I left to join DSU."

"Kevin's the guy you worked with in Nixon?"

"Right. We were too far into the Cyclops program to switch gears, but try and imagine Cyclops with a lidar array that spins continuously at high speed."

"Spinning lidar would give you a complete three-hundred-and-sixty-degree field of view with almost real-time information." Sam leaned back in her seat and closed her eyes. Her mind began to race through the hundreds of computer programs and millions of lines of code she and her team had built for Athena. She thought of the obstacles they'd encountered, and the workarounds they'd developed. A smile spread across her face as she imagined what she could do with the system he was describing. "How close were you to having it completed?"

"Kevin and I were close." He took a sip of wine and frowned. "I had wanted DSU to try to implement it, but Rusty felt it was too risky. I think he was wrong."

"Maybe you shouldn't be so hard on Rusty. The guy's sent robots to the moon. I'm sure he knew the risk wasn't worth the gain."

"So, you're taking his side?" Ted's tone was suddenly defensive.

"This isn't about sides. It's about the approach. Progress takes time, Ted."

"I disagree. Progress takes pushing boundaries. That was something I admired about Rusty. He pushes. Just not the way I thought he would."

"I'm starting to think that extra 'F' in your name stands for 'frenetic.'"

"My teammates might agree with you on that one," he chuckled.

"Do you know the children's story *The Tortoise and the Hare*?"

"I'm familiar with it, but I can't say I remember it well." Ted tossed a cracker in his mouth and swallowed the rest of his wine. "Let me guess. You're going to give me some lecture about slow and steady winning the race."

"It's Dani's favorite story. I read it to her all the time." Sam downed half her bottle of water. The dryness of the air in the plane, coupled with the alcohol and spending the day in the desert, had her completely dehydrated.

"You do realize that Cyclops blew past Athena to win the race today. Speed won the day."

"And nine women can't make a baby in a month."

"What?" Ted stared blankly at Sam. "That makes no sense."

"My point exactly. Some things take time, Ted. Like it or not, oftentimes, you have to do A, then B, then C. Adding more resources won't make something happen quicker. There are some things you can't rush."

"Nine women making one baby." He chuckled as he leaned back in his seat. "I'm going to have to remember that one."

"At Ashton, we've been very methodical in our approach to the DARPA project. If you rush things you run the risk of making mistakes. Mistakes can be costly. Mistakes can lead to consequences you have to live with the rest of your life." Sam glanced right out the window. The jet was banking and she could see the ground far below. The faint glimmer of lights outlining the roadways flickered through the darkness of the evening sky. She grabbed for her pendant and closed her eyes. "You must see the good in what we're doing, Ted. A world where vehicles drive themselves. A world without accidents from reckless drivers. A safer world. A better world. For my Dani. For everyone."

"It sounds like this is all very personal to you." He leaned closer. "Why is that?"

"Maybe another time, Ted."

18

Ted glanced at the clock display in the Ford Escape Kyle had rented for them. It was 7:05 p.m. as they pulled up in front of the Fisher Tuner workshop outside Nixon, Nevada. The darkening sky was enormous and awash in deep purples and oranges as he parked and killed the ignition.

"Only five minutes later than planned." He popped his door open and pocketed the key fob. "Allow me to give you the grand tour."

"I'm shocked we didn't get stopped by the police." Sam got out of the SUV and slammed the door shut. "You were going way beyond the speed limit."

"I told you to relax. I'm intimately familiar with these roads. The cops are never around. I had a heavily tricked out Mustang GT I used to drive here. I'd open her up regularly. She was a beauty. I wish I had time to show you the testing grounds we used." Ted fumbled through his pockets until he found the key Kyle had given him. "Or Wadsworth, where I used to live."

"Wadsworth? What an odd name for a town." Sam paused and scratched her head. "That sounds like a measurement for the maximum amount of gum you can safely chew before choking."

Ted let out a boisterous laugh as he unlocked the front door. The interior of the office smelled of grease and oil. He ran his hand along the side wall until his fingers came across the light switch for the office.

In a flicker, the office appeared before them. Sam stepped inside and closed the door behind her.

"Follow me." He opened the door to the main garage and hit the switches to turn on the huge overhead lights. The maintenance bay sparked to life. Ted paused to take in the surroundings, noting the familiar and the new. "This is where the magic happens. Well, it used to for me."

Three vehicles were crammed inside the garage. A black Jeep Wrangler was on a lift on Kevin's side of the shop. The area closest to the office, Ted's old space, had a dirt bike completely disassembled, along with a heavily modified bright blue Toyota FJ Cruiser. Ted frowned at not seeing Frankie parked inside. The Pontiac had been gutted and sold for scrap several months after he left for DSU.

The workbench Ted once used was littered with tools and equipment. Instead of replacing Ted with a full-time employee, Kyle had opted to do an internship program with some of the local colleges. Over the past two years, Kevin had taken on a number of different students as protégés, exposing them to hands-on development. Ted briefly surveyed his old desk before heading to the other side of the garage.

Kevin's workspace was crammed with a variety of gadgets, all in various stages of assembly. Half a dozen were covered in Do Not Touch sticky notes. A picture of Ted and Kevin sitting on Frankie's hood was pinned to the corkboard lining the back wall.

"What are these all about?" Sam ran her fingers across the edge of one of the yellow stickies. "It looks like someone doesn't like to share."

"That's Kevin." He smiled as he studied the components Kevin had marked with caution. "Looks like someone's been a busy boy."

Sam made her way past him to the far end of Kevin's desk. A black cylindrical object, two feet tall by a foot wide, caught her eye. She grabbed the slotted center section and wiggled it back and forth. A bright orange sticky note fell from the top. Ted immediately joined her to see what she was studying.

"Is this what I think it is?" she asked.

"That's it." He grabbed the sensor by its base. It weighed less than he expected. "This is the spinning lidar we were developing. Kevin's made a lot of progress."

"Wow." Sam bent down to get a closer look at the technology. "This could be a huge boost for autonomous driving."

"I told him to wait until after the DARPA Challenge so that we could finish it together." Ted slid the device back onto the table. He opened up a notepad resting beside the lidar system and began to read through Kevin's notes. He felt his blood pressure rise as he digested the information. "He's working off my designs. *Mine!* I'm going to have to have a chat with him when he gets back. He's changing things I explicitly told him not to."

Ted flinched at the feel of Sam's fingers along his shoulder. The tingle he felt from her gentle stroke surprised him. He exhaled slowly and turned around.

"Relax." She brushed his lock away from his eyes and slid her hand down his arm. "I'm sure he's only trying to perfect it."

He felt his pulse soften. Sam's blond hair and green eyes sparkled in the harsh fluorescent lighting inside the garage. The smell of motor oil was replaced by a flowery scent, coming from her skin and hair. Her presence was so calming. Her touch. Her voice. Ted smiled and ran the back of his hand across her hair, pushing it behind her shoulder.

"You look so different without that silly baseball cap on." He grinned as she took a small half step back and began to fidget with her hair. He noticed her blushing. "It's a good look."

"Thanks. Um, so, where are the parts that you need? We should probably get back to Reno."

"They're in the warehouse. I'll need a few minutes to find them. Why don't you wait outside?" He tossed the car keys to her. "The stench in here is nauseating."

She smiled, nodded, and headed back into the office. As soon as he heard the outside door close, he went into the back room. The warehouse, roughly half the size of the main garage, was filled with floor-to-ceiling metal shelves. The air was stale and dry. Kevin was responsible for maintaining the inventory of every item they stocked. He never allowed Ted, or anyone else, to add or remove items without following his strict rules.

Ted grabbed a binder resting on the table just inside the door to the warehouse. He flipped through and took a full two minutes until he found the entry for the magnetic shocks. Kevin had them listed as being in aisle 3, section D, shelf 2. Ted looked around for an empty box. There were several along the back wall. Taking the largest, he headed straight to the third aisle, binder in hand. Kevin labeled every shelf and section in the warehouse. Section D of the second shelf had four boxes. Each one had an inventory ID number, along with magnetic dampers/shocks scribbled on them in black ink.

"Bingo." Ted pulled the four boxes out and placed them on the floor. Most of the items were very familiar to him, given that he had designed and built them. The fourth carton contained components he'd never seen before. He checked the binder for the ID number listed on the box. The items were dated from late last year. "You son of a bitch. You've been modifying my designs."

Ted slammed the binder closed and flung it down the aisle. His mind was a blur, filled with months of developing new technologies for Cyclops while at DSU. He glanced at the shelves around him and shook his head.

"What else of mine have you stolen?"

He took a few minutes to study the modified design Kevin had built, but ended up selecting a slightly older set of dampers. He retrieved the binder and began searching for additional items he wanted to collect, figuring he might as well stock up on spare parts, just in case they ran into issues during the rest of the challenge.

Ten minutes later, Ted emerged from Fisher Tuner carrying a large cardboard box, sealed in packing tape. Sam was sitting inside the Escape, behind the driver's seat. The SUV was running, and the headlights illuminated the exterior doors as the sky was nearing complete darkness. Ted took a deep breath, taking in the crisp fifty-degree air. He'd forgotten how peaceful the desert could be.

He popped the back hatch open and slid the heavy box into the cargo hold, locking eyes with Sam, who was watching him in the rear-view mirror.

"I'm driving," Ted said. "Out."

"I prefer not to get killed."

He slammed the hatch closed and walked over to the driver's front door. He tapped the glass with his knuckles. Sam lowered the window and raised her right eyebrow.

"The tortoise will be driving us back to Reno." Her grin turned into a snicker.

"We're not going to Reno." He grabbed the door handle and pulled the door open, surprising her. "There's something else I have to show you. Out."

"Show me? What? Wadsworth?"

"Out."

He stepped aside as she hopped from the driver's seat, jumping in quickly and adjusting the seat and mirrors. As soon as Sam was buckled in, he guided them back to Route 447. Once there, he turned right and quickly accelerated.

"The airport is south," Sam said. "Where are we going?"

"It's a surprise. Something Kyle suggested."

Ted's iPod rested in the Ford's cup holder. A deep charcoal cord ran from the mp3 player's headphone jack to the auxiliary input on the Escape's dashboard. "Lunatic Fringe" by Red Rider was playing through the car's speakers. He had been frustrated at Sam's disapproval of his music choices during the car ride, so was keeping the volume down.

"We've been driving forever, Ted. Where are you taking me?"

"Were you this annoying when your mom drove you around as a kid?"

"Won't Kyle be expecting us?" She spun sideways in her seat so she could face him. "I think we should at least call him."

"Kyle knows where we're going. He gave me the tickets and insisted we use them."

"Tickets? To what?"

"That."

He pointed ahead, thrusting his arm above the steering wheel. Sam turned to see what was in front of them. A glow filled the sky so bright it was almost as if a small subdued sun was rising.

"What . . . what is that?" she asked with confusion. "Where are we?"

"Black Rock Desert."

"Black Rock? Why does that sound so familiar?" She focused on what was ahead of her. "Wait. Isn't that where they have that big event every year? What's it called? With the big fire."

"Yes. Keep going. You've almost got it."

Sam looked back and forth from Ted's grin to the ever-increasing glow in the distance, eventually throwing her hands up and shrugging.

"What do fires do?" he asked.

"What?" she paused.

"I'm trying to give you a hint. Fires burn."

Her jaw slowly fell open. She looked out the window and said, "Burning Man!"

"See, that wasn't so hard."

"Why . . . why are we going to Burning Man?"

"Kyle goes every year. This year with DARPA happening, Kyle gave his tickets to Kevin, but Kevin's out of town. Kyle didn't want the tickets to go to waste. He also felt a bit guilt-ridden about smashing Cyclops."

"That was very sweet of him."

"Oh, he's not all roses and sunshine. I'm pretty sure he's in Reno, probably at his favorite strip bar."

"Oh." She sat back in her seat. "Burning Man. Wow. I've. . . I've heard about it but I honestly don't know what happens there. Do you?"

"Brace yourself, Sam." He turned off the stereo. "Trust me when I say you've never seen anything like this before."

Arriving late in the week meant that traffic was fairly light. They parked at a campsite and immediately set off on foot to explore the city. Despite the free-spirited nature of the event, the city followed a rigid structure in its design. When seen from above, it was shaped slightly larger than a half-circle, with clearly defined rings and roads running from the center to the outer bands. Attendees got around on foot or by bicycle. The only vehicles allowed on the streets were service personnel or creative works of automotive art dubbed Mutant Vehicles.

As they headed out, a bicyclist came around the corner, almost hitting Sam. White and orange silk fabric covering a wire frame transformed the bike into a rolling clownfish. The elderly woman riding the bike smiled a toothless grin and waved apologetically as she continued on her way.

"This is all so bizarre," Sam said, coming to a halt. "Don't. . . don't you find this weird?"

"Very. Kyle brought Kevin and me here once. It was wild. I'd only been working at the shop for a few weeks."

Another bicyclist whizzed by, causing Sam to jump. Ted gently draped his arm around her shoulder and guided her to the side of the road. She smiled and pulled back.

"Was . . . was this supposed to be part of your initiation?"

"I guess." Ted laughed as he recalled how awkwardly he'd behaved back then. "In case you haven't noticed, Kyle's a bit of a free spirit. I remember him telling me I was too uptight and needed to learn to let go."

They walked a few more blocks, taking in the sights and sounds of laughter and excited talking around them. As they rounded a corner, Sam came to a halt. Two women, wearing only beaded necklaces and flip-flops rushed by holding hands, smiling and waving as they passed by.

"They . . . they don't have clothes on." Sam moved closer to Ted, keeping her eyes on the couple as they disappeared into a large canvas tent. "Is that allowed?"

"Pretty much anything goes, here." He reached over and gently took her by the hand. "Stay close. I'll keep you safe."

Dozens of camps lined the streets—cars, vans, and tents of all shapes and sizes. Some people were even staying in converted school buses. The smells were also pretty intense. Incense, all kinds of food, and marijuana permeated the air.

Ted pulled out a map Kyle had given him. The streets that led to the city center, the Burning Man location, were numbered like the hours and minutes on a clock face, making it easy for people to find their way around.

"We don't have that much time before we have to leave," he said as he looked between the map and the streets surrounding them. "I feel like we're at Disney. A very weird Disney. We should just hit the highlights. Maybe we can head to—"

"Look at that!" Sam ran ahead, pointing excitedly. "That's amazing!"

A few blocks ahead sat a royal blue semi-truck's cab perched on its front wheels. The grill pointed toward the ground. In place of a trailer-bed, the back of the vehicle was a series of chrome oil barrels, twisting and churning their way into the sky—the opposite end of the barrels connected to a second cab, this one light blue. The cab was looking down at the one secured to the ground. The sculpture made from real trucks and barrels resembled a two-headed coiled snake, ready to strike.

"This!" Ted said with joy as he ran ahead to meet her. "This is what I love about Burning Man. The artwork here is mind-blowing. These are real big rig trucks!"

"The barrels are filled with silk," a young man standing beside Ted said. He was wearing an oversized cream-colored linen shirt with no sleeves and tight black spandex shorts. His skin was covered in colorful tattoos of curvilinear and intertwining geometric shapes next to depictions of all kinds of creatures and plants. In the firelight, it looked like his skin was writhing. "The theme this year is "Green Man." Oil may power our vehicles, and pollute our world, but we need to remember oil started from life itself."

Ted and Sam watched as the young stranger clasped his hands as if in prayer, and then turned and sauntered away.

"The Green Man?" Sam asked. "Eco-friendly. Understanding the balance of man and nature. I like it. Maybe what we're doing with self-driving technology will one day contribute to that."

"The only green I want to see from our hard work is cash."

"Are you really driven by nothing but money, Ted?" She folded her arms and stared at him. "There has to be more to you than that. Don't you want a better future?"

"Of course. But you have to admit that the technology we're building will result in money. A ton of money. There's nothing wrong with that."

"I'm sorry if my goals are less selfish than yours. I have a daughter. I want a better future for her." She was suddenly fired up. "Tens of thousands die in car accidents each year. Think about how many lives we could save with autonomy."

"This is really important to you, isn't it?"

"I . . . I lost someone close to me. In a car accident. It was before I had Dani."

"I'm sorry, Sam."

"A drunk driver caused the accident. That's another statistic I could throw at you. Accidents like those can be prevented with what we're building."

Ted suddenly felt awkward. He'd unintentionally struck a nerve with her. He pointed to the road ahead and said, "Come on—let's keep looking."

They spent the next half hour roaming the streets, stopping to admire the heavily adorned Mutant Vehicles along the way. The creations ran the gamut from comical to thought-provoking to inexplicable; an electric golf cart was covered to resemble a giant bumblebee; a school bus had hundreds of movable plastic fish that appeared to swim back and forth inside it; a dump truck was made to look like a Venus flytrap

"What are you thinking?" Ted asked. "You've been rather quiet."

"I'm. . . I'm just taking it all in. It's amazing to see the sense of community here, you know?"

"I remember my first time here," Ted said as he nodded. "I got separated from Kyle and Kevin. I didn't have a map and quickly got lost. Two people noticed the look of dread on my face and came over to help. Within five minutes, we were all reunited. It was amazing. Complete strangers helping one another."

"Why does that surprise you?" She stopped and leaned against the side of a school bus painted with marijuana leaves. The smoke drifting from the open windows reinforced the paint job. "You shared with us, remember?"

"Huh?"

"The email you sent us regarding the sensor data."

"Oh, right." He felt a twinge of guilt and looked away, hoping she wouldn't see his reddening cheeks. "Well, you, um, seemed like you needed the help."

"Uh, huh."

"Back then, anyway. Before . . . before we met."

"You're not a very good liar."

"What?"

She rolled her eyes and continued walking, Ted quickly following. He continued, "I mean now that we've met it's obvious you have a great team. Ashton looks like a close-knit group."

"Nice recovery."

"I'm trying to compliment you, Sam." He was flustered and confused by her comments. He smiled and tried to redirect the conversation. "Athena's amazing. What . . . what do you think was your team's greatest achievement? I'm guessing the digital gimbal, right?"

"No. No, I'd have to say it was the methodology. Our testing procedures are some of the most rigid I've ever seen. It's that repeatable set of controls that let us perfect the hardware and software the team created." She glanced at him and smiled. "Maybe . . . maybe someday I can show it to you."

"I'd like that." He felt himself blushing again, but not because of her questions about the email exchange. Instead, he had this desperate desire to hold her hand, but he didn't want to push his luck. He pulled the map from his pocket and stopped to get their bearings. "They won't light the burning man on fire before we leave, but we can still see him. I just need to—"

"What's that?" Sam was several feet ahead of him, pointing down a road. "It looks like a temple."

Ted scanned through his map until he found what she was looking at. "It's called the Temple of Forgiveness. Let's go check it out," he said.

Sam smiled and rested her head against his arm. He pulled her close, and they continued toward the temple. The temple, like the Burning Man, changed themes each year. This year it was forgiveness. The massive structure, towering over fifty feet into the air, contained three distinct levels. The open-air design was made of intricately carved wood. In the center was the main altar, connected by four halls. Dozens of people made their way throughout the halls. Some held hands, while others sat alone with their eyes closed, lost in their thoughts.

Leading her into one of the halls, the two stopped against a wall. "Just like the burning man, they'll burn this down, too."

"Why?"

"Every year it's a different temple, and every year they burn it down."

"So, this is all about forgiveness?" Sam asked as she looked at him.

"I guess so," he replied.

"Do you have anything you'd like to ask forgiveness for?"

"No." He shoved his hands into his pockets and looked away. "Why would you ask that?"

"So defensive." She chuckled and grabbed him by the arm, withdrawing his hand from his pocket. She took his right hand in hers, gently stroking it in comfort. The temple's interior was awash in flickering torches, filling the air with the scent of charred cedar embers. Sam held Ted's hand in front of both of them. A slightly shiny, white line running from his thumb into his palm caught her attention. She pulled his hand closer to her face trying to make out the details in the wavering orange glow. "Is that a scar?"

"It's nothing." He briefly glanced at the reminder of the injury he'd suffered when he crashed Frankie into the dunes when he worked at Fisher Tuner. He flipped his hand over and gently took hold of Sam's fingers. "It was just a stupid accident. You'd probably think it was from me being reckless and arrogant."

"I . . . I don't know." She slid her arm around his. "I'm seeing a different side of you here."

"Is that a good thing?"

"Maybe."

Sam grinned and leaned her head against his shoulder, and he pulled her closer. She looked up, and they briefly locked eyes. Ted glanced at her lips. He paused briefly before leaning in to kiss her. He felt a surge go through him as Sam responded to his touch.

Sam was the one to break the moment, stepping a small step back. "How are we on time?" she asked, looking away, smiling from ear to ear. "We need to be back to Reno by midnight, don't we?"

"We do."

He smiled as they left the Temple of Forgiveness behind. He kept his arm around her as they made their way through the crowd. Neither one spoke. Eventually, Sam pulled away slightly, only to take his hand in hers. They remained that way until they reached the rental car.

The clock in the Escape's display read 11:52 p.m. as Ted flicked on the blinker to exit from I-80 West onto Route 580 South. Sam was fast asleep in the passenger seat. He was thankful she had drifted off shortly after they'd left. This way he could go as fast as he wanted without having to hear any complaints. He took the corner wide, distracted by how peaceful she looked beside him. He yanked the steering wheel quickly to recover, sending her head against the passenger window.

"Oh! Where are we?" Sam asked. She yawned and rubbed her eyes, pulling herself upright.

"We're almost at the airport."

"I won't ask how fast you drove." She looked at the clock and shook her head. "I'm guessing you broke a few laws to get us here."

"If I wasn't caught, then I didn't do anything illegal." He snickered and smiled. "We made great time. It's been quite an evening, hasn't it?"

"I have to thank you once again, Ted. Burning Man was amazing. In so many ways. I can only imagine what it would be like to actually stay there."

"Maybe we'll come back one day."

"That'd be nice."

She reached over and took him by his right hand. She turned his palm up and ran her thumb over his scar. "You're an interesting man, Ted Wolff with two 'F's. You might think you're in this for the money and fame, but there's more to you. I know it."

"Oh, do you?" he chuckled. "Maybe all those mind-altering fumes we inhaled back at Burning Man gave you the power of clairvoyance."

"I wish." She laughed and sat upright, turning to face him. "Then I could predict who'd win next week's challenge. I guess we just have to wait and see. What . . . what an amazing evening this has been. Tell me, Ted. Back at the temple, I . . . I felt like you had something more to share. We left in an awful hurry. Was it your scar?"

His smile faded. He let go of Sam's hand and gripped the steering wheel.

"Earlier tonight, you . . . you were talking about sharing." He cleared his throat as he debated the best way to clear his conscience. "Remember?"

"Sure. That was the whole point about Burning Man. That sense of community."

"I meant about Ashton and DSU sharing information. The email exchange we'd had."

"What about it?"

"Well, in the spirit of the Temple of Forgiveness, I feel I need to confess something to you."

"What? That the data you sent us was bad?"

He looked over at her and was shocked to see her grinning, looking almost exuberant.

"Well, it wasn't bad. It was, um, doctored." He slowed as they reached the exit.

"Doctored or not, Ted, the data was useless."

"I wouldn't call it useless. I just removed a few key sections."

"It was illegible, Ted. I know that's a breach of ethics but I really hadn't expected you to respond. When you did, I thought I'd get a feel for how advanced the DSU robotics program was but saw immediately it was junk. I know I should mind, but I really don't. I didn't tell the others about it. I didn't want Vin making a big stink."

"What I did to you with that doctored data has been eating me up all night."

"Ted, it's okay. Really . . . I see my psychic powers were right. Deep down, I knew you had feelings and a soul."

He shook his head in disbelief not knowing what to say.

"Tell me, what did you think of the info we sent to you?" she asked. "Did you look at it?"

"I know Harry started to. But we were so busy with our own issues that I don't know if he did anything with it. Why? Was it doctored crap, too?"

"Nope. It actually provided a fix for the tree-people issue you asked about."

"Get out of here! God, thanks. Now I feel worse!"

"Ted, honestly, I didn't think much of it. I knew you sent the data in a spirit of competition and really didn't spend more than five minutes thinking about it. Honestly, you really can drop it." She flipped the visor down and checked her hair in the mirror. "Anything else you need to confess? The temple is long gone, but I'm still open to hearing your sins."

"Well, how about this? During our email exchanges and before meeting you at DARPA, I thought you were a guy, an *ash-hole* guy."

"Sexist!" Sam said teasingly as she grabbed the lipstick out of her purse and retouched her lips. "I hope you weren't disappointed."

"That you were a woman?" He reached over and took her by the hand. "A beautiful, smart, and incredibly generous woman? What do you think?"

19

Harrison Air Base was twenty miles southwest of the original staging area DARPA had created for the forty competitors in the DARPA FAST Challenge. The complex had been built in the 1950s as a testing and training facility for urban combat. Dozens of streets were lined with homes and businesses, the buildings mostly facades, though a few had fully designed interiors without the electrical and plumbing. Back in the day, troops would train here for hostage-type situations, but the base had been abandoned now for over thirty years.

DARPA, with the assistance of Kyle Fisher, designed the final test—the Urban Challenge—to take place at Harrison Air Base. A three-mile course zig-zagged through ten looping streets. Obstacles included cars pulled by cables, as well as multiple stop and yield points, one a roundabout. Mannequins, meant to represent real humans, were placed throughout in key locations, along the edges of sidewalks or in the middles of crosswalks. With only three hours prior to the 9:00 a.m. start time, DARPA had provided all teams with detailed GPS and other relevant data, including speed limits and locations of the stop and yield signs.

"How's it looking?" Ted asked Nico. "Are we good?"

Nico was kneeling on Cyclops's hood doing a final inspection of the newly installed magnetic damper. The team had spent the previous few days retrofitting, calibrating, and testing the device on Cyclops.

The air was a crisp sixty-two degrees—the relentless wind gusts having given way to only a slight breeze. Despite the mild temperature, sweat poured down Nico's forehead. The pressure of the event was taking its toll on pretty much everyone.

"We're good." Nico sat back and wiped his brow.

Ted walked around to the front driver's corner of the vehicle. "And you two?"

Harry and Lori were sitting on the ground, cross-legged, their backs against either side of Cyclops's bright orange brush guard. Heads down, they were each engrossed in their laptop screens. Empty bottles of water and Red Bulls littered the ground around them. After several seconds, Lori closed her computer and let out a long sigh. Harry hit a few keys before finally nodding in approval. He looked at Lori and smiled.

"We're good to go, Ted," Lori said. She tucked her laptop under her arm and grabbed hold of one of the orange-painted tips on the brush guard to help herself up. She offered a hand to Harry, but he waved it away, continuing to look at his screen. "It all comes down to today. In this bizarre little military town."

The final group of competitors was lined up along the edge of the faux town. Many of the structures had shriveled over time, the brutal desert sun drying out wooden posts and beams. The once brightly painted buildings had faded to washed-out hues of yellows, blues, and greens, struggling to add some color to the harsh, mostly brown environment. This area had very few trees but those that had managed to eke out an existence were sick and ragged looking. The paved roads were cracked and rutted and covered in some areas with drifting sand.

"This reminds me of Wadsworth," Ted said as he surveyed the area.

"What?" Nico asked.

"Some place I used to live. Feels like a lifetime ago." He glanced past Nico toward the main gate that led to the big top. Rusty was approaching, his limp much more noticeable than usual. "Heads up, guys. Here comes trouble."

Rusty stopped a few yards from his team and studied the lidar and gimbal assembly atop the Hummer. He was decked out in olive and gray camouflage pants with matching long-sleeved shirt and cap. He took a long swig of coffee from his Marines thermal mug, drinking a bit too quickly and spilling it down the front of his shirt. Beads of coffee also clung to the tips of his handlebar mustache.

"No big speeches this morning." Rusty's voice was cracked and hoarse. Weeks of dry desert air had taken its toll on his vocal cords. "Today will decide if you are winners or losers. DARPA will penalize every screwup made during today's challenge. You can expect them to toss a surprise or two at us somewhere on the course. Are you confident Cyclops is ready?"

"Absolutely." Ted looked back and forth between Lori and Nico. They were nodding in agreement. Harry was still sitting on the ground, lost in his computer. "I guarantee you we'll take first place."

"I've told you before. There are no guarantees in life. Ever." Rusty coughed lightly to clear his throat. "Ted, I need you alone for a moment."

Rusty took a few steps back and waited for Ted to join him.

"What's up?" Ted asked, shoving his hands into his pockets as he stopped beside Rusty. "If you plan to lecture me about something I screwed up on, I really don't want to hear it."

"Have you talked to your family lately? Your dad, specifically."

"No. The last time I talked to them was when we were packing up to leave Pittsburgh. Why?"

"The auto workers have gone on strike. It's all over the news. Things are getting rough out there."

Ted paused and looked at the dozens of faded buildings off in the distance. He recalled the conversation he'd had with his parents when he made the decision to follow Rusty back to DSU. He wondered why Rusty cared.

"He'll be fine," Ted said flatly. "I have more important things to focus on."

Rusty was about to speak when Vin and Sam walked up. Athena

was parked close by and the Ashton team was busy making their final preparations for the race. Ralph Lorenski waved excitedly toward Ted. Ted gave him a slight nod but only smiled once he spotted Sam. She was in full Ashton team gear with her aviators perched atop her baseball cap.

"Rusty." Vin held his hand out and gave Rusty an enthusiastic handshake. "Today's the day."

"Indeed it is," Rusty replied.

"Win or lose, I can tell you this is a great day for the transportation industry." Vin pointed to the bleachers stacked next to the operations center. "Word has gotten out."

The stadium seats were filled to capacity, with dozens more in the standing-room only area leaning against the protective concrete barriers. Ted had been so focused on preparing Cyclops he hadn't paid attention to what was going on behind him. He cupped his hands around his eyes and scanned the crowded stadium.

"What's that group up there?" Ted pointed to the top two rows on the left side of the bleachers. A dozen people sat together in matching white collared shirts. "Is that Ford? GM?"

"GSI," Vin replied.

"GSI?" Rusty asked with surprise. He scratched his beard and gently nodded. "Interesting."

"What's GSI?" asked Ted.

Rusty, not without a hint of annoyance at Ted's apparent ignorance, answered. "Grant Systems International is a technology company based in Redwood City, California. They have call centers, data warehousing, networking solutions, and a whole host of software and consulting services. GSI are the ones that provide the mapping software used by a bunch of public-facing companies as well as the Marines and other U.S. military branches."

"Where's Detroit?" Ted scanned the rest of the stadium but couldn't see any other people grouped together in matching clothes. "They have to be here somewhere."

"I was told there are a total of three people from Detroit," Vin said. "Ford, GM, and Chrysler each sent one person."

"I don't get it." Ted frowned and looked at Sam. "Don't they understand how important this is? Especially for today's challenge."

"Their loss," Rusty replied.

Sam maneuvered her way past Vin and Rusty and led Ted to the backside of the Humvee, away from Vin and the DSU team. Lori looked on knowingly but said nothing.

"Don't focus on Detroit, Ted." Sam gently ran her fingers along the collar on Ted's shirt. "Let's just get through today."

He smiled as he gazed into her twinkling green eyes. She had this ability to immediately calm him. He was about to speak when he glanced over his shoulder at Lori, who was now staring from several feet away, smiling. Ted pulled Sam to the far side of the vehicle.

"Do you recognize this air base?" he asked. "This is where we flew out from with Kyle."

"Really? I was so nervous about the flight I hadn't noticed."

"Wish I'd known. It might have helped us prep a bit more."

"Always looking for an advantage, aren't you, Ted? Anything to win."

"At all costs." He couldn't help but laugh.

"I told you, slow and steady wins the race."

"You did." He grinned. "Ashton versus DSU. The tortoise and the hare once again go into battle. I think this is going to be a close one."

"I agree. Is your hardware all patched up?"

"Yes. We're ready to go."

"I'm happy for you, Ted. Truly I am. And thanks again for the birthday getaway. As much as I hate birthdays, you made this one special."

"It was my pleasure. But you should thank Kyle for breaking Cyclops."

"Kyle wasn't the one holding my hand at Burning Man." Sam ran her fingers across the back of his hand. "Besides, I like to think that maybe it was meant to be. Fate."

"Fate? Don't get all preachy on me, Sam." He looked back at his team to make sure they weren't watching. He leaned down and kissed Sam, happy they had been able to grab this moment. "See you on the battlefield, turtle."

"May the better man win, rabbit." She giggled, stood on her toes, and gave him a kiss on the cheek. "Good luck."

Ted could feel Sam begin to let go. He pulled her forward and gently kissed her again on the lips before she stepped back, popped her aviators down, smiled, and headed back to Athena, a few yards away.

He walked back around Cyclops to join his team. Vin was nowhere to be found, having already left. He glanced briefly at Sam as she walked away.

"I'm heading to the big top." Rusty pried the top off his mug and chugged down what was left of his coffee. "I want everyone inside in ten minutes."

Lori waited until Rusty was several yards away before she turned to Ted, crossed her arms across her chest, and raised an eyebrow.

"What?" he asked, doing his best to play stupid.

"How serious is it, Ted?" she said. "I've seen the way you two look at each other for weeks. I'm not blind."

"Blind to what?" Nico asked.

"Seriously?" Lori shook her head and looked at Harry, still sitting on the ground buried in his laptop. "I swear, one of these days women will rule the earth. Men are clueless. Clueless!"

Ted kept his mouth shut. He was thankful to be interrupted by the sound of a whirring Segway as Steve Wozniak rolled up. He circled the Hummer once before coming to a stop in front of Harry. Harry looked up at his idol but said nothing.

"Well?" Steve asked, a wry grin spread across his face.

Harry slammed his laptop closed and used the bars across the Humvee's grille to haul himself upright. Sand fell from the folds in his faded denim jeans. He wiped his hands across his light gray Apple hooded sweatshirt and nervously adjusted his glasses.

"Woz up?" Harry asked cautiously.

"Me!" Steve replied. "On my Segway!"

Steve leaned back and burst into laughter. His Segway immediately responded, and began going in reverse. Steve struggled to steady himself and, feeling somewhat embarrassed, rolled back to Harry's side.

"Best of luck today, Harry Palmer." Steve chuckled and leaned sideways, quickly zooming around Harry on his way to visit team Ashton.

Harry stood motionless for several seconds as he watched his idol speed away. He glanced down at the rainbow logo emblazoned across his chest and smiled.

"He knew my name." Harry spun around and looked at Ted. "He knew my name!"

Hours later, the inside of the big top was quieter than it had been during the past two events. Many from the eliminated teams had already gone home, and cooler temperatures had minimized the need for the giant air conditioners. The fans were running, but their motors were much less noisy than the huge outdoor compressors. The competing teams that remained were sitting at their stations, eyes fixated this final time on the overhead monitors.

The leaderboard showed Virginia Tech as being in first place so far, with MIT five points behind in second place. Oshkosh was the most recent to complete the course and finished third overall. The massive MTVR struggled on the narrow city streets, having to perform most tasks two to three times. Every other contestant had failed to complete the event. Ashton and DSU would be the final two competitors. Ashton's Athena was just starting the course. DSU would bring up the rear.

The Urban Challenge had proven to be the most complicated of the three tests by a large margin. What seemed simple on paper had vexed every team. Despite being only three miles long, and containing tasks similar to the first Qualifying Stage, the addition of fixed and moving vehicles and pedestrians, as well as having to navigate narrow streets, was more than most could handle. One entry failed to identify a gate at a railroad crossing and was completely T-boned by a freight train. Another simply stopped and exploded.

Rusty's hunch about DARPA throwing a twist into the mix proved correct. One of the intersections included a pickup truck that would be pulled out at the last minute via cable. Three of the competitors failed to adapt to this surprise and ended up disabling themselves due to high-speed impact. The crashes forced DARPA to repair or replace the truck prior to each new test run.

The clock at the front of the tent read 4:37 p.m. Nerves were high at the Ashton table but even higher at DSU. Lori had banished all pens from the area, to prevent Ted and Nico from nervously playing with them. Rusty refused to sit, and paced back and forth endlessly. Harry was on his fourth bag of potato chips and third Red Bull.

"Excuse me." Ted released a loud exhalation as he stood up.

"Where are you going?" Rusty asked. "We're next."

"I'll be back before we start."

He didn't wait to hear any reprimand from Rusty, sliding past Nico and Lori and walking over to Ashton's table. Sam was head down at her workstation when he arrived. Her aviators and baseball cap were on the corner of the table. Ted pushed them aside so he could take a seat on the tabletop beside her computer.

"How's it going?" he asked.

"Oh!" She looked up and smiled broadly at the sight of him. "Hi. Honestly? It's been fantastic. Athena hasn't missed a beat yet."

"I've noticed."

"One test to go. That dead-end street. It's been a challenge for everyone."

"I still can't believe TerraCrusher was able to get out of there."

"They took five tries and still clipped two parked cars. I'm sure that cost them in points." Sam turned her gaze from Ted to her screen. "We're almost at the end. Sorry, I need to focus on this."

He spun around and faced the overhead monitors just in time

to catch Athena turn down the dead-end street. The room instantly hushed as all eyes settled on the displays at the front of the tent.

Everyone assumed the last test in the Urban Challenge would be the easiest. It seemed simple enough. Drive to the end of a dead-end street, turn around and leave. The test, though, turned out to be much more complicated and was a culmination of everything that had transpired up to that point. DARPA had lined the road with many obstacles, both on and off the street. One driveway had a car that would back out without stopping. A parked van's door would randomly open in front of the approaching vehicle. Everything from utility poles to an open manhole cover stood ready to confront each combatant.

Ashton's Prius hummed along at twelve miles per hour, its engine off as it coasted along on battery power. Ted watched with mixed emotions as Athena easily conquered the first half of the street. Every surprise DARPA unleashed failed to derail the vehicle.

"I should get back to my team." He stood up and watched Athena grind to a halt in front of an unexpected van door opening. He turned and sighed as the Ashton team cheered. "Good luck, Sam."

His head hung low as he snaked his way through the different team tables. He couldn't bear to see Athena ace the test any longer. As he made his way back, he overheard two people discussing a damaged sensor. Out of curiosity, he looked up at the monitor showing the view from a helicopter. Athena was stopped at the end of the street, motionless. Ted quickened his pace to rejoin his team.

"What's going on?" Ted asked Lori.

"The van's door is malfunctioning," Lori said excitedly. "It swung wider than it should have and hit the sensors on the Prius. She's all confused now."

He didn't bother to take his seat, instead crouching between Lori and Nico. The DSU team, like everyone in the big top, had their eyes glued to the chopper feed. Ashton's Prius was on the move again. Barely. It appeared to be attempting to make a three-point turn, but it was unable to complete the final piece. Athena rocked back and forth, repeating and resetting her position.

"It's like she's in a loop." Harry tore open a fresh bag of chips and popped open a Red Bull. "I wonder how long until DARPA gets mad."

Three minutes ticked by before DARPA finally issued a two-minute warning over the loudspeakers. Vehicles competing in the Urban Challenge were disqualified by either self-inflicted damage or becoming stuck and unable to solve the test. DARPA had been generous during this phase of the competition, graciously allowing competitors many attempts at each part of the course. TerraCrusher took twenty minutes to navigate the dead-end street, and never got a single warning issued. There had been dozens of small errors and do-overs, where the vehicle would back up and repeat a section until it got it right. It was evident to everyone that the Prius was now stuck.

Almost as if the car heard the warning, Athena suddenly came to a halt. Thirty seconds passed, and the Prius remained still. Ted stood up and looked across the room at the Ashton table. Teams were not allowed to transmit changes to their vehicles once the test started. All they could do was watch. He could see Sam and Ralph in a huddle, talking to Vin.

"Look!" Harry said. Athena began to move backward. The Toyota turned its wheels left until Athena was facing the end of the street. "What's she doing?"

"That's my girl!" Sam cried out from the Ashton table.

Athena began to back her way out of the dead-end street. The exit was painfully slow. The sensor arrays on the back of the Prius were not as sophisticated as the front-facing ones. Slowly but surely, the Toyota snaked its way through the obstacles that had challenged it earlier. After several minutes, the Prius cleared the street, paused, and then turned around and headed back toward the start of the course. The damaged front sensor caused the vehicle to wander side to side until it finally reached the finish line.

"Wasn't that illegal?" Harry asked Rusty.

"It was," Rusty replied. "The dead-end street test mandated the vehicles turn around with a three-point turn before leaving."

The leaderboard went black. Two minutes passed before it flashed to life. When it did, it showed that Athena was now in first place. Rusty slammed his fist on the table and marched off toward the operations center at the front of the tent.

"Okay, *now* there's going to be blood." Harry tossed some potato chips into his mouth and looked over at Ted. "Did you see his temples? They were close to exploding."

"We need to get Cyclops ready." Ted sat down next to Harry. "I doubt DARPA will care what Rusty has to say. We need to win this thing."

Two minutes later, the loudspeakers requested DSU to prepare to launch. Rusty stormed up to the table, obviously angry and flustered.

"What'd they say?" Ted asked.

"They said the truck door malfunctioned and hit the Prius after it had successfully maneuvered around it. There was a debate whether they should allow Ashton to do repairs, but in the end, they were so impressed that she navigated the course in reverse they decided to give them a pass."

"Well, it's DARPA's competition," Ted said. "They do set the rules."

"Rules are meant to be followed!" Rusty banged his fist on the table. "They had no right to change them. I reminded them that Cyclops was also damaged, courtesy of a DARPA chase vehicle, and we had to go through hell to get it repaired to compete this week. They told me Ashton had aced the test up until that point, so there was no reason to spend hours or days having them repair it. The test was almost over when it had been damaged."

"They sort of have a point."

"Don't take their side, Ted. Giving Ashton some goddamn ingenuity badge is bullshit. *Bullshit!* This isn't the Boy Scouts!"

"Not under you, Sarge." Ted did not wait for Rusty to respond. He turned and faced his teammates. "Okay, troops, let's nail this."

Cyclops proved to be a beast, acing every challenge as easily as Athena, but at a faster speed. Their only problem had been the roundabout. The Humvee swerved to avoid another vehicle and crested the concrete curb in the rotary before continuing on. Rusty wasn't sure if DARPA would penalize them for that or not. By this point, he was so disgusted with DARPA's scoring system all he wanted was for Cyclops to be flawless.

"Here we go." Ted stood up and began pacing back and forth behind Lori and Nico. "The last test."

The Humvee stopped and took a left turn to enter the dead-end street. The road was very long, with few obstacles set along the first hundred yards. Cyclops accelerated to twenty miles per hour.

"Going a bit fast?" Sam asked.

Ted turned around, shocked to see her standing at the end of the table. He could feel his whole body lighten at seeing her. He jumped from his chair and walked past Lori so he could be closer to Sam.

"Of course," Ted replied. "Are you *hare* to see us beat you? See what I did there?"

Sam laughed and rolled her eyes. She moved closer to Ted and slid her arm around his waist. He responded by gently pulling her closer until her head was nuzzled against his chest. Lori, facing straight ahead at the screens, had a huge grin across her face.

"Here comes that stupid van," Harry said.

Cyclops slammed on its brakes and swerved to the left to avoid the van's door. The door was still malfunctioning and continued to swing open wider until it slammed into the side of the Hummer. Cyclops stood much taller than Ashton's Prius. The top of the van's door, still covered in bits and pieces of Athena's sensors, stopped several inches below the Humvee's roof, safely out of reach of the gimbal. As Cyclops roared by, the bottom of the van's door caught the Hummer's back wheel-well. Weighing over four tons, DSU's vehicle ripped the van's door off its hinges and soldiered forward.

Lori, Harry, and Nico jumped to their feet and started clapping.

"*That's* how you deal with DARPA's surprises," Rusty bellowed, finally allowing a smile. He took a few steps forward and cupped his hands around his mouth to project his voice to the operations center at the front of the room. "I don't want to hear about any deductions due to your faulty test equipment!"

Several people stood up and started applauding. DARPA's tests and equipment had proven to be cumbersome and error-prone throughout the past three weeks. Arguing with DARPA had been an exercise in futility, and many competitors had developed a disdain for the military's unwillingness to compromise when requested.

Once DSU completed their run, the competition would be over. You could feel the tension building in the room. Many around the room were on their feet and heading toward the front of the room to get closer to the overhead screens. Where before there had been quiet, it was now buzzing chatter and excitement.

Cyclops slowed to a halt upon reaching the end of the dead-end street. He immediately started to make a three-point turn but slammed into a set of traffic cones behind him. One of them got jammed under the rear bumper. The Humvee paid no attention to the crash and completed its set of turns and aimed for the road ahead. After a brief pause, Cyclops accelerated and began to retrace his course out. The door that had been ripped away lay tattered in the middle of the street. The traffic cone wedged beneath the rear bumper clung fast to the Hummer, digging a path in the sand covering the roadway. The Humvee rolled over the van's door. The crushed door grabbed hold of the cone, and after being dragged for several feet, yanked it free from the bumper. With the debris safely behind it, the Hummer cautiously made its way through the obstacles that remained between it and the end of the road. Five minutes later, Cyclops exited the street and turned right to head back to the finish line.

The big top erupted in applause. Lori and Harry embraced each other. Nico slapped Ted on the back, sending him and Sam stumbling.

"Quiet down!" Rusty bellowed, his smile completely absent, as he leaned forward at one of the DSU workstations. "We don't know what kind of penalties DARPA will hit us with. We weren't perfect. We clipped the rotary. We hit the door. Twice. Not to mention dragging that cone."

"He's not much fun, is he?" Sam whispered in Ted's ear.

"I'll be so glad when this is finally over, and I can get out from under him." Ted ran his lips across the top of Sam's head, taking in her scent, grateful she wasn't wearing her cap. "It's been twenty months of hard work and trial and error. I've had to put up with a lot of shit to get this far. Win or lose, it was worth it."

"I should be with my team when they announce the final score." She gave him a quick kiss. "Good luck."

Ashton had gathered at the front of the room, along with the other contenders. Ted watched Sam push her way through the crowd to join them. The overhead screens showed Cyclops making the final turn back toward the finish line. All eyes were focused on the leaderboard. The screen had gone dark as soon as Cyclops had exited the dead-end street. It took less than twenty seconds for the monitor to come back to life. DSU was ranked first, one point ahead of Ashton.

Ted, Nico, Harry, and Lori screamed and hugged. Lori could not stop the tears from running down her face. Even Nico found himself wiping the cuff of his shirt against moist eyes. Ted scanned the room to see if he could find Sam, but the entire Ashton team was lost in the throngs of people running up to congratulate DSU for winning. Ted and the rest of the team were greeted with slaps on the back and handshakes all around. Everyone was genuinely supportive and happy for them.

"One point?" Rusty shook his head in frustration. "DARPA is being way too kind to Ashton."

Ted watched in disappointment as Rusty stormed off toward the operations center at the front of the tent. Lori's smile faded when she noticed Rusty leaving.

"Where's he going?" Lori asked.

"I guess there is such a thing as being a sore winner." When they'd arrived earlier that morning, Ted had placed a small canvas backpack beneath the DSU table. He grabbed the bag and slid the zipper open. "Screw him. It's time to celebrate."

He reached into the bag and pulled out a bottle of Chivas Regal, along with five faux-crystal acrylic cups. He spread all five out in a row in front of one of the workstations and began to fill them.

"Yes!" Harry said. "You served this when we finished testing along the Allegheny River."

"Not the whisky again," Lori said. "You know it knocks Nico on his ass."

"Make mine a double." Nico laughed as he grabbed one of the cups. "I don't have to drive tonight."

Rusty returned to the table, a frown still pasted across his face. Ted, Nico, Lori, and Harry were all holding their cups. Rusty looked down at the bottle of whisky and the single empty cup.

"What's this?" Rusty asked.

"It's sort of a tradition of mine," Ted replied.

"A tradition?" Rusty picked up the bottle and inspected the label. "Nice choice, Ted."

Rusty picked up the empty goblet and filled it halfway with whisky.

"You should all be incredibly proud of yourselves." Rusty raised his cup. "The victory wasn't as decisive as it should have been. I just tore the director of DARPA a new asshole for their shitty scoring. But it was still a win."

"And it's just the beginning," Lori said. "I can't wait to see what's next. We've made history today, haven't we? You guys were the best team to work with. Congratulations, everyone."

"Cheers to that." Ted tipped his cup back, savoring the silky amber liquid as it ran down his throat. "Victory never tasted so good."

Rusty downed his entire cup and let out a long and slow exhalation.

"Good stuff, Ted." Rusty immediately poured himself another

half cup. "Excuse me. I need to go find Vin and ask him how second place feels."

Ted frowned as he watched Rusty disappear into the crowd. He took another sip of whisky.

"Did I miss him saying thank you?" Lori asked. "Or that he was proud of us?"

"I don't think he's capable of that," Ted replied.

"He's not." Nico emptied the rest of his glass and smiled. "I'm proud of us. And all of you. It's been amazing working together. Really."

"Same here," Harry said. "You've been like family to me. I can't believe it's over. What . . . what happens now?"

All four lowered their cups and as they looked at one another.

"Rusty said the military would get to use the technology that was created." Ted poured a bit more whisky. "But we get to keep the intellectual property. I think the sky's the limit. Detroit will be begging to hire us."

The tent had begun to empty out as the other teams slowly exited. Many called out congratulations as they passed by DSU. Ted smiled once he noticed Sam pushing her way through the crowd.

"Excuse me." He downed the rest of his whisky and tossed the cup onto the table. He met Sam in the middle of the crowd, took her by the hand, and led her to Ashton's abandoned team table a dozen yards away. "Hey there."

"Congratulations." She gave him a gentle kiss on his cheek. "You did amazing."

"We all did. If that door hadn't clipped Athena, you could have easily won this."

"Vin already went up and cried foul. They said we should have been able to maneuver around it. We cut it too close. At this point, it doesn't matter. All I want to do is get home. I've been away from my family for far too long. How about you? What's next? Fame and fortune, right?"

"Hopefully." He grinned and pulled her into his arms, kissing the top of her head and allowing his hands to caress her back. "I want to go to Detroit. And I want you to come with me."

"Detroit?" Sam pulled herself away from Ted. She shook her head, sighed, and sat down in one of the chairs scattered behind the Ashton team table. "I need to get home to my daughter."

"I don't mean tomorrow, Sam. But soon."

"You're crazy. What will we do in Detroit? The technology is nowhere ready to be deployed."

"Not yet, but it will be. It's only a matter of time. We've proven the technology works." He took her hands into his. "I want us to do this together, Sam. What you did with Athena was amazing. I know in my heart we will win over Detroit. Your software. My hardware. We're good together."

"The tortoise and the hare?" She smiled briefly before shaking it off. "You're moving way too fast, Ted."

"Am I?" He ran his thumbs across her hands and gently kissed her fingers. "Or are you being too cautious?"

"I . . . I don't know." She stared longingly into his eyes. "I'm . . . I'm feeling very confused."

"So, there's a chance?"

"How . . . how can we make this work? I live in California. You're in Pittsburgh."

"That's not my home, Sam. I don't really have one. Not anymore. I'm done with DSU. My plan is to go back west and figure out a way to conquer Detroit. I want you by my side when I do."

"Detroit? I can't think that far ahead. There's too much to figure out."

"Has there ever been a time when you didn't plan everything in detail?" Ted chuckled as he pulled her against his chest. "You told me you wanted a better future for the world. For your daughter. That won't happen in some lab at Ashton. GM, Ford, Chrysler, and others need to lead the way—with us showing them how it can be done."

She pushed him away so she could wipe the tears from her face.

The sight of tears initially shocked him. But then he was relieved when he saw a smile slowly form on her face.

"You're asking a lot of me, Ted. We . . . we barely know each other."

"I know enough. Take the risk, Sam. I'll do all the heavy lifting. I'll get the meetings set up. Figure out the travel. All of that. But we can partner ahead of time on what we want to show them—on how we want to present everything. We can do all of that remotely. Phone. Email. Then we can meet in Detroit once we have our materials ready. You can stay with your family until then."

"Can I think about it?"

"Sure." He leaned forward and kissed her deeply on her lips. "Trust me, Sam. Together we will change the world."

20

Terminal A inside Detroit Metro Airport was hectic for a Sunday at 7:00 p.m. Throngs of business travelers had departing night flights in preparation for Monday morning meetings. Ted struggled to carry his garment bag and two cups of coffee, while trying to keep his laptop backpack from sliding off his shoulder. He bumped and nudged his way through the crowd, feeling irritated at those in his way.

The monitor within sight of Gate 50 showed Sam's flight from San Francisco as having just arrived, albeit half an hour late, though no sign of any passengers yet. Once he was quiet and waiting, he had a sudden flood of realization of just how excited he was to be seeing her again. An image popped in his mind of arms outstretched, grabbing her, spinning her around, as they laughed together. The DARPA Challenge had ended six weeks earlier, but they'd remained in touch almost daily. Ted's heart began to race as the door to the gateway opened. He maneuvered his way past several anxious people and took a strategic position opposite the gate.

The first group of passengers to deplane were the first-class travelers. The bulk were white men in their sixties, looking exhausted and perturbed. Ted waited patiently as a mix of ages and genders, some children, filed past. He wondered if Sam would be as excited to see him as he was her.

His wandering mind came to a halt once Sam appeared in the

doorway. He smiled as she looked around, a bit confused. She was dressed casually in a pair of black jeans, a black turtleneck, and a bright emerald jacket that matched her eyes. She looked stunning. Even from afar, her eyes sparkled just as he remembered them. Ted felt himself begin to blush as she noticed him and waved.

"Ted!" Sam adjusted her small rollerbag carrying her laptop and quickened her pace. "You're here!"

Ted held his arms open wide, each hand holding a cup of coffee. Sam stopped a foot before him, dropped her bags, and took one of the cups from him. She was not going to embrace him and his smile instantly faded. Other passengers from the flight were pushing past them, only adding to Ted's displeasure.

"How, um, how was your flight?" he asked cautiously. His mind raced as he tried to figure out why she hadn't greeted him with so much as even a hug.

"Long. And the coffee was horrible. Is this decaf?"

"No. French Vanilla. Lori got me hooked on it."

"Smells wonderful." Sam took a long sip of coffee. "I know we were delayed. Have you been waiting long?"

"No." Ted struggled to hide his disappointment. "It's good to see you. You look great."

"Thanks."

He looked right into her eyes. All he could see was the woman he had so passionately kissed weeks ago at Burning Man. He used his free hand to brush Sam's hair back behind her shoulder and closed his eyes, leaning in to kiss Sam on the lips. She turned at the last minute, allowing Ted to kiss her cheek. He sighed as she pulled back.

"Are you okay?" he asked.

"I'm just beat. It was a long flight. I'm not used to flying, remember?"

"I remember. You must be tired. We should get the rental and head to the hotel. Let me help you with your bags."

"I'm fine." She slipped her handbag over the handles of her roller and began heading toward the main walkway. "I have checked luggage as well."

Ted grabbed his garment bag and backpack, realizing she seemed intent on keeping an emotional distance. He couldn't help but feel rejected but decided not to say anything, chalking it up to her being tired and awkwardness at seeing each other in person after talking so much on the phone.

"Are you ready to take Detroit by storm?" Ted forced himself to sound upbeat. "We have tomorrow to finalize and rehearse our presentation. We talked about making several changes, especially around some of our projections on adoption rates. Were you able to make those during the flight?"

"To be honest, Ted, I spent the flight missing my family. My Dani."

"Oh."

"Those weeks at DARPA really upset her. I explained to her that I would only be gone for a week this time. But she's young. She doesn't understand."

"Well, we can make the changes tomorrow," he said, confusion and more than a little frustration rising. Sam's cold reception was bad enough. He could push his feelings aside if it at least meant nailing their presentations. "I thought we agreed you'd have things ready by the time you got here?"

"What's with the attitude?" She stopped abruptly. "I'm sorry you don't have a family to care for, Ted. This has all been very stressful for me. I thought once DARPA ended, I'd go back to a somewhat normal life. Instead, I dove back into my work at Ashton, and partnered with you on pursuing things with Detroit."

His frustration subsided as he saw the worry and pain rippling across her face. He instinctively put an arm around her and pulled her close. Relief filled him when she didn't resist, and instead seemed to welcome it. He closed his eyes and kissed the top of her head, taking in her sweet intoxicating scent.

"I think we're both stressed." He turned, keeping his arm around her, and continued heading toward the baggage claim area. "Let's get your bags and head to the hotel. We can grab a late bite if you want."

"That sounds nice."

He grabbed her hand as they made their way through the terminal. They walked together in silence, but Ted didn't mind. He was just grateful to have Sam close by his side as they made their way to the carousel for her flight from SFO.

"What's our schedule?" Ted asked. "Tomorrow is prep, and we leave on Friday. But I can't remember the meeting order."

"For being such a brilliant engineer, your organization skills are lacking."

"I never claimed to be organized. That's your specialty."

"I won't argue with that." She smirked at him. "Tuesday is Ford. Wednesday is Chrysler."

"With GM on Thursday. Right. Then Thursday night, we celebrate our new jobs as executives in charge of autonomy at one of them. Do you think they will get in a bidding war over us?"

"Executives?" Sam laughed and shook her head. "Are you planning to move here?"

"Well, of course. Isn't that the point of all of this?" Ted frowned and shook his head as Sam took a few steps back and folded her arms defensively. He held up the garment and laptop bags. "Almost everything I own is in these two bags. I'm here to convince one of these companies that self-driving cars are the future. And that we have the technology and expertise to lead the way."

"So am I, Ted. But let's take it one step at a time. I never once thought of uprooting my life to relocate here. The cold air blasting in through the jetway is reason enough to avoid living in Detroit. I can only imagine what the dead of winter is like."

"Then what's the end game, Sam?"

"My family is back in California. My mother is dear to me. She helps me care for Dani."

"Sam, we're talking six-figure salaries here. You can hire another nanny."

"You don't understand." She shook her head and turned her attention toward the conveyor belt, now filled with luggage bags. "It's not about the money to afford daycare. Dani adores her grandmother. My mom is a wonderful role model for her. And for me. I'm just not ready to make that kind of change."

"So, what will you do if Ford waves a bunch of money at you to come work for them?"

"There are ways to work with the auto companies that don't involve relocating here. I always thought I would stay at Ashton, working with Vin on continuing to develop and refine the technology. Vin and I talked about a possible partnership with one of the auto companies. Maybe even one of their suppliers. This technology is still new, Ted. It's not ready for prime time."

"Look, Sam, we need to be united when we present to the executives this week."

"We will be. We both believe in what autonomy can and will do for the transportation industry. The presentation we are making is about the technology and what it offers. We agreed that we weren't going to go in and tell them how to do their jobs."

"I know."

"And we certainly aren't going to tell them to hire us. That's not in our presentation."

"I know, Sam. I just assumed once they heard what we had to say, they'd want to hire us."

"Maybe it will lead to that, Ted. Remember, this needs to be an organic process. A conversation. This week is about starting the discussion."

He grinned and pulled her into his arms. She slowly received his embrace and held him close.

"What?" Sam asked.

"My sweet little tortoise." He chuckled and kissed her gently on her cheek. "So methodical."

"Always."

They had opted to stay at a Holiday Inn outside Royal Oak, a central location for their Dearborn, Auburn Hills, and Detroit meetings. At Sam's insistence, Ted had booked separate rooms, but he made sure they were adjoining. Ted was alone in his room, flopped on his bed, wearing nothing but a pair of blue checkered boxers and a white T-shirt. He was staring at a PowerPoint presentation on his laptop. The time was just past 10:00 p.m. His eyes burned from the hours he and Sam had spent refining and rehearsing the material.

He sighed as he scanned through a scribbled set of notes. His fried brain was full. He walked over to a brown bag resting on the nightstand. Rustling through it, he pulled out pajama pants, put them on, grabbed two glasses, and removed the bottle of Chivas Regal whisky from the bag.

"You awake?" Ted asked as he knocked on the door that connected their two rooms. After a few moments, the door opened a crack, and Sam stuck her face in the opening. "Hi," he said.

"It's late, Ted," she said. "We've got a long day tomorrow. It's our final shot."

"I know." He held the bottle and glasses up and smiled. "A toast to our success?"

"Uh, aren't you being a bit premature? So far, we've struck out."

She opened the door and motioned for him to come in. He was struck at how beautiful she looked in her full-length, mint-green silk robe as she crossed the room. He closed the door behind him and put the bottle and glasses on the bureau. Sam's laptop was open and resting on her bed.

"Looks like I'm not the only one with last-minute jitters," he said, pointing to her computer and smiling. "The presentation's solid, Sam."

"Are you sure?" She shuffled over to her bed and sat beside her laptop. "I . . . I think we need to soften our delivery a bit."

"That's why you're taking the lead tomorrow. You said it yourself. I can be a bit too pushy."

"Well, you can." She laughed but remained focused on her computer. Ted cracked the whisky's cap open. When Sam heard it she looked up and said, "None for me."

He frowned and debated pouring himself a glass. He decided not to and walked over and sat on the opposite side of the laptop. After studying the screen for a few seconds, he dragged the computer away and slid closer to Sam.

"You'll do great tomorrow." He took her hand in his and began to massage her fingers. "Even if they reject us, we both know what the future holds."

"We do?" She stared longingly into his deep blue eyes. "You're, uh, talking about autonomy. AI?"

"That." He pulled her hand to his face and kissed her fingers. "And more."

She pulled her hand away and lowered her head. She paused a moment, then said, "I told you we should keep this professional."

"So, you don't have feelings for me?"

"I didn't say that."

"So, you do have feelings for me." He waited momentarily to see if she would respond. "Good, because I have feelings for you, Sam. Ever since DARPA. I thought we had something there. I can feel it again now. Can't you?"

"I . . . I do, too, Ted. It's just . . ."

"Talk to me."

"I . . . I can't look that far ahead."

"You can't or you won't?" He slid closer and put his arm around her. She rolled her head against his chest and sighed. He asked, "What are you afraid of?"

"I . . . I don't know. It's been so long."

"Same for me." He gently took her chin and tilted her head until their eyes were locked. "I'm falling for you, Sam Lavoie. You challenge me. You inspire me. I . . . I want . . . more."

He leaned forward and gently kissed her lips. She responded, and soon their embrace and affection became intensely passionate. As they fell back on the bed, she propped herself up on an elbow and said, "If we cross this line–"

"I know." He ran his fingers through her long flowing hair and smiled. "There's no going back. Trust me, Sam. Trust me."

The Renaissance Center, built in 1977, served, in part, as the world headquarters for General Motors. The complex situated along the river separating the United States from Canada included a total of seven buildings. The central tower served as a Marriott hotel. GM was one of several companies who had offices here.

The administrative assistant Ted and Sam had worked with to book the meeting with GM had not bothered to give them instructions on where to park, so they picked a public lot a couple of blocks from the complex.

The temperature was in the upper forties, and the wind gusting in from the river was damp and bitterly cold. Ted kept Sam close to his side as they reached the corner of Randolph Street and East Jefferson Avenue. Ten lanes of traffic, divided by a large island, stood between them and their destination.

"Wow." Sam squinted her eyes, tear-filled from the wind slicing across her face. She looked up to the top of the central tower. "That's impressive."

"Wait until you see inside. I brought us early so we could do a little tour before going upstairs."

"I hope today goes better than the last two. This weather sure isn't a good sign."

"Ford is being too shortsighted. And Chrysler seems to be spiraling into bankruptcy. I have a good feeling about GM."

"I hope you're right. So far, this week has been a bust. Do you think our presentation is off?"

"The presentation is great. You're great. It's the idiots that have been sitting across from us that have been the problem." He kissed her cheek. "Whatever happens today, I'm just happy to be here with you. Last night was pretty special."

"Can we not talk about this right now?"

"Are you having regrets?" He took a step back and slid a finger beneath her chin, tilting her head up. "I haven't been with many women, Sam."

"I know, Ted. Like I told you last night, you're the first man I've been with since having Dani. I'm trying to keep my emotions in check for now, okay? Let's get through today. Then we can talk."

"Of course." He smiled and kissed her gently on her lips. "One step at a time."

It took several minutes for them to reach the entrance to the Renaissance Center. Once inside, Ted led Sam to the GM Pavilion where they were greeted with an exhibition showcasing GM's history—from classics to current production models to concept cars. Over a dozen vehicles were spread out on multiple levels, each in pristine condition. Plaques displayed on posts in front of each vehicle gave the specs and history of each.

Ted immediately made his way over to a twentieth anniversary Turbo 1989 Pontiac Trans Am. To celebrate the car's twentieth year of production, GM replaced the V-8 engine with a turbocharged 3.8-liter V-6 borrowed from corporate cousin Buick. Paired to a four-speed automatic, Pontiac made only fifteen hundred of the cars, with the hope they would one day become collector's items.

"I was seven years old when this came out." Ted could not stop grinning as he took in the sleek lines of the pony car. "I had pictures of this plastered to my bedroom wall. Did you know that Pontiac had to subcontract the engine modifications out to a third party to make it fit under the hood?"

He looked over his shoulder expecting to see Sam, but she was nowhere in sight. He spun around to look for her. "Sam?" *Where did she go?* he thought as he began frantically searching. He stopped when he spotted her behind a big sign on the far side of the room next to two vehicles.

"What do you see?" he asked once he got to her side.

"This is incredible." She ran her fingers across the plaque in front of the two concept vehicles. "They did these five years ago. I had no idea."

The Hy-Wire and Autonomy concepts were GM's foray into a future of alternative fueled vehicles and a new way to design and build cars. Because they were only concept cars, though, they were never built with production in mind. Rather, they were made to test the waters of public reception. The 2002 Autonomy concept had what GM had dubbed the *skateboard chassis*, so named because of the four wheels connected to a large, long, six-inch-thick platform that housed everything needed to power and control the wheels, including a fuel cell powertrain. The design would simplify construction and lower costs.

A year later, GM built the Hy-Wire as an example of what a vehicle riding on top of the Autonomy chassis would look like. The sleek silver four-door was completely drivable, and GM allowed a good number of car experts to take it for a test drive to get their feedback.

"It's not self-driving, but it's all drive-by-wire." Ted knelt to get a closer look at the skateboard chassis. It wasn't a simple metal brick. The skateboard had an organic shape as it curved to meet each wheel. "I think they were trying to out-Prius Toyota by looking into fuel cells and electrification."

"I don't understand—what makes it autonomous? You said it's not self-driving. Why the name?"

"It has to do with the skateboard design. You could, in theory, drop any type of vehicle on top of the chassis. It could be a sedan, hatchback, or van. That makes the chassis autonomous from the vehicle class, if that makes sense."

"Of course. Ted, this shows they can be forward-thinking. We need to find a way to weave this into the discussion today. Imagine our self-driving tech on this type of platform? They have to see the possibilities."

"I hope so. We need a win after bombing at Ford and Chrysler."

"I feel good about this, Ted. I really do. Just don't lose your cool again like you did yesterday."

"I'll do my best, Sam."

"Follow my lead."

"Of course, my calm turtle." He pulled her close and kissed her on her head.

"Remember, this is a process." She ran her fingernails through his hair, combing it back away from his face. "We need to get them on board today. That's our goal. Everything else is secondary."

"You're in charge."

She smiled and picked strands of lint from Ted's navy suit. She adjusted his red and blue pinstriped tie and said, "You clean up nicely, Ted. Now let's go show them the future."

Sam found it difficult to focus on the meeting. The view from the thirtieth floor was gorgeous. Despite the cold temperatures and gusty winds, the clouds were few and far between. Visibility was clear, and from the massive windows one could see across the river to the city of Windsor and beyond. She kept a smile on her face as she listened to Ted go through the final set of slides. Deep inside, however, she knew they had failed to connect with the three men at the far end of the room.

Two of them had arrived ten minutes after the meeting had started, without bothering to introduce themselves. They'd also remained silent during the entire presentation. The only one who had spoken was David Foster, vice president of product development for GM. His attitude throughout the whole meeting had been condescending and dismissive. The stocky, barrel-chested man did his best to contain his expanding waistline by wearing a dark gray wool suit and an overly long, narrow, bright red tie. His shirt, one size too small, clung tightly to his neckline. When he spoke, the veins along his throat throbbed as they pulled precariously at the top button of his collar.

"You still haven't given me one good reason to believe *any* of what you've shown so far is worth GM's investment." David glanced at the hard copy of the presentation Sam had provided at the start of the meeting. He flipped back a few pages and frowned. "This has been a complete waste of our time. Your hour is almost up. I suggest you wrap this up."

For the first time since arriving in Michigan, Sam felt awash in anger. She did her best during the Ford and Chrysler meetings to remain polite and respectful, trying to listen and understand everyone's points of view. Perhaps it was the weather. Perhaps it was the long nights. Perhaps it was her confusion over what to do about her growing feelings for Ted. Whatever the reason, she'd had enough.

"Not one good reason?" She slid her chair sideways, pushing Ted to the side. Their presentation was displayed on a large screen at the end of the room. The current slide showed a graph with a twenty-year timeline that showed a rise in alternative fuel vehicles, a rise in autonomous vehicles, and a decline in personal car ownership. "There are three staring you in the face."

"I'm sorry, but what . . . what was your name?" David asked.

"Sam."

"I'm sorry, Sam, but I simply disagree with your projections."

"These aren't our studies. Ted explained that—"

"Then I disagree with *their* projections." David removed his thick glasses and tossed them onto the table. "These papers and projections you reference from these so-called industry experts are nothing but attempts to get attention. Go back to the seventies and the fuel shortage. Everyone predicted the end of large vehicles and the V-8 engine. Those all came roaring back, and better than ever."

"I'm sorry, but I don't think you see the big picture." She glanced over at Ted. She could tell he was shocked at how emboldened she'd become. "The future is coming. What we showed you today is the future of transportation."

"If you don't believe us, look at your own history," Ted said. "There was a time when seat belts were unheard of in a car. The same with airbags. Each decade sees the rise of new technology."

"Technology that people initially feared." Sam stood up and took a breath to calm her nerves. "Antilock brakes were designed to improve safety and prevent accidents. They were met with a mix of awe and trepidation. Now they're standard on every car built."

"You can thank the government bureaucrats for that," David said. "Damn regulations. There is no way the government will mandate self-driving cars. Ever."

"That's not what we're proposing." Ted tapped his laptop's backspace key to go to a slide that listed the technological breakthroughs pioneered on Athena and Cyclops. "These systems are the antilock brakes of the future."

"You're wrong," David said.

"Maybe if you'd been at DARPA, you would have felt differently," Sam said.

"I may not have been at that desert race, but Jeff was." David pointed at the man sitting to his left. "He wasn't impressed. Neither am I."

Sam waited to see if Jeff would chime in with his opinion, but the man never moved his gaze from the lovely view outside. Ted flipped open his notepad and started scanning through additional topics he and Sam had drafted last night, tapping his pen as he searched through the list nervously.

"What about your competition?" Sam slowly reached over and took the pen from Ted's hand and placed it out of reach. "What if they get there before you?"

"Competition?" David chuckled, looked at Jeff, and rolled his eyes. "We don't work in a bubble, young lady. I already spoke with Brad over at Ford. Bob too. They warned me about your pitch. I chose not to cancel out of common courtesy. We're all in agreement this is a dead end."

"What about others?" Sam said. "New technology is going to disrupt the transportation industry."

"Are you planning to take this to Toyota?"

"I was talking about competition from outside the established industry leads."

"Such as?"

"Well, look at Tesla."

"Tesla?" David burst out laughing, quickly followed by the other two gentlemen. "That company is nothing but a bunch of laptop batteries crammed into the back of a Lotus. Nothing more than a group of lefty tree huggers selling pipedreams to other lefty tree huggers. And before you start to lecture me about electric cars, let me remind you that GM made the EV-1. We invested a fortune in that battery-electric vehicle—money that never gave us a return on investment."

"We had a chart showing you the anticipated cost reduction of lithium-ion batteries over the next twenty-five years." Sam's voice and temper had calmed. She realized that, just like Ford and Chrysler, this was a losing battle. Ted's stillness surprised her. "If Tesla doesn't survive, someone else will step in to take their place."

"I'd like to see them try." David leaned back in his chair, the seat groaning in protest. "Building cars isn't easy. There's an entire supply chain that needs to be in place. That's why you don't see new car companies popping up all the time. It's just the opposite."

Sam looked over at Ted. He seemed lost, almost catatonic, staring at his notes.

"That's all the more reason for GM to be a leader with this technology," Sam said. "I was admiring the fuel cell concepts you had in the lobby."

"Do you know why they're in the lobby and not on the road?" David did not wait for Sam to respond. "Because, just like your robot cars, they were deemed not ready for prime time. If you ask me, they were another huge waste of our money."

"I found them to be rather elegant solutions." Sam sighed and glanced up at David.

"Expensive solutions to a problem nobody asked to be solved." David shook his head in disappointment. "Are we done?"

She flipped open her notepad. Just like Ted, she'd made a list of key points to raise at the GM meeting, based on lessons learned from their earlier outings this week. She sighed as she failed to see anything relevant to bring up.

"I feel we've made a strong case for where the industry is headed." She glanced at Ted. He looked up, but did not smile. She turned and faced David. "Can you at least tell me one good reason why you won't even consider this technology?"

"I'll give you five. One. Nobody is going to want to be seen in a car with all that ugly gear strapped to the roof. Two. Before you tell me about downsizing, I can tell you that it will be decades before they can shrink lidar down to a manageable size. Three. The expense of lidar is cost-prohibitive and, just like the size issue, a long way from becoming affordable. Four. Unions will never allow it. I'm not talking about those jackasses that build our cars. I'm talking about the taxi and trucking unions. There's no way they're going to let some robot replace them. And last but not least, this is America. The home of apple pie, baseball, and cars. People love their cars and trucks. Why do you think we make so many of them? All shapes and sizes. Our biggest seller is a pickup truck, and most people don't take advantage of half of what it's capable of doing. Why do they buy it? For the same reason they buy a Corvette. It brings them joy. What joy is there in a robot car?"

"I see," she said. "Then I guess we're done here."

Ted pulled his laptop closer and flicked off the dual-screen option that sent their presentation to the projector in the room. He quickly disconnected the cord and tossed the video cable aside. Jeff and the other man stood up and left the room without saying anything.

"Ted, when you started this meeting, you told me your father worked at one of our plants," David said. "Which one?"

"Lordstown," Ted replied. "My brothers, too."

"You must have grown up surrounded by car culture. It's got to be in your blood. I'm surprised you're on board with all of this."

"Because it's the future. Someday you'll see."

"Really?" David removed his glasses and used his tie to clean the lenses. "Tell me, Ted, what do you drive?"

"Nothing. I sold my car to pursue this dream." Ted flicked his laptop closed. "Sam's right. GM was on the right track with those concept cars. The same with the EV-1. Someone will be first to perfect this technology. And when they do, they will change the world."

"What did you drive?"

"Excuse me?"

"What car did you sell to chase your dream?"

"A Mustang GT."

"A Ford?" David frowned, stood up, and headed toward the door, leaving the folder with Sam and Ted's materials behind. "Lordstown builds Chevys, and you're driving around in a Ford. I'm sure your dad must be proud of you."

"You stopped building the Camaro in 2002," Ted said. "I went to the competition to get what I wanted. That's what we've been trying to explain to you. The future is autonomous cars, whether you like it or not."

"Nobody wants an electric or self-driving car." David stopped and stared directly at Ted. "Even a shitty Mustang. And they never will."

21

The heater installed in the outer wall of the Holiday Inn hotel room clicked softly before the fan roared to life. The hot air spewing from the vents smelled of burned dust. Luggage bags covered the queen bed closest to the heater. Sam sat on the end of the bed beside her rollerbag, staring at the rumpled sheets of the other bed. Images flashed before her of the moments of passion she'd shared with Ted, and she wondered if she had made a mistake by coming. Maybe she shouldn't have come—or agreed to work on anything with Ted. She shook the thoughts out of her mind and tried to concentrate on the phone call she was having with her daughter instead.

"That's right, Dani, Thanksgiving will be here soon. Will you help me bake cookies to share with everyone?"

The bathroom door squeaked as it swung open. Ted emerged, carrying his toiletry bag. He tossed it onto the nightstand beside the clock and sat down at the end of the bed facing Sam.

"Of course we can make chocolate chip. We can bake whatever kind you want." Sam listened intently as her daughter described the cookies she'd had on her last playdate. "Mommy misses you. I'll be home tonight before you go to bed. Can you put Gram-Gram back on?"

Sam did her best to ignore Ted, but she could see him packing his bag out of the corner of her eye. They'd said very little since waking up earlier that morning. Moments later, her mother came on.

"Hi, Mom. Thanks again for caring for Dani this week. No more travels for me. That's a promise." As she talked, she stood up and checked her bags piled on the bed. Everything was packed and ready to go. She tugged at the zippers and made sure she knew just where her driver's license was. She stopped and looked at Ted as she answered her mother's question. "I don't know what will happen. Thanksgiving and Christmas are all I can focus on for now. Listen, let me get going. I don't want to miss my flight. Love you."

She ended the call and tossed her phone into her handbag. The only sound in the room was the hum and rattle of the heater.

"Sounds like you had a nice call with your mom and daughter," Ted said as he sat at the end of the other bed.

"I was surprised my mother called me so early in the morning, but it was nice to talk to them." She pulled her bags to the edge of the bed. "So, what will you do next? Are you going back to DSU?"

"Pittsburgh? I told you Detroit was a one-way ticket, Sam. I have no plans to go back. I never want to see Rusty again."

"Then, where will you go?" She briefly looked into his eyes, but immediately averted her gaze as she checked her bags again. "You must have something else lined up."

"I . . . I don't know." He sat on the edge of his bed and lowered his head. "I really didn't have a backup plan. I never thought all three companies would reject us."

"How could you not have a backup plan?" She cautiously took a seat beside him. "Did you really think they were going to offer you a job?"

"I did. The technology we built is the future. I figured I would have to stay in the hotel and keep the rental a bit longer until I sorted out job offers."

"Job offers? *That* was your plan? But when I first got here, we agreed that wasn't our priority."

"You agreed it wasn't *your* priority, Sam. Some of us have to work for a living. I don't have some loving family with tons of money waiting to welcome me home with open arms." He briefly glanced at her before looking away. "Sorry. I didn't mean that."

She shook her head in frustration and sighed.

"I bet the farm, Sam. I sold my car to get to DSU. I drained my savings while staying there. My bank account is almost empty, and my credit cards are close to being maxed out."

"I had no idea." She slid her arm around him and began to caress his back. "Why didn't you tell me?"

"You've told me a thousand times that I take too many risks. I didn't want you to know how far I was willing to go. I thought that might put even more pressure on you this week."

"You should have confided in me, Ted." She ran her fingernails through the part in his hair. "Is there anything I can do?"

"There is." He reached up and took her hand and kissed it. "You can tell me what you want to do about us."

"Us?" She recoiled, sliding her hand from his. "Ted, how . . . how can there be an us? I live in California, and you . . . you don't have a home."

"I told you, I thought I would build a future here. Maybe even with you."

"With me?"

"Sam, I wasn't sure what would happen between us this week. I'm not talking about the meetings with Detroit. I'm talking about *us*. Ever since Burning Man, I've been unable to get you out of my head. Staying with you here, making love, . . . this has been amazing. You've got to see that, too? Don't you? But you seem so distant, especially this morning. What is it you're thinking? What do you want?"

Sam lowered her head and looked away. She felt her heart begin to race as she tried to search for the right words. She had planned every aspect of the Detroit meetings, but she hadn't planned for what had happened with Ted. She now had to ask herself what to do next.

"I . . . I don't know."

"You don't know? Where do you see our relationship going?"

"Relationship? Ted, we barely know each other."

"Oh, so, sex this week meant nothing to you? Was I just some hookup?"

She stood up and shocked herself by smacking him across his cheek. "How dare you!"

She spun around, gathering her bags from the bed frantically. Her hands shook, and the palm of her right hand stung from the blow.

"I'm sorry, Sam." Ted tried to put a comforting arm around her, but she yanked her shoulder away. "I . . . I deserved that."

"I told you I haven't been with anyone since I got pregnant with Dani. Anyone!"

"And I told you I don't sleep around. What's happened between us is special, Sam. It meant a lot to me." He took a few steps back. "Why are you suddenly shutting me out?"

"I was worried it was a line we shouldn't cross. I was thinking ahead. Where it could all lead."

"But we did cross it. And it was beautiful." He paused to take a deep breath. He rubbed his hand along the cheek she had smacked. "Why are you pulling away? We joke about you being the slow turtle, but you're more like a clam. Closed off and hard to open."

"That's not true."

"No? Then why have you barely looked at me today? Why won't you tell me what's going on? Why do you hate your birthday?"

"What?" Sam felt her entire body begin to tremble and quiver. Her eyes filled with tears. "What does me not wanting to celebrate my birthday have to do with anything?"

"It's another way you've closed yourself off. You can trust me, Sam. Show me that you can open up to me."

She paced back and forth, her breathing short and measured. She shook her head as she debated what to say, and even if she should say anything at all. She looked over at him, sitting on the edge of the bed. His blue eyes pierced her heart.

"Fine." She sat beside him but could not look at his face. She kept her gaze on her hands as she nervously rubbed her fingers together. "Remember how I told you that I lost a best friend to a drunk driver?"

"Sure."

"Well, that drunk driver was . . . was me." She was full on crying now, that old familiar rush of guilt and loss consuming her. She slowly removed the heart pendant around her neck, clutching it in her hand. As she wiped her tears away, she looked at Ted and said, "I . . . I wear this so I won't forget."

He pulled her toward him and wrapped his arms around her, feeling her shake as she sobbed. She relaxed a bit with his touch and composed herself enough to keep going.

"It was my sweet sixteen party. My mom had hosted this huge party for me, with dozens of friends and family. My best friend, Jackie, and I were rebels back then. Especially her. She kept spiking our drinks when nobody was watching. Anyway, I didn't have my driver's license yet. Neither of us did. We ended up in the driveway. Jackie stole the keys to my mom's car. We somehow thought it would be a grand idea to take a little drive, just around the block. Before I even got half a block down the road, I got too close to the ditch and flipped the car. Jackie's seatbelt wasn't on and . . . and . . ." she couldn't bring herself to tell him the rest.

She just sat there sobbing into his chest the memories of that dreadful night stirred up and fresh. Shaking her head, she wiped her tears away as she pulled back from him.

"It was a stupid, stupid accident," she continued, placing the necklace beside her. "The pendant used to be a charm on Jackie's bracelet."

"Sam, I don't know what to say. I'm so sorry."

"I . . . I was never charged for what happened. My mother lied to protect me. It was just down the road from our house and I ran to her when it happened. She told the police she had been the one driving. I was so upset, so scared, I just stood there and watched my mother make everything go away. It's haunted me my entire life."

"You were young, Sam. You didn't intend for that to happen. God, I'm so sorry."

Sam wiped her face dry, stood up, and walked over to her bags. "Well, anyway, there you have it. The clam is open, okay? The turtle stuck her head out. Happy?"

"I didn't mean to dig up painful memories, Sam. I was only trying to let you know you can open up to me. I wanted you to be comfortable with me. With us. And what may lie ahead."

Without saying a word, she turned her attention back to her bags. Once again, she checked the pockets to confirm everything was packed and secured. She glanced at the clock to see if it was time to leave for the airport. She suddenly wanted nothing more than to get as far away as possible. Just then she felt Ted's arm around her shoulder.

"Look at me," he said. "We're good together. Don't deny it. Connections like ours are rare. Can't we at least talk?"

"I can't do this, Ted. Not again."

"Again?"

Sam's body trembled as the tears returned. Everything was a blur as she scooped up her bags, tossing what she could over her shoulders and flinging her rollerbag onto the floor.

"Wait, are you going? Let me at least drive you to the airport, Sam. We can talk in the car on the way there."

"No. No, Ted. I need to go. I . . . I just need to go."

She rushed past him and stopped at the door. She struggled to open it while keeping her bags from crashing to the floor. He ran to her side to help.

"Please, Sam. Don't leave like this."

"I'm sorry, Ted. I have to. I can't do this. I can't."

She took one last look into his deep blue eyes. For a brief moment, she let herself imagine a future with him. Deep down, she knew he was right. They were indeed good together. But then she reminded herself of Dani and her mom, and Dani's father—and her dreams of being with Ted vanished in a puff. Part of her still wanted to drop everything and collapse into his arms. With new resolve, though, she pushed that thought away, lowered her head, turned, and left the room.

Ted stared at the cell phone cradled in his hands. Sam had left the hotel at 9:30 a.m. He was beginning to feel a little unhinged. Desperate. In the hour since she had walked out the door, he'd tried her phone multiple times but only got voicemail. His eyes burned and felt swollen. He couldn't remember the last time he'd cried so hard. His mind was racing. What was he going to do? Who could he call? Where could he go? He knew Rusty and DSU were an option he had no interest in pursuing. Kyle Fisher! He might have something for Ted. It only took a few rings before Kyle answered.

"Kyle!" Ted tried to sound upbeat. "It's Ted Wolff. Did I wake you?"

"Ted? No, of course you didn't. Where are you?"

"I'm in Detroit. Well, Royal Oak, to be exact. Sam and I came out here to see the big three. Show them what we did out at DARPA."

"How'd that go?"

"They're, uh, curious. You know these old companies. They tend to be a bit cautious."

"I see."

"Anyway, I'm not sure when they're going to come around to sign up with us. Sam had to get back home to California. I was thinking that, well, maybe I could get my old job back. Just for the time being."

He waited for Kyle to respond, his heart pounding through the silence that followed. Kyle clucked his tongue against the roof of his mouth, followed by a long, drawn-out sigh.

"Ted, you know I love you. You're a brilliant engineer. But I can't put you back in Nevada."

"Are you still doing those student workers? I'm happy to help play apprentice. You can cut my pay if there's a money issue."

"It's not that, Ted. Kevin is really pissed about what you took from the Nixon shop. Ted, you took more than just the magnetic dampers."

Ted lowered the phone and closed his eyes as images of what he'd shoved into that oversized cardboard box flashed up. "I took what was mine, Kyle."

"That's not how Kevin sees it."

He felt his hands begin to tremble. "My old notebooks . . . I can prove the lidar is mine. Don't believe Kevin. He modified my designs behind my back. He's . . . he's a liar."

"See, Ted. How can I have you working at the shop with someone you call a liar?"

"I'm sorry, Kyle." His voice began to shake. His world was collapsing, and he didn't know how to recover. "Maybe I can call Kevin—to smooth things over?"

"I'm sorry, Ted. I've spent the past several weeks calming Kevin down. He wanted to sue you. He wanted *me* to sue you. Lawsuits are never a good thing. They're always bad for business."

"Please, Kyle. I can do better. Maybe another shop? You must have something open somewhere else. You have operations all over the world."

"You've been gone for almost two years, Ted. Kevin's become one of my top guys. I can't risk losing him by bringing you back into the fold. Especially if you're just killing time waiting for Detroit to call you. There's too much bad blood with Kevin now. I have a company and a reputation to uphold. I can't have that bitterness pervading my business. You must understand that."

Ted closed his eyes as new tears welled up. He shook his head and took a deep breath to gather himself. He had to accept that Kyle was, unfortunately, a dead end. Ted needed to get off the phone. Immediately.

"Okay. Sure. Sorry to have bothered you, Kyle."

"No bother at all, Ted. You're a talented man. I'm sure you'll find something soon. You said Detroit was thinking it over, right?"

"Right."

"Give them time."

"I will. Goodbye."

As Ted pressed "End," he flung the phone against the pillows piled at the foot of the bed. Pacing back and forth, he forced his mind to go through the options. Part of him was in shock at Kyle's rejection. He was also feeling a rising anger toward Kevin. Like a pendulum, Ted felt his emotions swing between disbelief and resentment. He knew he could not go back to DSU. Like a loop, he could hear Sam's voice saying, "How could you not have a backup plan?" over and over again. With a heavy heart, he picked up his phone and dialed the only person he knew would not reject him. He sat down on the squishy hotel bed just as the call connected.

"Hello?" Barbara Wolff asked.

"Hi, Mom." His voice was lifeless and empty. He couldn't even pretend to sound upbeat. "How are you?"

"How wonderful to hear from you! I'm just lovely today. Where are you? Is everything okay?"

"I'm in Detroit."

"Detroit? For what?"

"I'm just checking out some job opportunities. I was thinking I could drive over and maybe visit for a bit. Thanksgiving isn't that far away."

"Thanksgiving?" Barbara's voice instantly changed from happy to suspicious. "My son wants to spend the holidays with his family? What's going on, Teddy?"

"Nothing, Mom. Look, I just figured—"

"Hold on while I get your father."

Ted lowered the phone and sighed. He was hoping he wouldn't have to talk with his father. The wall-mounted heater shuddered as it powered down. The quietness that permeated the room only added to his sense of loneliness.

"Ted?" John Wolff asked.

"Hey, Dad." Ted glanced at the clock on the nightstand to verify the time. "Shouldn't you be at work?"

"Your father's home sick with a horrible fever and should be back in bed."

"Union benefits, Son. Plenty of sick time for me. Your mom said you were in Detroit. Why?"

"He's looking for a job, Jack. Can you believe it? Three hours away, and he never bothered to call us."

"A job?" John coughed, his throat heavy with phlegm. "What kind of job?"

"It's nothing, Dad. It has to do with the technology from the DARPA competition."

"Well, how'd that turn out? Did you impress them with that amazing brain of yours?"

His heart began to race, and his chest tighten. He'd just wanted a simple conversation with his mother about coming home. First, Sam rejected him. Then Kyle. He wasn't sure he could handle a lecture from his father.

"I tried. We . . . we tried." Ted jammed his thumb and index finger into his eyes to try and stop the tears from falling. It was no use. He soon found himself sobbing uncontrollably. Ted pounded his fist against the bed, angry that his emotions were so out of control.

"What's wrong, Ted?" John asked with sudden alarm.

"What is it, Teddy?" Barbara said. "You can tell us. We're your family."

"I thought Detroit would listen. I thought they'd have a job for me." He could not stop weeping and struggled to connect his thoughts and words. "But they didn't. They rejected me. Us. Sam's gone. Kyle. Kevin. DSU. I have nothing now. Nothing!"

Quickly saying he had to go, he hung up and collapsed into the pillow beside him. He felt hollow. Dull. His future was draining away. He was alone and had no idea what to do. A minute passed before his cell phone rang. He sat up and wiped his face dry, clearing his hair from his eyes.

"Hello?"

"Why would you say you have nothing?" John asked, his voice softer than usual. "Come home, Ted. Together we'll figure things out, okay?"

Ted held the phone to his ear, unsure of what to say.

"I'm going to put your mother on." John coughed loudly. "See you soon, Son."

"Teddy? Where in Detroit are you? Do you need me to come get you?"

"No." His temples throbbed from the tears he'd cried. "I have a rental car."

"Then you need to come home. Right now. We don't want you to be alone." There was a long pause as his mother waited for him to respond. When he didn't, she continued. "I've sent your father back to bed. We both love you, Ted. We've always wanted what's best for you."

"I . . . I know."

"Just come home, and don't worry about anything. We'll take care of you. Your brothers will be so happy to see you. I'm sure you have old friends here as well. Will you come?"

"Okay."

Several seconds passed before his mother spoke. When she did, her tone was back to being its usual upbeat and cheerful self.

"My baby will be home for the holidays! I'm going to make that spice cake for dessert. Remember the one you always used to beg for?"

"I do." He was surprised to find himself smiling. "Thanks, Mom."

"Drive careful. And don't speed!"

"I won't. Goodbye, Mom."

He let the phone go by his side and exhaled slowly. His eyes felt like they were on fire, but he was relieved his tears had stopped. He was also surprised to find he was looking forward to going home. Ted knew his relationship with his parents and brothers was nothing like the close relationship Sam had with her mom and daughter. But he also knew he had no other options. Hearing his mother's excitement, and even his dad's heartfelt concern, brought him a bit of comfort.

He walked over to the bathroom. The fluorescent bulb above the mirror flickered on, casting a harsh white light. He was taken aback by how pale he looked. All the color seemed to have drained from his face, and his eyes were red and bloodshot. He grabbed a glass from beside the sink and filled it halfway with water from the tap. Just as he was about to take a sip, he thought back to those early days at DSU when Rusty asked the team if the glass was half full or half empty. Ted tightened his grip on the glass and watched his knuckles whiten as he squeezed. After a few seconds, he softened his grasp and swallowed the water, quenching his thirst.

Killing the bathroom light, he walked over to the two beds and gathered the rest of his things, throwing them into his garment bag, zipping it shut. He noted that his cell phone was resting against the pillows. Sitting down on the edge of the bed he picked up one of the pillows and put it up to his face. It still smelled like Sam. He inhaled deeply and held it there for a few moments before tossing it back against the headboard. Just as the pillow hit the mattress, he noticed a sparkle of gold among the sheets. Sam's heart necklace was lying on the bed.

He grabbed it, inspecting the clasp. It didn't appear to be broken. He watched the edges of the pendant reflect the light as it twirled, dangling from his hand. Opening the front pouch of his laptop backpack, he tossed the necklace inside. Flinging the bag over his shoulder, he reached for his garment bag and keys, and left the room.

22

It had been a brutal winter in Lordstown, Ohio, especially that particular February when temperatures regularly slid down to zero. Ted had forgotten how ruthless the dead of winter could be in this part of the country. He was thankful he had made it through to the end of April and spring was beginning to peek through.

The Lordstown Complex, located along I-80, spanned over nine hundred acres and included multiple facilities, including metal, paint, and assembly buildings. John Wolff had managed to get Ted a job working in the main assembly plant since January. His dad had to pull a few strings to make it happen, which Ted was grateful for, but he also knew it was the last place he wanted to be, for many reasons.

Inside the complex, Ted was perched on a catwalk, staring at the line of half-built vehicles below him. The procession of cars seemed to go on for an eternity. His mind was elsewhere. Five and a half months after Detroit, and all he could still think about was Sam. He hadn't heard from her once since she had left the hotel room in Royal Oak.

The whir and hum of motors and equipment were interrupted by the occasional voice of someone calling out from below. The sounds also masked the footsteps of his father walking up behind him.

"Working late?" John asked his son.

Ted glanced back at his dad before returning his gaze to the activity of the assembly line. "No, I was just enjoying some alone time."

"Your brothers were looking for you."

"Did they leave?"

"Yes, but they plan to come by the house this weekend for Sunday dinner." John waited for Ted to continue the conversation, but was met only with silence. "I hear good things about your performance, Ted."

"Uh-huh."

Ted watched two robots off in the distance, spot-welding a frame. The flying sparks of orange reminded him of the embers rising from the torches at the Temple of Forgiveness he and Sam had seen last September. He tried to ignore the cold, piercing stare he could feel from his father.

"What's wrong, Ted?"

"Nothing."

At 6'3", John stood even a couple of inches taller than his son. They shared similar features, including those deep blue eyes and short tempers. John's temper flashed now as he turned and grabbed Ted by the shoulder and twisted him around.

"Bullshit. You've been moping around since the day you came back home. Yeah, things didn't work out for you with that stint at DSU, and corporate Detroit rejected you, but you've finally got a real job. You should be happy. Do you know what I went through to get you in here? GM's been struggling with record losses lately. We suffered through that awful strike. I went to bat for you, Ted."

"I know, Dad. It's just that this isn't what I wanted. This wasn't supposed to be how my life turned out." He yanked his shoulder free from his father's grip and leaned against the bright yellow safety railing, casting a blank stare toward the assembly line below. "You don't understand."

"I understand you're brilliant, Ted. You're wasting your skills here. I know you deserve better."

"Excuse me?" Ted was shocked to hear such a glowing compliment come from his father. "Then, why did you bring me to work in this plant?"

"You have a future here, Ted. With your skills, I see you working your way up. Show them what you can do. You should be looking for ways to improve our processes or maybe the hardware. There are thousands of pieces that go into creating these cars. You see this stuff coming down the line. I know how much you love to tinker and build things." John put his arm around his son and pointed at the vehicles gradually making their way down the line. They were still just the core frames, without any mechanics or interiors installed. "Look down there. What do you see?"

Ted sighed as he let his eyes follow the direction of his father's pointing finger. Humans and robots were broken into sections, each with a specific task to perform. Stacks of materials, including components such as doors, suspension items, and engines, were aligned and waiting to be installed. Ted's mind drifted back to the GM Pavilion and the elegance of the Autonomy's skateboard chassis.

"You want to know what I see, Dad? I see waste. I see the past."

"The past?" John shook his head dismissively. "Have you seen the new turbocharged engine going into the Cobalt SS? That motor is cutting edge. It's very competitive."

"Sure, it's competitive. It's just not the future." Ted glanced back and forth between the robots and the people working down below. He remembered coming to this plant as a kid. The ratio of robots to humans was much lower twenty years ago. The tasks they could perform were much more basic. He thought back to the research paper he did in college about AI becoming smarter and more skilled. "One day, Dad, this entire factory will be nothing but robots."

"Bullshit. Those things break down. We're always maintaining them."

"Right. We will work for them. Not the other way around."

Ted turned and began to make his way down to the main floor. His father stayed close behind, stopping him halfway down the staircase.

"I know you wanted corporate GM to hire you, Ted. That hasn't worked out for you. But you can prove them wrong here. Work your way up. Show them how much better they can be. Prove yourself here, and they will give you a big job in a big office."

"You don't get it, Dad. They didn't hire me because they don't believe in me, or the technology that I showed them. Nobody does. Nobody except Sam."

"And what's she up to these days?" John knew the answer and continued to talk. "You have no idea because she abandoned you. The *only* ones who have been here for you are your family. I wish you would accept the life you've been given."

"I have!" The noise from the plant floor drowned out Ted's explosive response. "Just because I've accepted it doesn't mean I have to like it!"

He turned to descend the stairs, but his dad grabbed him again and stopped him in his tracks.

"If that technology you worked on is so great, then why didn't you join the military?"

"What?"

"You told me the military got to use all that tech. Why didn't they hire you?"

"We've already discussed this, Dad. Those jobs weren't for me."

Rusty had told Ted about some of the military job options he could pursue. Defense contractors, such as Oshkosh, were eager to build on the systems and components developed for the DARPA Challenge. He'd encouraged Ted to reach out to them, and others such as Lockheed-Martin. But Ted wanted nothing to do with weapons of war. Growing up in Lordstown, he was a car guy. His passion coming out of DARPA was to change the transportation industry. He'd tried to explain this to his father several times, but it always fell on deaf ears.

"You're too stubborn, Ted. I'll never understand."

"Exactly!" He could see the confusion, anger, and now pain in his father's eyes. He feared he might have pushed the conversation too far and regretted snapping at him. "I'm sorry. I know you only want what's best for me. It's . . . it's been a long work week, Dad. I'm wiped. I'll see you at home tonight."

Lordstown was small, with less than fifteen hundred homes spread across its twenty-three square miles. Ted had never understood why his parents chose to live here. Most who worked in the plant lived in Warren, ten miles away. But then again, the smallness of Lordstown reminded him of Wadsworth, the town in which he had picked to live in Nevada. He pictured someone else living in his old apartment, probably helping out around the place like he had. These were his thoughts on his drive home.

The speed limit on Route 45, also known as Tod Ave., was fifty miles per hour. It was a relatively quiet, tree-lined, four-lane road. Ted kept his car a couple of miles under the limit. Traffic was light, and he was in no rush to see his family.

Two months ago, much to the dismay of his mother, Ted had bought a 2000 Chevy Camaro. She'd wanted him to carpool with his dad or brothers or borrow her car when needed. But he'd felt trapped, wanted the freedom of his own wheels. The Camaro was jet black with too many miles on it, given its age. The 3.8-liter V-6 and four-speed automatic were a far cry from the high-performance Mustang GT he'd had in Nevada. The car also had its fair share of nicks and dents. The interior rattled horribly, and the stereo only worked when it wanted to. He didn't care. And his dad was glad he didn't buy another Ford.

His parents still lived in the house he grew up in. Built in the early 1940s, the tiny beige Cape Cod–styled home crammed three bedrooms and two bathrooms into fourteen hundred square feet. An oversized two-car garage sat at the back of the property at the end of a rutted blacktop driveway. Ted pulled his Camaro to the rear of the house, stopping just before the garage. He killed the engine, grabbed the brown paper bag resting on the seat beside him, and got out.

Through the covered porch at the back of the house, he could see his mother puttering around in the kitchen preparing dinner. Barbara was a stocky woman with long silver hair, often pulled back in a bun. His mother loved cooking for her family and had a collection of stained aprons to prove it. This evening she was wearing a yellow and white checkered one with Kiss the cook if you want to eat! scrawled across the front.

Ted unlocked the side door as quietly as he could and stepped inside.

"Jack, is that you?" Barbara asked. She stuck her head around the corner. "Teddy! How was work today? Are you hungry? I'm making lasagna."

"Work was fine." He closed the outer door and opened the door that led to the basement. "Let me know when dinner is ready."

He flicked the wall-mounted light switch, illuminating a dull, yellowed twenty-five-watt bulb overhead. The walnut-paneled walls and brown-painted wooden stairs were dark and confining. The steps creaked and groaned as he stomped his way to the basement. A dehumidifier hummed from somewhere in the darkness, attempting to alleviate the dampness that permeated the entire lower level.

Shortly after Ted was born, his father and some buddies from work had built a fourth bedroom in the basement. It was quite rudimentary, made of nothing but 2 x 4 studs and panel boards. Orange shag carpeting, from the smell most likely mold-infested, lined the floor. There were no windows to let in light. A small electric space heater kept it warm during the cold winter months.

Many years ago, Ted's oldest brother Steve had been the first to move into the basement bedroom. As soon as Steve moved out, Michael had insisted on taking over his room. Moving to the basement became a source of pride in the family—almost a coming of age event. When Ted moved back in last November, his mother had practically begged him to stay in one of the upstairs bedrooms, but Ted insisted on staying in the basement.

The downstairs bedroom took up half of the lower level. The other half was equally divided between storage and a laundry room. Over the years, the laundry room had morphed into a makeshift kitchen. A small dorm-room sized fridge hummed in a corner, and a microwave sat atop a shelf over the utility sink. During Ted's last year in college, Steve had installed a set of old pine cabinets from when the family had renovated the main kitchen. These held plates, dishes, and utensils, giving the basement everything it needed except a bathroom.

Ted flicked on the small nineteen-inch color TV that sat on top of a chest of drawers in the corner of the room. He reached into the brown paper bag and pulled out a bottle of Chivas Regal.

"I remember when you used to be special." He cracked the top open and took a swig of whisky. "Now all I use you for is celebrating Fridays. And one other tradition."

He grabbed his cell phone and dialed Sam. It had become his weekly ritual since early December. He waited patiently for the call to connect. After several rings, it went to voicemail—the same way it had done every Friday.

"Sam, it's Ted. But you know that." He took another sip of whisky. He let out a long sigh as the amber liquid slid down his throat. "You never return my calls. But you also have never told me to stop calling you. And you haven't blocked me. My little turtle, hiding in her shell. Part of me wants to believe that maybe you like hearing my voice. So, I will keep calling you in the hope that one day, you'll answer."

The nightly news broadcast broke for a commercial. An ad from a local dealer was pushing the Pontiac Grand Prix. Seeing the red arrow emblem briefly brought Ted back to testing Frankie in Nevada.

"Things are pretty much the same," he continued. "I'm working at the factory with my dad and brothers. The only good thing is I'm slowly saving money. Maybe by the end of the year I can finally think about making a change. I . . . I think of you often, Sam. I wish you would call me. At least let me know you got your pendant I sent to you."

"Teddy!" Barbara's voice boomed from the top of the stairs. "Dinner is almost ready!"

"Okay, Sam, I guess I should get going. I hope this message finds you and your daughter well. Take care."

He ended the call and turned off the television. Putting the cap back on the whisky bottle, he tucked it beside his bed against the paneled wall. The sound of his mother's footsteps seeped through the ceiling above his head. A small alcove in the corner of the bedroom, set back behind the bedroom door, contained a six-foot-wide writing desk. Ted pulled out the chair, the wheels snagging on the shag. Sitting down, he clicked on the chrome reading light nestled in the corner.

He picked up a copy of *Wired* magazine. There was an article he had been reading about the latest advancements in AI. The reporter had interviewed both Rusty and Vin. Stacks of cardboard filing boxes were crammed between the desk and wall, filled with old magazines and college papers. Ted knew one of them had the copy of the Vernor Vinge essay on AI replacing humans, as well as the research paper he did for college. He flung the magazine in the trash and stared at the hulking metal object resting in front of him.

"Will I ever get back to you?"

The spinning lidar unit from the Fisher Tuner workshop sat dismantled across Ted's desk, spread out in pieces. Next to it sat a yellow legal-sized notepad covered in formulas. He picked up the black ballpoint pen beside the pad, tapping it as he read through his notes. He stopped tapping and tried Nico's trick of spinning the pen across his thumb and fingers, but the pen just tumbled across his hand and into the wastebasket beside his chair. He frowned as he drummed his fingers across the main lidar housing.

"Why do I bother?" he said, as he flipped the reading lamp off and sighed. "This isn't my future anymore."

23

Rusty paused halfway down the steps that connected the Yerba Buena Public Square to Fourth Street. He arched his back and ran his hand along his spine, just above his waistline. A decade before, Rusty's hip injury had started to manifest itself in his lower back. The limited range of motion with his leg forced the muscles along his spine to adjust accordingly, resulting in pressure on two of his discs and the nerves beneath them. Remaining still for long periods exacerbated this problem. He'd just spent four days sitting for close to twelve hours each day, and he could feel every moment of it.

"Give me a minute, Vin." Rusty bent over and extended his arms and hands as far down as they would go. After a few seconds, he was finally able to touch his fingers to his shoes. He groaned as he felt his spine decompress. "I'm not getting any younger."

"Should I run ahead and find a boy scout to help you cross the road?" Vin laughed briefly at his joke until he noticed Rusty rubbing his hip. "Tell me, Rusty, will that pain ever go away?"

"No." Rusty continued to moan as he felt the tension leave his body. "I'll be fine, Vin."

"Always the tough guy. Not many people survive a fall from a helicopter. You should be thankful—"

"Stop, Vin." Rusty raised his voice as passersby shot curious glances toward him and Vin. "You know I don't like to discuss this. I never should have told you. Very few people know how I got this injury. Drop it, okay?"

"I didn't mean to dig up bad memories, my friend."

During his early twenties, while stationed at the military base in Yuma, Rusty and his team had gone out on a routine training mission. Their helicopter had run into heavy wind shear and a downdraft forced the pilot to lose control. Rusty had dove into the front seat and attempted to steady the chopper, but to no avail. He was thrown clear, falling from the helicopter shortly before it crashed into the mountains. He was the only survivor. Every time Rusty replayed the scene in his mind, he couldn't help but wonder if his actions to help his friend steady the chopper contributed to the crash. Was he to blame?

"I'm sorry I snapped at you," Rusty said as he struggled to clear his mind of those painful memories. "It's been a long conference."

He stood back up and rotated his upper body back and forth a few times. When done, the pair continued their way down the staircase. Vin attempted to give Rusty some support by holding his elbow, but Rusty shook it off.

The over eighty acres of the Yerba Buena Public Square was part of the Moscone Center in San Francisco, a popular site for large-scale conventions. The three main buildings contained over 700,000 square feet of exhibit space and over one hundred meeting rooms. Given San Francisco's huge volume of hotels, combined with the massive exhibit and public spaces the Moscone Center could handle, conferences with tens of thousands of attendees were not uncommon.

The International Global Robotics Association (IGRA) had selected the Moscone Center as the site for its 2008 conference. This year's event had pulled in more than 27,000 attendees from over forty countries. Rusty and Vin had reached the last day of the conference, Friday, September 19. Many attendees had not bothered to show up for the last presentations. The closing celebration had been held the night before at Treasure Island and was massive. IGRA had pulled out all the stops and created a circus-themed event to thank the attendees.

Elton John wowed the crowd with a forty-five-minute concert as the closing event. GSI, a platinum sponsor, had footed the bill for that elaborate show.

The last day's conference schedule was only a half day. Rusty and Vin were asked to repeat their presentation on autonomy from earlier in the week, as it had proven so popular. They ended up presenting to a crowd of over five hundred engineers and scientists.

"What impressed you the most at this year's conference, Rusty?"

"Artificial intelligence. The advancements in AI were, well, unexpected. We touched on it during our presentation, but a few other players out there are truly breaking boundaries."

"Agreed," Vin said, nodding in approval. "AI's capabilities are outpacing all original projections. We should get on one of those councils that are exploring its future—or perhaps form our own."

"I was thinking the same thing, Vin."

"The expected loss of jobs due to AI is truly shocking."

"The economy is shedding jobs at unheard of volumes, and yet AI is poised to obliterate even more."

"I'm afraid we won't recognize this world a few decades from now," Vin said. "It makes me wonder if the human race is even ready for the change."

"During the DARPA project, my team used to joke about the day robots would replace humans."

"I think we're a long way off from that, Rusty. Although I certainly won't dismiss the inevitability of that occurring." Vin gave Rusty a quick reassuring pat on the shoulder. "Looking back over these past few days, I think this was the best event yet."

"It was definitely the largest. I heard it was almost fifteen percent larger than last year. I'll take their word. You and I both missed last year's conference because of the FAST Challenge."

"Do you think the huge turnout is because of us—because of the buzz that came out of last year's DARPA competition?"

"Selfishly? Yes."

The two men laughed as they finally reached the bottom of the staircase. The sidewalk was packed with people leaving the conference. Cars and trucks honked as they crawled along in the stop-and-go traffic. The faint scent of garbage packed into overflowing trash bins filled the air.

"So much has changed since then," Vin said. "It's been exactly one year since we were in the Mojave."

"Progress waits for no one."

"Have you reconsidered my offer to stay for the weekend? I'd really love to give you a tour of our new lab at Ashton."

"I wish I could, Vin. I have too many commitments waiting for me back at DSU. This year's batch of new students is the worst yet. No structure. No commitment. I don't get today's youth."

"Did you ever?" Vin could not help but let out a hearty laugh. "Rusty, you do know you are a complete and total hardass? You run that place like a special-ops unit. I'm lucky I made it out in one piece. Your work ethics were brutal."

"And your work ethics today?"

Vin stopped as they reached the corner of Fourth and Howard streets. The temperature was a few degrees shy of seventy degrees. He closed his eyes and took in the warming rays of the sun. Eventually, a smile spread across his face.

"I'll take that as a compliment," Rusty said.

"I'm strict for sure. Structured. But in a gentler way. I'm sorry you can't stay. Sam was hoping to see you."

"Really? I didn't even know she liked me."

"She doesn't." Vin grinned and winked at his former mentor. "But she respects you and everything you've done. She wanted to show you how far she's taken Athena."

"Perhaps another time." Rusty was still wearing a lanyard with the conference pass dangling from the end. He slid it off and jammed it into the nearest trash bin. "I'm glad to hear Sam has continued to pursue what we achieved with DARPA."

"Have you heard from Ted?"

"No. All I know is he's working at a GM factory in Lordstown." Rusty shook his head in disappointment and let out a long sigh. "I don't understand that kid. He was wasting his life in Nevada, and now he's wasting it in Ohio."

"You can't fix everything, Rusty. Or everyone."

"Unfortunately."

"What you need is a wife." Vin squinted his eyes and crossed his arms. "It's amazed me that in all your travels across the globe, you've never found someone special. My wife, Sophie, is my rock."

"I prefer my rocks to be extracted from a volcano." Rusty winked at Vin in an attempt to avoid the lecture he could feel brewing. "Or the moon."

"As long as you're happy. You don't get lonely?"

"I have my work and my students. It's a full life." Rusty slapped Vin on the shoulder. "No need to worry about me."

"All right, my friend, I should head out. It was great to see you."

"And you."

The two men did a quick bear hug. Rusty gave Vin one final slap on the back before watching him cross the street and disappear into the crowd. Rusty then checked his watch—12:22 p.m. He decided to grab a coffee before catching a cab to the airport. He looked around and spotted a café farther up Fourth Street. He slowly made his way along, taking the time to twist and stretch his back along the way.

The line inside the café was over a dozen deep. Half of the people waiting to order were conference attendees, easily identified by the colorful lanyards wrapped around their necks. The tables were crammed with patrons. The air permeated with the smell of coffee, cinnamon, vanilla, and various fresh baked goods.

Speakers mounted on the wall behind the counter were broadcasting a popular noontime radio show called *Chris and Kris*. The married couple that ran the two-hour-long program would pick a different topic to debate each day. Their biting and sometimes caustic humor and real-life commentary always made for a lively and entertaining show. Rusty tilted his head away from the crowd so he could better hear the radio.

"Stop the discussion," Kris said. "It appears my wife forgot to pack our lunches. Again."

Several locals in the coffee shop began to laugh loudly. Rusty looked around somewhat confused and then returned his gaze to the line ahead of him. Despite the café having four employees working behind the counter, the line was not moving.

"What is this, the fifties?" Chris replied in a high-pitched shrill voice. "If we forgot our lunches, then *we* forgot them. Just because I still slice the crusts from your peanut butter sandwiches doesn't make me your mother. It makes you a child."

The man standing in front of Rusty burst out laughing. Rusty shook his head, not understanding the humor coming through the radio. He figured it had to be a local thing. Rusty took a few steps back as the man ahead of him shifted and bumped back against him.

"Oh, sorry," the young man said. "These two get me every time."

"If you say so," Rusty replied.

The man ahead of Rusty turned away and glanced back up at the speakers.

"Our listeners know what it means to not have food out here on Treasure Island," Kris said. "Nobody delivers our way. We entertain you daily, but will any of you bring us a coffee?"

"And a nice scone to go with it," Chris added. "Oh, or a deli sandwich? With sourdough, of course."

"Or a pizza?" Kris continued. "Oh, what I wouldn't give for a nice big pepperoni pizza right now."

"Your doctor, and our bathroom scale, would disagree with that last one," Chris added.

"They're right," the young man said as he turned back to face Rusty. "It's a huge waste of time. I'd know."

The man stood a few inches shorter than Rusty. His long wavy brown hair jutted wildly from an olive knit hat pulled down to his ears. He pointed to the black T-shirt he was wearing. Bright red words across the front proclaimed, UNCLE DANNY'S DEEP DISH.

"I can deliver ten, maybe a dozen pizzas here in town in the time it would take me to get across the Bay Bridge and back. And that's with no traffic. Traffic? Forget about it. It's just not worth it."

"I see." Rusty sighed and looked at his watch, and then again at the line ahead of the scraggly young pizza delivery man. "Is this place always this slow?"

"Not when these conference idiots aren't around." The pizza delivery guy pointed at two women dressed in business attire, sitting at a high-top table near the front door. "Look at them with their dumb badges hanging around their necks."

"Right."

"You know, last year they did a contest. The radio show. They wanted people to find creative ways to deliver them lunch from the San Francisco side. The first one there won a prize. People tried boats, bicycles, even a catapult."

"A catapult?"

"That one didn't turn out so well. I feel bad for them, being stuck out there. Their lunch options are, well, limited."

The young man shrugged and spun around. Rusty was relieved when the line finally shuffled a few steps ahead. He glanced up at the speakers to listen to the show.

"I'd give my right arm to get a slice of Danny's deep dish right about now," Kris said.

"Nobody wants that flabby arm of yours," Chris chimed in. "You may have to give more than a two-dollar tip to get someone out here."

"Isn't that the restaurant you work for?" Rusty tapped the young man ahead of him on the shoulder.

"It is," the man replied. "But my boss won't deliver there. Even though he loves the show."

"That makes no sense."

"Anyone he sends to deliver a pizza out to Treasure Island quits."

"Why?" Rusty was suddenly fascinated by this discussion. He wished Vin was still here.

"We work for tips. Traffic across the bridge can be a nightmare. I'm not going to risk getting stuck in traffic. That show would have to give me a fifty dollar tip to make it worth it. Even then, I'd probably pass."

"You'd give up fifty bucks? Why?"

"There's never a guarantee with a tip. Besides, who wants to sit in a car stuck in traffic for an hour or two to deliver a stupid pizza? Nobody I know."

"Nobody." Rusty smiled as the line inched ahead. "I see your point, kid. No human would want to do that. Would they?"

24

Ted eased his Camaro into his parent's driveway and coasted to a halt close to the main road. A car he had never seen, a new bright white Ford Fusion wearing Michigan plates, was parked directly in the middle of the double-wide driveway, blocking his way to the back of the house. Ted was exhausted after another long work week at the assembly plant. He worried his mother might have invited guests over for dinner. The thought of having to spend a Friday evening being social with strangers felt very depressing. All he wanted was to be alone.

"Great," he said aloud as he slammed his transmission into park. He killed the ignition and got out. "If this is another one of her surprise dinner parties, I'm outta here."

Halloween was two weeks away. Mrs. Wolff had a reputation in the neighborhood for getting a bit excessive when it came to seasonal decorations for the house. This year was no exception. The towering red maple tree in the front yard, barren of leaves, had a dozen ghosts and skeletons hanging from its branches. Fake spider webs, along with orange outdoor lights, were strung across the evergreen shrubs beneath the front windows. Plastic gourds of all shapes and colors were scattered across the porch steps, capped off with an expertly carved jack-o-lantern. The pumpkin's triangular eyes and jagged tooth smile greeted Ted as he made his way past, toward the back porch.

Ted's mother was alone in the kitchen when he walked inside. He looked around and cocked his head to try and hear voices coming from another room. All was silent, other than the clicking of an overly loud kitchen timer resting on the counter. The room was filled with the scent of garlic and butter-basted chicken simmering in the oven.

"Teddy!" Barbara wiped her hands along her apron, leaving streaks of herbs in their wake. Tonight's apron featured stenciled drawings of bread next to the words, come loaf with me. She walked over to the sink to rinse a large fork and spoon and asked, "How was work?"

"Whose car is in the driveway?" he asked.

"You have an old friend visiting." Barbara could not contain her excitement, her face radiating joy. "I so love surprises like these!"

"Who? Where?"

"Downstairs. Go see for yourself."

Ted looked at the sparkle in his mother's eyes. Whenever his mother had exciting news to tell, she would bristle with delight. She had that look about her now—more so than usual. Ted wondered who could be here that would make his mother so excited. He had been living at home for almost a year. During that time, he'd gotten much closer to his mom. He'd confided much to her, including the loss he felt when Sam had returned to California. His eyes widened at the thought of Sam waiting for him downstairs.

The basement door was open. He ran down the stairs, gripping the faded wooden railing for support. His feet pounded as they slammed against each tread, pausing at the bottom of the steps. He was suddenly overwhelmed with happiness, laced with worry. He couldn't recall the last time he felt this way. Then he remembered his excitement at seeing Sam at the Detroit airport. That's what he felt coming over him. His mind was immediately flooded with questions to ask her. He wondered why she'd stayed silent, and what brought her across the country to see him without warning.

The light in the laundry area was on, but the room was empty. There was also a dim light coming from the bedroom. Ted poked his head inside, but saw no one. Confused, he checked the darkened storage room, but, again, no one. He was about to head upstairs when he heard the office chair in the bedroom squeak.

He walked into the bedroom, farther this time, and turned to face the alcove recessed behind the door. He swung the door away to get a full view of the area. Someone wearing a baseball cap was sitting in his chair with their back to him, hunched over his desk. The small desk lamp lit the person from behind, masking their features. Ted flipped the wall switch for the overhead fluorescent lights. The chair squeaked loudly against its worn hinges as it spun around.

"Rusty?" Ted asked. He didn't even attempt to hide his disappointment at the sight of his old mentor. "What the hell are you doing here?"

"Nice to see you, too." Rusty pointed at the lidar array on the desk in front of him. "I see you've been busy."

Ted's shock and disappointment at not finding Sam waiting for him were almost immediately replaced by anger and resentment. Rusty was the last person he wanted to see. He was the polar opposite of Sam. After DARPA ended last year, Ted had traveled with the team cross-country back to DSU. The following week, Rusty had assembled everyone to tell them how DSU planned to use the prize money to upgrade the robotics lab. He also wanted Ted to stay on to assist with the expansion. Ted knew already he would pursue Detroit, despite Rusty's objections. The last words the two had exchanged were far from complimentary.

"I work on it when I have time." An unlaundered shirt lay draped over the back of the desk chair, pinned against Rusty's back. Ted turned off the desk lamp, yanked the shirt free, and tossed it over the lidar. "So, why are you here?"

"What's with the tone, Ted? Are you still angry? It's been a year." Rusty held up a bottle wrapped in a brown paper bag. "I come bearing gifts."

"I wasn't expecting to see you again. Ever." He folded his arms and leaned against the edge of the alcove. Rusty seemed uncharacteristically calm. "How did you even find me?"

"I have my connections." Rusty stood up, emitting a mild groan as he stretched his lower back. He glanced around the bedroom and shook his head. "You've been gone a year, Ted. Why are you still living in your parent's basement? I thought you hated them."

"I never said that. We just . . . just wanted different things for me. Look, I had no idea what to expect when I moved back here. The first few months working at the plant were miserable. One of the first things I did was start looking for apartments. But then I realized I could save a lot of money living here."

"For?"

"For?" Ted immediately felt like he was back at DSU again, on the defensive.

"What's your future, Ted?" Rusty held out his arms, motioning toward the small TV across the room and the unmade bed tucked in the corner. "All of this?"

"I just told you, I'm saving up. I plan to move out by the end of the year."

"And do what?" Rusty did not wait for a reply. "Spend the rest of your life working for GM? In a factory? Look me in the eye and tell me you're happy."

Ted glared into Rusty's dull, lifeless eyes. He'd never noticed how much their color resembled the hazy gray of naval ships. The staring contest lasted less than ten seconds before Ted lowered his head and focused on his feet.

"It's a job," he finally said, his enthusiasm non-existent.

"But are you happy?"

"How can I be? With the bankruptcy and constant shakeups, closings, layoffs—it's all a big crapshoot. If I left GM, where would I go? The economy is faltering, jobs are drying up. There's nothing else out there for me. This . . . this is all I have."

"All you have? What happened to the cocky guy who almost dismantled a Segway to show me how to tame the beast that would become Cyclops?" Rusty yanked the shirt off the lidar system. "This, Ted, this is your future. Why are you throwing it away?"

"Why?" Ted felt his blood pressure rise. He wasn't sure if his anger was just at seeing Rusty or if it was his invasive line of questioning. "Because I failed, okay? I tried. Sam and I tried to win Detroit over. It was a disaster. Happy?"

"Happy? No. And I know all the details from Detroit."

"You do?"

"I told you, I have my connections." Rusty set onto the desk the brown paper bag he'd been holding. He walked over to the bed and sat on the edge, patting the space next to him.

Ted stared at the lidar sensor, as a flood of memories of Sam arose. Her at DARPA, baseball cap and green sparking eyes, the calls they'd shared putting together their presentation for Detroit, the wretched meetings, and that awful last morning in the hotel. He had thought the Detroit execs would be wowed by the spinning lidar, his secret weapon for the advancement of autonomous vehicles. In the end, of course, the execs completely dismissed his ideas and their data and projections. A wave of hurt filled his chest. He just wanted to hear Sam's voice. See her. Touch her.

He shook off the thoughts and turned his attention back to Rusty. "Okay, I'm listening," he said as he slumped down on the bed where Rusty had patted.

"I was in San Francisco a couple of months ago at a convention. Vin was there, too. He says hello, by the way. Long story short, there was this radio show based on Treasure Island. They complained that nobody would deliver to them because of how far their studio is from downtown San Francisco. I called them up and told them I could do it with a robot car. They had me live on the air. I told them the future was robots, AI, and self-driving cars. I got loud and preachy."

"Not you," Ted said with a smirk.

"I was fresh out of the robotics seminar and pumped on everything I had experienced. I went on and on about how artificial intelligence would result in huge innovations and life-changing approaches. I mentioned that in the future food delivery would not be dependent upon whether a delivery person felt like waiting in traffic or not. They accepted my challenge."

"Do you really believe that?"

"What? About pizza delivery being replaced by robots?"

"I mean, in general. About AI." Ted paused, and with a wry grin said, "Rise of the machines?"

"I do, Ted. I was skeptical before, but the sessions I attended at IGRA in San Francisco really opened my eyes. It's not a question of if but when AI truly explodes across the world."

"Wow." Ted glanced over at the boxes stacked beside his desk. His mind drifted back to his college paper on artificial intelligence. "Maybe Vinge was right. So, this pizza challenge thing. Is there a prize?"

"A prize?" Rusty shifted sideways so that he could face Ted directly, the inner-spring mattress squeaking in protest. "Have you not learned anything these past few years? That was your attitude when I rescued you from that shit job in Nixon working for Kyle Fisher."

"Shit job? You didn't rescue me. Leaving Fisher Tuner was *my* decision. I was a fool to believe in you."

"And if I hadn't shown up at Fisher Tuner, where would you be today?"

Ted looked around the damp drafty bedroom. Even with the harsh overhead fluorescent, the dark walnut paneling sucked the light from the room. He'd asked himself the same question, wondering if he'd still be living in Wadsworth, or perhaps running the shop, or having a more senior position working for Kyle. In the end, it was all a guessing game. He couldn't change the past.

"While I was on the radio call, I mentioned a local pizza shop by name," Rusty continued. "There was this slacker of a delivery guy who had given me the idea to call the radio station with my challenge. The owner of the restaurant called in and said if I could pull it off, I'd get free pizza for life."

"Free pizza?" Ted started to laugh. "You're doing this for pizza? From San Francisco? I hate to break it to you, Rusty, but the pizza's going to be cold by the time they ship it to Pittsburgh."

"I offered to do it to make a point, Ted. To prove the technology worked. I could care less about winning the free pizza. This is about the challenge. That, and the one million bucks."

"What?" Ted was suddenly fixated on Rusty, studying every line on his face. "You're serious."

"Just as I was about to end the call, the guy, Chris, tells me they just had someone call in to sweeten the deal."

"Guy, Chris?"

"The radio show is hosted by this annoying couple. Anyway, some mystery caller said, and I'm paraphrasing here, but something like, 'If that's the same Rusty Abrams from DSU that won the DARPA FAST Challenge, I want to see that technology work in the real world.' Then she offers the million dollars."

"Who do you think it is? You must have recognized her voice."

"I didn't. It was a very brief on-air call. But I later confirmed with the radio station that the offer is legit and the person asked to stay anonymous."

"Holy shit." Ted looked around his room again. The space suddenly felt confining. "What, um, what will you do with the million if you win?"

"It goes to the school, of course. I've spent the last few weeks coming up with a plan of attack. Which brings me to you."

"Me?"

"You need this, Ted. You don't belong here. Deep down, you know it."

"I have a life now. A steady income."

"But are you happy? Is this the life you dreamed of?"

Ted stood and walked over to the alcove behind the bedroom door. He turned on the desk lamp, casting a shadow across his dream project. He ran his hand across the cool, polished black metal surface of the spinning lidar unit.

"I've almost got this working," he said softly. "I'm so close. But—"

"But what?"

"Why should I follow you again? I gave up my life once to do the FAST Challenge and look where it got me." He gestured around his room.

"Don't blame me for your poor choices, Ted."

"There he is." Ted sat on the edge of the desk, folded his arms, and glared across the room at Rusty. "There's the prick that smashed our equipment in the dead of winter along the banks of the Allegheny River."

"Don't lecture me about my methods. They get results. I doubt we would have won the challenge had I not pushed everyone beyond their limits." Rusty struggled to pull himself up from the mattress. He groaned as he stood up and limped across the room, stopping a foot from Ted. He softened his baritone voice when he spoke again. "Look, Ted, I'm here to give you a second chance."

Ted studied Rusty's weathered face. Aside from looking a bit older, there was something else different about his old mentor's demeanor. He seemed less threatening to Ted. Was it that he was just tired? Had Ted simply moved on with his life, and now Rusty's opinion didn't matter? He also noticed something in Rusty's eyes he'd never seen before—desperation.

"Bullshit. You're here because you need me to win. Just like last time."

"Excuse me?"

"Yes. That's it, isn't it?" He stepped forward, as Rusty took a couple of steps backward. "When you came to see me in Nevada, it was my magnetic suspension system that caught your eye. Now you want my spinning lidar. You need me, Rusty. Admit it."

"Now who's talking bullshit? Look, Ted, I can do this with or without you. This is your decision to make. You can stay here in this shithole or come to California with me to win this challenge."

Ted kept his gaze directly on Rusty's dull gray eyes. A sense of confidence wrapped itself around him despite Rusty remaining stone-faced and unflinching. He knew Rusty would never admit he was right.

But he didn't need him to. Ted backed away from Rusty and leaned back on the edge of his desk.

"So, if I agree to do this with you, Rusty, what's in it for me?"

"And there *you* are. The selfish, greedy prick hungry for money." Rusty joined Ted at his desk and sat beside him. "I'll make this easy for you. Come with me and help me win this thing. If we do, I'll give you fifty thousand. That will tide you over until you can get a real job."

"Make it a hundred," Ted said with a broad smile.

"If I say yes, does that mean you're on board? Or are you going to get greedy?"

Ted stood up and started pacing back and forth, scuffing his shoes across the worn shag carpeting. His eyes went from Rusty to his spinning lidar unit as he considered what this would mean. A calendar tacked above his computer monitor briefly brought him back to his days in the watch tower, with the endless project plans plastered to the walls.

"You mentioned you spent a few weeks working on this already," Ted said. "Did you commit to a date?"

"We have until the end of February."

"That's only four months. How will you get Cyclops prepped by then? We had almost two years for the DARPA Challenge."

"This isn't DARPA, Ted." Rusty approached him and gently took him by his shoulders, stopping him from pacing. "This is a very short five-mile preset course, from Uncle Dipshit's pizza parlor to Treasure Island. Half of that is on the Bay Bridge. There is no mystery challenge awaiting us. We can easily map this out ahead of time. We just need to do some practice runs and get clearance."

"Clearance?"

"I've already begun that process and have been assured by city officials that we'll have it in plenty of time, provided we can prove there's no real liability to them. That will be easy to do with some documentation of what we did with Cyclops and laying out specifics of what we'll do when. And, the radio show plans to make this into a big event."

"I see." He pulled away from Rusty and walked over to his desk. His spinning lidar unit was almost half the size of the rotating one they'd mounted atop the Humvee last year. He flipped open his notepad and scanned through the formulas scattered across the pages. "How are you going to get Cyclops out to the West Coast? Have you started lining up sponsors? Are you getting the entire team back together?"

"We won't be using Cyclops. We're going to use Athena."

"Athena?" Ted's concentration was shattered. "As in Ashton's Prius?"

"I called Vin as soon as I hung up from talking to the radio show. He's on the fence about doing this. He doesn't like the idea of running Athena on public streets. But I have him ninety percent convinced. As far as I'm concerned, it's a done deal."

"Does that mean Sam would be working on it, too?"

"I assume so. She runs the entire Athena project now. Why?"

"Does Vin know you are trying to bring me on board?"

"Look, Ted, I know about your history with Sam. You are both going to put on your grown-up pants and get over it. The stakes are too high."

"Does Vin know I'm coming?" Ted's excitement of working on the pizza delivery challenge was replaced by a mix of fear and joy over possibly working with Sam again. "Does Sam?"

"Why?"

"She hasn't spoken to me or responded to any of my calls since she left Detroit last year."

"Did you rip her a new asshole the way you laid into me when you left DSU?" Rusty's temples were throbbing, and the volume of his voice had risen. "It may surprise you to hear that neither me nor Vin give a rat's ass about your relationship with Sam. In fact, it never even came up during the discussions Vin and I had when we were talking through using Athena. You two will need to be strictly professional. We have to work as a team to get this done. Am I clear?"

"Crystal. I have no problem seeing her again."

"I will tell Vin you're on board. He can relay it to Sam however he sees fit. That, of course, assumes you're joining me. Are you? I'm not asking again."

"I am." Ted surprised himself at his quick response. He breathed out long and slow, glanced again at the lidar, and shoved his hands into his pockets. He felt his entire body relax. He fumbled around in his right pocket to retrieve his GM ID badge and tossed it onto the desk. "My future lies elsewhere, Rusty. It always has."

Rusty grabbed the crinkled paper bag he'd brought with him and handed it to Ted. Reaching in and pulling it out, Ted smiled at the sight of the Chivas Regal whisky.

"You know me so well, Rusty."

"I know you better than you know yourself, Ted. We'll win this thing. And this time, I guarantee you we *will* change the world."

25

Sam stared blankly at her reflection in the bathroom mirror. Her cheeks were pale, despite the extra rouge she was wearing. Strands of blond hair dangled from the silver tiara perched atop her head. She sighed as she frantically tried to tuck the strays back into her bun. As head of this year's Halloween committee at Ashton's robotics building, Sam had gone all out on her Cinderella costume. Her gown was silver, as in the original release of the movie, not the bright blue used in the marketing of the toys. It had taken her months to find the perfect replica. Her daughter Dani would wear an Ariel outfit when they both went out trick-or-treating that evening. Dressing up at work had seemed like such a good idea—before she had known Ted and Rusty had moved up their planned visit for next week and would arrive any minute. Vin had opted to drop that bomb on her only an hour before they were due to arrive.

Relatively small at just over 200 acres, Ashton's campus was carved into the hillsides of San Carlos, California, not far from Redwood City. Founded in 1925 by Charles Ashton and his wife Jean, it was much younger than its storied and prestigious sister institutions. Its engineering and mathematical sciences programs ranked among the top, not only in the United States but in the world, contributing to Ashton's excellent reputation.

Sam emerged from the bathroom adjacent to Ashton's main

robotics lab to find her lab partner and good friend Ralph Lorenski patiently waiting for her. Ralph was decked out as the Joker from the hit film, *The Dark Knight.* Like Sam, Ralph was wearing an authentic costume. Luckily for him, the local costume shop had had a perfect Joker outfit. The purple and white flecked shirt covered in hexagons was matched with a forest-green vest and coordinating checkered tie. Bright purple pants completed the look. Ralph had spent an hour trying to get his makeup just right. The final result was fairly accurate to the movie, despite Ralph being quite a bit shorter and wider than the movie character.

"Why so serious?" Ralph asked her, his grin made all the more exaggerated by his makeup.

"You know why," she replied, not bothering to acknowledge his attempt at humor.

The main hallway was surprisingly busy for ten in the morning. Most people were dressed in costumes, laughing and chatting loudly as they walked by. Ralph maneuvered Sam off to a quiet corner away from the noise.

"You knew he was coming, Sam."

"The original plan was next week. I wouldn't have put on a costume had I known he was coming today." She clutched the sides of her silver gown and rippled the chiffon back and forth in frustration. "I look ridiculous."

She felt her eyes begin to well up. She glanced at the stout clown trying to console her, and then looked away, forcing herself to focus on the parade of people marching past them.

"Nonsense." He took her chin in his purple gloved hand and tilted her face until she looked him in the eye. "You look beautiful, Sam. Trust me, I know pretty when I see it. Ted is going to take one look at you and melt."

She managed a brief smile. As authentic as Ralph's clothing was, his green and white wig ended up being ill-fitting and too small for his bulbous head. Strands of the fake hair dangled across half of Ralph's face. Sam brushed them away.

"That's the problem, Ralph. You know how I left things with Ted. You and my mother are the only two I've told."

"Given your past, Sam, it's completely understandable why you didn't feel ready. I know you've worried that you ran away from something special, but more importantly, you ran home to your daughter. She's your world. You're right to put yourself and your daughter first."

"I never gave Ted an explanation."

"Well, now's your chance to give him one, if that's what you think needs to happen."

"I suppose."

"Or not. Look, Sam, this pizza challenge is a fantastic opportunity. Not just for the half million the school will get. Think of the publicity! Athena will make history. If you don't know how to deal with Ted, then just tell him you want to keep things professional. Limit your interaction with him. We both know you're good at shutting people out when you need to."

"Was that supposed to be a compliment? Or are you saying I'm . . . I'm a clam?" She looked down at her gloved hands and furrowed her brow. "Or is it a turtle?"

"A bit of both." He tossed his head back and laughed. "I just meant you're very good at taking care of you. And doing what's best for Dani."

"True." She wiped her moist eyes and took a deep breath. "I guess I can focus just on the challenge. And make this all about the work."

"It's important we accomplish this, Sam. Did you forget we'll also get free pizza for life?" He patted his protruding stomach. "And not just any pizza. Uncle Danny's Deep Dish!"

Sam laughed and draped one arm around his shoulder as they walked. The hallway had quieted down, and the pair turned and made their way past the laboratory entrance where they kept Athena. A few doors later, they found themselves at Vin's office. His door was wide open. Sam stopped abruptly as soon as she heard the voices coming from inside. Each voice was distinct. Vin's faint Indian accent was overshadowed by Rusty's brassy boom. In between the chatter, she could hear Ted's nasally tone. Without realizing it, she instinctively reached up to touch the heart on the gold chain that lay beneath the black choker of her Cinderella costume.

"Are you coming in?" she asked Ralph. "I'm not sure what to say to Ted."

"Allow me to break the ice."

Ralph stepped in front of Sam and burst through the doorway. Vin's office was quite large, room enough for a circular conference table with four chairs. Ted and Rusty were sitting with their backs to the entrance. Vin was on the opposite side of the table. Before Vin could say a word, Ralph threw himself onto the tabletop directly between Ted and Rusty and spun around so that he landed facing them.

"Gentlemen!" Ralph proclaimed as he pointed at his mouth. "Can I tell you how I got these scars?"

"Shit!" Ted leaped from his chair, sending it rolling backward.

Rusty momentarily jumped, but after inspecting the costume, gave Ralph a nod and a smile of approval. Vin chuckled, while at the same time shaking his head in disapproval. Ted turned around to retrieve his chair, just as Sam entered the room.

"Wow," Ted said, looking stunned. "Sam?"

"That's Cinderella to you," Ralph said, sliding off the table. "Sorry to startle you like that, Ted."

Ted looked back and forth between Sam and Ralph, completely confused by what he was seeing.

"Ralph?" Ted asked as he leaned forward and inspected Ralph's makeup. "Is that you?"

"What?" Ralph responded. "This is how I normally look when I'm not in the desert."

"Okay, Ralph, that's enough." Vin stood up and pointed at the door. "Go find someone else to scare."

Ralph took a theatrical bow. As he did, his wig started to slide off.

He quickly caught it and chuckled as he tried to reattach it to his head. Sam stepped aside as he walked past her.

"My lady," Ralph said, gently kissing Sam's silver-gloved hand.

She watched him leave before turning to face the three men in the room. Ted was, unfortunately, closest to her. She cleared her throat and walked over to greet him.

"Ted," she said, her voice slightly hoarse. She coughed again. "It's been a long time."

"Too long." Ted blushed as he looked her up and down. "You look, um, amazing."

"Halloween." She managed a nervous laugh as she ran her hands across her grown, attempting to smooth out the wrinkles. She glanced over at Vin and scowled. "Had I known you were coming today, I would have dressed appropriately."

"That's my fault," Rusty said. "We were originally coming next week. But we have some big shot donors arriving at DSU on Monday, so I had to make some last-minute changes to our plans. I wrote Vin an email giving him a heads up, but he never got it. It turns out I forgot to send the damn thing."

"Nice to see you again, Rusty." Sam stepped closer and shook Rusty's hand. "It's been a while."

"Indeed, it has." Rusty stood up, grabbed his mug of coffee from the table, and took a long sip. "I hear you've made some amazing progress with Athena. We're looking forward to seeing your lab."

"Then let's start the tour," she said.

She turned and quickly left the office, ignoring Ted as she walked by him. Her gown was long, requiring her to lift the front edge slightly as she walked. The costume had come with white heeled shoes covered in reflective fabric but Sam found them incredibly uncomfortable. She opted, instead, for her most supportive pair of white sneakers. Once at the lab entrance, Sam took off a glove to place her hand on the biometric sensor beside the door, illuminating a red strip of light just above her fingers. After a few moments, the light changed from red to green, and a buzzer rang out. She swung the door open and motioned everyone inside as she pulled the glove back on.

Ashton's robotics lab was nothing like the one at DSU. The space was half the size of the vast workshop in Pittsburgh. What it lacked in size, it made up for in technology. Stepping into the lab felt like entering a sterile room. The walls, floor, and low hanging ceiling were white. Rows of cool white LED lights hung from above. One entire wall was dedicated to banks of computer servers. The opposite wall had a dozen workstations, each occupied by a student.

Sitting in the middle of the room was Athena. The Prius looked different from when it had competed in the Mojave Desert over a year ago, with a completely new sensor array bolted to the roof. The rear hatch was open, and a dozen black cables spilled onto the floor. Some of the cables connected to plugs in the ground. Others ran from the back of the vehicle to a standalone workstation several feet away. The small white desk had a single monitor and keyboard, with very little else covering it. Once everyone was inside, Sam led them to the Toyota and took a seat at the terminal.

"Athena has a new lidar configuration up top." She paused to log into the system. "We were inspired by your rotating setup on Cyclops. Ours works differently. We took the concept of our digital gimbal and expanded its integration with the revised lidar. With six arrays installed, we get a full 360-degree view with twice the detail we had a year ago."

"What's with the cameras?" Ted asked, pointing to the optical gear mounted to the roof. "That seems kind of low-tech."

"That's our latest project," Vin said.

"We use the cameras to provide a visual map of the streets." She used her mouse to open a folder on her screen. "So far, we've only done the campus."

"A visual map?" Ted stepped closer and stood directly behind her. "I don't understand."

"We call it EyeSpy. We visually record everything around Athena as we drive her around." Sam typed in a few commands, and the map on the screen zoomed in to an overhead view of the parking lot. The map was a rudimentary representation, with the roads depicted in gray and everything else in green. "We think that long term, there's a lot of potential with this technology."

She double-clicked her cursor on the street beside the robotics building. After a brief pause, the image changed to a static picture of the side of the building, including the parking lot filled with cars. Sam pressed the arrow keys on her keyboard. The screen began to pan, showing the road ahead, then the opposite side. Back and forth, it twirled. Ted and Rusty looked on in quiet astonishment. She tapped the enter key a few times, and the screen blurred as the image jumped ahead a dozen feet. She rotated the image to show them, now looking back toward where they used to be.

"You did this for the entire campus?" Ted asked.

"Most of it. It's all a bit tedious to do right now."

"Can we take Athena out so you can show us?"

"Not right now." She cleared her screen and launched another program. "She's still dreaming."

"Dreaming?" Ted squatted beside Sam so he could get a better look at the screen. "What are you talking about?"

"We drive Athena around during the day. She takes in a lot of information. I don't mean just the visual images we use for EyeSpy. We collect all the lidar and radar data, too. At night we plug her in and run this system we built—Data Recall and Mapping." Sam pointed at the top of the screen. The application banner read "DReaM" across the top. "It can take up to twelve or more hours for the computers to process the data. When finished, our self-driving and mapping software are updated based on the latest information. Right now, we're limited by the hardware we have."

She tried to keep her eyes focused on the screen, but she was acutely aware of how close Ted was to her, his chin only a few inches from her shoulder. She could smell his familiar, sweet musky scent. She briefly allowed herself to glance his way, all while keeping her head facing the screen. Ted's chin and jawline were covered in stubble. She wondered in the back of her mind when he had arrived and where he was staying.

"This is all very impressive," Rusty said. "Can we use any of it for the pizza challenge?"

"I'm . . . I'm not sure," she replied.

"Should I first ask if we're even doing the challenge?" Rusty became impatient, his tone one of frustration. "Forgive me, Sam, but Vin told me you were having doubts. He won't commit without your approval. Ted and I came a long way to hammer this out. What questions do you have? What can we do to get you to sign on with us?"

She suddenly felt everyone staring at her, including Ted. She turned to face Rusty, rolling her chair sideways, leaving Ted crouched behind her. Vin was staring at her, a look of concern on his face.

"We haven't taken Athena outside the university grounds yet. The campus streets are simple compared to the congestion of downtown San Francisco. I'm not sure we can use our new systems out there."

"Put that aside, Sam," Vin said, his voice calm and reassuring as always. "Those are easy issues to solve. You told me you wanted to know more about how the partnership with DSU would work. Ask away."

She stood up, clutched the lower part of her gown, and strode over to be near Athena and away from everyone else. The computers in the rear hatch hummed and whirred, their cooling fans bringing Sam a bit of comfort. She spent so much time in the lab, it pretty much felt like a second home to her.

"Well, I have a few concerns," she said cautiously. "The city may not allow us to take Athena out on public roads."

"With the radio show's help, we're getting that covered," Rusty replied. "We will have to do the delivery very early in the morning and on a weekend when traffic would be the lightest. The city plans to close off the roads to other traffic. Athena won't have to contend with other vehicles. Next?"

"How will we split the work?" Sam asked. Rusty's dismissive tone was beginning to annoy her. "What will DSU be doing versus Ashton?"

“That will be your call.” Rusty let out a long sigh. “Look, Sam, Athena is your baby, okay? But this was my contest to enter. You will be the lead on this. DSU resources are completely at your disposal.”

“Will . . . will I have to fly to Pittsburgh? Because I don’t like flying.”

“Not at all,” Vin said. “This won’t be like DARPA, Sam. Zero travel commitments.”

“What about my other projects?” She suddenly became very excited, thinking she figured out a way to avoid working with DSU. “Vin, my plate is already full. I can’t commit to something like this. Maybe we can get Ralph to be the lead?”

“That’s why you have Ted,” Rusty said.

“Excuse me?” she asked, her smile fading.

“Ted will be representing DSU,” Rusty continued. “He will be here full-time, completely dedicated to making this work. My people back east are just as busy as you, Sam. But they will make themselves available as needed. Ted? Ted’s got nothing else to do.”

“Thanks,” Ted said flatly. He was now sitting in the chair next to Sam’s monitor. “As far as I’m concerned, you’re the lead, Sam. We’ll do everything your way.”

“My way?” She surprised herself by laughing out loud. “As in slow and steady? You?”

“What’s that supposed to mean?” Ted stood up and folded his arms defensively.

Vin shook his head and clapped his hands together three times. Sam knew this was Vin indicating he’d reached his limit. He was a man of few words and fewer emotions.

“Everyone back to my office,” Vin said calmly. “Now.”

Vin turned and walked to the main exit. He did not bother to hold the door open and instead headed down the hallway to his office. He stood at the open doorway, his arm pointing inside. Sam entered first, followed by Ted. Vin thrust his arm in front of Rusty to prevent him from stepping inside.

"You two need to settle this," Vin said before slamming the door shut, leaving him and Rusty in the hallway.

Sam and Ted stood alone inside Vin's office. She glanced at Ted, trying her best to ignore the piercing stare from his deep blue eyes. She looked around, debating what to say. She wasn't sure if she should sit or stand, finally deciding to take a seat at the small circular conference table. Ted immediately sat next to her.

"We can't do this without you," he said. "Rusty's right. Athena is your baby."

She clasped her hands in her lap and stared at her silver gloves. She thought again how ridiculous she must look. There was no way she could have a serious conversation with Ted dressed like this. She struggled to yank her gloves off, tossing them on the table, then flung her tiara on top of the gloves and removed her black choker.

"I honestly don't know what to say, Ted."

"Let's start with the project. You mentioned some of your concerns in the lab. What else? Are you genuinely concerned about running Athena on public roads?"

"Yes. Well, no. Not yet. We always planned to take her out into San Carlos to start city-level mapping. That's been on our project plan for quite some time, but it's not scheduled to start until January."

"Still the planner. Aren't you?"

"Of course."

She smiled and looked into his eyes, this time forcing herself not to turn away. She thought he looked the same as he did a year ago, other than the stubble covering his jawline. She had so much she wanted to say to him, but didn't know where to begin.

"It would be nice to work together again, Sam. I thought we made a good team in Detroit."

"We did. It just didn't . . . didn't turn out as we'd hoped."

"Look, Sam, I'm here to work. If you don't want to talk about the past, we don't have to. This pizza challenge will be a public showing of what self-driving cars can do. This won't be us using dozens of slides to try and explain things to a bunch of auto execs. The radio show plans to have the local television stations broadcast this. We are bound to attract attention. Remember, there's that mystery donor, too."

"Right?" She perked up. "What's that about?"

"No clue." He rolled his chair closer to her. "I just know this is our chance to make a splash. With the world watching. I . . . I brought the spinning lidar with me."

"What spinning lidar? The one you and Kevin were building? Out at the shop in Nevada?"

"I've worked on it over the past year and I think it's about ready, though I haven't tested it yet. Maybe we could try to integrate it into Athena and use it for the challenge?"

"I don't know, Ted. That might be too much change."

"Maybe not. The data stream the system produces isn't that different from most other lidar units. We could try."

"Four months isn't much time. The integration alone would be at least a month. Figure another two months for initial static testing."

Ted leaned back in his chair and laughed loudly. He then bent forward and rolled even closer to her, resting his hands on top of hers.

"My little tortoise," he said softly. "Slow and steady, until the end."

Sam felt her cheeks blush. She couldn't deny that she was still intensely attracted to him. She felt her stomach turn sitting so close to him, holding his hands. So familiar and . . . comfortable. Then the image of her leaving the hotel room in Detroit flashed in her mind. She slid her hands out from Ted's and pushed her chair back a few inches. Slowly, delicately, she ran a finger along the heart on the chain around her neck.

"I see you got the necklace," he said

"I'm . . . I'm sorry, Ted. I should have called."

"It's okay, Sam. I'm just glad you got it."

"Not about the necklace. I mean, yes, thank you for sending it. I was already at the airport when I realized I'd lost it. I was so happy when it arrived in the mail." She felt herself welling up with tears. She bit her lip and slid her chair forward, taking Ted's hands in hers. "I'm sorry for not calling. For disappearing."

"It's okay, Sam."

"No. No, it's not. I . . . I trusted someone once. Many years ago. He lived far away and made a bunch of promises." She squeezed her eyes shut in a failed attempt to stop her tears from falling. "He hurt me, okay? It was the kind of betrayal that leaves a scar."

"Did I do something similar in Detroit? Was it something I said?"

"No, you didn't. I just wasn't ready, Ted. It was so much easier just to shut you out and focus on my work and my family. You were so far away."

"Did my endless phone calls drive you crazy?" He grinned as he wiped the tears from her cheeks. "I thought I might have come across as a bit of a stalker."

"Just a tad." Sam started to chuckle. She held his hands and allowed her heart to open a bit as she looked into his eyes. "If I'm being honest, it was nice to hear your voice every week. I remember the week you stopped calling."

"I eventually gave up."

"I almost called to see if you were okay. But . . ." She shook her head in disappointment. "I'm sorry, Ted."

"Look, Sam. We have a chance now just to move forward. We can keep things professional, if you prefer that. I thought we had something special. You didn't. Or if you did, you weren't ready. Everything in life comes down to timing. You're talking to the guy that went from Nevada to DSU to a GM factory. I never could have predicted or planned for any of that to happen."

"It almost sounds like you're talking about fate." She grinned as she studied his eyes. "Are you getting all spiritual on me, Ted Wolff with two 'F's?"

"Me?" He laughed and shook his head. "All I'm saying, Sam, is that last November wasn't our time."

"Ted, I . . . I—"

"I'm not saying now is our time. In fact, I think it would probably be best to focus on the work, okay? This pizza thing could open doors. I'll admit, though, the thought of seeing you again and working with you again was exciting. Correction, it *is* exciting! But, if all we do is win a million dollars, and then go our separate ways, so be it."

She leaned back in her chair and closed her eyes, letting her thoughts drift back to the weeks spent working with Ted to prepare for their meetings with the auto companies in Michigan. She knew they worked well together. They pushed and challenged each other. She missed that feeling she had working with him. She missed Ted.

"Just one thing," she said. "This isn't just about the money, okay?"

"Of course. There's also the fame and publicity." He grinned and winked at her.

"Bigger than that. I was talking about the free pizza. Ralph is insisting we win."

They both laughed. Ted leaned forward and ran his fingers across her chin. "You . . . you look good, Sam. You haven't changed a bit."

"Other than being a princess," she replied mockingly as she ran her hands across her gown.

"Other than that." He sat back in his chair and smiled. "So, are we good? Are we doing this?"

Sam looked straight into Ted's blue eyes and wondered if she was ready for the challenge. This would be a four-month commitment. Was she ready for what might happen? Would they be able to keep their relationship professional? She thought back to the conversation she'd had with Ralph earlier. How long was she going to keep hiding in her shell?

"Yes." She exhaled, releasing what felt like a year's worth of tension. "But remember, I'm in charge."

"Of course. I'm *hare* to serve you."

She winced and shook her head, laughing loudly at his horrible attempt at humor.

"Still as dorky as ever, aren't you?"

"You tend to bring it out in me."

She gently pushed his hair back with her fingers. Then she stood up, collected the rest of her costume from the conference table, and walked over to the closed door and stopped.

"Let's take it day by day, okay?" She asked.

"You're the boss."

"I'm going to hold you to that."

She flung the door open to find Vin and Rusty standing mere inches away from the opening. Vin smiled broadly as he looked at Sam and Ted.

"So, we're good?" Vin asked.

"I'm in," Sam replied. "When do we start?"

26

The only sounds in Ashton's robotics lab on a Friday just past 8:00 p.m. were the hum and whir of the computers. Most of the students had left long ago. Some wanted to get Christmas shopping done. Others had parties to attend. Sam rubbed her red sore eyes as she stared at the screen in front of her. Row after row of computations scrolled by, most of it a blur. She checked a second monitor, displaying the project plan for what was needed to complete Athena's upgrades before they could start their test runs for the pizza challenge. They were on track, thanks to the insanely long hours everyone had been putting in. Ted's hand rested gently on her shoulder.

"Hey," Sam said. She turned around and glanced around the lab. "Is . . . is it just us?"

"Didn't you hear Ralph say goodbye?" he replied.

"When was that?"

"Like, an hour ago."

"Shit."

"How's our girl?" he asked, pointing to the Prius, parked in the middle of the lab. "Is she ready for bed?"

"I was just about to put her to sleep." She activated the system's DReaM mode, leaned back in her chair, and sighed. "Sweet dreams."

Ted spun Sam's chair around and took both of her hands. She

smiled and began to caress his knuckles with her thumbs. She flipped his hands over and dragged a finger across the scar near his thumb.

"Well?" He rolled his chair closer to hers until the chairs touched. "What are you thinking?"

"I'm thinking we're on track." She said, nodding toward the screen with the project plan. "We can do our first dry run across the Bay Bridge next week. That depends on—"

"I wasn't talking about the challenge."

"Oh, right. You mean, the, um, closet."

"Yes, Sam. An hour ago, we were making out like teenagers in high school."

She burst out laughing and shook her head. "I never did that in high school," she said.

"Me neither." He kissed her fingertips. "But it was nice."

"It . . . it was." She stood up and walked over to Athena. The rear door was open, and the backseat was covered in papers. She could feel Ted staring at her, still sitting in his chair. "I . . . I don't have any regrets, Ted."

"Me neither. I know we both said we'd keep this professional, but I can't help how I feel."

She spun around just as he stood up. Her heart raced as he approached her, stopping beside her. He wrapped his arms around her, and she tilted her head back and kissed him. The gentle pecks almost instantly turned more urgent. Sam felt Ted guiding her into the backseat. She grabbed him by his shoulders and pulled him inside the Prius.

"We're not doing it here," she said. "I'm not that kind of girl."

"I never said you were." He kissed her again. "But I certainly wouldn't judge you if you changed your mind."

She laughed and held him close. Her mind and heart argued as she looked into his deep blue eyes. Was she ready to take this chance again? To risk getting hurt? Deep down, she knew he was different. She knew she was the one who kept pushing him away. She was the one hiding. She wiggled away from him and sat upright.

"Ted, if we're going to go down this road again, then we have to both be on board." She began to fidget with the pendant around her neck. "I . . . I care about you too much to make this something casual."

"Sam, that's not me. I've told you that before."

"I know." She took his hand in hers. "I've . . . I've got a daughter, Ted. She's my world. For you to be a part of that world, at some point, you're going to need to meet her."

"Of course."

"And my mother."

"Sure, Sam." He put his arm around her and pulled her close. "Whenever you're ready."

She nodded and said, "I'm . . . I'm surprised it took us this long to reconnect."

"Hey, I've been doing my best to be a perfect gentleman and respect your wishes to keep it all business. These past several weeks haven't been easy for me."

"You showed great restraint, Mr. Wolff. That's why I pulled you into the utility closet to kiss you."

In their embrace, both laughed. She felt so at peace in his arms. The endless weeks of flirtations and quiet moments were finally behind them. They could be back together again.

"There's no rush to meet them," she said. "But, I've told you that my mom can be a bit, well, overprotective."

"I'll just have to turn on that Wolff charm of mine."

"Good luck with that."

"What? It worked on you?"

"Oh, Ted." She laughed as she brushed a lock of hair from his eyes. "I'm not my mother."

Like the rest of her mother's house, the dining room table was opulently decorated for Christmas. Sam hastily adjusted the centerpiece—a three-foot-wide red marble bowl filled with gold and silver glass ornaments. Two solid crystal candlesticks flanked the bowl, each with a towering evergreen candle. There were place settings for four, yet Sam's mother insisted the table be expanded to its full length. Sam thought it a bit ridiculous but knew this was her mother's way of showing Ted that this was her home and she was in charge.

She left the dining room and made her way into the kitchen. Dani was hard at work, frosting freshly baked sugar cookies. Her mother was basting an insanely large turkey, freshly pulled from one of the three ovens. The aroma of rosemary, thyme, and apple pie brought a smile to Sam's face. Christmas music played softly from the overhead speakers.

"Are you planning to make ten gallons of turkey soup with the leftovers?" Sam asked.

Catherine, despite her 5'8" stature and slim figure, always commanded any room, honed by decades of building and running her business. Even when preparing a holiday meal, she was the boss of the kitchen.

"Nonsense," Catherine replied. "I'm going to send half home with you and then freeze the rest."

"Half?" Sam laughed as she joined her daughter at the island filled with desserts. She kissed Dani on the head and dipped her finger into the bowl of frosting. "Everything smells great, Mom. You've outdone yourself as always."

"It's not every day I get to meet my daughter's new boyfriend." Catherine slid the turkey back into the oven and adjusted the timer. "I want to make a good impression."

Sam walked over to her mother and gave her a peck on the cheek and said, "Just behave yourself, okay?"

"You've gotten very serious with this man very quickly." Catherine gave her a piercing glance. Sam knew the look all too well and folded her arms defensively. Catherine turned her attention to the potatoes simmering on the stove. "You're my only daughter. My only child. There's nothing wrong with me wanting what's best for you."

"Wanting what's best doesn't mean you have to be—"

The doorbell chimes rang out, startling everyone. Sam felt a flutter of both nervousness and relief and left the kitchen, making her way toward the front door. As she entered the hallway, she suddenly had second thoughts about choosing Christmas Eve dinner as the time to introduce Ted to Dani and her mom. But, as always, her mother had had the final say. When Sam had told Catherine that Ted had spent Thanksgiving alone and had no plans to fly home to be with his family for the holidays, his fate was sealed.

Catherine's home in Fremont was immense and impeccably furnished. Two living rooms flanked the front foyer, both decked out with Christmas trees. The smaller room had a fire burning in the stacked-stone fireplace. Stockings for her, Dani, and her mom hung from the walnut mantle. Sam continued down the hallway, her nerves taking over. When she reached the front, she stopped and took a deep breath as she opened the door.

"Hey," Ted said. He held up a bottle of wine and handed it to Sam. "Merry Christmas."

"Hi." Sam said, kissing him and welcoming him inside. "Merry Christmas."

"When you told me your mom's place was big, I had no idea." He looked back and forth between the two living rooms and shook his head. "This is a palace," he said with a nervous smile.

"The riches of being the boss of your own company. Everyone's in the kitchen."

She led him down the hallway, surprised to find her palms sweaty as she gripped the wine bottle. Her mother could have followed her to the door to greet Ted, but she knew her mom would prefer that he come to her. Everything was a power play with Catherine. Sam stopped at the entrance to the kitchen and took his hand before stepping inside.

"Everyone?" she said. "This is Ted."

Dani, her fingers covered in frosting, looked up, smiled, and waved. Catherine was busy brushing rolls with butter and sage, her back to the doorway. She spent a few moments finishing up before sliding them into the oven. She slowly turned around and gave Ted a detailed inspection from top to bottom.

"Hi," he said. "Nice to meet you."

Catherine wiped her hands across her apron and walked over to them with her hand outstretched for a rather formal handshake. Sam passed the bottle of wine to her mother, saying, "Ted brought this."

Catherine glanced at the bottle and frowned. She said, "A merlot? We're having turkey. I prefer a crisp white wine myself. No worries, I have plenty of bottles in the wine cellar."

Sam groaned under her breath as her mother deposited his gift onto the counter, sliding it into a dark corner. She'd hoped her mother would start things off on a positive note, but it was obvious they had a long way to go. She looked up at him and tried to smile.

"Really?" he replied. "I only drink red. I guess the merlot's for me."

Catherine and Ted stared at one another for a long moment until Sam slid her arm around him and led him to the other side of the kitchen.

"This is Dani," she said. "Dani, this is my friend Ted I told you about."

"Hi!" Dani raised a cookie and passed it to him. "I made these."

"Hey, kid." He took a bite of the cookie. "Thanks."

"Don't spoil your appetite," Catherine said. "We've got a lot of food to eat."

Sam tugged on Ted's elbow, hoping to get him to back down from the power struggle she could feel brewing.

"It smells great," he said. "And your house is beautiful."

"I've worked hard to get where I am." Catherine smiled as she turned off one of the ovens. "My Sam's got greatness in her future, too. She's brilliant."

"That she is." He pulled her close and kissed the top of her head. "It's the first thing I noticed about her. Well, that, and those dazzling eyes."

"You met at that desert competition, didn't you?" Catherine asked. "DARPA?"

"We did. The tech she spearheaded was groundbreaking."

"As was Ted's," Sam interjected.

"Yes, well, wonderful that everyone is groundbreaking, isn't it?" Catherine said with a plastered smile on her face. She turned and went to the fridge, removing a bottle of chardonnay. "Why don't we all move to the dining room? We can start the first course."

Dinner went smoothly for the next two hours. The minute Ted starting raving about Catherine's French onion soup, the tension in the room vanished. He told stories of the desert racing vehicles he'd helped design at Fisher Tuner. Catherine told Ted how she took a thousand dollars and turned it into a billion-dollar cosmetics company.

Though she could sense the one-upmanships, Sam was somewhat relieved. By the time dessert was served, her mom seemed genuinely smitten with him, especially when he'd recounted their magical evening at Burning Man. As Catherine began pouring coffee, Sam realized she should never have doubted Ted and that "Wolff charm" he'd promised to bring.

"So, tell me, Ted, what happens if this pizza challenge fails?" Catherine asked.

"Oh, it won't," he replied. "Our testing's going great."

"Always plan for the worst. That's how I built my empire. I was always planning two to three moves ahead. Like chess."

"I'm more of a checkers kind of guy."

Sam sighed as she sliced herself a piece of cherry pie, sensing round two of the tension coming. She chimed in, "Ted's right, Mom. We'll figure this out. Aren't you the one always telling me that positive thoughts lead to positive results?"

"True, but–"

"To answer your question, Ms. Lavoie—"

"Catherine, please."

"To answer your question, Catherine, I haven't given not completing the delivery much thought. Even if something goes wrong, the national attention will open up opportunities. Someone will want our technology."

"Isn't that what the DARPA competition was supposed to do?" Catherine clasped her hands and leaned forward. "I thought your big trip to Detroit with my daughter was going to change the world?"

He winced. That was a low one but he recovered quickly enough. "This time will be different," he said.

"There are no guarantees in life." Catherine stood up and walked over to Dani, whose lips were smothered in bits of frosting. She put her arm around her granddaughter and kissed the top of her head. "You never know what God has planned for you."

Sam felt her cheeks get flush. Was her mother really using Dani as a pawn in this little mind game she was playing? She looked at Ted, worried his ego would only escalate the discussion.

"And that's what makes life so exciting," he said. "The unknown."

"It sounds like you're quite the risk taker," Catherine replied.

"I think that's a fair statement." He looked over at Sam and smiled. "But I think I'm doing a fair job of playing by the rules this time round. Sam's grounded me."

"We're a good team," Sam added.

"I'd never hurt your daughter." He looked directly at Catherine and she did not back down. "I care for her too much."

27

Fifty-year-old Matthew Grant, founder of GSI, had been born to mixed race parents in Detroit, Michigan. He was brought to an adoption agency by his mother when he was less than a year old. Fortunately for Matthew, however, it hadn't taken him long to get a new home. He was raised just outside Ann Arbor by a nurturing family with three other adopted siblings, all older than him. An early growth spurt had his parents believing he'd end up in sports, but his passion had always been math and science. Quite successful now, Matthew strongly believed that success came with a strong responsibility to give back, which he did generously both personally and through his company.

He stared at one of six fifty-inch screens mounted on the opposite wall from his desk in his office at GSI's headquarters in Redwood City, California. The screens were stacked in two rows of three, their bezels firmly locked together. Normally, these screens were used to monitor multiple news sources and stocks, as well as real-time analytics on internal projects and company performance. However, on this day, Saturday, February 28, the center top screen was showing the local ABC station, as the rest of the monitors were black.

"The day is finally here, Lisa." Matthew leaned back in his chestnut leather executive chair and stretched his arms above his head. "Thanks again for coming in today."

"Are you kidding?" Lisa Phillips replied. "I wouldn't miss this for the world."

Lisa Phillips, Matthew's assistant, was an ambitious and dedicated twenty-nine-year-old who served as Matthew's eyes and ears whenever he could not be present. Her energy and enthusiasm were the reasons he had hired her. Although she could have easily watched the historic broadcast from the comfort of her Redwood Oaks townhome, she couldn't imagine sharing this experience with anyone but her boss.

"I think this will be different than your time at DARPA," he said.

"You really should have come out with the team to the Mojave—especially that final challenge."

"That intense heat didn't interest me. Besides, I knew I could count on you to cover the details for me. Your final report was, shall we say, most illuminating."

"What do you think? Will the pizza make it successfully to the radio studio?"

"With Ashton and DSU working together? I'd be shocked if it didn't. This is the beginning, Lisa. The beginning of the world changing."

The commercial on the screen ended and a reporter from the local affiliate came on, standing in front of Uncle Danny's Deep Dish pizzeria. The chyron on the bottom of the screen read Self-Driving Pizza Delivery. Is it the future? The time showed 7:45 a.m. Matthew had muted the sound, so that they couldn't hear the interview with the restaurant owner.

The wall of windows in Matthew's office provided panoramic views of southern San Francisco Bay. He spun his chair and briefly gazed outside, noting the peace and tranquility of the ecological reserve across the water. Northern California's weather was something he cherished, never too hot nor too cold.

"Oh, man," he sighed. "Winters were so brutal in Ann Arbor. I didn't have the luxury of owning a car, so I had to rely on public transportation. I cannot stress the word 'rely,' or really the lack thereof, enough. I spent way too many afternoons waiting for bus twelve-eighty-five.

And those bus stops are not designed for sheltering folks from the bitter cold, the wind, or the snow." He closed his eyes for a moment to remember that cold. "That wind would cut through your skin as you waited for a bus for God knows how long. If it ever even showed at all. I knew there had to be a better way to move people around. I'm not sure if you can relate. You're from Miami, right?"

"I am. Not much snow down there." Lisa paused and looked out the window, her smile fading. "For us, it was hurricanes. The worst one? Andrew."

"That's right. Hurricanes. Blizzards. Humans have enough to deal with in their daily lives. Driving in unsafe conditions shouldn't be one of them."

"Or delivering pizza."

He smiled and nodded in agreement. Picking up the remote control resting on his desk, he aimed it at the bank of screens on the wall. The center monitor went blank temporarily before all six burst to life. The broadcast was now divided across the entire set of screens, creating a single giant television. He hit another button to unmute the sound. Speakers embedded in the ceiling filled the room with the reporter's voice.

"Imagine a world where public transportation was fully autonomous," Matthew said. "You'd eliminate so many issues."

"And jobs."

"But new jobs would be created. Buses could be replaced with on-demand transportation. You could order a vehicle from a fleet waiting to take you wherever you wanted to go. The elderly could easily get to medical appointments or to see family members, children going from one divorced parent to another could be shuttled back and forth without either parent having to drive, people could watch a movie or their favorite show on their way to work. Brilliant. Or if it's truly a self-driving bus, you could track it on your phone to see how far away it is. Maybe even see how many open seats there are. The possibilities are endless." Matthew pointed at the broadcast on the massive screen across from them. “We’re about to witness the beginning of a new dawn in transportation.”

Ted awkwardly smiled as he looked into the TV camera aimed directly at his face. He’d just finished answering a barrage of questions from three different news outlets. Finally, the last of the crews stepped back.

He spent the morning relishing the endless flood of questions. He hadn’t thought of himself as someone who craved the center of attention, but found he actually enjoyed it. All told, he had done half a dozen on-camera interviews, and over a dozen for print media.

“Are we done yet?” he called out to Sam.

She was a dozen yards away, crouched close to the ground next to the open door of Athena’s front passenger side, busy scrolling through the mapping program on the laptop resting on the front seat. Once she was comfortable with what she saw, she stood up and closed the door.

“We need to get moving. The city shut down this route at six this morning and we only have until ten to get this thing completed.”

The police had erected a barrier to keep onlookers, including news media, away from Athena. Ted, computer in hand, had gone back and forth, inside and outside the barrier, for the past hour to talk with the press. He respectfully nodded as he stepped past the two cops monitoring the opening between a set of metal A-frame barricades.

“It’s eight now. We have two hours left.” He walked over to Sam and met her at the front of the Prius, tucking the laptop in one arm sideways and placing the other hand reassuringly on her shoulder. “Can you put the laptop in the driver’s seat for me? I’m going to go see where we’re at with the pizza.”

As he handed the laptop to Sam, he turned around and saw Rusty emerge from the entrance of Uncle Danny’s, carrying a box of pizza. Reporters swarmed Rusty, with camera people jostling for the best position. Ted laughed as Rusty snubbed the media, using his broad shoulders to barrel past everyone.

“I think Rusty’s as done with the hoopla as we are,” he said.

Rusty paused briefly to share some kind words with the police before bringing the pizza over to Ted. Ted squinted, washed in a sea of flashing lights as Rusty handed him the pizza.

"I'm starting to wonder if a million bucks are worth all of this," Rusty said.

"Didn't you say you wanted the public to see a robot car in action?" Ted put his arm around Rusty and spun him to face the cameras. "Smile for the world."

Ted waved the pizza back and forth as he grinned, keeping a tight grip on Rusty's shoulder. Rusty sighed deeply and forced the slightest smile to sneak out from behind his handlebar mustache. In less than five seconds, he pulled himself away from Ted's embrace.

"Let's get this show started." Rusty turned around to see Sam now standing at the back of the Prius's open hatch. He gave her a brief wave. "Good luck!"

Ted couldn't help but chuckle as Rusty, engulfed by cameras, microphones, and reporters, tried to exit the narrow opening. He was ultimately forced to answer a few more questions. Ted carried the pizza over to Sam at the back of Athena. The scent of garlic, tomato, oregano, and cheese wafted up to him. He peeked in the box to get a view of the amazing Uncle Danny's pizza and shrugged. He didn't see what was so special. It looked like any other pizza to him.

"I'm going to get the system ready to go," Sam said, leaving him behind.

One of the many advancements Sam and her team had made with Athena was in the computing power and complexity needed to run the latest self-driving software. For the DARPA Challenge, Ashton had stuffed eight computers into the back hatch. This time, Athena needed only three computers, mounted in a special cage in the backseat. The cargo area had been converted to a special oven that Ted and Ralph had designed to keep the pizza warm for the trip across the Bay Bridge. Ted wanted not only to show that a self-driving car could make the trip, but that it could be custom designed as an optimal pizza delivery vehicle.

Ted popped open the oven door and slid the pizza box inside, securing the latch. Because the unit had been specially designed for cardboard boxes, there was no fire risk.

Though Athena was fully self-driving, the city required that a driver ride in the vehicle at the ready in case even the slightest thing went wrong. Sam was already in the passenger's seat. Ted stopped briefly at the driver's door and waved to the crowd. Besides the reporters, close to a thousand people had come out to watch the event and see Athena leave the starting area. The route from Howard Street to the Bay Bridge and over to Treasure Island was completely closed off, and the city had set up multiple viewing platforms along the way.

"What's that thing on the roof?" The question came from a teenage boy leaning over one of the A-frame barricades. He pointed to the spinning lidar unit perched in the middle of the other sensors. "It looks dorky."

"Dorky?" Ted responded. "It's the future, kid."

He opened the driver's door and slid in without looking. He ended up sitting on a helmet and just missing the laptop, which got pushed to the area between the two seats.

"What the hell?" He grabbed the helmet and placed it on his legs. "Do I *really* have to wear this thing?"

"The city requires it," Sam said as she adjusted her chin strap. She struggled to get a comfortable seating position. "And you should know better than to challenge me on safety."

He didn't bother to respond. He slid the helmet on and immediately banged the top of his head against the ceiling, letting the safety strap dangle freely from his chin. He closed the door, grabbed the laptop, opened it and held it with his right hand, mainly to show the crowd he wasn't driving. Sam's computer would be doing the actual work, but he wanted everyone to be clear that neither of them were controlling the car. He stuck his left arm through the open window to wave at the bystanders.

"The future?" Sam asked. "Ted, we both know your spinning lidar is only partially integrated into the system. The main controls are still running off the primary array."

"They don't need to know that. Besides, I think it's impressive how much we were able to get done in the past four months. Both in and out of the lab."

"Don't get playful!" she blushed. "This isn't the time or the place."

"I promise not to bring up the endless nights of amazing sex." He glanced over his shoulder as best he could, fighting to keep his safety helmet from hitting the ceiling. "And I won't even mention the heat we generated in that back hatch. I probably didn't even need to build that custom oven. We could have just—"

"Ted!" She started laughing. "Focus on the challenge."

"I couldn't resist." He patted her shoulder and gave it a gentle squeeze. "From a technology standpoint, we've come a long way these past few months. I won't make a sleazy joke about my impressive hardware."

"Please don't." She turned her attention to her own computer that she had placed in the car, and began keying in the commands to start the route. "You proved me wrong, Ted. About your hardware—the one on the roof. I never thought we'd get any of that spinning lidar to work."

"Because I made you cut corners when you didn't want to."

"I only did that because this is a one-off challenge. Normally I don't take such risks."

"Maybe you should try to more often," he said, looking directly at her green eyes.

"Save it for later." She smiled at him, then pointed out the windshield. "The future awaits."

It took another ten minutes before Ted received the "go" signal. Sam initiated the program, and Athena slowly pulled out onto Howard

Street, heading southwest. The sidewalks were lined with onlookers watching the Prius drive by. Some were well aware of what was going on and eagerly waved at Ted and Sam. Others paid no attention, going about their morning wondering why the street was closed to traffic.

"Here comes the first turn," Sam announced, her eyes fixated on the map slowly scrolling across her laptop's screen. Athena was humming along at a leisurely twenty miles per hour. "This should be the easy part."

Watching Athena drive by herself still brought a grin to Ted's face. The drive-by-wire system gave him an entirely new perspective on autonomy. When he rode in Cyclops, he watched the servos and robotic controls run the show. This felt like the future happening now.

A loud thrumming from overhead awoke him from his trance. He looked out the window, craning his neck so he could see the police helicopter flying above them. Off in the distance, a second chopper from the local NBC affiliate was broadcasting their progress.

"This really has turned into a big production," he said, his voice filled with a mix of awe and pride. He waved to a crowd of people sitting in a small row of bleachers on the corner.

Athena slowed and came to a halt. After what he felt was too long of a pause, the car turned left onto Eighth Street and slowly accelerated to fifteen miles per hour.

"I wish you would have let me set the speed limits," he said with a frustrating sigh. "We aren't putting on much of a show for the cameras."

"Not now, Ted. We're approaching the tricky part. This one and the bridge exit will be Athena's biggest tests. Do you *hare* me?" Sam briefly laughed at her joke.

Athena once again came to a halt and then quickly turned onto Bryant Street without slowing down much. The speed took Ted by surprise. Suddenly Athena came to a halt in the middle of the intersection. He looked over at Sam, her eyes frantically scanning her screen.

"What's the problem?" he asked. "We've driven this route multiple times and done the simulations at least five times in the past month during testing."

Athena backed up several feet and stopped. The Prius rolled forward and immediately slammed on the brakes again. The car did this three more times before seeming to give up.

"She's confused," Sam said. "I . . . I don't know why. Hold on."

Ted closed his laptop, tucking it between the front seat and center area as he ran his hand across the top of the dashboard. "Come on, Athena. Talk to us. What's going on in that beautiful AI mind of yours?"

Athena was dead in the middle of the road. Ted felt helpless. He looked outside at a camera crew set up at the corner. A reporter was now pointing directly at the Prius. He suddenly had no interest in waving back. He looked ahead, only to find more people standing behind a row of concrete construction barriers. Two young children were holding a poster board plastered in a colorful rainbow of letters reading GO ATHENA! Ted smiled briefly and then frowned as he stared at the crowd.

"Sam, the barriers!" Ted pointed to the five concrete barriers jutting into the middle of Bryant Street just past the on-ramp to I-80.

"Shit!" Sam frantically looked back and forth between her laptop screen and the barriers. She opened the EyeSpy map to confirm the change. "We did this run on Monday. The construction is all new. I can adjust the programming. I think. But, I'm not sure how long it will take."

"Won't that be cheating?" he asked with a grin.

"Cheating?" she exclaimed. "Is it? No, seriously? It's not a problem to make adjustments on the fly, is it? Are we voiding the pizza challenge rules?"

"Well, we certainly can't just sit here dead in the road."

A window opened on Sam's laptop, a series of messages quickly scrolled by. Sam squinted her eyes as she read the information. A smile slowly spread across her face.

"Am I to assume that's good news?" Ted asked. "What did you do?"

"Nothing. I never made any changes."

"So, what then?"

"She's recalculating. Like we taught her! She's using the alternative data from the spinning lidar." Sam looked at him and smiled. "I think your lidar may have saved the day."

Athena suddenly lurched forward with a jerk, slamming Sam's helmet against the passenger side door window and catching both Ted and Sam off guard. Nothing could deter their smiles though. The Prius maneuvered past the construction site and entered the on-ramp. Moments later, they crested above Seventh Street and merged onto I-80, the Dwight Eisenhower Highway.

Because the roads were closed along the route, the eastbound side of the interstate had no traffic. Ted closed his window and took in the bizarre view outside the car. Behind them were four police motorcycles and two cruisers, all with their lights flashing. Athena settled in at a sedate thirty-five miles per hour, keeping herself six feet from the guardrail, precisely as programmed.

"We've got another three miles to go," he said. "It's going to take us several minutes at this pace."

The Bay Bridge is a double-decker design, with the eastbound traffic running on the lower level. In the city, the east and west lanes of I-80 were mostly side by side. There were multiple merges on both sides of the highway before crossing over the water. Sam had programmed Athena to know where these were, and to alternate sides and track when needed using the edge of the road. As Athena passed Second Street, the roadway snaked beneath the westbound side of the road. They were finally under the bridge.

"I feel like I'm in some post-apocalyptic movie. Five lanes, and we're the only ones on the entire lower deck." He craned his head around, trying his best to see past the edges of his safety helmet. He considered taking it off but knew Sam would object. "Doesn't it freak you out?"

"Huh?"

He looked over at Sam. He expected to see her staring at her computer, intently monitoring their progress. Instead, she was resting her helmet against the window, watching the scenery pass by.

"What's on your mind, Sam?"

"We make a good team," she said, taking his hand.

"So, no regrets?" he asked.

"No regrets."

"Good." He let out a quiet sigh of relief. "It's been amazing—all of it. Spending Christmas with you and your family were wonderful. You live in such a different world than I do. I've never had a holiday where people weren't yelling at one another."

"Dani adores you."

"Really? Huh. Well, I still haven't exactly won Catherine over."

"My mom's a tough nut to crack." She smiled and kissed his hand before letting it go. "She's just extremely protective of me, given, well, given my history."

"Ah yes, the mysterious past and pain. I told you, I'm not going to pry, Sam. But at some point, you'll need to tell me. You told me about your birthday. But I know there's a story related to your daughter."

"I know." She squeezed Ted's hand gently before letting go. "This isn't the time or the place."

His smile faded. He'd done this dance with her several times over the past weeks. Every time he thought she was about to open up, she'd retreat. He'd been as patient and respectful as he could be, but his patience was beginning to wear thin. He saw that the two of them were good together. This shell she chose to hide within, this wall she'd erected had to come down.

"When will it be the right time and place, Sam?" He asked without a little bit of annoyance. "The project ends today. Any time I try to talk to you about what happens next, you deflect. I want to be with you, Sam. Here in California."

"So, you'd move here?" She seemed shocked. "Permanently?"

"Yes. Why do you say it that way? Don't you want that?"

"Can we discuss it later, Ted? Please? I can only focus on one thing at a time."

"Fine."

The next few minutes passed in uncomfortable silence. He didn't want a repeat of what happened in Detroit, yet here they were again, him ready and her pulling away.

He forced himself to focus on the beautiful view, which did help somewhat. Even with gray skies, looking across San Francisco Bay was gorgeous. And he could just make out Alcatraz jutting from the smoky waters far in the distance. He wished that despite all the crazy hours spent on the pizza challenge that he and Sam had had time to explore San Francisco.

"The exit is coming up," she said.

The first ramp on Treasure Island was a sharp U-turn with a recommended speed of fifteen miles per hour. Sam had programmed Athena to take it at ten miles per hour. The Prius did as expected and smoothly wound its way from the bridge to Treasure Island Road. A childish grin spread across his face as the steering wheel spun freely. The thoroughfare ran along the southern side of the island, providing more spectacular views of San Francisco. He couldn't help but look back in awe at the picturesque city across the bay.

"We just watched Athena drive herself over that bridge." Ted put down his window, letting the fresh morning air inside, as he reached down again for his laptop to hold for the crowds. He pointed back toward I-80, fading in the distance. "This is historic, Sam."

Treasure Island was made of two sections. The hilly part housed I-80 and a huge Coast Guard Station. To the west was the main island with roads and businesses. Treasure Island Road was a slow winding descent from I-80 until it flattened out, passing Clipper Cove and the Treasure Isle Marina.

Athena turned right onto California Avenue. In comparison to downtown San Francisco, the fanfare in this less densely populated place was quite minimal. After a few more uneventful turns, they were in front of the radio studio. A small crowd, mostly press, was waiting to greet them, secured behind a row of barricades. A temporary gate that guarded the entrance rolled open to allow them access. The Prius came to a stop directly in front of the building.

"Holy shit," Sam said. "We did it."

"Was there ever a doubt? You're a brilliant engineer, Sam. Almost as good as me."

He winked at her as each closed their computers, put them down on the floor in front of them, opened their doors, and stepped out to greet the crowd. Applause, cheers, and whistling greeted them. Bulbs flashed. Reporters leaned over the barrier screaming out questions. Ted ignored them all, and ripped his helmet off, tossing it into the car. He walked around to the back of the Prius and opened the hatch to get the pizza. Sam joined him, still wearing her safety gear. Ted opened the oven door and immediately frowned.

"Shit," he said.

"What's wrong?"

"I forgot to turn the oven on." He pulled the cardboard box from the custom oven and started to laugh. "Do you think cold pizza will disqualify us from getting a million bucks?"

"No. But don't expect a tip."

Terminal One at San Francisco International Airport was mobbed with travelers. Storms along the eastern seaboard had resulted in hundreds of delays and cancellations. Tensions were high as passengers impacted by the weather sought options, several getting into heated arguments with airline agents. The overhead monitor showing Delta's departing flights indicated only half were on time, the rest delayed or canceled.

Ted was thankful his flight to Atlanta had not been delayed, although deep down, he would have welcomed staying with Sam for one more day. His long layover meant he wouldn't get to Akron until 8:00 p.m., an almost twelve-hour trek, assuming no issues arose. Then he would have to suffer through an almost hour-long car ride, listening to his parents. Maybe that would be a good thing, Ted thought to himself. He had many things to tell them. The time he spent with Sam's family over Christmas gave him a new perspective on his own family. He surprised himself by almost looking forward to being with them.

After the pizza challenge four days prior, Vin had taken the team out for a huge celebration dinner. Ted spent the following two days doing interviews. The days and nights had flown by. Suddenly, here he was at the airport, holding Sam tightly, tears in both their eyes.

"I told you, Sam, I'll be back by the end of the month. Early April for certain."

"Sure," she replied softly, her face buried in his chest.

"I just need to smooth things out with my family." He slid his arms from her waist up to her shoulders, pulling her away from him. "Of all people, you should understand how important family is. I'm coming back. I promise."

She lowered her head and struggled to keep the tears from falling, her hands trembling.

"Hey?" He asked, looking directly into her eyes. "Don't you believe me?"

"I . . . I . . . I need to tell you something, Ted. I need to explain to you why I pushed you away after Detroit. Why I'm such . . . such a clam. Turtle. Pick your shell."

He looking directly at her and held her chin. He said, "You can tell me anything. I'm right here."

"I told you how I was hurt once before—someone who scarred me."

"I'd never hurt you, Sam."

"Please, let me finish. If I don't get this out now, I never will." She took a deep breath and continued. "The man that hurt me was Dani's father. His name was Jeff. He was several years older than me and attending Berkeley. We'd been dating for a few months. The pregnancy wasn't . . . wasn't planned. I found out shortly after he graduated. He told me not to worry. He told me he'd be there for me. He had to leave but that he'd be back."

"But he never came back."

She sobbed and dug her fingers deep into Ted's arms. "He left me alone. He said he would be there for me."

"I won't leave you, Sam. You have to trust me."

"He made that same promise right here, in this very terminal." She looked around the bustling airport, drying her tears. "Practically in this very spot. He was even flying to Atlanta!"

"Sam—"

"He flew away, and I never heard from him again. He just disappeared. The bastard got me pregnant and ran! I spent months trying to track him down." She paused, lost in pain-filled memories. "But, after Dani was born, my world changed. I stopped looking. I . . . I had more important things to focus on."

"Sam, I'm not Jeff. Please don't lump me in with him. You have to know I'll come back. I promise."

"I love you, Ted. Please don't make promises you can't keep."

"Sam, I was the one who wanted to continue things after Detroit. You pushed me away."

"And now you know why."

He pulled her close and kissed the top of her head, gently running his fingertips along her back as he offered her little kisses over and over again.

"I love you, Sam. I'm coming back here. To you. I will get a job. Here. . . . Look, all I know is I want to be with you. I'd say I want to be *hare* with you but . . . "

She trembled in his arms, her tears turning to laughter. She wiped her face dry once more, leaned her head back, and kissed Ted on the lips.

"You're such a dork."

"You love it."

"I do."

"I'll be back. And I am not letting you out of my sight when I do. I will make *us* the priority."

He held her close again, rocking her back and forth. He felt her shudder as her tears formed once again.

"I can see my timing is bad," Lisa Phillips said. Matthew Page's assistant had been quietly standing a few feet away from them. "I'm sorry to interrupt."

"Do I know you?" Ted asked, releasing Sam from his embrace.

"Ted Wolff, and Sam Lavoie, correct?" Lisa asked.

"Yes," Sam replied.

"My name is Lisa Phillips." She extended her hand and exchanged brief greetings with Ted and Sam. "Can you please come with me? Ted, I know you have a flight to catch but this won't take long. There's someone very important for you to meet."

"What? Where? I've really got to go and, I'm sorry, but I have no idea who you are."

"I'm from GSI. My boss has asked me to bring you to him. I'll explain more. Don't worry about your flight, Mr. Wolff. You still have plenty of time to make it. My boss is only just outside that door."

Ted looked at Sam and shrugged. She nodded in agreement and somewhat skeptically, they followed Lisa to the closest exit several yards away. A metallic black Audi A8 with heavily tinted windows was idling curbside. As the group approached the car, the back door opened, and Matthew Grant emerged.

"Ted and Sam, so great to meet you!" Matthew enthusiastically shook their hands. "Matthew. Matthew Grant, with GSI."

"GSI?" Sam asked. "The mapping company?"

"Among other things," he replied. "I have to tell you that the pizza challenge was truly spectacular. The work you did with Athena was groundbreaking."

"Thanks," Sam said. "Wait. Matthew Grant? You aren't *with* GSI. You *created* GSI!"

Matthew smiled and nodded quietly. Sam's jaw slowly fell open.

"Wow," Ted said. "So, you saw the pizza challenge?"

"Lisa and I watched from my office. It was riveting. I talked with

Vin Malik late yesterday. I wanted to know about the engineers who built the tech that went into successfully completing the pizza challenge. After much wrangling, he told me you two were the superstars. I kind of had a feeling you were, based on what happened at DARPA in the Mojave last year."

"You were there?" Sam asked.

"No. I had Lisa go, along with a number of others from our core team. Lisa's my eyes and ears—sometimes even my voice. She profiled every key team member of the DARPA competitors for me." Matthew glanced at his watch and took a couple of steps closer to his car. "I know you have a flight to catch so I'm going to be brief. Self-driving cars are the future. GSI intends to lead the way. We're building an amazing team, and I want you two involved. More than involved. Sam, I want you to lead the software group. Ted, I want you on hardware. Let's take what you did with Athena last weekend and use it to change the world of transportation."

Ted looked between Matthew, Lisa, and Sam. Sam looked shell-shocked; the color had drained from her face. Ted's mind raced as it filled with questions.

"Lisa has all the details." Matthew sat down in the back of the Audi and closed the door. He immediately lowered the window. "Take your time to think it over, but I hope you say yes. Lisa?"

Lisa stepped forward and handed Ted and Sam each a manila folder. Ted ripped his open. It was an offer letter. After reading the first paragraph, he scanned through the document looking for a salary. He found it in the last paragraph. Six figures. Ted read it three times to be sure he got it right.

"Holy shit," Sam blurted out, her face buried in the folder Lisa had given her. "Is this for real?"

"I think it's a fair offer," Matthew said. "We don't need an answer today. Lisa's contact info is in there. I'm sure you will have plenty of questions."

"After you've had a chance to go over everything, please feel free to call me anytime." Lisa shook hands with Ted and Sam and jumped into the front passenger seat of the Audi.

"It's a good thing you caught the pizza challenge on TV," Ted said to Matthew.

"Caught it?" Matthew laughed and shook his head. "Who do you think ponied up the million-dollar prize money?"

The back window closed, and the sleek Audi pulled away from the curb, disappearing into the traffic.

28

GSI's building management team spent six months renovating a workspace in a relatively new building for the autonomous vehicle team. Since its beginnings, GSI's growth had been exponential, but the autonomy project was being done under the radar, at least as far as the public was concerned. GSI did not want anyone knowing what they were developing, so even those involved in building the project room had no idea who would occupy it. The space was light and airy, with ceilings soaring twenty feet high. Floor-to-ceiling windows allowed in plenty of light and offered stunning views of San Francisco Bay. Computerized blinds worked in concert with the heating and air conditioning system to optimize when to best use, or refuse, the warming rays of the sun.

The workroom was divided into four named sections: Create, Crash, Convene, and Café. The main workroom—Create—consisted of sixty L-shaped wall-free workstations, the open concept meant to enhance interactive teamwork. Employees had their choice of color for their desks, making the room bright and joyful. Crash was a recreation area, with beanbag chairs of different colors and a wide assortment of games. The irony of the lounge's name was not lost on anyone working on the self-driving car. Convene, as the name suggested, was a space for departmental and other meetings. Moveable and retractable walls would allow gatherings of various sizes as small as twenty-five or as large as five hundred. The café served a variety of breakfast, lunch, dinner, and snack options. Adjacent to Create were other rooms and facilities, including a comprehensive lab similar to that at Ashton, where people could refine and test the related hardware and software components directly on the autonomous vehicle.

"This workroom is amazing," Ted said to Sam.

"It's beautiful," she replied. "We're not in the Mojave anymore."

"I'm just glad we can officially kick this thing off."

Dozens of people swarmed about the new space, waiting for an opening ceremony of sorts to begin. Half were sitting in the rows of chairs facing the stage, while others stood about anxiously. Applause broke out as Matthew Grant entered the room and climbed up a short flight of stairs onto a raised stage area set up at one end. That was the cue for everyone to take their seats.

Ted snagged Sam by the elbow and maneuvered her around several people to make a beeline for a front-row seat. Ralph and Lori followed closely behind. Ralph, at Sam's request, had joined her at GSI. After relocating to California, Ted had contacted his three former DSU teammates and tried his best to entice them to get on board. Nico and Harry already had other projects and declined, but Lori jumped at the chance.

"It feels like this workspace took forever to finish," Ted said to Sam.

"Really?" she replied. "I think it's shocking they got it completed so quickly."

A hush fell over the crowd as Matthew held his hands up to get everyone's attention. "Good morning," he said. "I'm excited to see so many familiar faces as well as many new ones. Today is not only the first day of June, but it's also the first day we truly set about changing the face of transportation as we know it."

More applause, followed by cheers and whistles echoing against the concrete and glass walls.

"I'm proud to introduce your team leader," Matthew said. "Give it up for Vin Malik."

Vin, who had been standing quietly in the corner next to Lisa, smiled as he joined Matthew on stage. The men briefly shook hands before Matthew waved to the crowd and walked offstage to stand near Lisa. The applause for Vin was deafening, with Sam and Ralph on their feet cheering and yelling. Vin laughed and motioned for them to sit down.

"It's been great working with each of you these past few months," he said. He looked down at Sam and Ralph sitting in the front row. "Some of you much longer. But today is different. With our project center finally ready, we can now work side by side to bring this undertaking to life."

Vin clicked the remote in his hand. The motorized window blinds quietly closed as the lights lowered, darkening the room. An overhead projector that hung from the ceiling gradually brightened the screen hanging directly behind Vin, showing the official project name—Project Courier.

Vin spent the next half hour highlighting the team structure and key technologies that would be used to design the autonomous vehicles. Ted, Sam, and the other team leads were all asked to stand when their areas were highlighted. Vin praised the breakthroughs made by Ashton, DSU, Princeton, and others. He then recapped the DARPA FAST Challenge, including highlights from Lisa's reconnaissance mission. Ted was shocked to see specific details on the work done at DSU.

"Lisa's good," Ted whispered to Sam. "How'd she get this information? I don't even remember seeing her in the Mojave."

She shushed him and pointed back toward the screen. A new slide appeared with the words, Our Goals.

"As I've said repeatedly, perhaps too many times, what we did at the FAST Challenge was just the beginning." Vin paused in the center of the stage and clasped his hands behind his back. "As I look out at this crowd, I see the future leaders in autonomy, artificial intelligence, robotics, and mapping. A big lesson we learned working on Athena was the delicate balancing act between hardware and software. It's a dance—a give and take—a marriage."

Ted couldn't help but smile and glance over at Sam. He could see her grinning, refusing to acknowledge his stare.

"Everyone must think outside the box," Vin continued. "Never be afraid to challenge ideas. This is a total team effort. We win when the *team* hits its goals. So, what are our goals, you ask?"

A new slide appeared with "100,000" and nothing else.

"Our autonomous vehicle needs to complete one hundred thousand miles completely hands-free. That can be done in conjunction with the other goals, but even if all other goals are met, the project will not be considered a success until we hit that milestone. As for those other goals, there are ten. Ten feats that must be conquered."

He clicked the remote, changing the slide to show the list of challenges.

1. MARKET STREET
2. LOMBARD STREET
3. EL CAMINO REAL
4. NORTH BRIDGE LOOP
5. SOUTH BRIDGE LOOP
6. LAKE TAHOE
7. YOSEMITE PARK
8. SAN FRANCISCO TO NAPA
9. PACIFIC COAST HIGHWAY
10. SAN FRANCISCO TO LOS ANGELES

"Many of these may look easy," Vin continued, slowly pacing back and forth across the stage. "Some are even blatantly obvious, such as Lombard Street. Others have a few surprises thrown into them. For example, those of you not familiar with the area should know that the El Camino Real test will have over two hundred stoplights across a one hundred-mile distance. And the last one? Your target in Los Angeles is the Petersen Automotive Museum. There are a few ways to get from San Francisco to Los Angeles. For that challenge, you'll need to take the 5 with the rest of the population. We want to see a vehicle maneuver through heavy stop-and-go traffic."

Several groans surfaced throughout the room. Matthew, standing beside Lisa in the corner, chuckled loudly. He clearly got a kick out of the reactions across the crowd.

Vin spent time going through additional slides that spelled out the complexities of each of the ten challenges. The last slide showed the list of ten again, along with the other goal of hitting 100,000 miles. Vin clicked his remote to raise the blinds and the room lights.

"Okay, I'm sure this crowd must have some questions," he said. Several hands went up. He looked at the front row and pointed to Lori. "Yes, Lori?"

"Are we allowed to drive on these roads?" Lori asked. "I mean, the self-driving car. We did DARPA in the desert. To complete those challenges will require us to drive on dozens of public roads."

"I can answer that," Ted said, standing up and turning to face the crowd. "This came up during the pizza challenge. Technically it's not illegal under California law. We had two of us in the car, ready to take over if things went wrong. As long as we've got at least one person behind the wheel, we'll be fine."

"Ted's right. Our legal team has researched this thoroughly." Vin looked over at Matthew and nodded, acknowledging the painful number of weeks the legal team had spent working with state regulators. He then looked back at the crowd. Ted had his arm up. "Ted?"

"What happens when we meet the goals?" he asked.

"I've saved the best for last." Vin turned to Lisa and motioned her to come forward. "Lisa? Can you, please?"

In the back corner of the stage was a table with a white sheet draped over it. Lisa walked up on stage and rolled the table to the center, near Vin. Underneath the sheet, the outline of a variety of different shaped items could be seen, including a taller one in the center. Matthew walked up to join her. Together, they grabbed a corner of the sheet and pulled it away, revealing what was underneath.

A 1.5-liter Magnum of champagne was centered in the table, surrounded by ten smaller bottles of champagne. Each bottle had a folded embossed cream-colored card with a number scrawled across the front. The small cards were numbered one through ten for each challenge, and the larger bottle's plaque read "100k."

"What is that?" Sam asked Ted. "Champagne?"

"It looks like one bottle per test," he replied. "I would have preferred Chivas Regal."

"We will pop each of these once a challenge is completed," Vin said. "But don't worry, there's much more on the line than some celebratory champagne. Matthew, would you do the honors?"

"You are the brightest minds," Matthew said. "This won't be easy. With Project Courier, we are changing the very concept of transportation. So I want to make sure you are well rewarded. Once all eleven goals are met, each team member will receive a quarter of a million dollars as a bonus."

Gasps rippled throughout the room and a murmur built, as those in attendance exclaimed their surprise. Matthew looked up at Vin and nodded in approval.

"That's not all," Matthew continued. "Our team leads will each get an additional quarter of a million."

"Holy shit!" Ted could not contain himself. He thought back to that morning back in the hotel room in Ann Arbor when he had nowhere to go and called his family. He had gone to Detroit with Sam, thinking they would take on the automotive world. Now, here he was, less than two years later, in Silicon Valley, looking at a potential bonus of $500,000. He turned and placed a hand on Sam's shoulder. "I never thought I'd make that much money in five years, let alone one. Can you believe it, Sam?"

"I'm more in shock over the goals, Ted." She glanced up at Vin, standing on the stage, smiling. "Vin warned me this was going to be the greatest challenge of my lifetime. He wasn't kidding. But, Ted, you do realize this is going to take a lot longer than just one year."

"Bullshit. Look at this facility, Sam. All of these people. We're going to bang through those challenges in no time."

29

The Project Courier space was buzzing with activity. A dozen people were in line at the café waiting to grab a bite for lunch. The day's specials included a build-your-own taco bar as well as five-bean chili. No matter where you walked, you couldn't escape the fiery scent of cumin, chipotle, and jalapeños. In the Crash area, several people were flopped in beanbags with their food on plates. Three members of the robotics team sat at a small circular table playing a game of Monopoly. The fourth chair was occupied by a robot programmed to be the banker and distribute money to the other players. Laughter and smiles were everywhere, despite the long hours and enormous challenges everyone faced.

Ted sat at a small high-top table beside one of the floor-to-ceiling windows. His plate was filled with three corn-shelled tacos, stuffed with chorizo, cheese, salsa, sour cream, and guacamole. One of the tacos was half-eaten. He had a notepad open, both pages crammed full of disparate notes and formulas, many crossed out. As he took a bite, he scanned through what he had written, tapping his pen against the paper as he mentally ran calculations.

Flinging his pen down in frustration, he looked up at the sixty-four-inch flat panel monitor nestled high up the corner wall. CNN was interviewing David Foster, VP of Product Development at GM. Ted recognized him as one of the executives he and Sam had met with in Detroit. The audio was muted, but the conversation was closed captioned. David was discussing GM's decision to kill the Pontiac brand as part of their restructuring to deal with bankruptcy.

"Rest in peace, Frankie," Ted said softly.

"Is this seat taken?" Sam asked playfully.

"Sorry, I'm saving it for my beautiful and brilliant girlfriend." Ted flung his leg up, dropping his foot on the empty chair next to him.

"Wow. Beautiful *and* brilliant? That's quite the combination. You must be a very lucky guy."

"You have no idea."

Sam's choice for lunch was a mixed green salad tossed with lime-infused sliced chicken, pico de gallo, and savory black beans. She slid her plate across the table and shoved Ted's foot off the chair, taking a seat next to him.

"Good answer," she said with a devilish grin. She looked at the scratchpad of notes sprawled out in front of him. "How goes the battle?"

"Market Street is going to be the death of me." He looked across the Project Courier area at the milestone celebration table placed against the back of the stage in Convene. One of the ten bottles was open and emptied, resting upside down in a hammered pewter champagne bucket. The card for the Lombard Street challenge was now flipped face-down. The team still had nine challenges to complete, along with the hundred-thousand-mile task. "Why is this one proving to be such a pain in the ass?"

"Because it's the most unpredictable. Pedestrians don't always follow the rules, walking in opposite directions, or cutting diagonally across an intersection. And bicyclists? Two words of terror in San Francisco: bike messengers."

"I can't figure them out! Those maniacs stay inches away from the traffic around them, sometimes even holding on to a vehicle to go faster."

"Relax, Ted." She laughed and focused on mixing the contents of her salad bowl. "We've made great progress."

"How can you say that?" He was disappointed with her nonchalant attitude concerning the Market Street challenge. "We've been at this for ten months, Sam. Ten! And we've only completed one challenge so far."

"It took us eight of those months to tear down Athena and create Leapfrog."

"That was our first mistake. We should have built on Athena, not ripped her apart to start over. Vin's methodology is killing us."

"Though another Prius, Leapfrog is lightyears ahead of Athena. It was time-consuming, but it was the right approach."

Project Courier had taken a clean-sheet approach to the autonomy mission. Vin brought Athena over from Ashton to allow the team to perform an autopsy and see how she was designed. They meticulously went through each component, from hardware to software, to determine what would be used as part of the new design. Vin likened it to cleaning out a closet of old clothes, and flagging items to be kept, tossed, or evaluated. This allowed for what Sam felt was a rapid development of an entirely new architecture for their self-driving vehicle. Ted saw the whole process as moving too slowly and felt they should have simply used Athena as the starting point and refined everything.

"Leapfrog," Ted said as he dove into his second taco. "I hate that name, too. I'm sure Harry would have loved it."

"We're leapfrogging the competition." Sam reached across the table and gave his hand a gentle squeeze. Although their relationship was public knowledge, neither was big on displays of affection in the workplace. "I think you need to look at the positives."

"Such as?" He remained slumped in his chair, eating his lunch. He tried not to think of the plans he'd made for the half-million-dollar bonus awaiting him at the end of the project. That dream now felt indefinitely on hold.

"All of the early tests have already put us well over two thousand miles."

"So."

"So? That means the hundred-thousand-mile test will be done well before we complete the last seven."

"You think so?" Ted closed his eyes and started crunching the estimated distance per test, multiplied by the expected number of attempts needed. He opened his eyes, somewhat disappointed he never bothered to do the math before, and suddenly felt a glimmer of optimism begin to surface. He smiled as he looked at Sam, her eyes sparkling with hope. He began to relax. He grinned as he realized how quickly Sam could snap him back to reality. "Slow and steady wins the race, right?"

"Always." She smiled and took another tiny bite of her salad. "You should be proud of what we've done, Ted. Your spinning lidar is fully integrated into Leapfrog. It's a game-changer. When we wired it into Athena, I could see the potential, but I could never have predicted how brilliantly it would perform once its full power was unleashed. Have you told Kevin how well it's performing?"

"Kevin?" Ted glanced around the room, trying to remember which engineer was named Kevin. He was drawing a blank. "We have a Kevin?"

"Kevin. From Nevada. He built that with you, didn't he?"

"Hallaway?" He was stunned she would suggest such a thing. "That was *my* design!"

"Okay. Lower your voice. I'm sorry, I just remember seeing it on his workbench. That's all."

"I've told you, those were my designs Kevin was using." He tossed half his soda down his throat and closed his eyes briefly, taking a deep breath to calm himself. "The system we have today is lightyears ahead of those original schematics. Why do you keep bringing him up?"

"I don't keep bringing him up. I rarely mention him. I just thought he'd want to see how far you've taken the design. Don't you stay in touch with him?"

"No."

"That's too bad."

"This entire project is a big secret, remember?" He wiped sour cream from the corners of his mouth. "I couldn't talk to him about it even if I wanted to."

"True."

"Even when the cops stopped us at the top of Lombard Street and wanted to know what all the gizmos were on our car, we couldn't tell them."

"Gizmos." She chuckled as she recalled the conversation. "I had to stop you from going into a longwinded explanation of the technology."

"You were so fast on your feet. Telling them you were doing mapping research for GSI."

"I wasn't lying to them. We continue to refine the EyeSpy program started at Ashton. What amazes me is how quickly they bought it."

"Why wouldn't they? The world has no idea that Project Courier exists. They didn't even know who GSI was. As far as they were concerned, we were just two more geeks out doing geeky stuff."

"Geeks? Speak for yourself, you big dork."

A flash of light from outside caught Ted's attention. He turned to see a small bright red sports car whip around the corner and into the parking lot. Ted scanned the sleek lines of the blunt vehicle and immediately recognized it as a Lotus Elise. The car pulled into a parking spot, and after several seconds, Vin Malik emerged. Ted frowned as he watched him walk away. Something was different about the Lotus. It took a few moments for Ted to realize what he was seeing.

"Holy shit," he said as he leaned closer to the window. He turned and looked at Sam. "Vin bought a Tesla Roadster."

"They're already making them? I thought it was still in development."

"Tesla showed the prototype a few years ago. They nailed some deal with Lotus to ship them their Elise sports car so they can convert them into electric vehicles. They only started making the production version two months ago. I can't believe Vin already has one."

"Vin's got a lot of connections in the tech world. I'm sure he's on some VIP list. Maybe we can get him to take us for a test ride."

"Ride? I want to drive the thing."

"We predicted this, Ted. Remember? The rise of the EV. It was in our presentation we did in Detroit."

"Can we not discuss Detroit?"

"Sorry." She looked outside at the sports car and then back at Ted. "How're things with your family these days?"

"The same," he said with a heavy sigh. "Mom is incredibly supportive. She doesn't really understand what I'm doing here at GSI, but she's proud of me. But my dad and brothers still feel like I'm somehow betraying the family dynasty."

"That makes no sense. I'd really hoped they would have come around by now."

"This gag order on discussing Project Courier makes it impossible to share any details with them. I've kept it all high level, but my dad considers me to be a 'Silicon sellout' as he likes to call me. There's just no pleasing him."

"He'll come around someday." She stood up and walked around to his side of the table, resting her arms gently around his shoulder. "I believe in you."

"I know you do. Thank you." His plate was now empty, and his notepad stained with streaks of guacamole and tomato juice. "Are we still on for dinner tonight?"

"It will have to be a quick. My mom can't stay late with Dani."

"Oh. Right."

"It's a school night. We could get takeout and bring it to my place for the three of us to have together. Maybe we can all watch a movie? Would that be okay?"

"Not this time. Let's hit our usual place. We'll make it fast."

Donovan's Pub was a few blocks from Hoover Park, not far from El Camino Real. The bar and restaurant had a retro theme, including a jukebox styled like one from the 1970s, but with the internals of the latest machines. The back corner behind the bar had a pair of pool tables and a few 1980s video games, including Pac Man, Asteroids, and

Galaga. The right side of the bar was the formal restaurant, with the rest of the space filled with a mix of booths and high tops. The woodwork was dark walnut accented with golden brass fittings. Stained-glass lights hung from the ceiling, bathing the entire restaurant in a warm, comforting glow.

Ted and Sam were seated in one of the three booths on the bar side of the restaurant, away from the gaming area but close to the jukebox. Donovan's had a limited menu, but the quality of the food was always excellent. Ted was enjoying a heaping plate of corned beef and cabbage, while Sam had the appetizer-sized shepherd's pie. Next to them, the jukebox played "I Gotta Feeling" by The Black Eyed Peas. Ted spotted their waiter, Brandon, on the far side of the bar and waved to flag him down.

"Can I help you?" Brandon asked. The waiter seemed stressed as he rushed to their table. "How's the food?"

"Excellent as always," Sam replied.

"The food's okay. It's the atmosphere." Ted looked over at the jukebox and frowned. "Can you do something about this music? Do you have any classic rock?"

"The music? Uh, sure. I can look into that. We're a bit short-staffed tonight. I'm normally behind the bar."

"The music is annoying," Ted replied.

Brandon nodded hurriedly, turned, and walked away.

"Did you really need to be such an ass?" Sam asked. "He's obviously got his hands full."

"What? It's his job." He watched as Brandon walked past the jukebox, stepped behind the bar, and began mixing drinks. "You know how I am about my music."

"That doesn't excuse your behavior. What's with you lately?"

"It's these challenges." He sighed as he slid his knife through a chunk of corned beef. "Like I told you at lunch, I feel like we're moving too slowly."

"Nonsense. You've seen the project plan. We're a bit behind, but not by much."

"That's the problem, Sam. That plan has too much red tape. Vin's requirements for approving each test are ridiculous. We have to repeat things over and over again before he signs off. How many times have we finished a challenge only to have him review the data logs and reject it and tell us to do it all over again? It's bullshit."

"You've been butting heads with Vin since day one."

"Sam, when we complete a challenge and your laptop flashes 'Course Complete,' that tells me the challenge is a success. But not in Vin's eyes. He and that stupid quality team of his always find something in the logs they don't like."

"I told you early on that this was going to be a marathon."

"And here I thought Rusty's plans were too detailed."

"Enough about work," she said. "Let's talk about the weekend."

"What about it?"

"What do you mean? My mother is throwing that big charity fundraiser on Saturday. Remember?"

"Is that this weekend?" He frowned as he pushed layers of cabbage around his dish. "I was planning on working to try to get the project moving forward."

"Working? Ted, you know this event is a big deal."

"It is?" He realized he'd not only forgotten about the party, but couldn't remember any of the details about why she felt it was so special. "Why do I need to be there?"

"Seriously?" She flung her fork against the edge of the ceramic casserole dish. The tines chimed as they bounced off the side. She glanced at the dart board–style clock hanging near the jukebox. "Dani and her friends are singing. She's going to be front and center on stage. You should *want* to be there, Ted."

"If it's that important to you, I can try to swing by."

"You're completely missing the point." She drummed her nails along the curved side of her wineglass. "I've told you from the beginning that my family is my world. You need to be a part of that."

"I thought I was. I love you, Sam."

"And I love you, Ted. But I feel like I have one life with you and another with my mother and Dani. Getting those two circles to join has proven . . . well, difficult."

"Don't blame me. The issue is Catherine."

"My mother?"

"We both know she's not my biggest fan."

"I've told you not to take it personally. My dad left her. I was left alone after getting pregnant. She's just overly protective of me. She'll come around. But it would help if you made more of an effort, Ted. I mean, if I'm being completely honest, she sees how distant you are with Dani."

"That's not true."

"Really?" She folded her arms and glared at him. "How old is she?"

"What kind of question is that." He felt his heart begin to race. The look on her face told him she was serious. He was surprised to realize he hadn't the faintest idea how old her daughter was. "She's . . . she's five, right?"

"Six. What grade is she in?" she continued.

"What's with all the questions?"

"What grade, Ted?"

He paused and looked around the restaurant to see if anyone was staring at them. Sam's voice continued to escalate with each question. The Black Eyed Peas faded from the background, immediately replaced by "Bad Romance" by Lady Gaga. Ted shot the jukebox a look of disapproval.

"Second. She just started second. Right?"

"She's in first grade, Ted."

"Okay, so I was off a bit on my answers. But I was close."

"Close isn't good enough. Not after all this time together." She collected the napkin resting on her lap, wiped her lips, and tossed it over her dinner. "Now do you see why my mother has her doubts?"

"Not really." He shook his head in frustration. "So, what am I supposed to do?"

"You can start by making more of an effort to play a key role in Dani's life. The school party this weekend is a great way to start."

He looked across the table at her. Her anger and disappointment were on full display. He wanted to explain that he'd already ordered his team to work with him the entire weekend. But he realized she wouldn't understand. "Okay, Sam."

She stood up and grabbed her purse. "Speaking of which, I need to get home to Dani. Split the check?"

"No, I've got it."

She leaned down and gave him a peck on his cheek before walking quickly out of the restaurant.

He stared at his plate, inhaling the salty scent of beef. Despite this being his favorite meal at this restaurant, he suddenly found himself without an appetite. He closed his eyes and replayed the argument in his mind. He couldn't understand why she had gotten so upset. He also worried about carving out the time to get to Fremont for the party on Saturday. He didn't want to disappoint her, but he also couldn't make his team work the weekend without him.

"Was the shepherd's pie not to her liking?" Brandon was standing beside the booth, looking at Sam's plate. "Or will she be back?"

"Where's my music?" Ted replied.

30

Sam was trying to push down her rising anger as she struggled to stay focused on the team meeting. She so rarely got upset or raised her voice, at least when it came to her work. She had arrived at GSI two years before, bright-eyed and filled with hope, believing she could help change the future of transportation. She still felt that optimism, the feeling that anything is possible if only you set your mind to what needed to be done, she just wished everyone on the team, most notably Ted, felt the same way.

The hallway off the main workspace led to several additional rooms, including four conference rooms. Each room had been given a whimsical name, voted on by the team members. Today they were meeting in "Johnny Five," the nickname given to the military robot that came to life in the movie *Short Circuit.* The AI team that submitted the name had launched a fierce campaign to drum up votes in their favor, even building a miniature version of the robot that passed out cards that read VOTE FOR ME. Ted, in tribute to Harry Palmer, fully supported their choice.

Sam, Ted, Lori, Ralph, and six others were seated around a white oval table. A whiteboard at the end of the room displayed the date: February 10, 2011, and the list of the ten challenges. The list was in a grid, showing the names, number of attempts, and current status for each. The Lombard, Market, and two bridge challenges were shown as complete. Lombard had proven to be the easiest at ten attempts, whereas Market took fifty-two. The upper corner of the board also showed the total miles driven: 67,452.

"As I've stated repeatedly, Ted, I must disagree." Sam stood up, shoving her chair away and sending it rolling back until it bounced off the side wall. She briefly closed her eyes and bit her lower lip to calm herself. "We *cannot* do these tests in tandem. I'm fine not doing them in the order listed. In fact, it makes sense to do them in a sequence based on how our AI and mapping software will learn and grow. But doing two or more at once is out of the question."

"I still think you're wrong." Ted leaned forward and looked around the table for support, but all eyes were on Sam. "Leapfrog will learn quicker by attacking two different problems at the same time. The Lake Tahoe test is the complete opposite of El Camino Real. I think we will get done faster by doing them concurrently. Assuming Vin's quality team doesn't keep shitting on our successes."

"They're holding us to a high standard, Ted."

"Oh, please. The items they are rejecting are irrelevant in the real world. I swear, Sam. Ditch that review team and begin parallel testing the challenges and we can be done in half the time."

"This isn't a race."

"Isn't it?" He stood up and walked to the board listing the challenges and the status of each. "We've gone through El Camino Real seventy-five times already. Seventy-five! We're racing the clock, Sam."

"And that's exactly why we need to do this the right way. Besides, if you really want to go faster, focusing on El Camino Real is the way to do it. We are learning a lot from this challenge. The AI engine keeps getting smarter." She pointed at Ted's seat and locked eyes with him. She felt frustrated and disappointed that they were having this same debate again. They had had this very same conversation at least once a month for the past year. "Sit down, please. I want to show you something."

He reluctantly returned to his chair, falling into the seat, slumped over and obviously angry.

Sam set about connecting her laptop to a panel recessed in the center of the table. The overhead projector buzzed and sputtered as it whirred to life. After a few moments, it went dark.

"Shit," Sam said softly.

Lori took this as a sign to top off her coffee. She quietly excused herself and walked over to a small table in the corner of the room. A box of bagels sat beside containers of peanut butter and cream cheese. Three thermal carafes lined the back of the table, labeled REGULAR, DECAF, and HAZELNUT. Lori slid her mug under the last one and filled it to the top. She turned to see Ralph standing beside her, picking out a cinnamon-raisin bagel.

"Was he always like this?" Ralph whispered to Lori. "Back at DSU."

"How so?"

"Was he always such a dick?"

Lori glanced discreetly over her shoulder to be sure Ted was still on the opposite side of the room. She was glad to see him hunched over his notepad, scribbling away, though stopping now and then to tap his pen.

"Ted's always been a bit hyper," Lori replied. "He pushed us, especially Nico. But that's just who he is. I've never had to work for him, however. Just with him as a peer. Why? What's going on with the hardware team?"

"Things were fine at first, but in the last two months, he's sort of started to pit us against one another. And he doesn't hesitate to throw someone under the bus whenever there's a setback."

"Bring it to Vin. We're all on the same team, remember?"

"I know. I just don't want to rock the boat."

The lights in the room dimmed, a screen descended from the ceiling, and Sam walked over beside it. Ralph scooped up a glob of peanut butter and smeared it across his bagel. He and Lori quickly grabbed their seats.

"Stop signs," Sam said. "We all know them, right?"

She used a remote controller to click through a few slides. Each slide showed a standard stop sign, bright red coloring, eight sides, white letters, white outline. Some were mounted on large silver lighting poles, others attached to squat narrow hunter-green steel posts.

"Easy to spot, right?" She scanned the crowd, quietly acknowledging the nodding heads, then clicked ahead. "How about now?"

The slides continued to go by in rapid succession. The sky in the background grew darker with each subsequent picture. Some of the stop signs shimmered, their reflective coating highlighting their message. Other sat dimly lit in the blackness of night.

"As humans, we know these are all the same signs with the same meaning. Our brains recognize them, even in different lighting or in different locations."

"We know, Sam," Ted said dismissively. "Our AI engine needs to learn these things."

She ignored his comment and clicked ahead. The next slide showed a stop sign with an All Way sign beneath it. The street signs above it showed it to be the intersection of Grant and Lombard, very close to Coit Tower, a popular tourist attraction in the Bay area. Sam clicked ahead. The image on the next slide was identical, but the All Way sign had been digitally removed. She continued to progress forward through her presentation. Each subsequent slide showed the stop sign becoming bent and mangled until the final slide showed no stop sign at all.

"Everyone in this room knows that a deformed stop sign is still a stop sign. As drivers, we would know to stop. But what about this slide here, where the sign is missing?"

"Even a human driver who had never been there wouldn't realize it should be there," Ted said. "They'd plow right through it. Maybe they'd get hit, maybe not."

"Since that's a four-way stop, it's also possible an alert driver might notice the other three stop signs and at least slow down," Lori added.

"Great observation," Sam said.

"Fine, you win." Ted flipped his notepad closed and slammed his pen against the cover.

"This isn't a competition." She kept her cool, turned off the presentation, and raised the lights in the room. "If the autonomous vehicle is to succeed, it must be smarter than us."

"It needs to see things that aren't there?" Ted asked as he rolled his eyes mockingly.

"Yes!" she replied. "The car needs to be a better driver than the best of us. It must be the greatest driver in the world."

"You're talking about AI replacing humans," he said. "Just like Vernor Vinge predicted in the nineties."

"When you say it like that it sounds all doom and gloom." She placed her remote on the end of the table and leaned forward, her eyes scanning the room. She had everyone's attention, except for Ted's. Sam walked over to the whiteboard and pointed at the date. "What happened on this day fourteen years ago?"

One by one, the team members turned and faced one another, exchanging confused glances. Ralph reached into his pocket to pull out his smartphone.

"No cheating," Sam said sternly. "Anyone?"

"Deep Blue won its first chess game against Gary Kasparov," Ted said. "The computer would go on to beat the world champion decisively the following year."

"Correct." Sam shot him a smile but found herself disappointed by the scowl that remained on his face. "Only after IBM rewrote the code. They learned a lot in that first competition and came back a year later with a better, smarter machine—one that could beat the greatest. That's what we're doing with each of these challenges. That's what we do each time we take Leapfrog out on the road. We're making a better driver. Ted, remember the bike messenger that took our mirror off?"

"Which one? We got hit three times on Market Street."

"I'm talking about the last one. The one where you hit the kill switch to avoid a runaway shopping cart. You jerked the wheel and almost hit the biker."

"So?" He chuckled to himself. "The asshole kind of deserved it. He was going the wrong way."

"My point exactly. Our technology needs to be better than bad drivers, including the ones in this room."

She stared at him, doing her best to ignore the rest of the team members. Her dig at Ted did not go unnoticed by the rest of the attendees. The silence and tension in the room were painfully uncomfortable.

"Are we done?" Ted asked flatly.

"The meeting's over," Sam replied. She turned and faced the rest of the team. "Everyone can go. Everyone except Ted."

She kept her eyes on Ted, waiting for the team to file out of the room. From the corner of her eye, she could see Ralph make a pitstop for another bagel. As he left the room, Sam pointed at the door. Ralph got the hint and closed it behind him.

"What's wrong with you?" Sam asked. "You've been wound up the past few weeks."

"I just have a lot on my mind."

"We all do. Look, Ted, I get that we are all under a lot of pressure. And I know you like to cut corners. But we are making great progress. I don't get the rush. Even outside of work, you've been on edge." She leaned across the table and took him by both hands, squeezing them firmly. "Talk to me."

"Are we still planning to do the El Camino Real test tomorrow?"

"What?" She sat back, letting go of him. She couldn't understand why he was deflecting the question. "Yes. The team is wrapping up the final coding changes today. Why?"

"I have a feeling this will be the one." He stood up and grabbed his notepad. "I have to leave early today."

"Why? I thought you were coming over for a movie night with Dani and I."

"I can't. I've been trying to schedule something."

"I'm beginning to think you don't like her."

"You know that's not true."

"I just feel you put my family last, Ted. I know you aren't close with your parents, or even your brothers. But you could be with my family if you would spend more time with them."

"Oh, as if your mother would love that."

She was about to respond when a knock rang out against the glass door of the conference room. She looked over to see Ralph smiling and waving. The door opened, and Sam's daughter Dani came running inside.

"Mommy!" Dani cried.

She was dressed in red corduroy pants and a pink cotton sweater, a visitor badge clipped to her collar. Her blond hair was pulled into a ponytail with a pink ribbon. Sam rolled her chair to the side and flung her arms wide open, pulling Dani into a warm embrace.

"Well, this is a surprise," she said. She looked past Dani's shoulder at Ralph. He was still holding the door open. Ralph's face became awash with dread as he took a step backward. Catherine Lavoie stepped in front of Ralph and entered the conference room. Sam smiled and said, "Mom? What are you doing here?"

"I left you a voicemail earlier," Catherine said. She turned and looked at Ralph and waited for him to leave. Once the door closed, she turned and looked at Ted. "Ted."

"Catherine," he replied.

Catherine's piercing hazel eyes could halt anyone in their tracks. She always seemed to be studying everyone and everything around her. She could be having a conversation with one person while keeping her eyes locked on someone else. Even when she smiled, her eyes would often convey a different set of emotions. When she spoke, it was always with conviction. Catherine chose her words carefully, so there would never be any doubt or hesitation in what message she was delivering.

"There's an emergency board meeting that I need to attend." Catherine took a few steps into the conference room. "I sent the nanny home earlier. She's running a horrible fever. I'm sorry to bring Dani here, but I didn't have any other last-minute options."

"It's not a problem, Mom."

"Ted!" Dani ran over to him and flung her arms around his legs. He stood awkwardly, still holding his pen and paper in his hand and clumsily patted Dani on her head.

"Hey, kid," he said.

"Can we go play with Leapfrog?" Dani asked.

"You need to ask your mom," he replied.

"Of course we can," Sam said. She stood up and walked over to her mother and gave her a hug and kiss. "I'm sorry I missed your call, Mom. It's been a crazy day. I've been in back-to-back meetings."

"You need to take time for yourself," Catherine said. She ran a comforting hand across Sam's hair, tucking it behind her ears. She glanced at Ted and said, "And your family. Always make time for your family."

Ted continued to pat Dani on her head, eventually turning his gaze from Catherine to Sam.

"I'll call you tomorrow," Catherine said to Sam. "Again, sorry for the short notice."

"No apology needed, Mom."

Catherine blew a kiss toward Dani and left the conference room. Ralph was waiting for her in the hallway to escort her to the exit. Once the door swung closed, Dani let go of Ted and ran back to her mother.

"Any second thoughts on dinner and a movie with us this evening?" Sam asked him.

"I'll do my best," he replied. "I promise."

31

Sam was dripping in sweat. Outside Leapfrog, the air was in the low sixties, however the bank of computers in the backseat generated quite a bit of excess heat, often requiring the Prius's air-conditioner to be turned on, even when it was cold outside. She lowered her window, welcoming the fresh, cool air as it ran over her face and played with the tassels of her hair whipping behind her head. She briefly closed her eyes, allowing herself the relief offered by the wind. A series of beeps on her laptop interrupted her reverie, bringing her back to the task at hand.

The map on her screen showed them closing in on the end of the El Camino Real challenge. Of course, they'd been to this exact intersection ten times before. Each time there had been something completely unpredictable that caused the car to go offline, forcing the driver to regain control. A car would run a red light or back out of a spot without looking. The team had wrongfully assumed they would encounter conditions similar to the ones experienced on Market Street, but the sheer length of the El Camino test constantly threw new and unexpected surprises at them. Ted likened it to playing a video game and reaching the final level only to lose your last man. Game over. Start again from the very beginning.

The loop began and ended at Ashton University. They were only a few miles away, several blocks from San Carlos Ave. El Camino Real, also known as Route 82, was two lanes wide on each side. They had yet to make it past this intersection. Traffic was heavy, and they were stopped at a traffic light behind a long line of vehicles.

"If we make it past this light, we should be in the clear," she said.

"You say that every time we go out, Sam. There are how many lights on this route?" Ted asked.

"Two hundred or so. I can pull up the exact number in my program. Hold on."

"I really don't want to know. Man, this test has been brutal—so many variables we have to account for."

The light ahead turned green, and the traffic began to move forward. Leapfrog, as programmed, was slow to accelerate, which allowed a gap between them and the car in front.

"That's why we have to keep repeating it, Ted. It's the only way to—"

A tricked out Honda Civic, periwinkle blue, and with a muffler the size of a coffee can, tore out of a parking lot just ahead of Leapfrog, cutting across the opposite lane of traffic. The AI system slammed on the brakes and swerved to the left to avoid an accident and came to a stop diagonally across the empty center lane. The burble of the Honda's customized engine blared like an angry nest of hornets as the two-door coupe tore its way ahead, screeching its tires as it raced away. Sam immediately reached for the kill switch.

"No!" Ted blocked Sam's arm. "Wait."

They both jumped in their seats at the sudden blast of a horn shrieking from behind them. A pearl white BMW 328i was mere inches from their back bumper. Sam looked over her shoulder to see the driver pounding on his steering wheel. The BMW lurched to the right and roared past the Prius, cutting in front of it and across to a turn lane on the right side of the road. Leapfrog sat motionless in the center lane. More horns honked as traffic inched around the Toyota, like marching ants.

"Leapfrog hasn't released control back to us." Ted pointed at her screen. "Don't end the test. Wait."

The lane ahead of them was clear of traffic. After what felt like an eternity, Leapfrog straightened out and began to move forward toward the center lane. The little Toyota patiently waited until it could maneuver back into the left lane, returning to the programmed course.

"She figured it out!" Sam scanned through a log file on her laptop. "That's the first time she didn't release control back to us. Not for an emergency lane change like that one. When she gets crammed in diagonally like that, she's always given up."

"I had the team design a new douchebag program," Ted deadpanned. "With sub-routines for hideously loud and ugly Civics, as well as pretentious BMW drivers."

Sam burst out laughing. Although they weren't at the end of the course yet, she realized this event alone was a milestone for Leapfrog. "That was a close one, Ted."

"You wanted to hit that kill switch. You trusted me and took a risk. I'm proud of you."

"That BMW almost slammed into us. I just didn't want anyone to get hurt."

"I've told you before that you jump the gun too often with that kill switch."

"It's better to be safe than sorry, Ted. You know we can't cause an accident."

"We didn't. Relax, Sam, it's almost over."

"God, I hope so."

Her heart pumped with optimism as the scenery passed by and she looked over at Ted, thrilled to see he, too, was smiling. She took his hand and squeezed it, refusing to let go. They held hands for the remainder of the trip until the Prius reached Ashton Avenue.

"This is it," she said. "This is the final turn, Ted."

"Don't jinx us."

She found it hard to breathe. Her eyes darted between her laptop, the stoplight, and every car around them. The pounding of her heart resonated throughout her body. She glanced over at Ted, hoping he'd shoot her a smile or any sort of look to relax her. Instead, he looked just as nervous as she was. She knew that if Leapfrog made this turn, their greatest challenge yet would finally be complete.

The stoplight turned green, and the Prius whirred ahead, turning left onto San Carlos Avenue. Sam finally exhaled once the turn was complete. The road ahead was clear. They sat in silence as Leapfrog continued humming forward until it reached Ashton Avenue. The Toyota turned onto the campus and followed the short winding road to the Welcome Center, pulling into the parking lot and coming to a halt.

Sam looked down at her screen and waited for what felt like an eternity until a message flashed across the window: "Course Complete."

"Holy shit," she said, her eyes tearing up. She turned and smiled as she looked at Ted. "We did it."

"Assuming Vin approves it."

"It will pass. I've been working with his quality team to update our tests. Our last challenge passed the quality review on the first full completion, remember?" She returned her gaze to her laptop and began to scan through the log files. "I know what they consider a pass or fail now. My system won't flash 'Course Complete' unless we are truly done. Trust me. We nailed this."

"I would love nothing more than to have the El Camino Real challenge behind us."

"I think we clocked in over six-thousand miles just on this one test." She leaned over and kissed him on the cheek. "How many miles are on Leapfrog? I just realized we might need to plan on getting another Prius. I think we're going to blow way past that hundred-thousand-mile goal."

"Enough with the plans, Sam. You're one hundred percent convinced Vin will mark this challenge as complete?"

"Completely."

He smiled, his face beaming with delight.

"I've never seen you so thrilled to end a challenge," She said. There was something different about his grin. "What?"

"We should go celebrate."

"What are you thinking? Donovan's?"

"Not quite."

Ted was giddy, waiting for the car's gas tank to fill. Ashton's campus was not far from GSI's headquarters. He insisted they stop at a specific gas station to refuel. Sam stayed in the car, keeping her head buried in her laptop as she methodically read off key information from the log file. A snap from the handle indicated the tank was full. Ted returned the hose to the pump, grabbed his receipt, and jumped back into the driver's seat.

"Give me that," he said. He snagged Sam's laptop from her grasp. "We have one more program to run."

"What program?" she asked.

He smirked, refusing to answer her question. He logged Sam out of the system and then logged back in with his credentials. He scrolled through a list of files before finding the one he'd installed last week called "Future." It was a simple program that Lori helped him design. Lori had pressed him on what it was for, but he told her she would have to wait. He also swore her to secrecy. He initiated the program and gave the laptop back to Sam.

"What is this?" Sam stared at the screen with confusion. Leapfrog began to move forward, stopping at the exit to the main road. "Where are we going?"

"Be patient. And don't touch anything. Or read the details on the map's route. Just let the program run."

"This isn't for the next challenge, is it? We need to plan these routes in detail, Ted. Run simulations first."

"Relax, Sam. Sometimes it's the unplanned events that end up being the most special."

The Prius turned onto El Camino Real, accelerated, and settled into the traffic, humming along at the posted speed limit. Ted could barely contain the excitement he felt over what was waiting at the end of the route. He felt his cheeks redden as he replayed everything he had planned for today. He glanced over at Sam, smiled, leaned over, and kissed her. She gently pushed him away.

"And how did you get a program installed on my laptop?"

"You ask too many questions." He let loose with a nervous laugh. "It's a surprise."

She frowned and returned her attention to the view outside the windshield. Leapfrog began to make its way east, following Whipple Avenue toward Emerald Lake Hills.

"I have to get home to Dani, Ted." She was visibly frustrated. "What's this all about?"

He ignored her. He was afraid her questions might result in him accidentally spoiling his surprise. He folded his arms, smiled, and watched the view ahead. Leapfrog made a few more turns before coming to a halt. Sam's laptop flashed the message "Course Complete."

"We're here," he said, popping his door open, and turning off the engine.

The Toyota had stopped in front of a custom-built modern style home. The beige exterior was accented with brown and olive trim. A wide paver driveway led to a two-car garage. The front yard had been recently landscaped, with fresh plantings and new sod everywhere. Posted at the front edge of the property was a realtor sign with the word "Sold" dangling beneath it.

Sam joined him next to the sign and studied the property. He smiled as her jaw fell open.

"Did you buy this?" she asked.

"I closed on it earlier this week." He reached into his pocket and pulled out a set of keys. "Follow me."

"But Ted, how? This neighborhood is expensive."

He chuckled and took her by the hand. The white and tan checkered paved pathway was lined with pink, red, and white flowers. A welcome mat in a covered portico greeted them. He opened the oak-stained wooden door and motioned for her to step inside. The empty rooms echoed the thud of the door closing behind them.

"It's at the top of my budget," he said. "Well, it's actually way over my budget. But I can make the monthly payments until we get our bonus checks. Then I plan to refinance. It'll all work out fine in the end. What do you think?"

"I think it sounds risky."

"Don't you know me by now?"

She stepped into the middle of the living room and looked around. A staircase led to a catwalk on the second floor. The far end of the room had a polished stone fireplace. The opposite side was open to a very high-end kitchen. She excitedly began inspecting it. A long island separated it from the living area. Glass pendants dangled from the ceiling like icicles. The cabinets, counters, and walls were white, gray, and beige. Sam played with a few of the drawers and ran her hands across the stainless steel appliances. She looked back up to the catwalk.

"How big is this place?"

"It's got four bedrooms and three and a half bathrooms. The master is downstairs."

He took her by the hand and led her down the hallway to the master suite. Inside, French doors on the opposite wall looked out to the backyard.

"Is that a swimming pool?" Sam scampered across the plush carpeted floor to look outside. "Ted, this is way too much house for you."

His heart was racing wildly. Her face was plastered to the glass panes, taking in the beautifully manicured yard. His hands trembled as he reached into his pocket and withdrew the real reason he brought her here. He walked toward Sam and stopped a few feet away.

"You're right, Sam. It's too much house just for one person."

Sam turned around to find Ted down on one knee.

"What are you"—her voice faded away when she saw what was in his hand.

He flipped open a blue velvet ring box, displaying a 1.5-carat pear-shaped diamond. The gem was set in rose gold and surrounded by twenty smaller stones. He felt the world around him begin to move in slow motion. The pounding of his heart slowed, as did his breathing. Words he'd rehearsed endlessly over the past few months sat precipitously on the edge of his lips.

"Sam Lavoie," he said, his voice shaking. "You're as brilliant as you are beautiful. You're as caring as you are confident. You ground me. You make me see the world through different eyes. Better eyes. And you're the best thing that's ever happened to me. Nobody understands me the way you do. Nobody else ever will. I can't imagine spending the rest of my life without you. Will you marry me?"

When he exhaled, he felt weeks of tension rush from his body, as if every nerve and muscle finally let itself unwind. He smiled as he held back tears of joy. Sam stood wide-eyed and motionless, staring at the sparkling ring.

"Ted"—her lower lip began to quiver— "I . . . I don't know what to say. I didn't expect this."

"I'm glad I surprised you." He stood up and removed the ring from the case, resting it in his palm. "I was worried you were going to figure it out."

"Figure it out? I'm . . . I'm shocked. How . . . how long have you been planning this?"

"Since Christmas."

"Christmas?" She continued staring at the ring. "That big discussion we had during dinner? My mother had asked you about raising a family. You . . . you said your life was too consumed with the work you were doing. The two of you even got into that spat when you said babies scared you."

"They do! They're so . . . fragile. Look, Sam, that entire discussion was Catherine fishing." He grinned as he recalled that dinner from a few months ago. "She wants what's best for you. So do I. I love you, and I want to spend the rest of my life with you. It's that simple."

She pulled his hand closer and ran her fingers across the gold ring. "I . . . I don't know what to say."

"I assumed you'd say yes." He chuckled briefly, but his nervous laugh quickly subsided as he studied her face. "What's wrong?"

"Nothing. It's just that, well, getting married is a big step. I'm . . . I'm a bit shell shocked."

"I can see that."

She gently took the ring from him and ran her fingertip around the edge of the main stone. "It's beautiful, Ted. I never . . . I just—"

"What is it, Sam?"

"This is just a lot to take in. There's a lot to think about."

"Like what?" He felt himself becoming worried and frustrated. Each time he'd rehearsed his proposal in his mind, it always ended with her saying yes and crying. "I don't understand."

"If we get married, then Dani and I would live here."

"That's generally how it works, Sam."

"But, my mother's out in Fremont." She stared at the ring as she began to pace back and forth in the bedroom. "She takes care of Dani when I'm not around. You know that, Ted."

"Meaning what? You'll marry me if we live near your mother?"

"No, I didn't mean that." She stopped pacing and stared out at the pool. "I'm just trying to process this."

He felt his nerves subside as he realized Sam was being Sam, trying to analyze every possible input and output. A smile spread across his face as he walked over to the door and stood behind her. He leaned forward and brushed his nose against her hair, inhaling her sweet scent. He gently slid his arms around her waist and pulled her close.

"This isn't some complicated project for you to plan in detail, Sam." He began to sway back and forth, rocking her along with him. "You either want to marry me, or you don't. Don't overthink this. We can figure out your mother and daycare later. We'll find a way to make it work. I promise."

She looked down at the diamond engagement ring she was holding.

Her eyes quickly filled with tears. She turned around and looked up at him. "You . . . you really want to marry me?"

"I do. But it takes two. Do you?" He kissed her on her lips. "Take the risk, Sam."

She trembled in his arms, finally pulling herself away and walking to the middle of the room, cradling the ring in the palm of her hand. She spun around once, and with tears streaming down her face turned to him and said, "Yes. Yes, I'll marry you."

32

Eighteen months later, the team found themselves in the home stretch. A whiteboard to the right of the stage in the Convene section of the Project Courier area showed the current status of the ten challenges. The first nine were complete, with only the San Francisco to Los Angeles challenge remaining. The upper corner of the board indicating the total miles tested read 548,319, with the original goal of 100,000 miles long ago crossed off in red marker. Ted and Sam were flopped in two bean bag chairs in the Crash area staring at the board across the room.

"We've done this test forty-two times," he said, squirming to get a comfortable position. "How many more will we have to do?"

"As many as it takes," she replied. "We're so close. I know we'll get it done by the end of the year."

"Do you really think it'll take six more weeks?"

"Why? Do you think it will take longer?"

"Longer?" He flung his palms against his eyes and slid his hands across his face. "Sam, I wanted this done months ago. We can't keep dragging this out."

"Is this because of your debt?" She waited for him to respond. He remained silent. "You never should have bought that expensive house."

"I thought we'd be married by now." He leaned forward, causing the blue suede fabric to creak and groan beneath him. "You're still not ready to set a date?"

"Not until these tests are over." She wiggled her way to the edge of her bag and lowered her voice. "Imagine if we'd set a date last year, thinking this would all be over."

"Then we'd be married by now."

"Ted, we both know our lives are insane because of this project. When would we have found time to plan a wedding?"

"We could have run off to Vegas for a weekend."

"My mother never would have allowed it."

"Exactly." He grinned and winked at her. "I proposed to you well over a year ago."

"I know, Ted."

"It's November. We can't keep delaying this."

"I barely have time for Dani or my mother. This job is consuming everything."

"I'm starting to wonder if you're having second thoughts." He reached over and ran his thumb across Sam's diamond engagement ring, slowly caressing it and causing it to spin gently around her finger. "Are you?"

"You know that's not true. My mother's become obsessed with the wedding."

"Oh, I've noticed. Detailed planning must run in your family." He chuckled briefly at his joke. "I'm just happy she's finally happy. With me."

"I told you she'd eventually come around. I've never seen her this excited. She wants to make this a big event. Why are you in a rush?"

"A rush? It's been over eighteen months, Sam. Maybe if you'd at least move in with me—"

"No, I told you things are easier living in Fremont near my mother."

"We can arrange for daycare. We're going to have to at some point."

"I'm not discussing this again. Dani is happy having her grandmother to care for her. She loves her school and her friends. We'll move in with you after the wedding. That will be a big change. I can't do that to her while I'm still working these crazy hours."

He forced a smile to appear, although deep down he was very unhappy. He knew from experience not to try and come between Sam and her mother or daughter. That was a bond he would never be able to break, not that he wanted to. He looked over at the table at the back of the stage. Only one bottle was left standing. He knew they were close to completing the final challenge. He told himself he just needed to hold out a little bit longer.

"Sure thing, Sam." He gently squeezed her hands before letting go and leaning back in his chair. "But no more excuses after the final challenge is over. We're setting a date as soon as it ends, okay?"

She was about to respond when Ralph and Lori approached them.

"Are we interrupting?" Ralph asked Ted. "You've got that look on your face."

"What look?" Ted said.

"Have you seen what's outside?" Ralph asked, ignoring Ted's question. "Vin strikes again."

"And it sparked an argument between Ralph and me," Lori added. "Pun intended."

Ted struggled to pull himself out of the lumpy bean bag chair, finally reaching out to Ralph for assistance. He then helped Sam up, and the pair followed Ralph and Lori over to the floor-to-ceiling windows a few yards away. Ted looked outside at the parking lot. Several people were walking around, and two others zipped by on bicycles.

"What am I looking at?" Ted asked.

"All the way down at the end of the first row," Ralph said. "What do you see?"

Ted sighed, frustrated that his conversation with Sam had been interrupted before he got an answer out of her. He also wasn't in the mood for any guessing games. He searched the front row of cars, stopping at the last one. A sleek five-door sedan was parked at the end, the sun glistening off the bright red paint job. Ted squinted as he studied the muscular haunches over the rear wheels.

"Is that what I think it is?" Ted asked in amazement.

"The new Tesla Model S," Ralph replied. "I haven't seen Vin this morning, but I plan to ask him for a test ride."

Tesla's launch of its first in-house designed and built vehicle had been all the talk around the Project Courier team. Many doubted whether the upstart company could pull it off and produce a vehicle even remotely close to the prototype they'd displayed in early 2009. Three years later, Tesla proved the naysayers wrong when the Model S finally started trickling out of their plant in Fremont just a few months ago.

"Did he keep his Roadster?" Sam asked.

"Who knows," Ralph replied, staring out the window. "Anyway, Lori and I started debating where self-driving tech will first kick in. I know you two have your theories. But, when I look at that sleek sedan, I just can't picture it with a giant lidar array on the roof. I mean, look at that thing!"

Vin's Model S was parked fairly far away, but Ted could still make out the car's flowing lines. He chuckled as he tried to picture Leapfrog's cumbersome set of sensors bolted to the roof.

"I see your point, Ralph," Ted said. He looked over at Sam. "We're going to need to find a way to make our frogs pretty."

GSI now had three Toyotas retrofitted with autonomous hardware. After much debate, the team had settled on the simple names of Leapfrog-2 and Leapfrog-3 for the latest additions. The original Leapfrog had suffered too many engine issues once they passed two hundred thousand miles of testing.

"Aesthetics are the least of our problems," Sam said. "We need to focus on finishing this final challenge. Then we can look into downsizing the hardware."

"I told Ralph that taxis and trucks seem like the best place to start," Lori said, leaning back against the window. Vin's sleek sedan no longer interested her. "We should be able to go after that market first. Bulky hardware won't matter with those vehicles."

"And I told Lori that even if that's true, at some point we need to make the hardware attractive enough to easily integrate into a car that someone would want to be seen in." Ralph tapped the glass, pointing in the direction of Vin's new ride. "Nobody's going to want to own a self-driving car if it doesn't look as sleek as that."

"Why do they have to own it?" Sam asked, taking a position next to Lori. "Why spend all that money on a robot?"

"What?" Ralph asked, genuinely confused. "You do realize that's the whole point of Project Courier."

"Nobody ever said the autonomous car needs to be owned," Sam replied. "Look at Where2."

"The ride-sharing app?" Ralph asked. "Zimride does something similar, don't they? I don't see your point."

"Where2 is currently piloting their program here in the Bay area," Sam said. "They intend to go national and then global. Right now, they seem like a cost-effective alternative to a taxi. You launch the app, enter a destination, and someone comes and gets you and takes you where you want to go. People like that can get different classes of cars, too. But what if they could replace car ownership?"

"You mean like Zipcar?" Ted asked. His frustrations with Sam from earlier were fading away. Her passion for the autonomous car project was one of the many qualities that attracted him to her, even though the project was also delaying their marriage. "In some cities, people use Zipcar because it's cheaper than owning a car."

"My point exactly, Ted. Take that Tesla outside. Slap our autonomous technology on top of it. Now put it in a charging station somewhere. You open up an app, pick a route, pay for it, and the car comes and brings you to your destination. When it's done, it either goes to the next customer or back to the charging station."

"So, you see car ownership going away and being replaced by fleets owned by Where2 and Zipcar?" Ralph asked.

"It's a definite possibility," Sam said. "This technology we built will be a disrupter—a major one. Who can really predict how it will end?"

Ted looked out at the parking lot. A second Tesla Model S passed by, this one white. He closed his eyes and tried to imagine an empty parking lot, replaced by a drop-off/pick-up area, and a line of driverless Teslas queued up to shuttle people away.

"I think it's going to be a difficult transition," Ted said. "Think of all the issues we've run into during these challenges. We've got hundreds of thousands of miles under our belt, and we still aren't there yet."

"But we're close," Sam said. "Look at how far we've come these past three years. Remember the first time a squirrel ran out in front of Leapfrog? The software didn't know what to do. Turn left? Turn right? Stop?"

"I still say squirrels should just be run over," Ted interjected, laughing out loud. His smile faded as he realized no one else appreciated his attempt at humor. "Look, the issue is the human driver in the non-autonomous car. If you look back at most of our failures, it's people getting in the way and not following the rules. I can see a clash between autonomous vehicles behaving perfectly, and humans behaving badly."

"Maybe we dedicate lanes just for the autonomous cars," Sam said. "The current HOV lanes could be used for them."

"Maybe," Ted said. He glanced back at the table with the champagne bottles. "We'll never know what the future holds until we conquer the final test. Let's get back to work. I want to complete this last challenge well before Christmas."

Rush hour on the 405 was an oxymoron. Traffic was at a complete standstill. Ted and Sam were waiting to exit onto I-10 East, having just completed over 370 miles of their trip from San Francisco. They had all four of Leapfrog-3's windows lowered a few inches, allowing a cool breeze to drift into the car. The date was December 14, and they were on their fiftieth test run of the final challenge.

"How are we doing?" Ted asked, lowering his window a few more inches. The temperature outside was fifty-three degrees. He would have been able to enjoy it a bit more were it not for the clattering of a diesel pickup truck idling next to them. “I’m almost afraid to ask.”

“Seven miles to go,” Sam said. “We’ve reached this point five times before. The I-10 always seems to kill us.”

“I would just like to make it to Fairfax. That’s the exit off the 10, right?”

“Yes. After that, it’s two miles to the museum.”

The diesel engine beside Ted rattled to life as the vehicles began to crawl ahead. Once they got to the ramp to get onto I-10, the traffic cleared, and Leapfrog-3 accelerated. They passed beneath an overpass before stumbling upon more stopped cars. The engine on the Prius shut off as the hybrid used its battery to coast to a stop. Suddenly a motorcycle roared past them, clipping the driver’s side mirror.

“Damn L.A. drivers.” Ted gave the mirror a quick inspection, noting the dent on the outer edge. He glanced over at Sam. “That hit wasn’t our fault. Don’t tell the quality team about it. And don’t even think of hitting the kill switch.”

“I know.”

“Do you think we’ll always need a kill switch?” He stared at the shiny red button attached to a black metal box popping out of the center console. “Even when we have full autonomy. I know the goal is to eliminate the human driver, but we never really talked about a failsafe option long term.”

“No.” Her response was immediate, without hesitation. She kept her eyes fixated on the map on her laptop. “Our testing has proven that human reaction times are too slow to re-engage when the system shuts down. I’ve looked at the data, Ted. Yours is the worst.”

“Mine?” He was taken aback. “What, are you spying on me?”

“No.” She laughed as she gave him a smirk. “I’ve documented all of our test drivers. Ralph. Lori. The entire team. If you look at how fast Leapfrog responds to an event and then compare that to a human response, it’s no contest. The robot wins. But when you look at the AI system giving up midway through an event, the human response to take over is horrible."

"It's amazing you fit so much brainpower in that pretty little head of yours." He leaned over and kissed her on her cheek. "It's one of your many sexy qualities."

"Don't change the subject." Her cheeks became beat red. "Remember the deer we hit in Yosemite?"

"How can I forget? We both screamed our heads off. That thing came out of nowhere."

"It blindsided us. We came around that corner, and it just jumped right out. Leapfrog had no clue what to do and shut down. You were too busy screaming to take control, and we hit it."

"That stupid animal cracked the windshield. Set us back weeks with repairs."

"That's not the point, Ted. You weren't paying attention. Neither was I. We were both too busy looking at the scenery."

"Well, it's a gorgeous park."

"We were complacent, thinking we didn't have to pay attention. We got lazy. You got lazy behind the wheel."

"You're just mad that we hit a deer and got blood all over the hood. I told you, Sam—"

"Don't give me your spilled blood speech, Ted."

"It was just an animal, Sam. That was the only real accident we've had on this project, other than some minor fender benders and curb strikes. Nobody's died in over half a million miles. That's impressive."

"That deer could have been a person—a child." She paused as she collected her thoughts. "You're a brilliant man, Ted. I truly believe Project Courier wouldn't have been a success without you. I just wish you wouldn't dismiss these close calls. Imagine if the next Einstein or Beethoven is in one of these car accidents. We can reduce that chance by eighty or ninety percent with autonomy."

"Did you just equate me to Einstein?" He smiled. He glanced over at Sam and quickly sobered when he saw she was not smiling. "I get it, Sam. I do."

The traffic began to move, as did Leapfrog-3. Sam frowned and focused her attention on her laptop. He reached over and gently took her by her chin, tilting her face back toward his.

"I *do*, Sam. And you're right. I wasn't paying attention when we hit that deer. I should have been ready to take control." He pointed to the steering wheel. "Maybe the vehicle of the future won't even need this thing."

She glanced at the dashboard and then looked back over her shoulder, darting her eyes everywhere. A smile spread across her face, and her eyes lit up.

"The entire concept of interior design will change," she said. "A car without a steering wheel. I never thought about that. We're going to have to add that to the list of research items once we finish this challenge."

"Then let's finish it. How are we looking?"

"We're almost at the exit for Fairfax. If we can make it there, I think we'll be fine. We've run that road before to map it out. Fairfax is a mix of residential and small businesses. Narrow. Only a couple of lights if I'm not mistaken."

"You sound so confident," he said.

"I have a good feeling about this one."

The Prius reached the end of the Fairfax exit and waited at the light to take a left-hand turn. Traffic was still busy, but Ted was relieved to be off the 10 finally. Fairfax Avenue's lane count varied sporadically, depending on the location. Once off the exit, there were five lanes—two on each side as well as a center turn lane. Once past Venice Boulevard, the northbound lane dropped down to one. Traffic lightened up, and Leapfrog-3 hummed along at the posted thirty-five miles per hour speed limit.

"This is going too smoothly." He craned his neck to look out all sides of the vehicle. The road was now lined with beautiful trees and homes with manicured lawns, set back behind concrete sidewalks. "Nice neighborhood, though."

As they passed Pickford Street, the single-family homes gave way to small apartment buildings. Ted felt his chest tighten as the light stayed green, and they passed through the intersection. He glanced over at the map on Sam's laptop. He was afraid to ask how much farther they had to go, but he knew it had to be less than a mile. He started to believe Sam was right. They were finally going to complete this test.

The intersection with Saturn Street had a sign for drivers to yield to pedestrians. There was no crosswalk, just a series of white arrows painted across the street. A tall, overgrown evergreen shrub blocked the view around the corner. Without warning, a small gray-colored pug appeared on the corner, his bright blue leash leading up to a young woman in her early twenties. The woman's left hand had a tight grip on the short leash, and a mobile phone was locked in her other hand. She was lost in her screen, oblivious to her surroundings. The dog did not bother to stop at the curb and continued to trot out into the street, with the owner mindlessly following along.

"Shit!" Sam screamed, lunging for the kill switch.

"No!" Ted grabbed her wrist and yanked her arm back.

Leapfrog-3 detected the dog and immediately slammed on the brakes. Ted and Sam both lurched forward against their seat belts.

"What the hell, Ted?"

He checked the laptop's screen to confirm the program was still running, relieved to see that Leapfrog-3 had not relinquished control. Then he felt a set of eyes piercing him. He looked out the windshield to see the woman standing a foot from the front bumper.

"Asshole!" The woman picked up her dog and shook it at him. "You almost ran us over! Pay attention to the signs!"

"Why don't *you* watch where you're going!" he yelled back through his open window. "Asshole!"

The woman presented him with her middle finger before continuing across the street.

"Are you crazy?" Sam asked. "Why did you stop me?"

"We're too close, Sam. Leapfrog did as programmed. I wasn't going to have you ruin it when we're almost there."

She was about to say something when the Prius began to accelerate. She furrowed her brow as she studied her screen. The map indicated they were on track to reach their destination in two more minutes.

"What were you saying about the self-driving car needing to be faster and better than the human?" he asked. "If you'd hit that kill switch, Leapfrog may have stopped braking, and I wouldn't have had time to regain control. We probably would have hit the dog—or the woman—or both."

"Good point, Ted. I'm sorry, I guess my nerves are just completely on edge. We're almost there. My heart's been racing since we got on Fairfax."

"Mine, too." He took her hand and gave her engagement ring a gentle kiss. "We're going to make it, Sam. I promise."

Traffic slowed once more as they passed Pico Boulevard. Small businesses began to spring up around them. Sam checked her laptop, counting the number of remaining intersections. She squeezed his fingers as she counted each one off.

"San Vicente is the last big cross street," she said. "After that, it's two blocks until we reach the museum."

"Have you ever been to the Petersen?" Ted asked.

"No. You?"

"No. My dad talked about it often. It's only been there for twenty years or so. The guy who opened it published lots of car magazines, like *MotorTrend*. I always read that as a kid. The museum has a lot of classic cars. I think the exhibits change often." He looked over at her to see she was lost in her computer screen. "You do know we're going inside when we're done."

"In the museum?" Sam pulled herself out of her laptop. "I'm starving. Can we at least eat first? We've got a long drive home, you know."

"Sure. I think they have a restaurant and bar inside. I wonder if they serve Chivas Regal?"

"What, you didn't bring a bottle?"

Ted laughed as they cruised through the intersection of Fairfax and San Vicente. The next cross street was Eighth Street. As they got closer, he noticed the museum ahead on the right. The building covered the entire block between Wilshire Boulevard and Eighth Street. The stoplight turned red as they reached the corner. He looked at her laptop.

"Are we done?" he asked, pointing at the corner of the museum. "It's right there."

"The program takes us to the front entrance on Wilshire."

"Dammit, Sam, if we fail in the next block, I don't care what the computer says. We made it. Game over. Success."

"We'll make it, Ted."

He took her hand once more. The light soon changed green, and the Prius lumbered forward, the small battery barely getting them into the intersection before the engine fired to life. They cruised along in light traffic until they reached Wilshire Boulevard. Ted held his breath and squeezed Sam's hand as they turned right. Sam's laptop soon beeped, flashing "Course Complete."

"Oh my God," she said.

"I can't believe it. The final test."

"Holy shit, Ted! We're done! All ten!"

He hit the kill switch and took over control, taking them around the side of the building to loop back toward the parking garage entrance. He found an empty space on the side of the street, pulled over, and turned off the engine.

"That leaves only one more unanswered question, Sam," he said.

"What?"

"Can we *please* set our wedding date now?"

The Project Courier room was packed beyond capacity. The core team was seated in the Convene area with all eyes on the main stage. Executives from other divisions and departments stood along the sides of the room and wherever they could find space. The table holding the eleven bottles was in the center of the stage, looking exactly as it had for many months. The Magnum was empty, and nine of the ten champagne bottles were upside down in their hammered pewter buckets. Matthew was holding the tenth bottle, with Vin standing by his side.

Each champagne bottle had been hand-picked by Matthew and came from a different part of Italy. The last bottle to be opened was a particularly dry variety from the Conegliano-Valdobbiadene region. Matthew and Vin were engaged in small talk as they prepared to pop the cork.

"This is the start of a new day . . ." Ted said to Sam. He, Sam, Lori, and Ralph were seated in the front row, only a few feet from the stage. "And, a new bank account."

"You and your money," Sam said as she rolled her eyes. "I'd tell you there's more to life, but why bother?"

"You know that's not true." He leaned closer to her, pressing his lips against her ear. He ran his nose across the top edge of her earlobe, pushing her hair back. "I'm still waiting for the wedding date."

"My mother's working on it." She glanced over at him and winked. "We completed the challenge three days ago. We'll figure the date out this week."

"Is that a promise?"

"Yes. Now, hush. It's starting."

Matthew raised his free arm and waved his hand, motioning for everyone in the room to quiet down. He waited politely for several seconds before realizing there was too much excitement to get everyone's full attention. He moved forward to the edge of the stage.

"I want to welcome everyone here this morning," Matthew said, his voice echoing down from the overhead speakers. "We started this journey in June three-and-a-half years ago. During that time, we achieved what many thought to be impossible."

The lights dimmed, and the screen behind the stage flashed to life. The first slide displayed Project Courier, causing the crowd to explode in cheers and applause. Next came a montage of information, listing the ten main challenges and the overall goal of reaching 100,000 miles. Pictures and videos taken throughout the project's life showed team members working together, as well as some epic failures along the way. Laughs and even some tears sprinkled throughout the room. It was a short video, lasting less than five minutes. The last thirty seconds were a rapid-fire succession, showing the table of champagne bottles flip from unopened to empty until there was one upright bottle remaining. The lights came back up as the crowd applauded.

"I think I speak for everyone when I say no matter how this champagne tastes, it is without a doubt the finest bottle up here." Matthew nodded toward Vin, presenting him with the bottle. Vin twisted the cork a few times before it finally released, sending white foam exploding everywhere. "Congratulations everyone!"

The applause grew louder, with many people stamping their feet on the floor or pounding their hands against their chairs. The noise and thrum became rhythmic and tribal. Matthew and Vin held the bottle high in the space between them. Soon Matthew motioned the crowd to calm down and retake their seats.

"I wish I could personally thank each and every single one of you," Vin said. "In fact, I intend to do that once these formalities are over. Speaking of which, I'm sure many of you are wondering what happens next, now that the challenges are done. Matthew?"

Matthew smiled and said, "We're taking our technology to Detroit!"

The room erupted in applause, with many people, including Ralph and Lori, jumping to their feet. Ted and Sam remained seated.

"What?" he said to Sam, his smile erased from his face. "Did you know this was coming?"

"No," she replied. She stared at Vin, hoping to make eye contact with him, but he was too busy waving and pointing to various people in the audience. "The plan was always to build the core technologies. I thought phase two was to make it something we can easily implement. I guess they want to do that through a partnership with Detroit."

"But we already tried that, Sam. They didn't listen."

"No, Ted. *We* tried it. GSI hasn't. I think Matthew will have a bit more sway than us."

"Are you saying Matthew Grant is more influential than Ted Wolff?"

"That's precisely what I'm saying."

They laughed, their chortles getting lost with the clamor echoing throughout the room. He took her hand and kissed her engagement ring. On stage, Vin motioned for everyone to settle down.

"We have a lot of work to do before we talk with Detroit," Vin said. "We don't want to just show them our results. We need to go to them with a specific plan on how they can use this technology. They don't know it, but I want Sam Lavoie and Ted Wolff to spearhead this effort. Give it up for them."

Ted and Sam half stood up and waved as they looked around the room.

"Great," he whispered to her. "Back we go to Detroit."

"I'm sure this time will be different," she said.

"Before taking Project Courier to the next level, we have one more bit of business to do." Vin stepped aside, allowing Matthew to take center stage. "I believe Matthew has something to share."

Matthew turned to the side of the room. Lisa was standing quietly in the corner. She smiled and knelt slightly to retrieve a black leather bag from the floor. She carried it up the stairs and handed it to Matthew. After shaking her hand, Matthew reached into the bag and retrieved a handful of envelopes.

"Bonus time," Matthew said, waving the envelopes above his head. He did not wait for the laughter and applause to die down before continuing. "I saved the best for last. Lisa will be coming around to hand these out. Thank you. All of you. Now, please, everyone, enjoy the rest of the afternoon."

Four members of the kitchen staff appeared from the hallway, wheeling tables to the café. Champagne bottles and flutes covered one of them. The other tables were filled with a seemingly endless variety of foods. Meats, cheeses, bread, salads, plates of pasta, stir fries, and other delicacies. The room became filled with delicious aromas.

"I can't believe this day is finally here," Ted said to Sam. He pulled her close and hugged her, not caring if he was too public in his affection for his fiancée. "All these years, and we finally have our bonuses."

"We have a lot more than that, Ted. We've got a meeting to plan. Vin just put us in charge of the Detroit presentation. This . . . this is big. The first thing we should—"

"The first thing we should do is get married."

"Oh, right." She laughed as she brushed his hair back. "You'll be happy to know my mom's already scheduled interviews with four different event planners."

"Four?! Let's try to keep it simple, okay?"

33

Sam paced back and forth across the thick Berber carpet in her mother's bedroom. She paused and looked through the French doors overlooking the backyard. Ted's request for an intimate wedding had ended with two hundred people seated outside waiting for the ceremony to begin. She couldn't complain. Her mother had worked several miracles during the last few months pulling the event together. A knock at the door broke her from her trance.

"Come in," she said.

The door opened and Ralph entered, closing it behind him. He looked her up and down, "Wow, you look beautiful." He adjusted the pink tie clinging to his collar as he walked over to her. "Remember when you dressed as Cinderella for Halloween? Well, you just put her to shame."

"Stop," Sam said with a chuckle. She turned and looked at the full-length mirror nearby. Her gown was her mother's, worn at Catherine's insistence. Sam felt it a bit old fashioned, but she knew she had no choice. The white lace top and long sleeves felt too formal to her, as did the veil. "I'm so nervous, I want to puke."

"Relax. It'll all be over soon." He tugged and smoothed the tight-fitting sleeves of Sam's gown. "Everyone out there loves you."

She looked out the window again. She could see Ted's family and what seemed like half the Project Courier team, including Vin and

Matthew. Her mother had invited a long list of friends and business associates, too. Sam grinned as she recalled Ted's suggestion to elope to Vegas.

"Where's the honeymoon?" Ralph asked. "Or is that a secret?"

"Ted wanted to wait and surprise me, but I told him I needed to know. We're . . . we're going to Paris."

"Paris!" He hugged her and went back to adjusting her sleeves. "I've never been. It's on my bucket list. That's a long flight for someone who doesn't like to fly."

"I know. But . . . it's Paris. And my honeymoon."

"You deserve it, Sam. Are you ready?"

The door swung open, and Dani came running into the room carrying a white wicker basket filled with white rose petals. She flung her arms around her mother and said, "It's time! It's time!"

Sam kissed the top of Dani's head and looked up at the open doorway to see her mother standing there, fighting back tears. Ralph put a reassuring hand on Sam's shoulder before turning and leaving. Catherine entered and closed the door.

"One . . . one of the violinists canceled at the last minute," Catherine said. "We should be okay with just the two, but I'm worried the music—"

"I'm sure the music will be fine," Sam said, laughing as she held her arms wide open to hug Catherine. "Everything's perfect, Mom. You outdid yourself—like you always do."

Catherine kissed her on her cheek, wiping tears away, as she asked, "Are you ready?"

"No. But if not now, when?"

"What?" Catherine stepped back and looked her up and down. "Are you having second thoughts? What's wrong?"

"I'm joking. I've never seen you so nervous."

"It's not every day your baby gets married." Catherine pulled Dani close to her side. "You . . . you know things didn't work out with your father and I. I just want to make sure you're happy."

"I've never been happier." Sam took Dani by her hand and walked to the door. "Come on, Mom. Time to give me away."

The mid-May weather in Fremont was picture-perfect: sunny and mid-70s, with crystal blue skies. Sam's heart raced as her feet walked across the petals spread by Dani. She could feel every eye focused on her as she approached Ted.

He looked dashing in his black tuxedo and pink cummerbund. The gentle breeze threatened to dislodge his gelled hair, but to no avail. Sam couldn't stop grinning as she reached the end of the aisle and looked into his deep blue eyes.

"Are you ready?" he asked.

"Why does everyone keep asking me that question?" she said with a grin. "Are you, Mr. Lavoie?"

The ceremony was brief, and the dinner that followed, extravagant. Ted took great pride in impressing his family with the opulence of the event Catherine had planned. Her property spanned several acres. Huge white tents covered the dining area and dance floor. The band played for hours, entertaining guests late into the evening.

Sam sat at a table with Ted's parents and Catherine, recounting stories of some of the more exciting moments of the GSI challenges. Ted sat there with interest and watched his dad sparkle. His mom glanced over at him and gave a gentle nod of approval. Ted leaned over and took Sam by her hand, saying, "I'm sure Sam would love nothing more than to spend another hour telling you about our adventures, but we've got a busy day tomorrow."

"Our flight to Paris isn't until two," Sam said.

Ted stood up and waited for her to follow his lead. "It's almost midnight," he said.

"It is?" She stood up and looked around the dining area. There were only a few dozen people left. "Where's the night gone?"

"My Teddy's right," Barbara said. "You should get going. That flight tomorrow sounds dreadfully long. I . . . I'm so happy to have you in our family, Sam." Tears welled in her eyes as she turned to her son. "You did good."

"Thanks, Mom." He kissed his mom on her cheek and gave his dad a brief hug, then looked around the tent. "Where are the guys?"

"Dance floor," Barbara said.

Ted looked over to see his brothers and their wives and two other couples slow dancing to a song he didn't recognize.

Sam walked over to Ted's parents and gave them each a kiss. She said, "If we don't talk tomorrow, have a safe flight home."

Ted led Sam over to the empty head table. He and Sam hopped onto the edge and sat back and held hands.

"What a day," he said. "Your mom hit it out of the park."

"I knew she would." She rested her head against his shoulder and sighed. "Paris. Eleven hours on a plane."

"First class. We'll be pampered."

"Are . . . are you sure we shouldn't bring our laptops?" She sat up and turned to face him. "What if something comes up while we're away?"

"GSI can survive a week without us. Besides, we finished building the presentation for Detroit last week. Vin and Matthew approved it. Relax, Sam. Let's go have fun."

"You're right. I'm just getting nervous about next month's presentation."

"So am I." He stood up, pulled her from the table into his arms, and gently kissed her lips. "But let's worry about Detroit when we get back. Paris awaits."

34

It was a beautiful mid-June Friday morning in Redwood City. The temperature had settled in at eighty degrees, the sun's golden rays casting out from powder-blue skies. The parking lot alongside the Project Courier building was jammed with Teslas. Earlier that year, a dozen charging stations had been installed along one end of the parking lot. The company was in the process of converting a lot across the street to park and charge electric vehicles. Rows of covered charging stations were being erected, all with solar panels blanketing the roofs.

Off in the distance, a fleet of six black SUVs came barreling around the corner. The first two were Cadillac Escalades, followed by two Lincoln Navigators and a pair of Dodge Durangos. The vehicles slowed as they approached the parking lot, coming to a halt in the street. Eventually, they turned in to a designated visitor parking area. Matthew had made sure there would be room for them to park. Lisa waved to the vehicles as they approached the building.

"Here they come," Ted said, leaning his face against one of the floor-to-ceiling windows.

"Detroit," Sam said. She slid her fingers up and down Ted's back in an attempt to relieve some tension. "Six months of preparation, and it all comes down to today."

One by one, the doors on the black SUVs began to open, each ejecting a portly executive in either a gray or navy suit. Some vehicles had four people exit, others five. Ted started to count them as they began to group around Lisa.

"Is that right?" he asked. "They brought twenty-six people?"

"Men," Sam added. "Twenty-six men."

"Why so many?"

"Maybe it's a good sign. Maybe it means they're serious."

"I hope so," Vin said. Ted and Sam both spun around, surprised by the appearance of their boss. "Matthew couldn't get much of a read on their response to his invitation. They brought their top people. I know you both had a bad experience with them in the past, but I'm keeping a positive attitude today."

"This is an army compared to the reception Ted and I received in Detroit."

"I have my reservations," Ted said flatly, turning a cautious eye back to the window. He was surprised that despite the warm weather, the executives were all wearing suits and ties. "Did anyone tell them it's casual dress here?"

GSI didn't have a strict dress code. Much like the bright and airy Project Courier workspace, the atmosphere was generally relaxed and comfortable. Jeans and T-shirts were not an uncommon sight, although most of the men preferred collared shirts. Ted considered himself formally dressed today, with khakis and a button-down, short-sleeved, blue-and-green-checkered shirt.

"I need to head downstairs to join Matthew for the meet-and-greet. We're going to do a facility tour first, followed by test rides for our guests." Vin pulled out his cell phone to check the time and frowned. "They're a half hour late. We may need to adjust the schedule. Lunch will be served at noon, and then it's showtime at one. Are you ready?"

"As ready as we can be," Sam replied. "I'm with you, Vin. I feel good about this."

"You should. You've put together a stellar presentation."

"If anyone can win them over, it's Sam," Ted said.

"Agreed." Vin slid his phone back into his khakis. "I'll text you when we are ready to bring them up."

Ted smiled and waited until Vin was out of earshot. He and Sam were alone in the Crash area. He led her to one of the tables, and they sat down together.

"What's wrong?" she asked. "You look concerned."

"Did you see the attendee list?"

"Yes, why?"

"Those same assholes that laughed in our face are all here. All of them!" He clenched his fists together and cast a glare back toward the windows that faced the parking lot. "I don't trust them, Sam. I don't."

"Hey," she gently wrapped her hands around his fists and began caressing his fingers. He unclenched his hands, taking Sam's into his. "The presentation we've prepared is nothing like what we showed them all those years ago. We were so cocky and wide-eyed back then—especially you. If anything, the test drives alone will blow them away. By the time they get to the meeting, they are going to be begging to partner with us."

Ted felt all the tension leave his body. As always, Sam had a way of talking him down, bringing him inner peace. Her green eyes glistened as she leaned in to kiss his lips. He welcomed her touch, the hairs on the back of his neck tingling. He glanced down at their interlocked fingers, admiring their wedding rings.

"Mrs. Sam Wolff with two 'F's." Sam held her hand out and admired her wedding ring. "I'm going to need to think of what that second 'F' means for me."

"Oh, that's an easy one. 'Fantastic.' 'Flirtatious.'" He paused and scratched his jaw. "'Frugal'?"

"I think you better quit before you say something you'll regret."

"'Fierce.'" He gave her a quick peck on the cheek. "We should get ready for the tour and test drives. Ralph and Lori are probably waiting for us downstairs."

He stood up, and taking hold of her hand, they wove their way through the tables, bean bags, and gaming tables, stopping in front of the stage in the Convene area. The table that once held the champagne bottles was long since gone. The whiteboard that used to track the project challenges now listed the schedule for today's events with the automotive executives.

"I hope this works, Sam. We need Detroit to partner with us."

"It will all work out. Just as long as you behave yourself."

"Me?" Ted started to chuckle, but Sam's stern eyebrows told him she was serious. "You're running the presentation, not me."

"You don't like Detroit, Ted." She brushed his hair away from his eyes. "Don't show that today, okay?"

"I'll do my best."

Sam slid her fingers over her pendant, gently wrapping her gold chain around her index finger. She cleared her throat as she studied the notes resting beside her laptop. The timer on her screen indicated they were forty-five minutes into the presentation to Detroit. She looked up and smiled at the thirty-one people sitting in the conference room. The attendees were split into two groups. Five people from GSI sat to her right, their faces awash in disappointment, frustration, and confusion. Ted looked the most perturbed, nervously tapping his pen like a jackhammer. The battalion of twenty-six men from Detroit sported faces covered in scowls. Half were not even paying attention, their interests buried in their phones. Those who were listening made no attempt to hide their boredom.

Just as Sam was about to speak, one of the doors opened, and Lisa stepped inside. Several heads turned, distracted by her entrance. Lisa waved politely and held the door open for staff to bring in coffee and pastries. The scent of freshly brewed coffee and sugary sweets filled the room, giving Sam a tiny jolt of energy.

"As we explained to many of you during the test rides earlier today, we got here by completing ten key challenges." Sam clicked to the next slide, which displayed the list. "What's important to know is we logged over half-a-million fully autonomous miles, across three different test vehicles."

"On public roads?" Robert Anderson, VP of Vehicle Planning for Chrysler asked, his voice filled with shock. "Someone mentioned that during the test drives. You didn't use proving grounds?"

"Proving grounds?" Sam asked, somewhat confused.

"That's what automakers—real ones—use to test their new cars." Robert turned and looked at Brad Kenner, SVP of Research and Development for Ford. "Do you believe this shit?"

"Can you imagine if we tried to test new technology by driving around Ann Arbor and Detroit?" Brad shook his head in disgust. The egg-shaped executive ran his fingers through his salt and pepper beard, scratching his nails against a pair of hidden chins. Brad rotated his chair slightly so he could face Matthew Grant. "You're lucky the state didn't shut you down."

"Typical liberals," David Foster said as he chuckled. "Only in California. At GM, we do things by the book—and follow the law."

"We followed the law as well." Ted's tone was terse, and his comment unexpected. "Do you think our legal team didn't vet this? The vehicles weren't out there driving around empty. Every test had two people on board, including one ready to take full control when necessary."

"And how many crashes did you have?" David asked.

"None," Ted replied.

"Bullshit," Brad said. "There's no way you didn't have any accidents with that many tests."

"We had some issues," Sam said. Her voice was elevated but calm as she tried to regain control of the conversation. She feared the discussion was becoming too heated. She shot Ted a look she knew he would understand. He needed to dial it back. "They were all minor. Our biggest was a deer that clipped the car. We never crashed. No injuries. No lives lost. The car never went wild, losing control."

"I remember hearing about some spectacular crashes at DARPA," David said.

"With all due respect, that was almost six years go." Sam took a moment to look each attendee from Detroit in the eye. At least those who were paying attention. "The systems we have today are lightyears beyond what we had back then. We ran countless simulations before we started a single real-world test. The technology works."

Sam's eyes settled on David's. She felt like he had positioned himself as the alpha male in the room. Perhaps if she could win him over, the others would fall into line. Unfortunately, David showed the same look of contempt he'd had all day. In fact, it was the same look he'd had when she and Ted gave their first presentation to him at the Renaissance Center in Detroit in 2007. Sam broke her gaze and pivoted to Vin for help.

"Let's talk about the future," Vin said, his voice upbeat. "We'll give you copies of our test criteria and results to view on your own time. Sam, can you jump ahead to how we see our technology working in the vehicles of tomorrow?"

Several Detroit executives took this opportunity to grab some coffee and snacks. Two left the room to use the facilities, and three others to make phone calls.

Sam skipped through three dozen screens that documented their ten challenges. With each keyboard click, her heart sank. She tried to ignore the months the team had spent pulling this valuable information together, only to have it all brushed aside. She shot Ted a glance, hoping to get some emotional support or encouragement. Instead, she found him trying, and failing, to twirl his pen across his thumb and fingers. The screen on the wall settled on the slide she was looking for, titled COURIER IN THE CAR. She glanced around the room to see several people still getting coffee but decided not to wait for them to return to their seats.

"As you saw during the test drive, and earlier in the presentation, our sensor array gives us a complete three-hundred-and-sixty-degree view around the car." She felt her confidence begin to return as she found herself back on familiar ground. "We can see everything from an inch to hundreds of yards away." She clicked the slide ahead to show various pictures of the equipment attached to the Prius. "You'll notice that we've been able to integrate some of the smaller sensors quite easily. Others, such as Ted's brilliant spinning lidar array, we've reduced in size by fifty percent from when we first started. We've already adapted our technology to two other test cars, giving us a total of three autonomous vehicles. The technology can be replicated and installed easily, given advancements in drive-by-wire systems. Let me pause here and see if there are any questions."

Robert Anderson raised his hand.

"Yes?" she asked, hoping for an intelligent question.

"Where's the restroom?" Robert asked. The tall, slim man stood up and slid his phone into his pocket.

"Oh, I can show you," Ralph said. He rolled his chair back and made his way past Lori, patting her reassuringly on her shoulders. Once at the back door, he held it open for Robert. Ralph turned toward Sam and feigned screaming in terror, then rolled his eyes and followed the Chrysler executive into the hallway.

"This is where we see great potential with a partnership," Sam continued. "We have the technology. You have the vehicles. Together we can find a way to integrate and downsize our equipment. It should be both seamless and visually appealing. We will also want to integrate this with your in-car display systems."

"You call that appealing?" Brad asked as he pointed at the image of Leapfrog. "There's no way we'd put anything remotely close to that on a Lincoln. I don't care how much you shrink it down. Nobody would buy one."

"Really, Brad?" David interjected. "The last time I checked, nobody was buying your Navigator. Maybe a wart on the roof would give it some sizzle."

Brad was about to respond when Ted stood up and leaned forward, and as Sam noted, he was poised to get on a soapbox. She raised her hand to get his attention, but it was too late.

"Why are you being so shortsighted?" he asked, darting his gaze between Brad and David. "Lincoln sales have declined over the past twenty-five years. Compare that to what Mercedes and BMW have done." Ted noticed David chuckle. "And Caddy is just as bad. All of you have lost ground to Germany and Japan."

"Ted, I think—" Sam attempted to take control of the discussion, but he ignored her.

"Remember when Lexus came out of nowhere?" he asked. Sam shot him a look of disapproval. He understood her concern, and when he spoke again, his voice was calmer. "Mercedes didn't know what hit them. Why? Lexus offered a better product with better technology at a better price. Toyota did the same thing with the Prius hybrid. They were the first and continue to be the leaders."

"We've got the Volt now," David said. "It's better than a Prius."

"Is it?" Ted asked. "Time will tell."

Vin reached over and gently took Ted by the elbow, guiding him back to his seat.

"The point I believe Ted is trying to make is that disruptive technology can have a big impact on industry leaders," Vin said. "The Prius is a great example of that. That first generation was a homely little car. But Toyota proved its hybrid system could work. They lost money at first. My guess is GM is losing money on these early Volts. Correct, David?"

David leaned back and folded his arms, refusing to answer.

"We believe this technology to be a game-changer," Sam said. She smiled and nodded toward Vin. "Someone will be first with it. Will it look a bit odd? Perhaps. That's something we believe we can partner on. Will it be expensive? Yes, but those costs will come down over time. In order for this to come to market, we need to work together."

She surveyed the room but saw little interest on the faces of the men in suits. She was surprised to see Matthew slumped in his chair, looking defeated. He'd been so upbeat during the tour and test drives. The door opened, and Robert and Ralph returned. They both stopped a few feet into the room. Ralph looked at Sam and shrugged, confused by how quiet the room was.

"What did I miss?" Robert asked as he took his seat.

"Don't ask," David replied.

"I see your point, Sam," Brad said. "Being first can be expensive, but long term, you have the potential to be the leader. You can make a name for yourself. Prius is synonymous with hybrid technology and efficiency. That car and name have put a green shine on Toyota."

"Exactly!" Sam was thrilled they were finally getting a positive response.

"In your testing, you indicated the driver could take over at any time," Brad continued. "If we can adapt this to be an advanced cruise control and get rid of that shit you have all over the roof, then we might have something."

"Sort of like a super cruise control?" David asked. "Interesting."

"No," Sam said. "That's not what we're talking about. Our testing showed a direct correlation between self-driving capabilities and driver reaction times. Meaning the smarter and more accurate the autonomy was, the longer it took for the driver to regain control in an emergency. The driver always got too comfortable thinking the AI system was in charge. We don't want to go in that direction."

"So, then, this is all a waste?" Robert asked, picking at patches of dry skin at the end of his nose. "Who would want a high-tech cruise control if the handoff to the driver is poor?"

"We aren't talking about cruise control!" Sam struggled to keep her composure. "The goal is *full* autonomy."

"This is the same pitch you made back in 2007." David removed his thick-beveled eyeglasses and tossed them onto the table, taking a moment to rub his eyes. He turned to Matthew and said, "When you invited us to come here, I told you I was skeptical. We all were. You said you'd taken the DARPA technology to an entirely new level."

"And we have," Matthew replied. He glanced back and forth

between each of the three Detroit lead executives. "Surely, you have to see the potential."

"The potential?" David said. "Possibly. The technology has been fine-tuned and streamlined compared to those monsters that roamed the Mojave Desert. But this isn't ready for primetime. Not by a longshot. I agree with Brad. Re-engineer this to be something we can integrate into the vehicle, so it's not so ugly. But dial back the cruise feature to better alert the driver. Full self-driving isn't an option."

"I must disagree with you." Sam began to flip through her presentation, looking for a slide she'd prepared to address this very issue. "Give me a moment, please."

"Gentlemen, I'm not sure we're on the same page," Matthew said. "Our goal is to reinvent the concept of transportation as it exists today. We aren't looking to dumb down our technology to make a better cruise control system. This is full-blown autonomy—taxis without drivers. Delivery trucks automated to move packages between facilities. The possibilities are endless. As Sam stated, this technology will be a disruptor. Whoever brings it to market first will be the one to lead the way. GSI doesn't know how to build cars, but—"

"And you never will," David said.

Matthew opened his mouth to continue to speak, but instead, let out a sigh. He shook his head in disappointment and leaned back in his chair.

"Tell that to Tesla," Ted said. His voice was much calmer now. "Back in 2007, you laughed them off as a toy car filled with laptop batteries. Now they have a gorgeous five-passenger vehicle with over four-hundred horsepower that can hit sixty in under four seconds—all of it without an engine. And they're only getting started."

"Try driving across the country in one," Brad said as he scratched at his beard. "Or towing a boat. Tesla has no clue what they're doing. They won't last."

"Brad's right. Besides, the country would never trust cars to drive themselves. There are already too many rules and regulations in place for human drivers. How would the insurance industry work? Who does the cop write the ticket to? A robot? Removing people from the equation raises too many issues. I don't think you've really thought this through."

"Similar arguments were made about ATMs," Sam said. "Who'd want to go to a machine for money? You can't talk to it if you have a problem. ATMs are everywhere now. Technology advances, whether we like it or not." She noticed Robert was heads-down typing on his phone. "Do you remember the first cell phone? It was the size of a brick. If someone told you back then that one day that phone would not only fit in your pocket, but would also let you send emails, would you have believed them? Or would you have laughed them off and told them they were crazy?"

"That's different," Robert said, taking offense at Sam appearing to target him. "You're not talking about scaling down the size of some hardware. You're talking about changing the very nature of driving and vehicle transportation."

"I agree," David said. "We don't invest in pipe dreams. Find a way to get that crap off the roof. Maybe integrate it behind the front grill. Make it invisible. Do that, and we can talk about doing an advanced cruise control system. That's all I see here."

Brad and Robert nodded in agreement.

"Again, gentlemen, we haven't built an advanced cruise control system," Matthew said. He stood up and walked to the front of the room, taking a position beside Sam. He turned and pointed at the image of Leapfrog on the screen. "We've invested years proving full autonomy is possible. Just because we can't build cars doesn't mean this technology isn't the future. Progress this disruptive cannot be stopped. There's no going back. Partner with us, and together we can change the world."

"I'm sorry, Matthew, but despite what you've shown us today, I must disagree," David said flatly. "Autonomy isn't the future. At least not for us. Not now. There are too many risks."

"Then I guess there's nothing left to discuss," Matthew said. He turned to Vin and frowned. "Can you please escort our guests back to their vehicles? We're done."

Sam looked over at Ted in complete shock. One by one, the executives from Detroit shuffled out of the conference room. She noticed that most even chose to leave behind their copies of the presentation she'd prepared. Ted joined her at the front of the room, feeling completely deflated.

"What do we do now?" she asked. "Where do we go from here?"

35

Ted rested his forehead against the window and stared out across the parking lot. Detroit's rejection six months ago had left him shell-shocked and lost. After silently counting twenty Teslas, he stopped. It seemed like every week a new one showed up. Across the street, GSI had completed construction on the first half of the new solar-powered charging station. Another dozen plug-in vehicles, including Leafs and Volts, were quietly charging their lithium-ion batteries. He closed his eyes and tried to enjoy the music filling his head. His wireless headphones were playing "Desire" by U2, the song streaming from the iPhone tucked into the front pocket of his denim jeans. A tap on his shoulder broke his concentration. He turned around to find Ralph standing behind him. His arms were folded angrily across his chest.

"Hey," Ted said, popping the headphones from his ears. He slid his hand into his pocket and retrieved his phone, muting the music. "What's up?"

"What's up?" Ralph's tone was peppered with nervous frustration. "You tell me. You're late."

"Oh. Right. The meeting."

"Yes, the meeting. It's already half over. You missed quite a bit."

Ralph spun around and marched through the Crash and Convene areas toward the hallway with the conference rooms. Ted was in no rush. He took another look outside and wondered if he should submit to peer pressure and get a Tesla Model S. He decided, as he did every time he asked himself this question, that he loved the thrill of his BMW M6 too much to give it up. The M6 was not a practical car, as Sam often pointed out to him, especially now that he was married and had a stepdaughter. But driving his M6 was one of the few points of joy currently in his life, and he wasn't about to give it up anytime soon.

Several co-workers were relaxing in the Crash area. A few were sunken low in the bean bag chairs. Two others were sitting at a high-top table, ignoring each other as they both tapped away at their Androids. Ted couldn't help but notice how joyless the room felt. Christmas was only a few weeks away, but the mood everywhere was dour. He took minimal pleasure in knowing that he wasn't the only one still depressed from Detroit's rejection. Shortly after that disastrous meeting, Matthew and Vin had made several changes. Ted was part of those who disagreed with the company's new direction.

He wove his way across the room and down the hallway. Each conference room was filled with different meetings. He realized he couldn't remember which room Vin's meeting was in and had to stare through the glass walls until he finally saw the room with Sam and Vin inside. They, along with several others, including Lori and Ralph, were in the KITT conference room, named after the self-driving car from the 1980s television show *Knight Rider*. Ted yanked the door open and stepped inside.

"Nice of you to join us," Vin said, pointing to an empty chair beside Sam. Ted opted to take a seat at the back of the room, close to the exit. "Just to catch you up, Ted, Matthew has signed off on building the LSV. We're going through the details and next steps."

Ted stared blankly at the screen behind Vin. A bulbous pod-shaped car was prominently on display. The picture was a conceptual image, designed on a computer by someone from Sam's team. Ted thought it looked similar to a Volkswagen Beetle but much smaller and with none of the whimsical charm of that classic design.

"I also announced the LSV project lead." Vin waved his arm toward Sam. "Say hello to your new boss, Ted."

"What?" Ted darted his eyes between Vin and Sam. Vin seemed overly happy to break the news to him. Sam's cheeks were flush with a nervous smile spread across her face. "When did that happen?"

"Matthew and I have been discussing this for a few weeks," Vin said. "I told Sam just before the meeting."

"I'm just as shocked as you, Ted," Sam added.

Ted glanced around the room and felt all eyes on him. Since joining GSI, he and Sam had been equals—peers. In some ways, he wasn't surprised that Vin picked Sam over him. They had a long history together at Ashton, and the two were in lockstep when it came to project planning.

"It's . . . it's a dotted line report," she said. "Just for the project. I'm not technically your boss."

"But Sam will drive the project." Vin smiled and nodded. "She will set the pace, milestones, and have overall project planning authority."

Ted could feel the veins in his temples throbbing. He wondered how much she would dictate how he ran his hardware team, and how Vin's excessive red tape would further slow the project down, just as it had with the ten challenges. He had a long list of questions, but realized this was not a good time to raise them. Part of him wondered if his concerns even mattered.

Vin waited to see if Ted would say anything. When he didn't, Vin moved to the next slide. The header read, Low Speed Vehicle. Beneath the title was a series of bullets outlining the target capabilities for the vehicle the team would be designing.

"As you are all aware, the LSV has many advantages," Vin said. "With a maximum speed of only thirty-five miles per hour, we can avoid most regulations. This will be a big advantage when it comes time for certifications and approvals. Before we get to the timeline and milestones are there any questions?" Vin noticed a hand go up in the back of the dimly lit room. "Yes, Ralph?"

"Are we calling this thing Tadpole?" Ralph asked. "Maybe Leapfrog Four?"

Ted rolled his eyes. Sam and a few others laughed.

"That's a good point," Vin replied. "We will need to name this little guy, won't we? Perhaps another contest like we did last time?"

"How about we just call it Lazy Slow Vehicle?" Ted asked. He looked around the room but was greeted with nothing but sour stares. He did notice Lori smiling. "Seriously, why are we doing this? It's just a golf cart, right? A self-driving golf cart. Is that how low we've fallen? Is that all we can achieve?"

"Ted, I think you're being very unfair," Vin said. "By downsizing and integrating this technology into an LSV, we will accomplish two things. First, we will prove full autonomy works as part of a completely integrated system. Second, we will bring it to market faster and at a lower price point compared to a full-sized vehicle."

"Bring it to market?" Ted asked. "Where? Golf resorts?"

"The possibilities are endless," Sam said, her tone suddenly defensive. "Universities could easily invest in a system like this. I think you're being shortsighted. I have to agree with Vin on this one."

"Of course you do," Ted said dismissively. He looked down at the empty space in front of him and realized he had forgotten to grab his pen and pad. Having nothing to fiddle with, he suddenly felt even more anxious. "We should have tried other companies. Screw Detroit. There are other players out there."

"The LSV is just the first step," Sam said. She stood up and positioned herself beside Vin. "We need to start small and then scale up. We avoid many risks by deploying the technology on a low-speed vehicle. It makes perfect sense. It's the next logical step in the process."

"Step, step, step!" Ted felt his frustration rise to a full boil. He could feel every set of eyes in the room staring at him, many filled with disappointment. He didn't care. "We spent years getting Leapfrog to work. We now have three of them up and running. But you want to go backward to a toy car? This stupid LSV will do nothing to change how transportation works. Wasn't our goal to be a disruptor?"

"That's still the goal," Vin said.

"When?" Ted struggled to temper his anger. "We moved too slow on Leapfrog. I know we could have completed those ten challenges in half the time if you'd just listened to me."

He hoped to get some sort of positive reaction or support from someone else in the room. Instead, he was met with silence. The only sound to be heard was the whirring fan from the projector hanging from the ceiling.

"Are you done?" Sam asked.

Ted looked over to Lori and Ralph to see if perhaps they might have something to say. Ralph had his head hung low, avoiding eye contact with everyone. Lori had a blank look on her face as she stared back at Ted.

"Just one more thing, boss," Ted said. "Given the shape and speed of the vehicle, why don't we call it Tortoise?"

"Oh!" Ralph suddenly perked up. "Maybe we can name it after one of those ninja turtles?"

Ted kept his eyes locked on Sam. He knew nobody other than her would understand why he picked that name. The last bits of his anger slipped away as he saw her face soften across the dim room. Her eyes began to shimmer as tears pooled at the edges of her eyelids.

"Excuse me," she said.

He stood up as she quickly made her way to the exit, thrusting his arm out to stop her, but she shoved him aside and flung the door open. He followed her into the hallway and grabbed her elbow. Sam yanked herself free but he lunged forward, grasping both of her arms.

"Stop," he said. The conference room directly across the hallway was now empty. He opened the door and pushed her inside, closing the door behind them. "I'm sorry, Sam."

"How could you?" She burst into tears and turned away. She noticed a table in the far corner with a box of tissues. She grabbed a few and blew her nose, dabbing her eyes dry. "You are constantly angry, Ted. Just what is the problem?"

"Because, Sam, GSI's going nowhere. Project Courier was a dud. Admit it!"

"I will not! I poured my life into that project. Years! So did you. We all did. What's wrong with you? It's because Vin made me lead, right? That's it, isn't it?"

"No." He lowered his head, refusing to admit she was partially right. He began to wonder how the entire LSV project would play out with her dictating his plans and strategy. "You've always been his favorite, Sam."

"So, you're jealous?"

"No. It's just that, well, I think having you as the lead will slow things down. It will slow *me* down. My team."

"Ted, I'm willing to work with you on this. Don't get bent out of shape because I'm in charge."

"It doesn't matter." He exhaled slowly to calm himself down. He could see that she was still rattled and angry. Rolling a chair forward, he spun a second one around for Sam. Once they were both sitting, he took her hands into his. "This company is going in the wrong direction. Can't you see that with the LSV we're moving backward?"

"No."

"Ever since Detroit snubbed us, this place has been in a downward spiral. Vin is leading us to a dead end. The LSV is not the answer. Half the team is still in shock over Detroit rejecting us. I don't know about you, but that kickoff meeting wasn't filled with joy."

"Your entrance certainly brought the mood down."

"Really? Nobody's been happy lately. Walking the halls feels like being in a funeral parlor."

"I'll admit that the morale around here has been a bit low, but now that we're moving forward with LSV, I expect things to perk up eventually."

"You're wrong, Sam." He let go and leaned back in his chair. He stared deep into his wife's green eyes, looking for any sign of a connection or understanding. "I . . . I think it's time we start looking elsewhere. Maybe even form our own business. Perhaps a consulting company. We can look for investors."

"What?" She stood up and backed away from him. "Have you lost your mind? I just got promoted."

"Wait. Vin promoted you? I thought this was just a project assignment. Did you get a raise?"

"Can we talk about this outside of work?"

He closed his eyes and thought back to the long nights and weekends he'd committed to the ten challenges. After all those months, it was his wife who got the promotion. He realized Vin would never support him, or champion his work ethics and methodologies. If he was going to see his dream of self-driving cars become a reality, her promotion solidified his belief that he couldn't do it at GSI.

"I've already started looking into other options." He stayed seated and watched Sam as she nervously wandered about the room. "I have feelers into both Toyota and Mercedes. A few others. How do you feel about moving to Germany?"

"Germany!"

"I'm joking, Sam. Sort of." He let out a soft chuckle as he felt a sudden clarity on what his future held. "Mercedes has offices in Atlanta, although it might be fun to live in another country."

"Ted, I'm not moving to Atlanta," she said, taking a seat next to him. "And I'm not leaving GSI. We're making great progress here."

"That's all we've made. Our designs are nothing but ideas and prototypes. Sam, this technology should already be in production vehicles. Now we're looking at building glorified golf carts. It's wrong. All of it is wrong."

"You aren't seriously thinking of relocating for a new job, are you?"

"I definitely need a career change, Sam. I don't want to move, but I wouldn't rule it out. If you want to stay at GSI, that's fine. Not me. Would Vin let you work remotely?"

"Ted, we've only been married since May. Dani is still adjusting to her new school and struggling to make friends. If you are serious about changing jobs, you need to keep it local. Moving is out of the question. Even if Vin said I could work remotely, I wouldn't."

"Why?"

"You don't get it, do you?" She closed her eyes and rotated her chair away from him to face the hallway. Vin's meeting had ended and the team members were filing by, each staring into the conference room as they walked by. "This is my chance to lead a ground-breaking project. There's no way I'm giving that up."

"But what if my only option requires me to move?"

"Move? Did you hear anything I said? There's no way I'm moving Dani again. Not this soon. She's too young for so much change."

"Change is good, Sam. Maybe you should try to shield her a bit less."

"Excuse me?"

"You and your mother have always babied her. Made it all about her."

"Is that it? Or is it because it's not all about you?" She shook her head and wiped her eyes dry. "I've always cherished our differences, Ted. But now I fear they're going to drive us apart."

"Don't say that, Sam. We'll work this out. If moving is off the table, then I'll stick with local options. I know there are better jobs out there." He rolled his chair forward and spun Sam to face him. He took her hands in his and kissed her wedding rings. "Everything will be fine. I promise."

36

Rusty shoved his hands deep into his pockets as he gazed down through the watch tower window overlooking the DSU robotics workshop floor. It was Friday, twelve days before Christmas. Two students—the two Rusty was the least impressed by—were busy toiling away attempting to secure a new radar sensor to the front of a six-legged autonomous drone. The vehicle was intended to be a new proof-of-concept, showcasing the lab's latest AI software. The floor should have been bustling with twenty or more students. Instead, it looked like a ghost town.

The lab's exterior windows howled and rattled in their frames, battered by blustering winds. Rusty hadn't bothered to use the DARPA or pizza challenge winnings to upgrade the building's doors or windows, much to the chagrin of the faculty and students working in there. Instead, he had poured all of the funds into the hardware and software he felt were needed to continue to keep DSU at the forefront of the robotics and artificial intelligence edges of science. The hinges on the exit door behind him squealed as the door slowly opened. He turned around to see Nico Lee enter, cradling an empty cardboard box in his arms.

"Leaving early?" Rusty asked. He checked his Seiko and frowned. "It's noon."

"I still have a lot of packing to do at home." Nico placed the box on the chair in front of his workstation. His desk was filled with several academic awards, as well as a few pictures of his wife and two infant children—twins. He began placing them in the container. "Why? Do you plan to dock my pay?"

"That's out of my control."

"And I'm sure that eats you up inside."

Nico began to rifle through his desk drawers, randomly selecting items and tossing them into the box. He paused when he got to his DSU mug. After looking at it briefly, he decided against taking it with him.

"Are you sure you're making the right move?" Rusty asked, surprised to find himself feeling slightly anxious. "You've been a great teacher to the students here. I had my doubts when you applied for the job, but they've come to respect you."

"Have you?"

"What's that supposed to mean?" Rusty asked angrily.

Nico placed the last of his personal belongings into the box and folded the flaps, locking them into place. He walked over to Rusty and pointed through the window toward the two students working down below.

"I remember being in their shoes," Nico said. "Those first weeks as a student were nerve-racking. I was terrified of you. We all were. When I became a teacher here, I thought that would have changed. I thought you would have seen me as a true colleague."

Rusty frowned and shook his head. He couldn't understand Nico's point of view. Rusty had delegated many responsibilities to Nico and felt he'd performed admirably. The students regularly praised "Mr. Lee" as they all called Nico. Rusty found Nico's style to be too low-key, but he often relished the good-cop/bad-cop role they often took when dealing with the students.

A crash on the shop floor below broke Rusty's concentration. He looked down to see the radar assembly intended for the rover now in several pieces scattered across the floor. He pounded on the glass and whipped the window open. "I'm sending that bill to the financial aid department!" He slammed the window shut and looked back at Nico. "We both know the only reason you're leaving is for the money."

"That's not the only reason. Look, I'll admit Where2 dangled a lot of cash in front of me. But you have to know the other reason I'm leaving."

Rusty stared blankly at Nico. He was truly at a loss for words.

"It's you, Rusty."

"Me?"

"You still treat me like a student."

"I do not!"

"Maybe not all of the time, but often enough. I'm your peer. I deserve better."

"My peer?" He leaned forward and glared into Nico's eyes. "How many robots have you built for NASA? How many trapped miners have your rovers saved? We aren't equals, Nico. We just work together."

"My point exactly." Nico walked over to his desk and gave a last look around to make sure he'd collected everything he planned to take with him. "I've made significant contributions to this department, Rusty. I swear, I think nothing will ever be good enough for you."

"I demand the best, Nico. Not just from my students, but from everyone."

"You demand the impossible. You push beyond limits."

"And do you think you'd be where you are today if I didn't?"

"You mean leaving?"

Rusty frowned and folded his arms across his broad chest. He was disappointed Nico didn't understand his methods. The students below were frantically trying to reassemble the radar sensor. Rusty caught his reflection in the glass panes. His beard and handlebar mustache were snow-white, the orange flecks having disappeared with age.

"Think about it, Rusty. Where2 is taking your entire undergraduate staff and me along with them."

"Where2 is a joke of a company, Nico. You're making a foolish decision. Those bastards had no right coming in here and taking my students!" Rusty glanced at the mess on the floor below. "They left me with shit."

"If you're talking about Tom and Debbie downstairs, they're leaving, too."

"What?" Rusty stormed across the room, his right hip sending jolts of pain down to his foot. He ignored the aching and stopped mere inches from Nico. "You can't gut this place, Nico."

"You're really going to try to blame this on me?" Nico laughed as he picked up the box he'd packed and swung the door open. He glanced back over his shoulder and said, "If you want someone to pin this max exodus on, try looking in the mirror."

Rusty glared at Nico's back as he disappeared through the door. The hinges creaked just before the door slammed hard against the frame. He debated going after him, but realized it was pointless. He reminded himself that Nico was not always the best co-worker, often pushing back and contradicting him in front of his students. Maybe this was for the best, he told himself. Maybe it would be better in the long run.

He limped as he crossed back over to the watch tower's window. He'd overslept this morning and forgotten to do his exercises. Digging his fingers deep into his right hamstring, trying to relieve the tingling pain he felt, he looked down at the shop floor, just in time to see Nico and his two students exit the building. Rusty debated if he should say or do anything when they looked up before leaving. No action was needed. Neither Nico, Tom, nor Debbie bothered to acknowledge him as they left the lab. He watched as the corner door slammed shut. The shop floor was barren. He stood alone in the watch tower, surveying the vast empty workspace below.

Turning around and walking over to Nico's workstation, he picked up the DSU mug Nico had left behind. Rusty felt his anger spike as he looked around the room. He walked over to the window that looked down at the lab floor. The scattered remains of the broken radar assembly were piled beside the half-built rover. He launched Nico's mug through the window and watched as it smashed against the lidar assembly bolted to the robot's roof.

"Everything can be fixed. Everyone can be replaced."

He ran his hand along his back and right leg, the throbbing now worse than ever. Lowering himself to the floor, he began doing the morning's forgotten physical therapy sessions, but stopped after the first half dozen stretches and sat upright, groaning from the pain. The hum of the industrial heaters coming on was the only sound filling the empty building. He realized he'd had students leave his program in the past, but never the entire team. This was a first. He shook his head and went back to doing his stretches.

"Nico will come to realize he made a mistake. He'll be back. They all will."

37

Oliver Yan thrummed his fingers across the polished edge of his mahogany desk. As VP of Advanced Mobility Research, the twenty-nine-year-old Long Beach native was tasked with vaulting Where2 to the forefront of self-driving technology. He'd been in the position for less than a year, but had assembled a team of the best and brightest in the industry. A skilled and ruthless negotiator, Oliver prided himself on his ability to recruit anyone. In his mind, everyone had a price, and it was only a matter of crafting the most enticing proposal to win them over.

"You're continuing to be a disappointment," Oliver said. The drumming of his fingers grew louder as he leaned forward across his desk. "I hired you six months ago, and we are somehow eight months behind schedule. How many more people do you need to get us back on track?"

Harry Palmer fidgeted nervously in his maroon leather chair, springs creaking as his weight shifted back and forth. After leaving DSU in early 2008, Harry had taken a position with Boeing. He'd been happy there, until Oliver approached him with an offer that at the time, seemed too good to pass up. The beads of sweat forming across his brow indicated the second and third thoughts he was having about his decision to join Where2.

"It's like I told you, Oliver, this isn't about throwing bodies at a project. We need more time."

"You've had more than enough time, Harry." Oliver folded his arms and leaned back in his jet-black executive chair, cocking his head sideways. The northeast view from his office at Where2's headquarters gave him a view of San Francisco Bay far in the distance. He closed his eyes and recalled the day he had seen the great pizza challenge broadcast. It still amazed him that after all that time, GSI had yet to put a self-driving car into production. "Where2 needs to be first. We need to be first. You need to be first."

"I understand our objectives."

"Then tell me what you need."

"Well, you've got Nico Lee coming here. He called me last Friday when he left DSU to tell me how excited he was. That's a big win."

"But will it be enough? I know you and Nico were two of the key players for the DARPA Challenge. DSU bested everyone else at that event."

"You also pulled in people from Ashton and Berkeley. The team is fantastic, Oliver."

"But is it the best?"

"Well, technically you don't have *everyone* that was on the DARPA DSU team."

"You're talking about Ted Wolff, aren't you?"

"Yes. And others."

"Damn GSI." Oliver stood up and strode to the window. He clasped his hands behind his back, taking his right wrist in his other hand. Oliver was a delicate man with thin, almost fragile, features. He twisted the skin at the base of his hand back and forth in frustration. "They've proven to be the most savvy of adversaries. They seem to have a death grip on their employees. I haven't been able to pry a single one away."

"We've been using their software to run our systems. Do you think they've caught wind that we plan to dump them for the new mapping applications we're building? Speaking of which, the code I inherited appears to be—"

"Our contract with GSI is locked in for another two years. There must be another reason. I can't understand why their people won't join us."

Harry paused and watched Oliver begin to pace back and forth in front of the window. He said, "It's because of Vin. They love him."

"Nonsense. Everyone has their price, Harry. Even love and devotion can be bought."

Harry started to chuckle. Oliver spun around and walked back to his desk, taking a seat on the corner. Harry rolled his chair back to put some distance between them.

"What's so funny?" Oliver asked. That smile on Harry's face made Oliver curious. He wondered if he'd struck a nerve.

"If anyone can be bought, it's Ted."

"I told you, Harry, we tried. Six months ago, right after you came on board. He'd just gotten married and said GSI had big plans. He shut me down before I could give him any details and then ignored my calls. As I said, GSI has proven impossible to raid."

"I hear things there have gone south recently. Something to do with a change in direction."

"Really?" Oliver's lips slowly spread into a Cheshire cat's grin.

"You may want to try again."

Oliver stood up and slapped Harry on his shoulder. He took a step back and waited for the other man to take the hint. Harry slowly pulled himself out of the chair and adjusted his shirt, tucking it back into his pants.

"If it's as bad as it sounds, there may be others looking to leave." Harry headed toward the door, opened it, and looked back at Oliver. "Ask Ted. Maybe he can get Lori Preston. She's a mapping genius."

Ted killed the ignition on his BMW M6 and checked his phone. He was running ten minutes late. The parking lot at Donovan's Pub was bustling with an energetic Friday lunchtime crowd. It was Friday the 20th, only five days before Christmas. Many employees were planning to take the following week off, so were leaving work early and going to the pub. The roads and businesses were congested with travelers and last-minute shoppers.

The inside of the restaurant was just as hectic as the outside. He looked around until he spotted Oliver Yan tucked away in a booth in the far corner. Oliver waved as soon as he saw Ted, who maneuvered his way around customers and the wait staff, crassly pushing some aside.

"Hey, sorry I'm late," Ted said. He extended his arm and shook hands with Oliver. "Traffic was a mess. It's nice to finally meet in person instead of by video chat."

A waitress approached as Ted sat down. He requested a glass of water and waved her away.

"No apology needed," Oliver replied. "Look, Ted, I'm going to cut to the chase. Like I said on the phone, Where2 wants to be first to market with an autonomous vehicle. We need *you* to make that happen."

"Harry called me yesterday. It sounds like you've got an impressive team already in place."

"But I want the best."

"I'm sorry I wasn't more receptive to your calls earlier this year."

"You blew me off before I could give you the details."

"Your timing was bad. We were getting ready to pitch our solution to Detroit. And I'd just gotten married."

"How'd that go? Detroit, not the wedding." Oliver laughed briefly but stopped when he realized Ted was not laughing. "That bad?"

"Detroit didn't go well. It was a mistake to believe they'd be ready for a partnership." He paused as the waitress returned with his water. He took a long sip from the glass and stared at the ice cubes. The way they reflected the light reminded him of Sam's engagement ring. "Lately, it seems the same could be said of my wife."

"Oh—" Oliver paused, unsure of how to respond. "I'm sorry to hear that."

"Nothing to apologize for, Oliver. Tell me more about Where2's plans."

"It doesn't surprise me that Detroit rejected you. Trust me, Ted, they aren't ready for the future we have planned. The days of personal car ownership are numbered. Within the next decade, Detroit will be building self-driving fleet vehicles that meet our specifications. Or they will simply cease to exist."

"You sound very confident about that. But Where2 can't build cars. You need a partner for that. And Detroit has shown no interest in this technology." He paused and studied Oliver's face. He seemed overly self-assured. "Wait. Do you have one? Did Detroit reject us because they already signed on with you?"

"Not Detroit, Ted." He leaned forward and smiled. "We already have a signed agreement with a major European manufacturer. I'm not at liberty to say which one. But they intend to supply us with a small group of test vehicles to retrofit with our self-driving systems. Long-term, they want to be our supplier."

"Wow."

"It's only a matter of time before the other companies, including Detroit, Asia, and the rest of Europe, realize they need to get on board. Sink or swim."

"What about your employees? All the drivers who work for you now?"

"Our drivers aren't employees. They're work-for-hire. They'll adapt and find different jobs. Everyone needs to be ready for the changes that are coming." Oliver leaned back and clasped his hands in front of him. "Look, Ted, the world is evolving. Kids today don't want to own a car. They like spending their time and money on phones and video games. Besides, they're too in debt to afford a car. Or a house. We're proving that a sharing economy works. Everything is moving in that direction. Don't get me wrong, Ted. We love our drivers. But self-driving cars are coming. We can't sit back and let someone else take the lead."

The waitress returned to the table. Before she could ask if they were ready to order, Oliver waved her away.

"Harry tells me you're the guy who invented most of the self-driving hardware on top of the Hummer that won DARPA," Oliver continued. "What was that vehicle called?"

"Cyclops."

"Right. He said they wouldn't have won if it hadn't been for you."

"He's right."

"I've got Nico Lee starting next month. But the team won't be complete without their leader."

"Leader?"

"I want you to have full control of the project. I've had Harry trying to steer the ship. He's a bright guy, but he's no leader. Nico and the others from DSU will flush out the team, but I need someone with vision, Ted."

"Full control?" Ted said softly. He tried to temper his enthusiasm. Vin's red tape. Sam's slow, plodding methodology. The overly detailed project plans. All of it would be history. Every word coming from Oliver's mouth rang out like the most perfect note in the most perfect song.

"It's all about you, Ted."

"When Sam and I"—He paused and fiddled with his wedding ring, briefly closing his eyes— "When I joined GSI four years ago, I thought the plan was to change the world. We all knew that the day would come when autonomous vehicles ruled the roads. The plan was to solidify the technology and take it to Detroit to show them the future."

"And?"

"When Detroit rejected us, the company changed course. The gears at GSI turn too slowly for me. Their new direction is one I can't support. The future you describe is the right way to go."

"I'm glad to hear we're on the same page." Oliver glanced around, leaned forward, and lowered his voice. "Ted, I want you to know that Where2 is looking beyond self-driving technology."

"How so?"

"We see enormous potential with the AI engine we're building. It's just the beginning."

"Of . . . ?"

"Of a whole new world. Autonomy is going to be a major disruptor to many industries, not just transportation. Artificial intelligence will change everything."

"Rise of the machines," Ted said quietly under his breath. He smiled and asked, "What's your timeline?"

"That depends on you. We have prototypes in the early design phases. But it's all on the drawing boards. I want to be ready to have a vehicle ready to show our suppliers in January 2015."

"That's less than thirteen months away." Ted paused and thought back to the years spent at GSI following Vin's strict quality testing methodology. There were so many opportunities to move the project forward, but Sam and Vin mandated everything be done by the book—their book. "Nico and Harry won't be up to speed on the latest tech I've got at GSI. But they're sharp, and I'm sure I can get the rest of the team up to speed."

"Whoa, Ted. Hold on. I don't want to get into any lawsuits due to patent infringements or stealing intellectual property."

"I can bring you what I brought to GSI. Trust me. My technology can do much more if pushed to its limits. I have a lot of changes I've wanted to make, but others deemed it too risky. I'll build you a much better system." Ted's pulse raced as he began to think of the freedom he'd have at Where2. "You said this would be my team?"

"Yes."

"So, I get to set the direction—the timeline—the rules."

"As far as I'm concerned, Ted, you're the king." Oliver reached into a brown leather satchel resting beside him. He retrieved a manila folder and slid it across the table to Ted. "This is my offer."

Ted pushed his glass of water aside and used his napkin to dry the shellacked tabletop dry. He pulled the folder closer and tore it open.

The figures on the first page took him back to that day at the airport when Matthew Grant had offered him and Sam jobs at GSI. Just like last time, he was shocked by what he saw. He flipped through the remaining pages, scanning for any other salary-related information. He closed the folder and clasped his hands across the packet.

"Well?" Oliver asked.

"This . . . this is double what I make today." Ted took another sip of water and cleared his throat. "And I'll have full control?"

"Total and complete." Oliver smiled and pulled another folder from his bag. He passed it to Ted, sliding it beneath his hands. "Where2 plans to go public in the near future. This outlines your potential stock option package."

The waitress returned again, and this time Ted flicked her away. He opened the file and read through the single-page letter, silently running the calculations.

"When are you going public?" he asked.

"Too soon to say, Ted. Look, this offer is just the beginning. Those stock options are just the beginning. You ride this thing to completion, and we see success, the sky's the limit."

Ted darted his eyes back and forth between the offer letter and the stock option details.

"So, is it a yes?" Oliver leaned back and frowned. "I'm having trouble getting a read on you, Ted. I've put my best offer on the table. What else do I need to do to win you over?"

Ted collected the two packets and slid them off the table, resting them by his side. He tried to remain calm as he ran through the offer again. The stock options were unknown, since they would be based on whatever value Where2's stock was on whatever day they went public. But he knew it could easily be an eight-figure payout.

"I know you've built a great team so far, but I'm going to need the best if we're to hit your deadline."

"Harry said you might have others you wanted to bring along. I think he said her name was Lori?"

"Lori Preston. Also Ralph Lorenski, if possible."

"Anyone else?"

Ted paused and briefly entertained the idea of asking Sam to join him. He couldn't imagine her leaving Vin. He also couldn't imagine her agreeing to follow his timeline and methodology. He knew he needed to be free if he was going to succeed.

"No," he said. "Those are the only two."

"Wasn't there someone else? The one from Ashton. What's her name?"

"My wife. She won't leave."

"Oh." Oliver's eyes widened as he sunk deep into the booth. "Ohhhhh. Gotcha. Sorry. I didn't mean to crack that open."

"It's nothing."

"Okay, well, listen, Ted, why don't you take the weekend to think this over? I'm going to need an answer by the end of the year at the latest."

"That won't be necessary, Oliver. I'm in." Ted thrust his arm across the table and opened his palm. Oliver smiled and grabbed Ted's hand, shaking it enthusiastically. "And I'll do my best to get Lori, Ralph, and anyone else on board. When do you need me to start?"

"Well, I assume you will want to enjoy the holidays and give a proper two-week notice."

"I'd like to hit the ground running as soon as possible. A week's notice is plenty. Once they hear I'm leaving, they'll surely want me gone."

"How does Monday, the thirtieth, sound?"

"Works for me."

"Perfect. Welcome to Where2, Ted."

The drive back to the office from Donovan's Pub took less than fifteen minutes. Ted almost got into two accidents on the way. He couldn't not stop staring at the twin manila folders resting on his passenger seat. His mind was a noisy echo chamber as he thought through how he would structure his department and what sort of partnership Where2 had formed with the European automaker. He parked his BMW at the first spot he could find and ran his fingers across the blue and white roundel on the steering wheel. Could BMW be the mystery partner? He smiled at the prospect of possibly working with them. He debated bringing the offer letters with him, but opted instead to toss them into his trunk.

The building was fairly quiet. Ted's heart raced as he searched for Sam. He checked the conference rooms, but all four were empty. He went to the main lab to find only three people inside—Sam, Ralph, and Lori. They all stopped talking when Ted burst into the room.

"Hi," he said, slightly out of breath from running into the building. He looked between Ralph, Lori, and Sam a few times before allowing his eyes to settle on Sam's. "Can I have a word?"

"Sure." She handed a small clipboard to Ralph.

He led her outside the lab and into the closest conference room. The motion sensor flicked the lights on as soon as they stepped inside. He walked to the back of the room. He wanted to be as far from the hallway as possible. Sam joined him, and the two sat next to each other.

"That wasn't a very long lunch," she said. "Is everything okay?"

"I didn't eat," Ted replied. He rolled his chair closer to her. "I have some news, and I wanted you to be the first to know. Maybe . . . maybe this will end up being a good thing. For us."

Sam leaned back in her chair and folded her arms across her chest. Ted couldn't help but notice the lack of sparkle in her eyes. She had taken Dani to her mother's seven days ago and not come back. Catherine had convinced Sam to take a break from the stress and the escalating fights. Ted hated to admit it, but he found the peace and quiet of the house relaxing without the two of them there. His work relationship with Sam had remained cordial at best. He often wondered if seeing each other day and night was contributing to the breakdown of their marriage. He wondered if having separate jobs would bring her back home.

"I got a job offer today," he said.

"What?" She sat bolt upright in her chair. "From?"

"Where2."

"Where2?"

"Yes." He glanced through the glass walls to confirm the hallway was empty. "It's an amazing opportunity, Sam. They have big plans for autonomy. They want me to lead their initiative."

"Harry's there now, isn't he?" She leaned forward. "I heard they raided the undergraduate class at Ashton."

"DSU, too. Nico just accepted a position with them as well."

"Wow." She leaned back and stared deeply into his eyes. "Are you seriously considering their offer?"

"I already accepted."

"What?" She shook her head in disappointment. When she spoke again, her voice was filled with confusion and disappointment. "Did it occur to you that maybe we should discuss this first?"

"Where? At your mother's?"

"At least Dani gets some love there." She sighed and stared at her wedding rings. "You keep making these decisions without me. Just like when you bought the house before we got married. Or that stupid BMW."

"I wanted to surprise you. We're making so much more money now."

"You make these big decisions that impact more than just you, Ted."

"All my choices are the right ones. So is going to Where2." He rolled his chair forward and took her hands. She resisted at first, but he refused to release her. "Where2 understands, Sam. They're moving forward with full autonomy. In real cars. Not that golf cart Vin has planned. Their vision is my vision. It used to be yours, too. Taxis and trucks that drive themselves. Remember?"

"That's still my vision, Ted. We're just going to prove the technology with the LSV. Our methodology shows us that—"

"Your methodology's taking too long." He flicked her hands away and stood up. He began pacing back and forth. "By the time Where2 has a self-driving taxi for sale, you'll still be testing golf carts in a lab."

"There's no way Where2 will pass us, Ted. No matter how many people they hire. Look how much trial and error we went through during those ten challenges?"

"We should have finished those in half the time. No thanks to Vin."

"He was right to make us go slow! Look at all the knowledge we gained during that time."

"I plan to take that knowledge with me when I leave."

"What does that mean?"

"Where2 has given me free rein to run the project the way I see fit. I told them I'd have something for them in one year."

"A year?" She snickered and rolled her eyes as she stood up. "You're dreaming, Ted."

"No, Sam. You're wrong." They were now standing on opposite sides of the room. Ted was wrought with confusion. There was a time when he and Sam were in perfect synch with their hopes and dreams. Lately, he had felt like he didn't understand her motivations. He shoved his hands in his pockets and lowered his head. "Why don't we talk it over tonight. Work isn't really the best place for this conversation. Dinner? We can order in."

"My mom's having some of Dani's friends and their parents over tonight."

"Oh."

"Besides, Ted, is there anything to discuss? You sound like you've made up your mind."

"I have."

"So, all we have to talk about is you convincing me why you're right, and I'm wrong." She paused briefly, but he had no comeback. She shook her head as she walked past him, stopping at the exit. "Good luck at Where2, Ted. I hope you know what you're doing."

38

Lori sat quietly at the small circular table, her hands clasped, gaze locked on the closed office door. To her right, Harry swayed his legs back and forth, his chair rocking and creaking to the movement. Nico was seated to her left, lost in the stream of information on his phone screen in one hand, pen dancing across his fingers in the other. The three of them had been waiting in Ted's office since 11:00 a.m. for a meeting Ted had requested earlier that morning. It was now eleven minutes past the hour.

"Where is he?" Lori asked. "I have an appointment at noon."

Ted's office was a mess. The only clean space was the table where the three of them were sitting. His main desk was made up of three sections, all of which were piled with binders and folders. The walls were covered with copies of project plans and three whiteboards plastered with computations and formulas. Even the floor had boxes with random pieces of hardware piled in them and were spilling their contents to the ground.

"Do we follow the ten-minute rule?" Harry said. "If the meeting organizer isn't here for his own meeting, then we leave."

"Good luck explaining that to the Big Bad Wolff," Nico said, never taking his eyes away from his phone. He'd given Ted that nickname five months ago shortly after coming to Where2. It had caught on with everyone on the team, unbeknownst to Ted. Nico looked up and opened his palm, catching his pen as it rolled from his fingertips. "I passed him on my way here. He was running to talk to Oliver and told me he'd be a few minutes late."

"We'll just have to wait. Otherwise, we'll have to face his wrath later." Harry stopped fidgeting and looked at Lori. "Was he this bad at GSI? I mean, Ted was always a bit full of himself at DSU, but we were all good friends back then. Now, he's, well, he's really kind of a dick these days. Sorry."

"No, you're right," she said. "He's a total dick. To answer your question, I didn't report to him at GSI. But his team often complained about his attitude. Ted tried to recruit this guy Ralph to come to Where2, but Ralph told me he hated working for him. Ralph used to complain to Vin about him, but Ted's designs were groundbreaking. That's probably why Vin tolerated him. I also think Ted was sort of kept in check by Sam and Vin. Everyone was guided by the methodology those two started at Ashton, and I know that always annoyed Ted. It's almost like he's been unleashed now that he's running the show."

"He's gotten ridiculously bossy," Nico said. "It's like Rusty rubbed off on him."

"You can't argue with the results," Harry said. "Look how far we've come these months, and we're ready to move testing from the lab to the road. That's insane."

"Is it?" Lori asked. Although they were the only three in the room, she lowered her voice, almost to a whisper. "Harry, you've seen the coding. A lot of what Ted's introduced this year is directly from what we were doing on Project Courier."

"Oliver told us Ted was bringing us the next generation of autonomous software," Harry said. He leaned back in his chair, clasping his fingers behind his bald head. "I mean, I can see code from our days at DSU. But it only makes sense, right? I'll be the first to admit that many of my software designs are based on what was done for DARPA."

"But did you bring those programs with you?" Lori asked. "Did you take anything from Boeing?"

"No," Harry said, lowering his eyes. "Well, I mean, I took *some* stuff. More like reference materials and documentation I'd created. Why? Are you saying Ted took the actual programs?"

"It looks like it," Lori replied.

"I wonder if Oliver made him," Harry said. He glanced at the door before looking back and forth between Nico and Lori. "I have a theory. The mapping software I inherited seemed to have a lot of GSI components."

"Are you talking about GSI's mapping engine?" Nico asked.

Suddenly the office door swung open. The handle slipped from Ted's hand and the door slammed against the backstop. He looked upset. He closed the door and approached the small conference table in the corner of his office, opting to stand rather than sit down with everyone else.

"Do I look different?" Ted asked, his tone curt and mocking. "I should. Because I just got my ass chewed out by Oliver!"

Lori tried not to show her annoyance at his hysterics. She considered glancing at his butt and making some sort of joke, but could see by his beet-red face that that would not fly. A sense of dread washed over her as she wondered if Oliver found out Ted was possibly using GSI's code.

"Have you heard the latest from our friends over at Tesla?" Ted asked. "The Model S will debut a new feature later this year. They're calling it Autopilot. How the hell are they beating us?"

"Relax, Ted," Nico said, his tone as calm and laid-back as always. He put his phone down, flipping the screen facedown. "They aren't using lidar. It's a different approach than our design."

"How can you be sure?" Ted asked.

"I know some people over there," Nico replied.

Lori felt her pulse return to normal, relieved that Ted's discussion with Oliver had nothing to do with her concerns about the coding.

"Nico's right, Ted," Lori said. "The tech is different. In my opinion, it's a glorified cruise control."

"Harry, did you know about this?" Ted asked. Harry lowered his head without replying. "Great. Why the hell am I the last to know?"

"You've got a full plate." Lori glanced at the clock on her phone, calculating how much time she needed to get to her appointment. She knew she needed to speed things along. "We didn't want to bother you with Tesla's system when we all agreed they weren't a threat. So, why are we all here in your office? This is your meeting, remember?"

"Originally, I wanted to talk about Monday's test launch." Ted seemed to calm down, pulling out the chair in front of him to take a seat at the table. "But now I think we need to revisit the overall timeline. If Tesla's really going live into production later this year, we're going to need to redouble our efforts."

"What?" Nico asked, his voice slightly raised. "You've already got people working seventy to eighty hours a week. Staff members are burning out, Ted. We need to do this the right way. If you ask me, we shouldn't even be testing on the road next week. It's too soon."

"I agree with Nico," Harry said. "There are too many holes in the coding. The simulations are showing—"

"Enough simulations!" Ted slammed his fists against the table. "That's half of what we did back at GSI. We need real-world data to move this project forward. I want the Volkswagen ready for Monday. I don't care if people have to work all weekend without any sleep. If it takes nine women to make that baby, so be it."

"What?" Lori asked. "What the hell does that mean?"

"It means we're going to do the impossible," Ted replied. "Road testing starts as planned."

Lori looked at Harry and then at Nico. She knew they shared her frustration and disappointment with Ted's attitude and work ethic. Lori refused to look at Ted. After less than four months at Where2, she was already regretting her move. Although she didn't take Ted's outbursts personally, she found them to be incredibly counterproductive. She began to wonder if Vin and Sam would allow her to come back. Then she remembered Oliver required everyone to sign a non-compete clause, meaning she would need to wait a year before seeking employment with another firm working on self-driving technology. Lori sighed audibly, disappointed she had let herself fall into this trap.

"I want a full staff meeting at one o'clock," Ted said. He stood up and walked over to his desk, retrieving his keyboard from beneath a stack of papers. "Have everyone clear their calendars. I want all team leads ready to walk through the project plan to see where we can speed things up."

"I have lunch plans," Lori said as she stood up. "I may be a few minutes late."

"Cancel them," Ted replied. "I want everyone there on time."

"But it's important. It's a doctor's appointment I made months ago. I'll be back as soon as I can."

Sam closed her eyes, allowing herself to enjoy the warm, moist steam rising from her lunch. The aroma of garlic, oregano, tomatoes, pepperoni, salt, and mozzarella felt decadent and she had yet to take her first bite of pizza. The din of the crowded, noisy restaurant fell away as she imagined herself at a small café in Italy, enjoying an afternoon meal before taking a pleasant siesta. She opened her eyes and carved a petite wedge from her small deep dish pizza. The pie was hot, so she nibbled bits of it from her fork, the gooey cheese dripping straight onto her chin. She looked up when she saw her lunch date finally arrive.

"You still come here?" Lori asked. "After all these years?"

"First of all, Uncle Danny makes the best deep dish pizza in town," Sam said, tossing another chunk of pizza into her mouth. "Second, I did win free pizza for life."

"It smells amazing. I don't know how you keep that tiny figure of yours."

"I only come here once a month. It's all about control, Lori." Sam wiped the corners of her mouth dry. "Are you sure you don't want to eat? I'm not going to finish this. I can have the waiter get you a plate."

"No, it's fine. Like I said in my text message, I can't stay long. Ted called an emergency meeting for one o'clock. So, how are things at GSI? How's Vin? Ralph?"

"Everyone's great, Lori. We all miss you. The real question is, how are you?"

"I'm . . . I'm fine."

"You don't seem fine. Honestly, you never get rattled. When you asked me to lunch, you said it was urgent. Are you unhappy at Where2? I'm sure Vin will take you back. All you have to do is ask."

"Where2's rough, Sam, but I can deal with it. It's a love-hate thing, you know? There are times, like today, when I second-guess my decision. But then I remind myself that the work we are doing is incredible—groundbreaking in some areas. It's the main reason I went there."

"And the money." Sam waited for a reaction, but didn't receive one. She sliced into her pie, taking time to secure a chunk of pepperoni onto the fork. "I know Ted threw a shitload of cash at you. It's fine. I just want to make sure you're happy there. What's the hate part? My husband?"

Lori smiled nervously and looked out the window.

"I married him," Sam responded, shaking her head. "I know what he's like."

"Hey, isn't your anniversary soon? The wedding was last May around this time, wasn't it?"

Sam was about to slide another piece of pizza into her mouth but paused, just as the cheese brushed against her lower lip. She put the fork back onto her plate.

"It's tomorrow."

"Wow! Congratulations. What do you have planned?"

Sam immediately felt her eyes well up with tears. She wasn't expecting Lori to ask about her anniversary. She pushed her pizza dish away, stealing a glance at her wedding rings. Bits of tomato sauce were sprinkled across the rose-gold edge. Sam wiped her fingers on her napkin.

"I'm sorry," Lori said, somewhat taken aback. "What's wrong?"

"It's just that you remembered my anniversary, Lori. Ted . . . Ted didn't."

"What?"

"I mentioned it to him months ago. I wanted to plan something amazing, you know? I even thought we could go back to Europe."

"But you hate flying."

"I know," Sam allowed herself to laugh, but it was only momentary. "I finally stopped asking. I told myself he was planning something special. I'd hoped things would get better when Ted went to Where2. So did he. But now he works these fourteen-hour days. Weekends. I never see him. Who knows, maybe he will surprise me with an exotic celebration this weekend."

Lori's phone buzzed with a text message notification. It was from Ted, reminding her not to be late for the meeting. She quickly typed a reply.

DOCTOR'S OFFICE IS BUSY. DOING MY BEST.

Lori jammed her phone into her purse and leaned forward, taking Sam by her hands.

"Sam, I hate to disappoint you, but we have a critical launch on Monday. Ted's expecting everyone to work the weekend. I guarantee you, he will be there with us. He plans on taking the test vehicle out himself and wants to make sure we hit every deadline."

"Of course he does." She patted Lori's hand and forced herself to smile. Pulling her lunch plate closer, she went back to eating her pizza. "Can we not talk about Ted or my anniversary? Tell me about what you're doing at Where2. You called it groundbreaking. Or is it something you can't share?"

"That's the million-dollar question." A rolled-up red-and-white-checkered napkin rested on the table between the two women. Lori slid the napkin closer and peeled it open, removing the fork hidden inside. She jammed the tines into Sam's pie, extracting chunks of tomato and pepperoni. She slid the pizza into her mouth and smiled. "Damn, that's good."

"It's the best."

"Sam, I asked you to lunch because I feel like I don't know who else to turn to."

"What's wrong?"

Lori stole another bit of pizza from Sam's dish. She wiped her chin dry and motioned for the waiter, requesting a glass of water.

"Harry started at Where2 almost a year ago," Lori said. "He and a few others did a lot of the foundational work for their autonomy program. Then Ted and Nico showed up in January, followed by me in February. Now it's mid-May, and we're already moving from the lab to the road."

"That's Ted," Sam said dismissively. "He's always in a rush."

"But think about it, Sam. That's five months since he came on board."

"Well, you said he's building on what Harry and the others did. How long has the program been active?"

"It's . . . it's . . . Shit. Maybe this was a bad idea."

"What, Lori?" Sam slid the pizza dish to the side and took Lori by her hands, squeezing them firmly. She waited for Lori to lock eyes with her. "You can trust me. You know me. What's going on?"

Lori exhaled and briefly closed her eyes. She slowly released Sam's fingers.

"When I got there, Nico told me they were already deep into a heavy rewrite of some of the software programs. Within weeks, our simulations became shockingly accurate. The team was thrilled, including me. It took several weeks before I started connecting the dots."

"What dots?"

"Sam, GSI's fingerprints are all over the software protocols."

"What do you mean?"

"I mean, I see lines of code I wrote for Leapfrog. Your code, too."

"*My* code? I don't . . . are you saying Ted stole the autonomy software?" Sam was stunned. She lowered her voice as she scanned the restaurant for any familiar faces. "*All* of it?"

"No, not all of it. Honestly, much of it is new. Harry did a lot of great work. But most of the lidar controls are pretty much what Ted designed for Leapfrog. And I know parts of your AI engine are intertwined in the core protocols."

"Mine?" Sam shook her head as she tried to digest everything Lori was telling her. "Did you ask him about it?"

"Sort of. He's my boss. I didn't want to rock the boat. I attempted to make light of it a couple of weeks ago. I tried pointing out how so much of what I was seeing reminded me of Project Courier."

"And? What was his reaction?"

"He got this condescending attitude. He said something like, and I'm paraphrasing here, but he said that Project Courier only happened because of his advancements with the lidar array. He brought that knowledge to GSI and could finally advance it at Where2."

"Really?" Sam's cheeks became flush with anger. "*His* advancements made it a success? I guess the rest of us were just making shit up?"

"I'm sorry, Sam. I keep telling myself I'm wrong. But the code speaks for itself. I know what I wrote. I know what you wrote. It just doesn't feel right, you know? We all take stuff when we change jobs. I have my own protocols and procedures I use for my mapping systems. But this . . . this is different."

Sam stared at her pizza. Her appetite suddenly vanished and her stomach churned as she tried to figure out what to do next. Should she confront Ted? She could already hear him making excuses. Sam knew if she took it to Vin, all hell would break loose.

"It's fine, Lori. I'm glad you told me." Sam looked at her phone. It was a few minutes before one. "You'd better get back to your meeting. You don't want to upset your boss."

"What are you going to do, Sam?"

"I . . . I don't know, Lori. I honestly don't know."

The oversized red numbers on the digital clock on the nightstand read 10:20 p.m. The clock was angled directly at Sam. She'd been in bed for twenty minutes. Despite her best efforts, she could not calm herself. Every beat of her heart pounded hard within her chest as she ran through the list of questions she wanted to ask Ted. Intertwined in these thoughts was the conversation she'd had with Lori during lunch. The thought that her husband could be or likely was a thief was almost too much to bear.

Her daze was broken by the hum and rattle of the garage door from downstairs. She pulled herself upright, evening out the folds in the white cotton bedsheet resting across her waist. She heard the sound of the hallway door open and close, followed by a set of keys rattling on the marble kitchen counter. She twisted and twirled her engagement ring back and forth, unconsciously changing its direction with each thud of her husband's footsteps coming up the stairs. The bedroom door swung open.

"Finally," she said.

"Why are you home?" Ted asked.

"It's nice to see you, too. You almost sound disappointed."

"Well, it's Friday. You usually go to your mother's for the weekend."

"I took Dani there earlier tonight."

"Oh." He crossed the expansive master suite and entered the bathroom. "Why didn't you stay there? Do you have plans here?"

"Do I have plans?" She chuckled lightly, raising her voice to be sure Ted could hear her in the other room. "Why would I?"

"What?" He emerged from the bathroom with a toothbrush jutting from his mouth. "What's with the cocky attitude?"

"Oh, I don't know Ted, I thought you might have a surprise planned for me."

"For what?"

"You really are amazing, Ted." She flung the coverlet away, tossed her robe on, and marched across the room, stopping at a cherry dresser.

An eight-by-ten wedding photo framed in solid pewter sat in the center. She grabbed it and brought it to Ted. "Do I need to ask you again?"

"Shit." He took the picture into his hands, allowing his toothbrush to droop from his jaw. "It's our anniversary. I'm so sorry, Sam. I've just been busy with work. Why didn't you remind me?"

"Don't turn this around on me!" She snatched the photograph and flung it onto the bed. "I asked you months ago. You kept telling me we'd figure something out. I finally stopped asking, hoping maybe you'd surprise me."

"I'll make it up to you." He tried to pull her close, but she stepped away. Putting his arms up, he turned into the bathroom and finished brushing his teeth. The bathroom light went off, and he returned. "I will, Sam. I promise."

She was now sitting on the edge of their California King bed, feeling lost in the six hundred square foot bedroom. She looked around and suddenly felt like a stranger in her own home. She pulled her emerald silk robe tightly around her waist as Ted came and sat by her side.

"You know work's been killing me," he said, trying to take Sam's hand, but she pulled away. "I have to work this weekend. Maybe we can grab dinner tomorrow night."

"Dinner?" Sam stood up and walked to the other side of the room. She didn't want Ted to follow her. His close proximity made her uneasy. "It's our first anniversary, Ted. This should be a celebration. It should be special."

"I'm sorry, Sam." He slouched forward, resting his chin in the palms of his hands. "I know I've been distant. But so have you. It's not like we've been seeing eye to eye lately. I thought my going to Where2 would give us some distance—some good distance."

"Don't act like you took that job to save our marriage. We both know you did it for the money."

"It's not just the money, Sam. We're making great progress. We start testing on public roads Monday."

"Monday? So soon? That seems awfully fast." She took a deep

breath. He had just given her the opening she was looking for. "Tell me, how is it that you started there less than five months ago, but are already out of simulations?"

"What can I say? I'm good." He smiled and winked at her.

"Or is it that you're a thief?"

"Excuse me?" He stood up and slowly made his way across the room, stopping less than a foot from his wife. "What's that supposed to mean?"

"Don't make me ask, Ted." She folded her arms across her chest. Her worry and fear from earlier were long gone, as anger and resentment began to expand from within. She leaned forward and looked into his eyes. He took a step back. "I know, Ted. I know about the data."

Ted continued to move backward, Sam matching each of his footsteps until they reached the bed. She gave him a gentle nudge with her right hand, forcing him to sit down. She glared at him until he finally lowered his eyes.

"I went through the log files on the backups we have of the Project Courier data."

"You what?" Ted's head snapped back as he glowered at her.

"I discovered over eight gigabytes copied the night you resigned. You didn't cover your tracks, Ted. I'll admit, it took me a while to find the proper security files. You were good, just not thorough. As always, you were in a rush."

She stared deeply into his blue eyes, hoping for the slightest sign of regret. Instead, she saw emptiness. A few strands of his chestnut brown hair slowly fell in front of his face, obscuring his right eye as it always tended to do. She didn't bother to flick it away.

"That was *my* data." He stood up, forcing her to back away. "I brought that knowledge to GSI. I expanded on it. I improved it. It has been and always will be *mine*."

"Yours?" Sam was both disappointed and enraged. "What about the dozens of other people on Project Courier? Are you saying they contributed nothing? What the hell was I doing there that entire time? Bowing down before the genius of the great Ted Wolff?"

"I only took what was mine, Sam. You saw the files. All the configuration-related documentation. I built that."

"You took more than that, Ted."

"How did you even know to go looking? Why would you go diving into backup files?" Ted's jaw fell open as the pieces suddenly fell into place. "You talked to Lori, didn't you?"

"It doesn't matter how or why I found it, Ted. The fact is you copied an enormous amount of data the day you resigned."

"I'm no thief."

"No?" She turned away, suddenly disgusted by his attitude. "Is that what you told Kevin?"

"Who?"

"Kevin in Nevada. Was that *his* lidar you took the night we went to Burning Man? Or yours?"

"How can you ask that? You've seen the work I've built. You know what I'm capable of."

"Do I? I think I'm just starting to learn how far you're truly willing to go."

Sam lowered her head and crossed the room, flinging the double doors of the walk-in closet open. She fought back tears as she grabbed the nearest suitcase and began shoving clothes inside.

"Let me guess," Ted called out from the middle of the bedroom. "You're going running back to your mother, aren't you?"

"Give me a reason to stay."

"Do you want an apology? Okay, fine. I'm sorry I took the data. I spent years developing it at GSI, and then Vin decided to slap it on to a golf cart. Remember our dreams of moving the world forward? That's what's driving me, Sam."

"Do you love me?" She stepped in the middle of the closet doorway so she could see him. It was a simple question—one that should be easy to answer after a year of marriage. She was brokenhearted to see him taking so long to answer her.

"Of course I do," he finally said.

She didn't believe him. His words rang empty in her ears as if he was telling her what she wanted to hear. Her marriage had fallen apart so quickly. She still couldn't believe he had forgotten their anniversary. It was time for him to prove his love.

"Then cancel the test you have planned for Monday."

"What?"

"Let's go away for the weekend to celebrate our anniversary—or take the entire week. Let's jet off to Italy or any place that's not here."

"I can't do that, Sam. There's too much on the line. Too many commitments."

"Too many commitments?" She shook her head in disgust as she sadly realized she was fighting a losing battle. She went through a few more drawers, collecting what she could, filling her luggage with whatever would fit. "Your family should be your biggest commitment, Ted. That's the problem."

"I told you I'll make it up to you."

"That's not good enough. Not this time. It's our anniversary."

"I told you I'm sorry."

"You're always sorry." She took a moment to wipe her eyes dry. She turned to face her husband—the man she had fallen in love with years ago. The man she had dreamed of spending the rest of her life with. She had once admired Ted's brilliance and confidence. Now when she looked at him, all she saw was the cocky, overly smug guy she had met in the desert. "You don't understand."

She looked at the mess of clothes jammed into her bag. She had no idea if she'd packed everything she would need. She didn't care. She zipped the bag shut and slammed her shoulder into Ted, pushing him aside.

"When will you be back?" His voice quivered with confusion. "Can we talk about this more?"

"Can we?" Despite her best efforts, she could not stop the steady stream of tears running down her face. "It's up to you, Ted. Every decision you make seems to be about you. And I've had enough."

"I can do better, Sam. I promise."

"You need to stop making promises you can't keep. Let me know when you're ready to focus on us."

She turned, lowered her head, and left the room. As she struggled to carry her bag down the staircase, she realized she was still in her robe and nightgown. She didn't care. All she knew was she wanted to get as far away as quickly as possible. She grabbed her keys from the kitchen counter and wondered if this would be her last time seeing this house.

39

Ted cradled his cell phone in both hands, keeping it just below the rim of the steering wheel. He alternated his gaze between his phone, the road ahead, the laptop to his right, and the instrument panel behind the steering wheel. He couldn't help but smile at how smoothly this test was going. The traffic on Guadalupe Canyon Parkway on this Sunday evening at 10:00 p.m. was almost nonexistent despite it being just four days before Thanksgiving. Thankfully, because of the hour, any holiday traffic was long gone. The Volkswagen Touareg was in full self-driving mode and had performed flawlessly the entire evening.

He wanted to send a text message to Sam but couldn't think of what to say. Scattered around his laptop were piles of papers and notepads. Lost within the mess was an envelope he'd received yesterday. He was still somewhat shocked by the contents, but deep down not all that surprised. Sam, citing irreconcilable differences, had filed for divorce.

The last few months had been a roller coaster for him—personally and professionally. As progress at Where2 accelerated, his marriage had unraveled. He had eventually taken Sam away for their anniversary, but the four-day trip had been strained and less than joyful. Initially, he was happy he had at least convinced her not to move out of the house. But as the weeks passed and Ted spent most of his time at work, their relationship faltered. He increasingly found himself coming home to an empty house, with Sam opting to stay at her mother's.

On the rare occasion when she was home, they would often end up fighting. By July, they'd decided to try couples therapy. Because of his workload, though, he often had to skip the sessions, much to Sam's disappointment. By mid-September, Sam and Dani had moved out of the house and into a two-bedroom townhome where Dani could continue at her same school. He had hoped to spend the November and December holidays with Sam and her family. He kept telling her everything would change in the following year once Where2 could begin marketing their self-driving taxi. The papers from Sam's lawyer confirmed that she had given up. He didn't take them seriously, though. He would fix everything next year, once things at work calmed down.

He opened his "Rock-It" playlist from a music app on his phone. He turned on the stereo and waited for the Bluetooth. After a few moments, "Burnin' for You" by Blue Öyster Cult began to reverberate all around him. He smiled and turned up the volume. He checked the car's speed—forty-five miles per hour and keeping centered within the lane. A sign flashed at the side of the road confirming the forty-five miles per hour speed limit.

Guadalupe Canyon Parkway was a four-lane winding road adjacent to the San Bruno Mountain State Park, twenty minutes south of San Francisco. This evening's test involved a mix of city and highway travel that included the downtown area, US-101, I-280, and a mix of urban and suburban roads. The peace and quiet along the winding mountain road marked the midway point of the test. Ted was sure this would be the final run prior to certification. He'd pushed his team hard all year to exceed every goal he'd set. They, and the Touareg, nicknamed Scorpion after the eighties German rock band, had performed spectacularly.

He checked the data scrolling across the screen of his laptop. He thought back to his days of testing Frankie in Nevada. The data on that computer were so primitive compared to what he was working with today. He couldn't help but smile at all the advancements. A flash of high beams flickered in the rearview mirror, distracting him. He squinted and adjusted the mirror. Whoever was behind him was accelerating quickly.

Ted debated bumping up the speed on the VW, but figured it was easier to let the other vehicle pass. He found himself chuckling, realizing that Sam's cautious attitude still had a way of affecting him. Eventually, the car began overtaking him. He was surprised to see a second set of high beams behind him.

"What the hell?" Ted said.

He glanced over his left shoulder as the first car pulled alongside. It was a red Tesla Model S. The passenger window lowered, and the person stuck their hand outside and raised their middle finger. Ted was about to return the gesture, when the person reclined their seat and pointed at the steering wheel. Nobody was driving the car. They waved at Ted and closed the window.

"Autopilot," he grumbled. Tesla's Autopilot system had debuted a month before. Where2 had already bought a Model S equipped with the self-driving technology, and Ted's team had dismantled it to study their competition. He turned his head to face the other vehicle. "Your hardware sucks!"

The red Tesla pulled ahead. Ted bumped Scorpion's speed up to fifty miles per hour. The laptop responded with three short chimes, followed by a long pause indicating he was now exceeding the posted speed limit. He ignored the warning.

He checked his rearview mirror as the other vehicle slid sideways to pass him. He could tell by the headlight design it was another Model S. Sure enough, a few seconds later, a second Tesla pulled up beside him. This one was jet black. The passenger window was down. The driver was actually in the driver's seat but instead of steering the car, the person was making a video of the event.

"What idiots." He focused on the road ahead and turned his attention back to his music, quietly singing along.

He notched the speed up to fifty-five miles per hour. He was catching up to the red Tesla. The other vehicle faded away behind him.

The laptop still blared a speed warning. He briefly considered slowing down. Part of him wanted to get far away from both cars, but he knew he might risk ruining the test. He wondered what Sam would do. He quietly laughed as he tapped the cruise speed back down to forty-five miles per hour. The digital speedometer behind the steering wheel began decreasing—fifty-three . . . fifty . . . forty-seven. The alarm switched from the speeding warning to the ominous, steady, continuous blare that Ted dreaded hearing. His heart went to his throat as the self-driving system returned control to the driver.

"Shit!" Ted raced to grab the steering wheel to keep the Touareg centered in the lane of the curving road. He looked ahead to see what had caused the system to go offline, and his jaw fell open. A petite woman walking a Great Dane was directly ahead, both were standing a good two feet inside the roadway. He would hit them. Ted panicked. There was nowhere to safely turn. The right side of the road was filled with trees. To the left was the narrowest of openings. The back of the red Tesla was even with his front wheels. The black one was behind him somewhere in his blind spot. But how far back, he could not be sure. In a split-second decision, Ted impulsively jerked the wheel to the left to try to snake between the two cars to avoid the woman and her dog.

Ted's reaction time was too late. The Touareg hit the dog, the leash dragging the owner. The animal's howls of pain lasted only a second, echoing in the blackness of night. The front of the VW hit the back corner of the red Model S, forcing it into an uncontrollable spin. He kept both feet against the brake pedal and swerved back to the right. His instinct was to get away from the red Tesla but then the black one plowed into the rear of Scorpion, sending Ted crashing into the steering wheel as the airbag deployed. A thump against the driver's side mirror caused him to turn just in time to see the body of the driver of the black car fly past his window.

The red Model S spun into the opposite lane of oncoming traffic, slamming sideways into a minivan. Ted looked in horror as the minivan shuddered and wobbled, unable to steer. The Tesla and minivan merged into one, with the Tesla forcing the other vehicle into a guardrail until both cars slid to a stop.

The stereo in the VW somehow continued to play. Ted's ears rang from the explosion made by the airbags. He looked around, checking his hands and seat belt as his heart raced uncontrollably. He caught his reflection in the rearview mirror glimpsing his face. He gasped as he noticed a few small lacerations across his nose and forehead. Horror overtook him as the reality of what had just happened began to sink in. He struggled to catch his breath. His hands trembled as he fought to release his seat belt. Once free, he flung his door open and fell to the ground.

One of Scorpion's headlights was still on, aimed straight ahead, showing a clear road. Ted checked the front of the car. The passenger's side, around the headlight assembly was dented and smeared in blood. He ran behind the car in a frenzy.

The black Tesla, the driver's window shattered, was wedged at an angle into the rear of the Touareg. Ted wheeled around as he recalled seeing the driver's body fly by his window. He suddenly spotted someone resting in the shadows just beyond the reach of the VW's one working headlight. He sprinted ahead and stopped just short of the body. Ted felt a wave of nausea as he took in the sight. The driver was completely mangled—head, arms, and legs all twisted into impossible positions. A pool of blood was forming beneath the man's deformed head. At least he assumed it was a man. He honestly couldn't tell. He knew there was nothing he could do to try to help the person. He turned and ran across the roadway, backtracking to the other wreckage.

The red Model S had pinned the minivan against the guardrail. The front corner of the navy Dodge Grand Caravan was utterly demolished and the electric vehicle was jammed beside the driver's side of the van. Ted grabbed the door handle of the Tesla and yanked it open. Inside the young man was covered in blood. Ted was relieved to see the man's eyes darting back and forth.

"Hey," Ted said, his voice shaking. "Are you okay?"

The driver rolled his head to face Ted and attempted to speak. Instead, he coughed, spraying Ted with blood. Ted stumbled backward, his hands trembling as he attempted to wipe his face clean. He fell to his knees beside the open door.

"I'm . . . I'm going to get help," Ted said. His hands were still shaking as he searched his pockets for his phone. He realized it must be somewhere inside the VW. Just as he was about to stand up, the man inside the car reached out and grabbed him by his shirt. Ted leaned forward and gripped his arms. The look of terror and fear in the driver's eyes sent a chill through Ted's body.

"I'm sorry," the driver said. "Tell my . . ."

"No!" Ted cried. The man's eyes remained open as he let go of Ted. Ted shook him, trying to get him to stay conscious. The man's frail body flopped back and forth in his grip. "Don't you die on me! Don't you die! No . . . no . . ."

He gently let go of the guy and tilted his body back against the seat. He stood up and started walking back to Scorpion to get his phone. An infant's cry stopped him in his tracks. Ted spun around and ran to the front of the minivan. A woman was unconscious in the driver's seat. The entire driver's side of the Dodge was blocked by the Tesla crushed against it. The smell of gasoline and motor oil filled the air. Most of the minivan's engine was either shredded or pushed into the firewall that protects the passenger compartment from the engine bay. Sparks flickered from wiring dangling from the destroyed engine bay.

Ted ran around to the guardrail, finding the Dodge sandwiched between it and the Tesla. Climbing atop the rail, he peered inside the front of the van. The woman behind the steering wheel was covered in blood. She barely even looked old enough to drive. He couldn't tell if she was alive or not. He moved a few feet back to check the second row. The baby, now screaming, was in an infant seat in the back. A wave of relief went through him as he saw that the baby seemed unharmed. He pulled at both door handles with a sick feeling knowing there was no way he was going to get them opened.

"Think, Ted, think!" He looked around and found a rock resting along the embankment. He grabbed it and ran back to the van. He realized he couldn't smash the glass without spraying the child and didn't want to risk doing the same to the driver. His temples throbbed as he struggled to figure out what to do. How could he be able to crunch complicated math formulas in his head but have no idea how to get that baby and driver out of this van? His thoughts stopped dead when he saw the orange glow on the opposite side of the minivan. "Shit!"

Hopping the guardrail he rushed to the middle of the road, finding flames licking one full side of the Tesla. He knew he was running out of time. With the rock still in his hand, he ran to the back of the minivan and smashed the window of the hatch. Inside, the baby's screams grew louder. Acrid smoke filled the air. Ted studied the jagged shards of glass along the base of the shattered window to figure out how he could safely pass through the opening. It suddenly dawned on him to pop the hatch. He dropped the rock and tried the handle. The hatch groaned and creaked as it moved an inch before stopping completely. The passenger's side was dented and mangled from the impact with the guardrail. He yanked and pounded and kicked the door but could not get it to work itself free. Tears streamed down his cheeks as the flames around the Tesla rose.

Picking the rock back up, he cleared the edge of the shattered window as best he could. Smoke was filling the inside of the van as he stepped onto the bumper, dragging himself through the opening. He cried out as bits of glass sliced into his torso and legs. The rear of the minivan was filled with bags and a stroller. He wrestled with them as he crawled to the child—a baby girl dressed in pink, her mouth open and tongue flailing in a tightly drawn face that shook as she screamed.

"Hey little girl," Ted said, his bottom lip quivering. The baby turned and looked at Ted, crying even louder. "It's okay. Stop crying. I'm . . . I'm going to get you out of here."

A glow pulsated behind him. He coughed and turned to look out the driver's side of the minivan. Flames were now dancing between the Tesla and Dodge. He wiped back tears as he struggled to figure out how to free the child seat.

"Lady, are you okay up there?" He leaned forward and grabbed the woman by the shoulder. Her lifeless body slumped sideways against the center console. Ted's breathing was erratic. He could not seem to get enough air into his lungs and felt the world around him begin to spin. Squinting, he looked at the belts connecting the child and seat and ran his fingers across the straps as his hands shook wildly. He could feel the heat of the flames as they began prying their way inside the van. "How the hell does this work? I can't see anything!"

Ted's mind was a blur. His thoughts drifted to Sam and her daughter. He knew Sam would know how to operate something as simple as a child seat. Sam. An emptiness spread throughout his whole chest. He wished she were here. She would know what to do.

Smoke poured in through the minivan's shattered windows. He coughed as he tried to rip the child seat from its anchors. The infant's cries turned into gasps and screams. He gave up and grabbed the baby, pulling at her through the straps. The child fought back, flailing her arms in confusion.

"I'm trying to save you!" The flames rumbling and crackling rose higher around them. He sobbed as he wrestled with the baby and the child seat. The walls of the van felt like they were collapsing around him as each second passed. He cried in pain as his back began to tingle. He spun around to find the fire inside the van. The fabric on the ceiling ignited. Still, he fought to free the tiny, helpless infant. The heat on his back was becoming too much. He could feel the skin on his back start to burn. The tight confines of the van were filled with the smell of oil, gasoline, and melting vinyl and foam.

Ted looked at his hands with anger, as if they were to blame for his inability to free the child. The glow of the fire shone across the inside of the van, illuminating the blood dripping from his hands. He wiped them dry to see how badly they were cut. He stopped for a split second when he noticed the scar on the palm of his right hand—from Frankie many years ago.

"No!" He shifted to the back cargo area and tried to pull the baby through the top of the straps. "Please, God, help me! Help me!"

Flames crawled across the ceiling of the van, hot red tentacles searching for something to embrace. Ted's body shook wildly as he took one last deep breath. He knew this was his last chance. The bitter taste of burning lithium-ion coated his throat. The heat inside the van made it impossible to see clearly. His face was wet with sweat and streaming tears. With a single primal roar, Ted gave one last pull. He howled as the baby girl slid up and back into his arms.

"Thank you!" He held the girl tight against his chest and spun backward atop the bags and stroller in the back. He looked through the shattered rear window. Thankfully, the fire had not yet reached this part of the vehicle. The escape route was clear. The bottom edge of the window was covered in bits and pieces of blood-covered shards of glass. He shielded the baby from the heat and flames with his own body but there wasn't room for both of them to go out of the vehicle at the same time. He was going to have to get out first and then grab the baby. Gently he put her down next to one of the bags in the back. The sharp glass shards lining the back broken window made it impossible for him to get himself and the baby out without getting cut. He was going to need to clear some of the shards first. Spotting a pile of reusable shopping bags near his knees, he grabbed two to cover his hands as he took hold of the shattered rear hatch.

The car was emitting sickening pops and groans and the roar of the fire had reached a deafening level, drowning out the screams of the baby. He carefully swung his right leg through the jagged opening, using the canvas bags to protect himself as best he could. The heat was unbearable. He closed his eyes and flung the rest of his body through the window. The bag covering his left hand snagged a piece of glass, slicing his hand open. He crashed to the ground, landing on his right shoulder. Exhaling a sigh of relief as he pulled himself up to his knees, he coughed several times to clear his lungs. "I'm coming, baby girl."

The detonation of the Grand Caravan's gas tank was instantaneous. The blast blew the back hatch off the van, slamming it into Ted, sending him and the rear door a dozen yards backward. The sound of the explosion echoed against the towering trees lining the roadway, their leaves aglow from the flames that raced into the sky.

Ted came crashing to the ground a few seconds later, landing in the embankment next to the guardrail. Dazed, it occurred to him slowly that he could not hear a thing, the world had gone silent. At first, he didn't understand what had happened. He rolled onto his back and stared up at the stars dotting the night sky. He rolled his head sideways to see the Tesla and Dodge completely engulfed in flames. He realized in horror that there was no way the baby had survived the blast.

With all his strength, Ted willed himself to stand up. His knees and hips buckled as he struggled to balance himself. Even at this distance, the heat was intolerable. He took a few steps forward before falling to the ground. He sat upright on his knees and looked down at his torn denim jeans and blood-soaked shirt.

"What have I done?" he cried. "God help me, what have I done?"

40

Ted stared listlessly at his hands resting atop his legs. His head hung low, his back slumped. Oliver had been yelling at him for fifteen minutes straight. Ted knew before entering his boss's office that his career with Where2 was over, and he'd mentally tuned out of the berating he was receiving. His left hand was bandaged. The lacerations across his body from the accident were somewhat severe, requiring stitches in both legs as well as his left palm. His left thigh and hip were heavily bruised.

"Are you even listening?" Oliver asked. "Look at me."

"I hear you," Ted said as he slowly raised his eyes. "Can we just cut to the chase?"

"Chase? That's an interesting choice. Tell me, Ted, were you busy chasing those Teslas before the accident?"

"The question's been asked and answered. Repeatedly. All I've done since coming back to work is answer everyone's questions. Are we done?"

"We are. Senior management held an emergency meeting last night. The vote was unanimous."

"I'm fired." Ted let out a long, slow sigh. Aside from his physical wounds, he felt emotionally shattered. But he was surprised, now that the moment was here, that he actually felt relief. Everywhere he went at Where2, he felt judgment. The eyes. The whispers. He wanted it all to end. "I thought you would have at least waited for a full review of the data before firing me."

"Your guilt or innocence is irrelevant. We can't risk the exposure, Ted."

"Oliver, I told you. There was nowhere to turn."

"This isn't just about the accident, Ted." Oliver shook his head as he began rifling through a pile of papers on his deck. He paused to inspect a stapled collection before passing it to Ted. "We've been contacted by GSI. They're claiming patent infringement and theft of intellectual property. Your lidar controls are being challenged."

"What?" Ted's heart sank as he scanned through the pages. He didn't waste the time reading any of the details. He thought back to the fight he'd had with Sam six months ago. Her discovery about the stolen data had never surfaced again. He was shocked to see it now spelled out in black and white. He tossed the papers onto Oliver's desk and returned his gaze to his injured hand. "Everything I brought to Where2 was mine."

"The lawyers will have to decide that. Look, Ted, you're a great engineer. There's no way we would've gotten as far as we have without you. But, at the end of the day, you're a liability. We need to cut the cord."

Ted ran his fingers gently across his bandaged left hand. The stitches still ached, the wound throbbing in sync with the beat of his heart. He flipped his hand over and rubbed his injured palm against his thigh, accidentally brushing against another set of stitches on his leg. He looked up and asked, "What about the project?"

"I'm putting Nico in charge. The partnership with Volkswagen is on thin ice, but I'm confident we can keep them. The future and vision are still there, Ted. Just not with your involvement."

Oliver stood up and shoved his hands into his pockets. Ted pushed his chair back and struggled to stand up, his left leg wobbling in protest. He turned and slowly walked to the closed door, slightly dragging his foot. He had no interest in shaking Oliver's hand. Instead, Ted stopped at the door, and without looking back, said, "I never thought anyone would get killed. I'm so sorry."

"You better pray they don't find you personally at fault. If I were you, I'd lawyer up. Good luck."

Ted turned the polished nickel door handle, took a deep breath, and entered the hallway. His office was one floor down from Oliver's. In spite of his injury, he decided to take the stairs hoping to avoid seeing anyone else. Once inside the stairwell, he fell back against the steel door in a sob. Five days ago, he had been heading out on what should have been the final test of his autonomy system. People died. An infant. Right in front of him. He had no job, his wife had filed for divorce, and he was facing at least one potential lawsuit.

How did I get here? he wondered. His ears echoed with the cries of the baby girl trapped in the minivan. He could not get her screams out of his mind. *I tried. I really tried.*

Using his forearm to wipe his face dry as he fought to calm himself down, he descended the stairs and opened the door to the hallway. Lori, Nico, and Harry were all standing outside his office door waiting for him.

"What's the news?" Lori asked.

"Are you okay, boss?" Harry said.

Nico remained silent as Ted limped his way between the three of them, ignoring their questions. He went into his office, closed the door, leaving everyone outside. Wincing, he sank down to the floor and leaned back against the door. He rolled his head sideways, pressing his ear to the wood. He tried in vain to hear conversation on the other side. He waited in relief as their footsteps became fainter, followed by silence.

Gazing at the mess all around him, he struggled to his feet and walked over to the row of boxes lining the wall. He dumped the largest one out and brought it to his desk, scanning the stacks of papers and personal belongings.

He reached into his pocket to get his phone. As he sat in the chair, jolts of pain shot through his legs. He dialed Sam's cell and waited for the call to connect. He hadn't seen her since the night of the accident. She'd rushed to the emergency room, but Ted had sent her away as soon as he was discharged. He was so racked with guilt, he only wanted to be alone.

All week, he had kept her at a distance, despite her repeated calls and attempts to see him. Suddenly more than anything in the world, he wanted her touch. To hold her. Smell her hair. Kiss her. He felt so completely alone. A sense of helplessness washed over him with each ring. He felt his eyes well up with tears as he got her voicemail.

"Hey, it's me," he said, his voice quivering. "I thought you should know I just got fired. I guess it was inevitable. I've . . . I've never been fired before. I've always left on my own. There's also a lawsuit. GSI is going after Where2—and me—about the tech we're using. But I'm not blaming you, Sam. Even if . . . It's not important. It doesn't matter. What matters is that you were right. You were right, okay? I was reckless and foolish. I was so much better when I was with you. We were such a good team. I screwed up. I ruined everything—my job—our marriage. I . . . I just wanted to say I'm sorry."

Ted pressed "end" and sat still. He felt nothing—almost like he was floating above his life and not fully connecting with any of it. He gently placed his phone on his desk and scanned the room. The project and test plans were taped to the wall. Ted's dream of building a self-driving car was over. He felt utterly lost.

41

David Foster paced across the oyster-colored woven carpet in his office, staring across the Detroit River toward Windsor, Canada. The wind today was coming from the south, carrying damp cold air from Lake Erie. With Christmas less than a week away, the last thing David had wanted was a late-day meeting with his rivals. But recent events left him no choice. Brad Kenner fidgeted in his large cherry wood chair with green leather back and seat, as he checked e-mail on his phone. Both men turned when Robert Anderson from Chrysler entered the room.

"Sorry I'm late," Robert said, groaning as he lowered himself into the chair next to Brad. "Holiday traffic out there is a real bitch. Couldn't we have done this on the phone, David?"

"I thought it best to meet in person," David replied. He remained standing, gazing out the window, his hands clasped behind his back. David leaned forward, keeping his nose less than an inch from the cold glass. "We need to talk about last month's fiasco with Where2 and Tesla."

"The crash?" Robert asked. He shook his head and smiled. "It just proves we were right. The technology isn't ready."

"I'm not so sure." David returned to his desk, taking a seat across from the other two. He picked up a stack of newspapers and magazines. One by one, David began tossing them onto the desktop in front of Brad and Robert. "*The New York Times. The Washington Post.* Even *Wired* magazine. They're not talking about the crash being a setback. They don't even care about the people who were killed. Do either of you even know the name of the guy walking the dog?"

"It was, um, hold on." Robert's cheeks reddened and his eyes darted around the room. "I vaguely remember reading it."

"That was a trick question," David said. "It was a woman walking the dog."

"What's your point?" Brad asked.

"My point is that all the buzz is about how Tesla and Where2 have vehicles that can drive themselves. The press doesn't seem to care about the accident. They all seem to be blaming the human drivers!" David rifled through the newspapers to find *USA Today*. With deliberate gruffness, he flipped through the newspaper until he came to the article he wanted. Adjusting his glasses, he read, "Where2 refused to comment on their long-term goals. However, they did confirm they believe the self-driving car is a future that can't be ignored." Turning and looking from one to the other, he said, "The article goes on to talk about GSI and the cars they are testing."

"GSI's autonomous cars are low-speed vehicles," Robert said dismissively. "They aren't a threat to us. Where2 shouldn't have been testing that technology on public roads. That accident will cost them dearly."

"Not so fast, Bob." Brad leaned back in his chair, dragging his fingers across his silver beard. He glanced around nervously. "We all know that Where2 raided a lot of talent from our companies. I've kept in touch with one of my engineers. I thought he would've stayed with Ford forever. Anyway, he told me that preliminary reports show the accident was unavoidable."

"Bullshit," Robert said.

"The black box data show that even a human driver would have struck that woman and her dog." Brad stood up, shoved his hands into his pockets, and started walking in circles around a conference table a few feet away. "Where2's Volkswagen was rounding a corner and had nowhere to go. That idiot was walking her dog in the middle of the road. At the speed those cars were going, there was nothing that could've been done."

"Tell that to the lawyers," Robert said. He stood up and walked over to Brad. "Speaking of, isn't GSI suing Where2 for stolen tech? I heard that hotshot lidar engineer took a bunch of data with him when he jumped ship."

"It's worse than that," Brad said as he stopped and leaned back against the conference table. "According to my inside guy, Where2 based their mapping software on GSI's systems. The whole foundation of their AI engine relies on stolen mapping and lidar controls from GSI. Where2 modified the shit out of GSI's systems without telling them. Where2 is screwed. GSI will devour them."

"Where2 has very deep pockets," David said. "All those venture capitalist investors will continue to back them. They'll want a return on their investment."

"Will they?" Brad said. "GSI is fifty times the size of Where2. This could easily turn into a costly and drawn-out lawsuit. Investors may decide to walk instead of spending years fighting with GSI. We've all been down this road before. Lawsuits take forever."

"I'm not so sure." David motioned to the empty leather chairs across from him and waited for Robert and Brad to sit back down. "Matthew Grant has built an empire—an extremely profitable empire. I don't think that company has ever seen a bad quarter. All of us use GSI's mapping systems in our vehicles. Like him or not, he's got a very positive reputation in the industry. From what I know of Grant, I expect him to make this go away very quickly. He won't want his company's image tarnished."

"I hadn't thought of that," Brad said. "A long legal battle is the last thing GSI will want. How do you think it will end?"

"I'm not sure." David tossed his thick glasses onto the stack of newspapers and magazines. He rubbed his weary eyes and stared back out through his office windows. Without the clarity of his eyeglasses, the muted hues of the Canadian town morphed into a blurry sea of smeared colors. "But I give Where2 a fifty-fifty chance of being in business six months from now."

"If Grant's half as savvy as he appears to be, he should just buy Where2," Robert said. "Take the good parts and throw away the rest."

David and Brad both turned and stared at Robert, looking somewhat surprised by his comment.

"What?" Robert asked. "That's what I'd do. Besides, does any of this really matter? Do either of you really see either GSI or Where2 as a threat?"

"My concern, gentlemen, is we seem to be at risk of losing a seat at the table." David slid his glasses back on and grabbed a copy of *Wired* magazine. "Do you know how many executives from Ford, GM, and Chrysler they interviewed for their article? None."

"Tesla, Where2, and GSI are the darlings of the tech world," he continued. "And they are dominating the discussions on self-driving systems. I'm worried we're going to be perceived as being late to the party."

"David, we've all been contacted about the Where2 accident," Brad said. "Our communications team has been all over this debacle. I've personally given four interviews."

"To the mainstream press, sure. But not to the tech industry." David briefly studied the cover of *Wired* before letting it fall onto the stack of papers and magazines in front of him. "Kids today have different priorities. Times change. People change."

"We adapt as well," Brad said. "We always have."

"Twenty years ago, GM did a pilot electric vehicle program with the Impact," David said. "We turned that into the EV-1 and ran a lease program in California."

"I remember," Brad said. "You guys caught all of us by surprise. That little car had quite the cult following—until you killed it."

"It wasn't profitable. The battery technology back then was much too limiting. As you know, we caught a lot of shit for ending that program and destroying those vehicles."

"I don't think you're giving yourself enough credit," Brad said. "Everything you learned on the EV-1 led to the development of the Chevy Volt."

"Be that as it may, Brad, we both know we sell the Volt at a loss." David sighed as he shuffled through the newspapers and magazines strewn across his desk. "It hasn't become the Prius-killer we'd hoped for. Long-term, we expect profitability to change. We're just not there yet. My point is that all the buzz around EVs is centered around Tesla. GM pioneered it, but we aren't in the mix. As I said, we're not even in the discussion."

"Tesla has yet to make a profit," Robert said. "Who knows if they ever will. That car they're building has to cost them a fortune to make. They lose thousands on every unit."

"Even so, they're stealing market share from Mercedes and BMW." David flipped open a copy of *Automotive News* and tossed it to Robert. "Everyone seems to be trading in their S-Class or 7-Series for the Model S. Gentlemen, we can no longer dismiss Tesla as a minor distraction. I recommend we also begin to view GSI and Where2 as major threats."

"But why?" Robert flung the paper back at David without bothering to read it. "Neither one owns an auto manufacturing plant. They have no idea what it takes to build a car."

"And neither did Tesla," David said.

The three men sat in silence, awkwardly glancing from one to the other. Outside, the brutally cold December wind blasted across the Renaissance Center, whistling loudly against David's office windows.

"I hear Apple is thinking of doing a car," Brad said softly.

"Jesus." Robert grabbed the copy of *Automotive News* he'd just tossed back to David, turning to another article about the Where2 accident. "If Where2 is investing in self-driving technology, what about all the drivers they employ? What happens to them?"

"More importantly, who buys the cars?" David rotated his chair to take in the spectacular view through the bank of windows. "Think it through, guys."

"People order a Where2 instead of driving themselves," Brad said, his chair squeaking as he shifted from side to side. "So down the road if self-driving cars become a real thing, will people even want to own cars? What will happen to dealerships?"

"That, gentlemen, is why I called you here." David turned back to his desk and leaned forward. "What if Where2 perfects their self-driving taxi? What if GSI decides to follow in Where2's footsteps? What if Tesla perfects its Autopilot system and successfully ramps up its Fremont plant to half a million cars or more? Electrification. Battery technology. Autonomy. Artificial Intelligence. Transportation as a service. It's time we accept the inevitable. Given our expertise in supply chains and manufacturing, we lead. We do not follow. We need to become major players in this future world. At all costs."

42

Ted smiled as he glanced around Donovan's Pub, remembering the times he'd spent here with Sam and others when he had worked at GSI. He thought about the great team they'd assembled for Project Courier. During his employment at Where2, he had never made the time to come to Donovan's, or for that matter, meet up with his old co-workers. He closed his eyes and tried to think back to the last time he'd been here. He wasn't sure, but he knew it had to have been with Sam. The restaurant was quiet. He was alone. The bar was empty except for pair of busboys scampering around the pub, doing a final cleaning of the tables. He glanced at his phone—10:20 p.m.

A couple sitting at a booth near the jukebox stood up, gathered their belongings, and walked out. Ted was the only one left. He looked over at the darkened music player and frowned.

"Would it be possible to get some music?" he asked Stacey, the bartender. He'd been chatting with her over the past forty-five minutes. "It's kind of quiet."

"We're closing soon," she said. At barely five feet tall with cropped dark hair, Stacey looked like a little doll in the universal bartender uniform—black slacks, white button-down shirt, and black vest. Her sleeves were rolled up, exposing a colorful set of tattoos covering her arms. "You've been here for a while. Did someone stand you up?"

"No, stuck in traffic," he replied.

"Oh, all right," she said. "I'll play you some music while you wait. What's your poison?"

"Thanks so much. Rock. Classic, if you don't mind."

The jukebox stood almost as tall as Stacey. She reached behind the rear leg and flicked a switch. The machine, though digital, was styled to resemble an antique player—arched front corners with curved glass tubes filled with faux neon lights. One by one, each light flashed to life. The solid oak sides and front were slotted with rounded brass grates. She studied the touchscreen nestled into the front of the player, scrolling as she decided what to play before pressing the selection and making her way back to the bar.

Ted waited patiently for the music to begin. After a few seconds, "Drive" by The Cars began. He sighed and let out a low laugh.

"What?" She asked. "This is old, isn't it?"

"It's fine. Thank you." He slid his empty glass away just as she went back behind the bar. "One more. Please?"

"Are you driving? This stuff is strong."

"No, I'm not."

"Ah, Where2." She pulled out a bottle of Chivas Regal and poured some into his glass. "You gotta love em', right?"

"Right." He unlocked his phone. His Lyft page was still up. For a flash, he wondered if they'd be following Where2's push into self-driving cars. He shrugged it off and swiped through his screens, lamenting the excessive number of apps he'd accumulated. He paused when he noticed he still had the Where2 app on his phone, frowning as he pressed his thumb on the icon and deleted it.

The front door to Donovan's swung open. Ted swiveled his head and felt his heart in his chest. A smile spread across his face as Sam hurried across the restaurant.

"Hi," she said, pausing beside him. "I'm so sorry I'm late. Did you get my text? Traffic was awful."

"No apologies necessary."

He felt a wave of relief as she took the stool next to him and spun it to face him. He looked straight into her sparkling green eyes and was struck, as he had been so many times before, at how beautiful she was. They hadn't seen each other in almost four months, since the night of the accident. He wanted to pull her close and kiss her, but he didn't know what she was thinking or feeling. Before he could make up his mind, Sam leaned forward and gave him a gentle kiss on his cheek.

"You look good," she said as she fidgeted in her seat, trying to get comfortable. "Are you fully recovered?"

"Excuse me," Stacey said. "Last call. Can I get you anything?"

"Chardonnay, please." Turning back to him, she looked concerned. "So, how are you, Ted?"

"I'm . . . I'm better. Finally." He pulled his gaze from Sam and stared into his whisky. The doctor's appointments, stitches, X-rays, and physical therapy sessions paraded before him in his mind. "It's been quite a process."

Sam grabbed the glass of wine Stacey poured for her and took a huge gulp. "I know we haven't spoken. . . . I've been worried."

"I just needed time. I had a lot of things to work through. One of them I just finished." Sitting on the counter to the left of him was a white sealed envelope with Sam's name scrawled across the front in blue ink. He slid it to his right until it was resting beside her glass of wine. "I know this is way past due."

She picked up the envelope and briefly inspected it. He was surprised to see that she still wore her rings. He looked down at the wedding ring on his own hand. After all these months, neither had removed their rings.

"Are these the divorce papers?" she asked.

"I've been meaning to sign them. There's just been so much happening."

"Ted—"

"It was unfair of me to make you wait so long."

"Ted—"

"Sam, when I first got these papers, I tossed them aside and just took for granted I'd be able to change your mind. I kept thinking once that final road test was completed, I'd be able to focus on us and win you back. I didn't know how utterly stupid and blind I was being. I'm surprised you put up with me as long as you did. After the accident, I lost my job. Hell, I pretty much lost everything. I have no one to blame, though, except myself."

"Ted! Stop!" Sam glanced over at the bartender. Stacey was at the other end of the bar, doing her best to act like she wasn't listening to their conversation. "I'm not here for the papers, Ted. I'm here because I'm concerned about you. You were such a wreck that night in the hospital. You're talking to the tortoise, remember? The master at retreating into a shell. . . . Talk to me."

"Where do I begin?" He took a sip of whisky and winced. As he slid the glass away, he looked down at the scar on the palm of his left hand. The injury from the Where2 accident was almost a mirror image of the wound he'd gotten from crashing Frankie in the desert. He looked back and forth between the two scars before clasping his hands together, tears welling up. "That accident left me broken, Sam. I was embarrassed and ashamed. I couldn't face you. So many people died that night. That baby girl. Her . . . her cries were terrible. I still hear them. I tried, Sam. I had her in my arms. I tried."

Sam leaned forward and flung her arms around him. He pulled her close, resting his cheek on her shoulder. Her scent brought with it a flood of emotion. He squeezed her tightly, so grateful to be embracing her once again. He wiped his eyes dry and pulled away, leaning back on his barstool.

"You did what you could," she said. "You tried to save her."

"It wasn't enough." He chugged back the last of his whisky. "And it never should have happened."

"But Ted, you weren't at fault. Nobody could have avoided that crash. I've read the reports. The black box data from all three vehicles proved it. The guy in front of you wasn't in the driver's seat. The guy behind you had turned off Autopilot. Your car didn't know what was coming. Sensors can't see around corners and through trees or buildings. They're no different than humans in that regard."

"It *was* my fault! I rushed the testing. And you always said the self-driving car should be smarter than a human. It should be the *best* driver. The hardware couldn't see ahead. But the software should have known we were heading into a blind corner and were completely boxed in. The car should have forced me to slow down well below the speed limit, just to be safe. By the time I took over, there was nothing I could do." He stared across the bar, his words bringing him right back to that night. "Four people died, Sam. All those years working with you at GSI and we never once killed or even injured anyone. My . . . my arrogance killed those people."

He lowered his head and closed his eyes as the minivan's deafening explosion flashed to mind. He turned to Sam and said, "They are right to be bringing me to court."

"I told you, Ted, the data will show you weren't at fault."

"We'll see if the courts agree." He reached over and held her hand. "I also have the minor issue of the data theft. I'm sure GSI is planning to hang me out to dry." He sighed and stared at his glass. "One . . . one lawsuit at a time, I guess. Right?"

"Maybe not."

"Why . . . why would you say that?"

"Well, if GSI acquires Where2, they'll get all their technology back in house. Maybe they'll even drop the lawsuit."

"If they acquire . . ." He leaned forward and looked at her grin. "What makes you think that will happen?"

"Lori and I have been talking. Apparently, the acquisition is all the buzz around the Where2 offices."

"Interesting." He rubbed his eyes and sighed. He tried to imagine a scenario where, even with an acquisition, Vin and Matthew would not seek retribution. "I . . . I can't think that far ahead."

"You've gone through a lot." She reached over and ran her fingers through his hair, flipping back the lock dangling in front of his eyes.

"So, what will you do when all this is over? What's next for the brilliant Ted Wolff with two 'F's?"

"You know me, always looking ahead." He smiled and winked at her.

The music faded, with just a hiss from the jukebox, and the bar became eerily quiet. He watched as Stacey organized the racks of bottles and glasses behind the bar.

"Oh, yeah?" Sam leaned back on her stool and let her eyes study his face. "I've only heard one rumor."

"Rumor? Does nothing stay secret in this town?" He shook his head and sighed. "What have you heard?"

"Something about a new EV company. Is . . . is it true?"

"Assuming my investors fall in line, then yes."

"Ted! That's fantastic! So, you're planning to take on Tesla?"

"Not quite. Remember how we always said the adoption of autonomy should begin with the taxi and trucking industries?"

"Yes."

"That's going to be our target—trucking and shipping. We're going to build trucks and vans in all shapes and sizes. Highly modular. Fully autonomous. Tesla can have the luxury car market to itself. We're going elsewhere."

"I'm impressed, Ted." She draped her hand on his shoulder. "Congratulations."

"Thanks. It all hinges on what happens with the trial. The . . . the manslaughter trial. My investors have no intentions of admitting their involvement publicly unless the trial ends in my favor. Only then can we move forward."

"I'm glad you've got people who still believe in you." She squeezed his hand and smiled.

"Me, too." He was surprised at how well his conversation with Sam was going. It brought him back to old times—better times. "It's not the only thing on my plate."

The jukebox suddenly went silent. Stacey was in the process of turning it off and powering it down. Ted glanced up at the dartboard clock hanging above the music player. It was just past 11:00 p.m.

"Remember our discussions on the Vernor Vinge essay?"

"The one about AI replacing humans?" Sam laughed and shook her head in bewilderment. "What does that have to do with . . . Wait. Don't . . . don't tell me you truly believe AI will evolve to replace us."

"Not physically. But intellectually? Think about it, Sam. From chess games to self-driving cars, AI continues to get smarter. It can do things better than we can." He noticed Stacey making her way toward them. "You have to stop and ask yourself where and how it ends."

She was about to respond, when Stacey collected their empty glasses and began wiping the bar top clean. She smiled at them and said, "I need to close up."

A shot glass with a paper receipt was resting on the counter in front of Stacey. Ted retrieved it and, after giving it a quick scan, pulled a one-hundred-dollar bill from his pocket, and slid it inside the glass. He passed it back to Stacey, "Keep the change."

"So, I'm guessing you've already figured out the end game," Sam said. "Care to tell me?"

"I don't know how it will end, Sam. Nobody does. That's what my other project's about."

The interior lights flashed on and off, startling both Ted and Sam. He glanced at the far end of the bar. Stacey was hastily emptying the cash register. One of the busboys was standing in the doorway that led to the storage room. He had his hand on a bank of light switches.

"We need to go," Ted said.

He slid off his barstool and took Sam by her waist, leading them to the front door. His hip had been damaged in the accident, causing a very minor limp. The awkward gait was one that he would keep with him for the rest of his life. He'd gotten good at hiding it, but halfway across the restaurant, Sam stopped abruptly.

"Are you limping?" she asked.

"It's nothing to worry about. I'll be fine." He shifted his weight slightly to get his balance by leaning against her. "Thanks."

Once outside, the Donovan's Pub sign went dark and the deadbolt to the entrance clanked loudly behind them. The building was shielding them from the wind as they stood in the doorway.

"So, what's this new AI plan you're cooking up?" she asked. "Some fancy new hardware like an advanced lidar system?"

"The opposite." He chuckled. "The future's in software, Sam. Something I learned from you."

"Well, my digital gimbal did come close to kicking your ass at DARPA."

"It did." He shared a laugh with her. "And every major advancement we made at GSI came down to the software. The same at Where2. The AI engine was the key. The hardware was always secondary."

They stepped off the curb and followed the walkway to the parking lot. The farther they got from the building, the stronger the wind became. Ted shoved his hands deep into his pockets. As they crossed the lot, he felt his fingers slide against the scars on his legs and, again, his mind filled with the image of the exploding minivan. He did his best to shake it off.

"I'm building an AI engine," he said. "That's my new project, Sam."

"Is it another funded partnership?"

"No. This . . . this is all me. I want to build the most advanced AI engine the world has ever seen. This won't be limited to self-driving technology. It will be . . . bigger."

"Sounds ambitious, Ted." She watched him rub his injured legs. "But when has that stopped you before?"

"I'm just looking ahead. AI's the future."

"If you aren't getting funding, then how—"

"No more questions, Sam. Not tonight."

"Sure." She smiled and nodded. "Another time, maybe."

They started to walk again, doing their best to deal with the blustery wind rushing along the side of the restaurant. Ted noticed Sam clutching the divorce papers with both hands. He gently tapped the envelope and she looked up at him. "Everything's signed, Sam. But, I . . . I don't want this to be the end for us. I've missed you."

"I've missed you, too. These papers can wait. No rush, right?"

"Right."

"Besides, we have a lot of catching up to do. I have a million questions about this AI future of yours. And your new EV company." She glanced around the empty parking lot. "Where's your car? On the other side?"

"No, I took a Lyft here. I'll get another one home. Where did you park?"

"I'm out back around the corner."

They walked along the side of the pub. The last set of lights inside the building went out. Sam wrapped her arms across her chest to stifle the wind. Ted instinctively put his arm around her and pulled her close. Having spent so many months alone, it felt good to have someone support him. Not just someone. Sam.

"How's your family doing?" she asked.

"They're fine. My mom freaked out about the accident and wanted to come and take care of me. I haven't told them about the divorce, though. I know that won't go over well. My dad's upset about the firing and lawsuit, but he told me he trusts I will land on my feet. How's Dani doing?"

"She's good. She asks about you."

"I missed her birthday in December. She turned twelve, right?"

"She did. We didn't expect you to remember, Ted. That was shortly after the accident."

"No, Sam. There's no excuse. I haven't been there for her. Or for you."

Once they reached the back of the building, the rear door of the pub flung open. Stacey and the rest of the crew filed out, ignoring Sam and Ted. He noticed a pearl white Tesla Model S parked in a corner beneath a lamp post.

"Is that yours?" he asked Sam.

"I picked it up a few months back as a Christmas gift to myself."

"Wow, look at you buying such a fast, powerful car. My little tortoise got herself a rocket sled."

"That's not why I bought it. I wanted to go green." She paused a few feet from the sleek five-door and let her eyes wander across the sculpted forms. A smile spread across her face. "I do have to admit it's kind of a blast to drive. Responsibly, of course. Never too fast."

"Never." He chuckled and shook his head. "Admit it, Sam, a bit of me rubbed off on you."

"Maybe. But just a bit." Her smile faded as she looked at the envelope in her hands. She turned and looked up at him. "We . . . we were a good team. Weren't we?"

"We were."

She opened the driver's door of her car and tossed the envelope inside, before gently taking Ted's hands, rotating his palms face up. She angled them to get a look at his matching scars which she softly kissed. One, then the other.

"I miss you, Ted. I miss what we once had."

He stared into her eyes. Even in the harsh light beaming down from the lamp post, her eyes glistened. He felt a lump in his throat as he recalled the day he first saw her—the baseball cap—aviator sunglasses—her long blond hair in a ponytail.

"When Kyle flew us to Reno, we talked about the future. You told me how you wanted to build a better world for Dani. It was specifically for her. I never understood why at the time." He leaned forward, tilted his head down, and kissed Sam on her cheek. "I do now."

"Maybe that's what the second 'F' in your name is for." She grinned as she flicked his lock of hair away from his eyes. "'F' is for 'finally.' You finally figured it out."

"Right." He laughed and pulled her into his arms. "Some things can't be rushed. I learned that from a beautiful woman."

He rocked her back and forth in his arms, quietly taking in the comfort of being near her. The warmth of her body pressed against his. He didn't want to let go.

"Can I drive you home?" She asked, her face buried in his chest. "We can crack open a bottle of wine. Or whisky, if you prefer."

"Don't you need to get back to Dani?"

"She's staying with friends. Girls' sleepover party."

"She's at that age already, isn't she?"

"They grow up fast, Ted. We all do."

He ran his fingers through her hair as she tilted her head back. He slid his hand across her cheek, gazing into her eyes, then leaned down and gently kissed her on the lips.

"Not everyone, Sam. Some of us take a bit longer."

Alex Schuler Collection

(Science Fiction and Action-Adventure)

ISBN: 978-1-933769-82-0

In a near-future world dominated by artificial intelligence, the country's leading scientist has programmed "ethics" into the decision-making of all machines, but when his algorithm finds that he is a threat to mankind, he must go on the run (and off the grid) to escape execution.

ISBN: 978-1-933769-90-5

In a continuation of the Code Word series, when a nefarious military team activates a new AI to retake control of the weapon systems, a team of hackers must help the Organites escape before they are exterminated.

ISBN: 978-1-933769-86-8

When a group of parents and children are sucked into an actual Dungeons and Dragons adventure, a father must resolve his own anger and guilt to reconnect with his son and survive the adventure.

ISBN: 978-1-933769-88-2

Mankind must put aside its deep divisions and come together to face an AI-driven network that threatens humanity's very existence. But when an attempt to use EMP technology to stop all computers fails, our motley group of heroes must enter the network itself to destroy the enemy from within.

ISBN: 978-1-64630-038-9

In a continuation of the Code Word series, the battle between humanity and the AI is interrupted by the invasion of our solar system by a Von Neuman Machine.